A PASSAGE OF REDEMPTION

a novel

For my friends in Hoyt Lakes...

pat mcgauley

Pat McGauley

a shamrock book

A Passage of Redemption

Published by PJM Publishing
2808 Fifth Avenue West
Hibbing, MN 55746
Email: shatiferin@aol.com
Author's website: patmcgauley.com

Without limiting the rights under copyright, no part of this publication may be reproduced in whole or in part in any form without the prior written permission of both the copyright owner and the publisher of this book.

Copyright: (Pending) est. November 2012

Library of Congress (EPCN) control number: Pending

ISBN: 978-0-9724209-7-6

First edition: November, 2012

Shamrock Books from PJM are published by Bang Printing in the USA.
Cover design by Renee Anderson, Express Print One, Ltd.

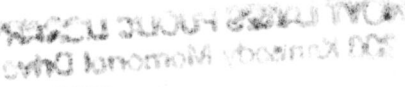

THE MORANS, A FAMILY CHRONOLOGY:

Twelve years ago, Minnesota author Pat McGauley began a novel titled To Bless or To Blame. That story led to a sequel the following year...then a third book. Over the past decade this author has written a series of novels featuring five generations of a Hibbing, Minnesota family through the entire twentieth century. This story, the seventh, continues what was started years ago. In brief, and in the order of publication, the previous novels were:

-*To Bless or To Blame*, everything begins with the adventure-drama of the rise and fall of Iron Range titan, *Peter* Moran in the early 1900's.

-*A Blessing or a Curse* is a love story touched with political and moral intrigue. *Kevin* and Angela Moran meet and marry and begin a family of their own.

-*Blest Those Who Sorrow* is an far-reaching psychodrama that completes McGauley's 'Mesabi Trilogy'. The story takes the reader from Hibbing to St. Paul, to California and then to Europe. It is set in the depression of the 1930's and pre-war 1940's.

-*The Hibbing Hurt*, set in the fifties, tells the story of a racial murder in Hibbing, Minnesota, and the rogue Hibbing cop, *Patrick* ('Pack') Moran, who solves it. The romance element involves disgruntled schoolteacher, Maddie Loiselle.

-*Flag* focuses on Pack's son, *Amos* Moran, a rebellious teen, who flees his family roots in Hibbing and finds himself in love and in trouble in Flagstaff, Arizona.

-*Saint Alban's Day*, set in the 1990's, is a political and a spiritual adventure involving Amos and Sadie Moran and their two children, Meghan and *Mickey*. Mickey is the last Moran genitor of the century.

In the prologue to this novel, a family tree will depict these six generational lineages of the Moran clan.

ACKNOWLEDGEMENTS

Before my story was 'press worthy' I had to prevail upon several of my valued friends. I needed the eyes of trusted others to examine the many mistakes, character inconsistencies, plot gaps, and/or redundancies that evidenced themselves throughout my manuscript. These readings occurred after the first and the second writing of this story–there was a third and fourth rewrite following each of the four reviews.

After months of work, when I finally decided to put this manuscript to bed, it is what it is and the imperfections are mine alone. I am too impatient to be a stylist: I have a reminder sign of that mantra taped on the wall above my MacBook: it reads simply, *'Story not Style'*. To those friends of mine who have volunteered hours of their valuable time reviewing each and every page of *A Passage of Redemption* I am deeply indebted. Many, many thanks to Jim Otterbeck, Richard Dinter, Jim Huber, Andrew Miller, and Charlie and Norma Grant. Their collective insights have contributed greatly to the content, flow, and grammatical accuracy of this story. Thanks and thanks and more thanks!

PAT MCGAULEY

Dedication:
*For Colin Isaacson, a dear friend
who left us much too early.*

A Passage of Redemption

*"I write a book at least three times—
once to understand it
the second to improve the prose
and a third to compel it to say
what it still must say."*

Bernard Malamud

PROLOGUE:

At the onset, I'd like the reader to know that an actual experience inspired the concept for a doppelganger story. My daughter Erin and I were taking our annual camping trip–this particular year it was a loop out East and included Quebec City, Bar Harbor, Boston, and the Big Apple–before heading back through the Poconos to Minnesota. I had done a similar trip once before and knew where the best campsites were located and how to find the attractions that would be of interest to my nine year-old companion. Certainly, seeing Lady Liberty, Central Park, and fifty other Manhattan sites in New York City were a must. Previously, I had done a Gray Line tour and thought that means of touring to be the most time-efficient way to see much of the city as well as provide us with an authoritative interpretation.

Already, I've gotten ahead of myself. The night before our planned outing to NYC, we camped at a pleasant park outside of Peekskill, which is located on the Hudson River, north of the City. Nearby was a railroad line into Grand Central Terminal. We were up early and boarded the train before seven. I gave Erin the window seat looking out upon the picturesque Hudson landscape to our immediate west; I took the aisle. The train trip would take about an hour.

I watched my daughter's eyes grow bigger as we passed sights she had never seen before. I was content to enjoy the ride through her eyes. The hard seats were uncomfortable, my shoulders were sore from sleeping on the cold earth in a thin bag, and I was still suffering from the car-lag of driving countless hours in my little Civic the previous day. I remember having a aggravating kink in my neck as well. I stretched and yawned, and Massaged the back of my neck, hoping to shake my aches and pains, glancing as I did so across and then down the aisle behind me…

All of a sudden I was awestruck!–not twenty feet behind me, was the most haunting sight of my life!

Sitting three rows back was a man with steel gray hair, a square jaw, and piercing blue eyes. Our eyes locked for a long moment. Peering at me from over the spread of his newspaper was my father… In his every feature, my dad–Richard–was connecting his gaze with mine. A lump the size of a baseball formed in my throat for those few frozen seconds… I was so gripped with emotion that I had to turn away and catch my breath. My father had passed away in 1969–seventeen years earlier. Every thread and ounce of logical explanation screamed–no!–this cannot be. Yet, I would have bet my life that this man knew exactly who I was. That momentary link between us was beyond surreal. After allowing my heart rate to settle down for a few moments, I turned slowly back in his direction. At this glance, however, his face was hidden behind another passenger and the *Times* he was reading.

I was tempted to go back and introduce myself, tell the 'stranger' that the resemblance between him and my father was so uncanny as to be almost beyond belief. I didn't. The train was crowded and I thought it best to wait for a few minutes and not embarrass either one of us. While I was experiencing this genuine Rod Sterling moment, Erin was completely engrossed in the river traffic, and the lush countryside north of the City. I didn't interrupt her thoughts, nor did I say anything to her about what I had just experienced.

Long minutes, and two or three stops later, I looked back to see if the man was still reading his newspaper–but, as fate would have it, the man was gone. I can only imagine that he got off at one of the stops after our initial encounter.

I wondered if I would ever see my father's double again. I wondered a lot of things–and, from time to time, I still do. Who was that man on the Peekskill train? Why his apparent 'interest' in me? Of course, I will never know. Since then, and to this day, I have not shared this experience with any other person. In fact, it wasn't until I started writing this story that I told my daughter what had happened that morning for the first time.

Thus, this novel, rooted in something both personal and mystical to its author. According to Wikipedia: "In fiction and folklore, a *Doppelganger* (noun) is a double of a living person–or, a 'double-walker'...." As you might imagine, an author may spend hours contemplating various title options. Doppelganger seemed to be the obvious title choice. One reader, however, suggested that this story evoked a richness transcending the paranormal, and that my tale was actually mistitled. At the time I didn't agree.

Things change–sometimes dramatically, sometimes in subtle ways. I was biking on a sunny Saturday morning in late July, contemplating the final rewrite that was nearly completed. I still had loose ends to tie together in the Epilogue to this story. For reasons I can't explain, I realized that one of my characters hadn't hadn't taken his final bow. This character would have wanted to say something profound about the journey my protagonist had just completed. Then it struck me. I had somehow misunderstood my own creation. This was not a story about Doppelganger! For sure there was a compelling paranormal thread sewing everything together but... the heart and guts of the story was something else–something transcending the psychological. In my final rewrite I was *saying what must be said*. Thank you Bernard Malamud for opening my eyes to a truth you learned long before I have. In this last rewriting I understood my story in a different way. This is the story of a young man's passage. The young man is a priest. A priest who experiences '*a passage of redemption*–spiritually, emotionally, and physically.

The Moran Family Tree

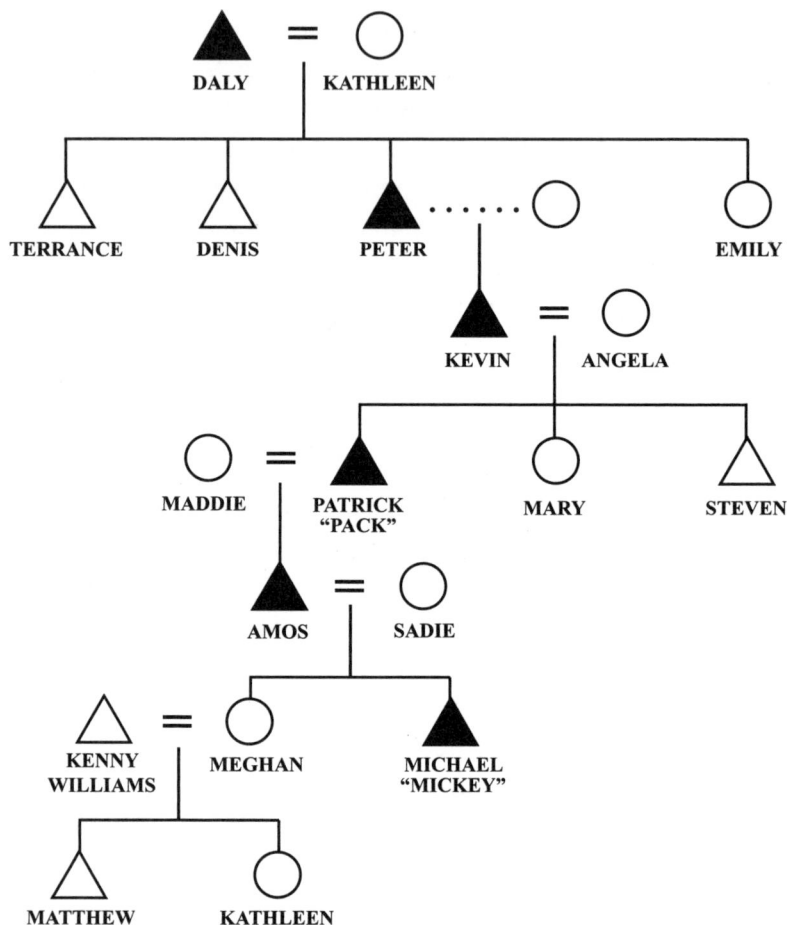

Pat McGauley

The Slade (Moran) Family Tree

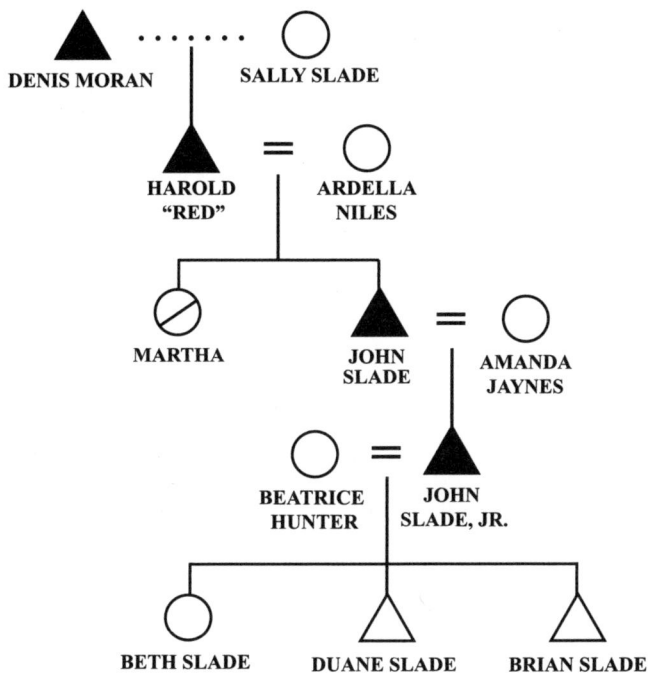

A Passage of Redemption

INTRODUCTION:

Kevin Moran was the first to discover a previously unknown strain of the Moran family. As with nearly everything else, he shared what he had learned with his wife, Angela. Although the two of them would never reveal what they had learned to anybody else, they did make provision for their secret to be passed on to another generation of the Moran family. Their grandson, Amos, was to be the beneficiary.

Kevin Moran was a prominent Hibbing attorney, civic leader, and philanthropist. He passed away in March of 1998, nearly three years before his wife. His death came several years after the completion of what he and Angela often called the 'family trees project'. Kevin's diligent research is the underpinning of this story. It should also be noted that Kevin was a fastidious man, thorough and orderly in all of his affairs. His attention to every detail of his research enabled him to reconstruct five previously unknown generations from his paternal heritage. This 'other' lineage was as divergent from his known roots as night is to day. As would be expected from a man of Kevin's nature, impartiality and detachment characterized each step of his research. Further, if one reality evolved from his study it was simply that there is a measure of good and bad in every person as well as in every family.

The genesis of Kevin's project dated back nearly fifty years to the autumn of 1928 when he was a twenty-two year-old law student at the University of Minnesota. He came upon a news item in a Minneapolis newspaper explaining that a fugitive known to have used several aliases, including the Moran surname, had been arrested in Hibbing, Minnesota. Following his arrest, the felon– named Denis Moran– had been tried in a Duluth district court, found guilty on several counts, and sentenced to a lengthy prison term. Kevin's innate curiosity led to his discovery that the convicted man was, indeed, his relative. Denis Moran was an estranged uncle and a man that he had never before seen nor met. Intrigued at having a notorious relative, he arranged a visitation with his late father's brother at the Minnesota penitentiary in Stillwater. Kevin met his uncle Denis for the first time in early November, the weekend before Thanksgiving of 1928.

While visiting, Kevin learned that his gruff and intimidating uncle had secretly followed his growing up in a West Duluth neighborhood and had come to know a great deal about his childhood experiences. Uncle Denis related that he had watched his nephew walk to St. James Elementary School from a parked car on numerous occasions, had watched him learn to drive an automobile under the tutelage of his foster father, and years later watched Kevin play high school baseball for the Denfeld *Hunters*. Ironically, Kevin would also learn that Denis' arrest had resulted from a clever, but ill-fated, attempt to withdraw a large amount of his nephew's trust money from a Hibbing bank. "I wuz jus hard-up, ya know, and kinda pissed at yer dad. Lookin' back, what I did wuz really stupid," Denis admitted with a thin, almost devious smile. "Like mosta da things I done."

Early conversations between the two men were mostly superficial, skirting most of Denis' shadowed criminality and centering mainly on the news of the day and Kevin's pre-law studies at the University. Both men preferred wading slowly into the waters of years lived in different worlds. Ensuing visits with Denis revealed familial events and episodes long secreted and deeply buried the dust of time. From this intriguing uncle, Kevin was able to piece together missing pieces of the puzzle that had been much of his own life's complex history.

In February of 1929, Kevin learned that Uncle Denis was dying of tuberculosis. When last he saw his uncle alive, Denis revealed an emotional side that the young law student had not seen before. Denis acknowledged a torment that brought tears to his deep-set, bushy browed, green eyes. Before leaving his uncle, Denis made an unusual, and seemingly innocent request– a 'personal favor' to use the man's own words. That request would ultimately inspire Kevin's family history project.

"I'd be beholdin' if you'd find a woman name of Sally Slade–I think that's still her name but I can't be sure 'bout that no more." Kevin found an envelope in his jacket pocket and wrote down the name. "Anyhow, last I knowed she was still livin' in Duluth. Just tell'er that I died." he said. "I 'spoze she might'nt even remember what my name wuz. We spent a little time together, her and me. Not much... but she might 'member."

Denis' breathing was labored and his thread to life was thin. The disease had progressed to that advanced stage where he was acutely aware of his imminent mortality. His hoarse words became nearly inaudible and Kevin had to lean over the bed, close to his mouth and his putrid breath: "T'was some time ago son, and I heared some things, ya know... some things..." His last earthly word was as nebulous as the man himself – things!

In order to honor his uncle's request, Kevin would need to dig deeply into his diseased uncle's life. He was left with little more than the name of a woman, maybe living in Duluth, from unknown years back in time, and some things his uncle had heard about. That was it! But, that couldn't be *it*... Kevin was convinced that Uncle Denis had been holding something back. Maybe something important, something left hanging in his uncle's cluttered closet. There had to be a missing chapter that might reveal things his uncle wanted him to know but hadn't yet found a way to tell him about.

The dying man had played around the edges of his deep-seated jealousy and a fierce anger toward Kevin's father. Denis had said many times, and in many different ways, that he felt his life would have been so much better if only his brother, Peter Moran, had loved him–respected him. "He treated bote me an daddy like he was shamed 'bout us–had me roughed up by some cops once den had me runned outta town. Dat was the worse thing ever happen ta me–'fore I got caught, I mean." His, and Peter's, 'daddy' died of a stroke in far-away Oregon many years before.

Before his death, however, Denis had dictated a letter to a ward nurse in the prison infirmary and asked that she mail it to Kevin's dormitory address at the University in Minneapolis after he had passed away. That letter contained the 'missing chapter' of his uncle's troubled life. In an eleventh hour confession, his single page letter revealed that Denis had killed his brother, Peter. *"No sense going to the grave with that still on my conscience,"* he acknowledged. Up until this time the local authorities had considered Peter Moran's unresolved death to have resulted from a self-inflicted gunshot wound. It was well known that Kevin's father had been under tremendous stress at the time.

Kevin kept Denis' letter locked away with his collection of diaries and research notes in a cedar chest and never revealed its contents. Everything that Kevin learned while researching the 'family trees' project was carefully transcribed in a collection of notebooks. Along with the letter and notebooks were photographs, various news clippings, along with other relevant items of interest. Through the years, this trove remained stored in the bowels of the attic in his home on remote Maple Hill south of Hibbing. Angela was aware of the trunk and of its importance to her husband. Kevin was the kind of person who needed to be preoccupied with something–anything! He also needed time and space all to himself, 'inner time' he called it. Angie not only respected that need, but also discovered that she could happily isolate herself for long hours in her upstairs art studio without feeling any sense of guilt or remorse.

Although Angie never read the contents in their entirety, she believed that one day a book might be written about its contents. On one occasion she enquired why his project was kept shrouded in secrecy and not shared with anybody else, not even their only son, Patrick. Kevin said: "It's just my gut feeling, hon, it's nothing personal for sure. It's just that Pack has known about my research but never, not even once, has he evidenced any curiosity." Angie understood that. She knew that their son was usually too caught up in himself and his own interests to have much connection to the lives of his parents. She let the matter drop. In the back of her mind was a hope that their grandson, Amos, would not turn out to be as apathetic as his father. No, she told herself, I'll see that he doesn't. The Moran story is going to be told–come hell or high water!

A Passage of Redemption

1/REMINISCING

Mid-September: 1996

One autumn evening, the two soul mates were engaging in a conversation that older couples often find a need to have. They were sitting in an old hickory glider with newly oiled hinges on the western side of their deck. They were nestled together, holding hands, and had a woolen blanket draped across their knees. A harvest moon hung above the crowns of majestic pines lining a distant hillside, then sloping down to a small pond. In the stillness they could hear the whisk of wind in the aspens, the shrill chirp of crickets near the pond, and the snorts of restless horses in the corral below. Their Maple Hill property held a lifetime of memories and the two of them often relived those precious times while sitting outside in the cool of the evening.

They reminisced, as they often did, about their children, their friends, family celebrations: Birthdays, anniversaries, holidays, and events special to the two of them. 'Remember when?' always invited a rich nostalgia that allowed them to relive those times of laughter, those times of tears. Their family, like every family, had a wealth of happiness as well as a modicum of tragedy. If they were prone to dwelling on memories past, they also ventured thoughts into those unknown realms beyond the moment. Both had spiritual dimensions that went beyond their Catholicism. Matters of faith, fidelity, compassion, and a collage of Christian values were topics that they could openly share without feeling self-conscious or vulnerable. Both realized that nearly all of their allotted years were now behind them. In their years together, the reality of life's inevitable conclusion had touched them in ways that were unique to each. Kevin's needs for space and isolation as well as Angela's bouts of amnesia brought tensions that bonded their union. Feelings and needs presented opportunities to search their souls for meanings beyond the mundane gossip about what friends and neighbors were doing. Kevin had inherited great wealth from a father he never knew and willingly shared that bounty with those in need. His philanthropy left its fingerprints on hundreds of lives over decades of giving; more often than not in an anonymous manner.

"Patrick has too much time on his hands these days. That's probably why he's always dabbling in that political party blarney." Angie broke a lull in their conversation with a sharp criticism. Their oldest, Patrick, was 'Pack' to everyone but his mother who despised the crude nickname. He was a former cop and a more recent activist in the Democratic Party. He and his wife, Maddie, had one child–a son named Amos.

Kevin nodded without immediate comment. He and Pack had gone fishing at Sturgeon Lake only twice during the past summer, and hadn't made their 'guy's trip' to a Twins game this season. "He's got some strong views about how things ought to be, not that I agree with many of them." He chuckled to himself at the recall of a recent argument the two of them had had. "Seems like he believes the government can solve all our problems. I'm inclined to think too much government gets to be too expensive. I fear a day will come when we are spending far more than we take in with taxes. Or, that the taxes we have to pay for our debts will compromise the future of our grandchildren."

Angela didn't like politics, period! "Whatever?" Her tone was one of exasperation. "Sometimes I really wonder if they know what they're doing. All I care about is having honest people making honest decisions without all the malarkey that goes on." She waved a dismissive hand, her way of changing the topic. "Did you get out to the cemetery today? We've got to put out some fresh plants–some flowering ones. Both the alyssum and the begonias looked terrible last weekend. Maribec must be turning in her grave." Angela's voice strained, "how that girl of ours loved flowers." Their middle child had been their greatest sorrow. Mary Rebecca was wed to an abusive Jack Daniels, had battled depression for years, and died from a liver disease in her early fifties.

"That's taken care of, my dear. I spent an hour out there this afternoon. Put some fresh plants at Tony's grave, too." Kevin often wandered through the north Hibbing cemetery and the spacious Bennett Park across Third Street from the gravesites. "So many of our friends... It's hard to imagine how life has gone on without them." Kevin swallowed a lump in his throat.

Angela gave his hand a squeeze. Her husband was a sensitive man and his emotions often caught him off guard. Both listened to the soothing sway of the glider without speaking for a few moments, each sinking into a meditation of private thoughts.

"I heard Amos' name is being mentioned for that judgeship vacancy. Do you know anything about that?" Angie said.

"That speculation has come up more than a few times before, hon. He says that he's not interested–he wants to grow his firm for a few more years."

Angie smiled at any mention of their only grandchild. "He's always had a good sense of priority, knows what he wants, how to get it."

Kevin chose not to offer a contrary perspective. Amos had made more than a few misjudgments along the way. When his grandson erred, Kevin–even more than his own father– always helped him find a way out. Angie, however, was convinced that Amos could do no wrong.

"Did you get Steven's birthday card in the mail?" Angela asked.

"Jeeze, no I didn't. Sorry, I forgot all about it. I've lost track of the years–how many is it now, forty?"

Steven was their youngest. He lived in a whirlwind, was independently wealthy, and found little time for his family or the community where he grew up. Talking about Steven and his 'big city' lifestyle was a conversation depressor. Success had been his 'Holy Grail' and personal relationships seemed only to get in the way of his corporate obsessions. "I'll run the card in to the post office in the morning, dear... should get to him in plenty of time."

"We must have Amos and Sadie over this weekend. I've got a huge prime rib roast... his very favorite. I'll call him in the morning." Angie was quick to redirect the conversation to something more pleasant than their deceased daughter or their wayward son.

Kevin nodded, knowing that his wife was destined to revert back to their grandson at some point. However, though Kevin was more pragmatic in most regards, he was almost equally devoted to Amos. His grandson had followed his grandfather's footsteps into law school at the University. And, like Kevin, had built a successful legal career for himself.

An hour had passed, and the looming orange ball had centered itself in the starlit heavens, to the left of the Big Dipper, and seemed to have moved toward the south. Kevin and Angie's conversation would return to where it had started.

"What are we going to do with all of this?" Kevin mused as his open left hand swept across the silhouette of horizon before them. Their Maple Hill acreage was probably the finest real estate in the northern reaches of the vast county. Angie stirred uncomfortably next to him. The subject of estate matters roused deep and conflicted emotions in both of them.

"This place has pretty much defined our lifetime together," Angie said. Kevin couldn't add anything to her observation. It was here where Kevin had proposed, where they had made love for the first time, where they had raised three children together. He smiled inwardly as the memory settled into another dimension. Some might frame his reminiscence quite differently; some might say that it was here that they first had a sexual experience. To Kevin, that first time was lovemaking in a breadth almost defying description, a sharing of each other that bonded them in a way that had never been compromised.

"I often think of that day... under the pine trees... down by the pond," Angie said, her beam was knowingly subtle as she imagined that Kevin was sharing a similar thought– their spirits were often in a harmony that bordered upon the surreal. She closed her eyes, allowing quiet moments to pass between them. She was trying to frame difficult thoughts into words that the two of them together could contemplate. Angela knew as her husband did, that important decisions had yet to be finalized before one of them passed away. The inevitable death of a beloved spouse was not a topic lending itself to pleasant discussion. Yet... both were lingering at the edges of sharing their feelings about what should be done with their treasure. Patrick, their oldest son, was the obvious and logical heir to the Moran family's estate. But convention was never a major consideration in the Moran matriarch's decision-making process.

Kevin glanced to his right and noticed that Angela's eyelids were nearly closed, he put his arm about her. Angie opened her eyes, smiled, cuddled herself under Kevin's arm. He adjusted the blanket on their lap and pulled her sweater over her shoulder. "You've got something on your mind, sweetheart?"

"You know my feelings, Kevin. But, it's not... "

Kevin let her thought drop without comment. He had already amended his will. Angela's wishes and his were nearly always in sync: "I think Pack will handle our decisions well," he said. Angela agreed but with noticeably less optimism, "I think so, too. I hope so." Their grandson, Amos, would be the executor and primary benefactor of the Moran estate.

Kevin added, "Amos will take good care of his dad; we both know that. He's never been materialistic, and he's never indicated that there's anything of ours that he would like to have."

"Neither has Patrick. They don't covet a thing of ours–is that something we should be proud of–or remorseful about?" Angie touched a tissue to a tear in the corner of her eye. "I just don't know." She sniffled, "What will become of our lovely home, Kevin?"

Both knew that neither Patrick nor Amos had ever expressed any interest in the Maple Hill mansion that had been in the Moran family for nearly a century.

Kevin shook his head on a question that had no answer. Talking about it always seemed to discomfort the two of them.

A chill in the autumnal air reminded them that it was getting late. "There is something I need to tell you before we go inside. In the library, left middle drawer, I've taped a key for that trunk in the attic."

"The 'family trees' project trunk?"

Kevin nodded. "When the time comes, I'd like the key to go to Amos."

Kevin had a deep sense of karma. He knew that his project was more than a scholarly exercise. He knew that one day the knowledge contained in the old cedar chest would be of some value. He also knew that his own death would precede that of his wife. In fact, Kevin knew many things that nobody knew he knew. Things! Things that only his grandson would come to know. Thusly, the weight of the family legacy would be passed from Kevin to Amos. Just as Kevin hadn't asked for the burden of his family's lore, neither had Amos.

2/ ONE DAY IN THREE PLACES

December 6, 2011: Fifteen years later...

Then, until now, the only person that Amos had shared his knowledge with was his wife, Sadie. The Moran diaries remained as Grampa Kevin had left them: stored in the same old cedar chest. Only the attic where they resided had changed, the trunk had moved from the mansion on Maple Hill to Amos' residence in the Home Acres neighborhood of Hibbing.

Amos, now retired from his law practice, had turned down

numerous political appointments, a district courts judgeship, and more than a few business opportunities. While living in Hibbing during the summer months he found time for volunteer activities in numerous community projects: the local historical society, Fairview Hospital, Salvation Army, and the local food shelf. The iron mining community on the Mesabi Iron Range of northeastern Minnesota had been, and would always be, home to the Morans. Nevertheless, after years of brief family vacations in southwestern Florida, Amos and Sadie finally purchased a three-bedroom home on Banyan Boulevard in Naples. The long, grey northern winters they left behind were a topic of conversation rather than an endurance test.

Within a few blocks west of their new Florida home was Lowdermilk Park on the Gulf of Mexico, and to the south the Naples Golf and Country Club. These days, Amos and Sadie split the year into near-equal halves, enjoying the entire winter in sun-drenched Naples. Despite significant tax advantages, Amos would not consider making Florida his 'official' residence. "My Minnesota roots are too deep," he would say.

In Hibbing, the name Moran was deeply embedded in civic involvement and philanthropy and to those who had lived in the community any length of time, the Moran name meant respectability, even notoriety. In Florida, however, the Morans were able to relax and live in relative obscurity. Amos subscribed to the E-edition of the Hibbing Daily News so his computer could keep him 'in touch' with events at home whenever he wanted.

Then, in early May, upon returning home with his rich Florida suntan, and settling into familiar routines, Amos would invariably find himself in the attic looking for something he had stored there. When up there among the cobwebs, Amos would notice that old cedar trunk and be reminded once again of his grandmother's wish– Angela had wanted him to share the Moran story that Kevin had meticulously detailed. There were times when Amos felt a sense of betrayal or guilt for failing to honor her last request.

~

Slipping her feet into down-lined boots, and pulling a jacket over her blue terrycloth bathrobe, Meghan Moran Williams stepped gingerly onto the back porch of her two-story colonial. On this December Tuesday morning she was greeted with a wind-chill of nearly twenty below zero. "Zikes", her frozen word hung in the air like a bit of cartoon dialogue. She shivered. "This sucks," she mumbled to no one but herself; the thought of another four months of this brutal northern Minnesota winter was daunting. Her Hibbing Tribune hadn't arrived yet so she quickly pulled the door shut on the icy draft, then retrieved her sugar-saturated cup of coffee on the kitchen counter next to her cell phone and her Tuesday 'to-do' list. The WMFG radio's weather report said that the high temperature for this December 6th would be minus four. Enough bad news for a day that had hardly even started, she turned off the radio.

Another 'same old' day lay ahead and Meghan would have to suck it up and get the ball rolling. She hollered toward the stairway, "Six-thirty up there! Yoo-hoo; get a move on!" Those thankless routines of a wife and mother could grind a woman down. This morning, she was feeling very ground down. Maybe this would be a good reading day, her book club was reading Marquez' Love in the Time of Cholera , and meeting at the Dinter's house on Thursday.

Eighteen hundred miles south and east, Meghan's barefooted father, slid open the screen and stepped onto the porch to retrieve his Naples Daily News. The irrigation sprinklers were finishing their early morning spray and the air held the fresh scent of wet grass, and fragrant flowering magnolias. Bordering the porch were vibrant purple bougainvillea, sprawling white plumbago shrubs, and tall firebush. Amos Moran breathed deeply, as a light western breeze stirred the rich, salty aroma the Gulf only a few blocks away. The eastern sun, visible beyond the palm trees bordering his manicured yard, was already warming the morning air. He would enjoy his first cup of coffee and read the sports page under the shading umbrella at the glass patio table. His first 'task' of this Tuesday morning would be checking on the score of Tubby Smith's Minnesota Gopher hoopsters who played some division II team the night before, then he'd see if the Twins had made any deals–they needed more than bullpen help to recover from the disastrous previous season–then, after reading the important stuff, he'd page to the financial section to check on his portfolio. Later that morning, Amos would bicycle for an hour or two down Gulf Shore Drive to Gordon and beyond Port Royal to the south. Before the afternoon heat, he would hit some golf balls at the local driving range.

~

On this same December morning, Brian Slade stood near the magazine rack in the Super America convenience store off of Payne Avenue in St. Paul. Brian considered purchasing a copy of the Pioneer Press so he could scour the want ads for job listings; but consideration was as empty as his pockets. He had six dollars and some change but that money had to last him for a while–how long he wasn't sure. He wasn't sure about much of anything these days. What to do? Where to go? How to earn his next dollar? Brian was two weeks without work and twice fired in the past three months. Making circumstances even worse, he carried the baggage of two felonies and an ex-con label. Getting any kind of job, from flipping burgers to washing dishes to any other mindless task, was a challenge he simply wasn't up for any more. How many 'Nos!' (and its derivatives) 'not right now', 'maybe in the summer', or 'we'll keep your application on file' could a person possibly cope with? In his darkest moments, and there had been quite a few lately, he had thoughts of closing the garage door and letting the car run until the carbon monoxide fumes put him to sleep–so easy and so painless. But, Brian didn't have a car or a garage anymore. And, he'd readily admit, he didn't have the guts to end his misery that way. The list of things Brian Slade didn't have would run from the Super America down the hill to the Mississippi River two miles away.

A magazine cover pictured an overweight mother and her obese son; the story caption read: 'Ten simple ways to lose ten pounds in ten days'. Brian suppressed a laugh, and mumbled under his breath: "How about one simple way–eat less! I've been doing the 'eat less' program for some time now–and, it works." The fact that he was able to find humor in his own loss of weight was encouraging, but the persistent hunger was a bummer. Don't let things get you down, Brian, he reminded himself, you don't have to look very far to see people who are a lot worse off than you are.

The Asian woman at the register eyed him with an obvious and growing annoyance. "Wan buy sompin?"

Brian shrugged, buttoned his lightweight jacket and went back outside. Two of the Payne Avenue street people approached, "Any change for coffee this morning, Bry-man?" Moon Monahan, Moonie to some, Moonshine to others had a missing-toothed smile, a boxer's flat nose, and eyebrows that would have made Andy Rooney jealous. Moon wore layers of old clothing that carried the odors of barrel smoke and mold. It was common street knowledge that Moon had graduated from prestigious Carleton College years before his problem drinking put him on the streets of St. Paul. Tagging along behind him pushing a rusted grocery cart was Annie Watts: Tugboat to some, Raggedy to others. Once a beautiful woman, the bleak years and the cheap wine had put her on the skids as well. Wrinkles hung like paper bags under her hazel eyes and her pale cheeks made her red nose more conspicuous. The two denizens of the street had been companions for as long as anybody could remember.

Brian fumbled in his pockets and felt the two quarters he might have used for the morning paper, "Make sure it's for coffee," he admonished. Moon stepped closer, reeking of cheap wine and bad hygiene: "Is that all you have for your brother and sister today, Bryman? Two-bits apiece?"

Brian was an easy mark for people who had less than he did. In the back of his thoughts was the nagging fear that, if he didn't get his act together soon, he might one day be hanging out at the same fire-barrels under the Interstate 35E bridges. He kept his five and a one buttoned in his back pocket.

What the hell, he thought to himself, then reached behind, "I've gotta keep something for myself. Here's my last dollar." Mickey's smile was equal to the pair of smiles given back to him.

"God bless you," said Annie.

"Maybe some day He will," Brian said. For some weird yet wonderful reason, Brian Slade believed that God might bless him.

3/ DECEMBER 2011

A day is a day is a day. But, so many circumstances shape it differently for every person in every place. The national and world news for December sixth, as reported in all three daily newspapers– Naples, Hibbing, and St. Paul– was essentially the same. Barak Obama was campaigning in Osawatomie, Kansas and espousing his populist economic vision while using some of the same phraseology that Theodore Roosevelt used in that same city nearly a century before. Voter opinion polls on the Republican primary in Iowa had Newt Gingrich distancing himself from Mitt Romney, Rick Santorum and the rest of the GOP field. Romney maintained his lead in the New Hampshire polls. Election year politics were already heated and it wasn't even election year yet. Amos, like millions of Americans, thought it was too much politics much too early.

The *Dow*, having gone through dramatic swings almost daily for months, reflected the early Christmas spending bonanza and was settling comfortably above the 12,000 level. Encouraged that his portfolio was healthy this morning, Amos Moran would give little credit to the current administration. The economy remained sluggish and the unemployment rate far too high to suit his liking.

State and Defense Department sources expressed grave concern over the *Drone* spy plane that had been captured by the Iranians. More bloodshed as President-for-life Basir al-Assad sought to quell the uprising in Syria. A Pakistan-affiliated suicide bomber in Kabul, Afghanistan killed sixty-five Shiites at a Moslem worship site. The withdrawal of US forces in Iraq was continuing on schedule. The Middle East was, as it had always been, a cesspool to Meghan Williams' way of thinking, and the departure of our troops was too little and too late.

Brian Slade had no idea what a *Drone* was, probably couldn't find Afghanistan or Arizona or Africa on a world map– yet, despite not knowing why the United States was in Iraq or Afghanistan, he would support American troops whenever and wherever they might be needed. He loved his country despite the realization that this bountiful homeland did not seem to reciprocate his affection.

Amos was a hot-stove-league baseball enthusiast and the winter meetings in Dallas preoccupied his morning reading. Every fan was waiting to see whether Albert Pujols would stay a Cardinal or go somewhere else. Prince Fielder was still a free agent, too. Amos Moran was a die-hard Twins fan and hoped against hope that his team would resign his favorite player, Michael Cuddyer. Meghan Moran Williams, a disgruntled Vikings fan, hoped that her team would do something, anything!–this season had become another total disaster. Brian Slade wore a faded Wild cap but couldn't name a single player on Minnesota's professional hockey team.

Before going to morning Mass at St. Ann Church in Old Naples, Amos would give his daughter Meghan, back in Minnesota, a call to confirm that her mother still wanted another Dickens's Village piece for Christmas. Sadie, Amos' wife of nearly thirty years, had finally given him her abbreviated gifts list. Sadie was of the mind that there were too many with too little in the wider world, and wanted to do more to help those in need this season.

"We have everything we could possibly want and then some," she told Amos. "Why not feel good about ourselves on Christ's birthday this year." She planned to donate $500 in the names of both of their children (and their two grandchildren) to *Doctors Without Borders*, her favorite charity. Both Amos and Sadie would make a trip back to their home in Minnesota for the Holidays so they could enjoy their grandchildren and, though they wouldn't readily admit it, enjoy the brisk temperatures and snow-covered landscape for two weeks. Amos' parents, and their son Mickey, from Duluth, would join them for their traditional family celebration. This year their daughter Meghan and her husband, Kenny, would host the gathering.

4/ A DOWN DAY X TWO

Still depressed with thoughts of winter and routine, Meghan contemplated her morning: Start a load of laundry, make a grocery list, grocery shop at Super One, then make it to Anytime Fitness for an eleven o'clock workout. The workout on her schedule brought the trace of a smile. She would skip morning Mass at Blessed Sacrament today. It was simply too cold outside. No, to be more honest with herself, she simply didn't feel up to going. Lately the blahs had been her companion for most of the day.

Upstairs, she could hear Kenny taking his shower and the children beginning to stir. Kenny had been taking more time getting ready lately and was overusing the obnoxious new cologne he had picked up somewhere. Hmmm, what was that all about…? Brushing off the notion that her husband had wandering eyes, she pushed herself away from the table and her crossword puzzle book. "Get off your butt, Meghan… the daily grind begins now!" she said to the coffee pot. Everyone would be making their own breakfast this morning; there was cereal, milk, toast, and juice aplenty–eggs in the fridge if anyone had the ambition to do something with them. She would get out the ironing board and press Matthew's slacks and Kathleen's blouse before starting the first load of washing. Kenny had offered to give the kids a ride to Assumption School this morning, so one chore could be checked off of her list.

By eight o'clock, the house was quiet and Meghan could collect her thoughts. In neat piles spread across the kitchen table were Christmas cards that had to be signed and addressed and mailed. The holiday season was adding to her stress and it would only get worse as Christmas got closer and the kids were home on school vacation all day. The artificial tree was up but remained untrimmed, she still hadn't finished her shopping, gifts still needed wrapping… add to the mix, she and Kenny were hosting the family gathering this year. When would it all end?

She hadn't quite bargained for the life she was living. But who cared? Kenny was always too busy to even notice, mom and dad were in Florida, her female friendships were superficial… she would have to talk with her brother Mickey soon–before she did something foolish. Mickey always understood, always supported; but this was going to be a different conversation, this was going to be far more difficult. Meghan was dreading what had to be said. Mickey's world and hers seemed miles apart and the distance was growing.

~

Brian Slade needed to come up with twenty-three dollars in order to purchase a round-trip Greyhound bus ticket to Duluth where he might be able to sponge a few days of food and lodging from his sister. His older brother, Duane, living in nearby Roseville had cut him off after the last twenty dollar 'loan' and told him "get a life, and stop by for a visit after you've had something to eat and you've taken a shower." Duane Slade had made it clear that he wasn't going to be a bed and breakfast provider any longer.

Bad luck, bad choices, and what was becoming a bad attitude best defined why Brian Slade found himself in the doldrums this Christmas season. At times he wished for a return to the routine tedium of the Ramsey County jail where he wasn't half freezing to death and hungry most of the time. Owing two months rent, he had been locked out of his apartment on Maryland Avenue two weeks before. Now, his only address was bunk number twelve at the Salvation Army shelter, and that tenancy would expire in April.

He watched Moon and Annie amble away, lit a Camel near the end of his pack, cursed the habit, tucked his gloveless hands into his light jacket pocket, and kicked an empty *5 Hour Energy* bottle into the street. It was nearly eight on this frigid Tuesday morning and he was searching his thoughts for something to do… some place warm to go. From somewhere, an idea hatched, and he found himself walking into the wind toward the Catholic Church of the Good Shepherd on Van Buren Avenue. He might take advantage of Christian warmth on this bitter morning; he'd find a pew in the back of the church and let the chill ease out of his bones. After that, what? Probably the soup kitchen at the shelter where he would see the familiar faces of the St. Paul street denizens once again.

5/ FATHER MICKEY

Whenever Father Michael 'Mickey' Moran went to bed with something unresolved weighing on his thoughts, sleep would come in short spasms, if at all. Earlier in the evening his sister Meghan had called. She was planning a trip to Duluth on Saturday and wanted him to join her for lunch. She claimed to have some remaining Christmas shopping and needed to find a few things at the Miller Mall. Mickey, however, was already committed to participating in a youth retreat at Saint Scholastica College. "Sorry, sis. I'm tied up most of Saturday–probably until early in the evening. I'm joining

Father Mario for..."

Meghan interrupted, "Mick..." a long pause... "Mick, the shopping is mostly an excuse to get away from things up here. I've gotta talk to you. It's important. How about dinner? Later? Whenever you can get away."

Mickey's post-conference evening plans with clergy friends could be rearranged. His sister's emphasis on *gotta* spelled her sense of urgency. "Sure... I think I'd be able to do that. Would you like to come by the Rectory or should we meet somewhere downtown?" On quick reflection, he realized that downtown might be easier for both of them.

They would meet at the Pickwick on Saturday night.

Shortly after Meghan's call the phone rang again. Father Timothy Haglund, one of Mickey's St. Paul Seminary roommates, and estranged friend, was on the line. The two priests had not kept in touch with each other and usually each conversation would begin with mutual and sincere apologies for allowing their friendship to flounder. No apologies this time. Tim blurted his first words before Mickey had time to say hello: "Mick sorry if I caught you at a bad time but I'm in crisis mode really bad tonight worse than I can ever remember." The string of words ran without a comma to slow them down. Then the labored inhale of a heaving sob. "I just can't keep it up, the act, Mick, the act of all this. I simply can't fake it any more. I'm sorry but... Jeeze, I'm getting sick to my stomach again." Mickey let his friend catch his breath and vent it all out before edging in a word. Tim's reactions to stress had always been dramatic; his personality explosive, his judgments often rash. Many times in the past Mickey needed only to settle him down and help him define a perspective that he could manage, a perspective of his own; not one of Mickey's own design. Mickey, and others at the seminary, often considered Tim to be a misfit. He was bright academically but inept socially.

"Tim, cool it a minute. Okay! Let's start over... as calmly as you can." Like many priests in his own diocese of Duluth, Tim was probably frustrated with the 'new Mass' language that had been mandated only weeks before. For many priests, especially the older ones, the new *Sacramentery* was tedious and awkward, but that issue shouldn't have caused Tim to be hyperventilating over the phone. There had to be something more critical. He'd let his friend explain. "What's happening, my friend?"

"I'm not going to get into everything on the phone... but, we've got to talk. Soon, Mick, this can't wait much longer... the pressure's getting intense... I don't know if I can make it through another weekend. Honestly! You're the only one I can tell about what's going on." Tim paused, sniffled for several moments: "When can we get together?"

Father 'Too Thin' Tim was an Ichabod. Everything from his nose and mouth, his chin and shoulders–everything was uncommonly thin. At six four, even his size fifteen shoes seemed misplaced under his toothpick frame. Maybe that was God's way of anchoring him against the wind. Tim hailed from the flat country outside of Roseau in the northwestern corner of Minnesota. His stoical father was a marginal farmer, his mother an assertive Federal border agent.

Tim's current parish was St. Lucy's in Forest Lake, a short drive north of the Twin Cities but a long two hours drive from west Duluth where Mickey lived. Tim had been a cleric there for the past five years, meaning he'd been passed over for a pastoral assignment of his own more than once. Mickey could imagine how frustrating it must be for him to be aware of his fellow seminarians moving ahead with their ministries while he was stuck in a rut. But, he also knew that Tim had more on his plate right now than feeling trapped at St. Lucy's Church.

Before Mickey could contemplate his calendar, Tim said: "I'll drive up to Duluth if you'd like–how's Sunday afternoon, after your ten o'clock Mass?"

Mickey felt the twinge of a headache about to settle in the back of his head. Looking up at an old color photo of a smiling Pope John Paul II on the wall opposite where he was sitting, he took a deep breath, relaxed his grip on the phone and regarded the calendar on his desk. The second day of Mickey's youth retreat commitment would finish up in the early afternoon on Sunday. "Do you want to stop by here at the rectory or..." Mary Alice Murray, his seventy year old housekeeper-slash-cook, could fix a pot roast that was absolutely to die for.

Tim's voice was subdued, "No... I'd rather be somewhere away from a church–any church for that matter." Tim was heavy on the *any*. Mickey puzzled, but offered the compromise of driving to Hinckley and meeting his friend at Tobies; a popular restaurant about halfway between their two locations, at seven on Sunday evening. Tim's gratitude was profuse while saying his good-bye, "I really owe you, Mick. You've always been... " he swallowed the word 'savior' before it came out and chose "my best friend," instead.

Mickey cradled the phone and regarded his beloved Pope John Paul II once more, said a quick prayer for his hurting friend. What was it this time? While in the seminary, Tim experienced a crisis-a-week, twice retreating to his family's farm in Roseau, only to return to the campus with a new determination a few days later. Most men weren't cut out for the sacrifices required of priesthood. Mickey wasn't the only one who wondered if Tim didn't fit every definition of a vocational misfit. If it were not for the incredible shortage of priests, Tim might have washed out before being ordained. If he were a betting man, Mickey would wager that Tim was struggling with his decision. Again! If that were the case, he might be hard pressed to dissuade his friend. A leave of absence among the Roman clergy was not uncommon, and quite often the healthiest path for healing doubts that could not be resolved while wearing the collar. Both were nearly seven years out of the seminary–was there any truth to a 'seven-year-itch' syndrome for the clergy as well as for married people?

While still mulling his sister's apparent dilemma, and Tim's appeal for help, Mickey considered getting back into the Jon Hassler book, *North of Hope*, a novel he was reading for a second time. Maybe some fiction would offer an escape from the realities of the moment. But, as inviting as the worn leather Lazy Boy recliner appeared at the moment, he knew he wouldn't be able to concentrate on the story.

Once again, Mickey realized that his time didn't really belong to him any more. Free time had become a stranger from a past already too far behind to remember clearly. Service to others was becoming more like servitude to his priestly vows every year. Even time for prayer had become difficult these days, especially meaningful prayer. And this was the beginning of Advent, the coming of the Christ season, the one time of the year when every Christian should be uplifted, inspired. Christmas, however shameful it was to admit, had become stress season: What gift to get for dad, for mom, for Meg, for his brother-in-law Kenny Williams, for his niece and nephew, his housekeeper, Father Mario…? The list and the budget-busting required to show his affection toward loved ones who already knew that he loved them dearly went on, and on… This shouldn't be what Christmas was about–yet, Mickey was finding himself increasingly caught up in things secular and decreasingly focused on things sacred. At least that was how it had been since his Saint Gerard's assignment.

With Christmas only short weeks away, Mickey hadn't even made a gift list, much less done any shopping. If only he had an assistant pastor… or even a deacon, someone to share the pastoral obligations–if only! What a shallow thought, he reminded himself–this parish had become a low-maintenance operation. He sighed against the tightness that knotted between his shoulders, outstretched his arms in a liberating yawn, he might as well wish for a month's vacation in southern Florida with his parents as for any help from the Bishop.

Mickey's office was small, and like most of the rectory it was furnished with an eclectic mix of furniture probably dating back to 1923 when the residence was built. Essentially, everything in the room had been there when he arrived in mid-summer nearly six months ago. More than likely Mickey's predecessors had left the room as bleak as they had found it; a tradition of apathy that was easy for him to conform to. The wall to the right of his desk was dominated by an antique oak bookcase whose shelves were lined from one end to the other with volumes of leather-bound religious books. Neither he nor anybody else had ever bothered to pay them any attention. Opposite was an antique mahogany table with drawers that had become almost impossible to open and close. His desk was crowded into a corner under a frosted window, and a mismatched credenza behind the desk squeezed his swivel chair uncomfortably close to its writing surface. On the credenza, Mickey's only additions to the space were evident: Photos of his niece and nephew, other family members in assorted poses and places, a desk clock with the Minnesota Twins logo, and autographed Joe Mauer and Justin Morneau baseballs in plastic cases. Leaning against a corner wall behind his desk was his cherished Martin acoustic guitar. Aside from those few personal effects, everything from the threadbare sofa and Oriental rug were old and musty with age!

Despite the comfort his recliner promised, at this moment Mickey was too stressed to be sedentary. When something unresolved festered in his thoughts, Mickey became a pacer. A pacer needed to have an adequate space to get from one thought to the next. He didn't. Crossing the small room with hands clasped behind his back, shoulders stooped, and head down… he pivoted sharply and repeated the four short paces the dimensions allowed. After several repetitions and no resolutions, he headed for the hall closet by the entry foyer. Despite the intimidating cold outside, he decided to take a walk. While walking, Father Mickey usually found it easier to get a handle on whatever was bothering him. He would pray that his mind would unlock and he would be able to see things more clearly.

6/ SAINT GERARD'S OF BENTON PARK

Before slipping into his Sorrell boots resting by the rectory's side door, Mickey regarded the Nativity scene on a shelf below the Bishop's suggested display of a Pope Benedict XVI photograph. He had purchased the crèche set at a neighborhood garage sale in west Duluth years before and had assembled the pieces that afternoon. For some unknown reason, Mickey felt a compulsion to kneel down and contemplate each of the wood-carved pieces. Whoever had crafted the intricately detailed figures had been a masterful woodworker. Mickey had always held a special affiliation to Joseph, the carpenter who taught Jesus his trade. Of the many saintly attributes, Joseph's obedience to the will of God was among the most admirable.

"Dear Saint Joe, I pray that your simple love and your devotion might guide me through this holy season. I ask that you bless me with your wisdom as I try to comfort and console those who seek my help. And, Blessed Mary, please help me to be worthy of the promises of your Son, Jesus." He blessed himself and felt a little bounce in his step as he retrieved his jacket and made for the door. The thought of his priestly vows crept into his thoughts as he got into his jacket: Poverty, celibacy, and obedience. Of the three, obedience was the most challenging for Mickey. In seminary, he was often reminded that 'without obedience, a priest a ship adrift at sea'. That advice, however, had fallen on deaf ears–right or wrong, Mickey believed that his Lord, not his Bishop, gave him personal directions.

It was nearly ten o'clock when his hand turned the door handle– the phone was ringing again. Rather than pick up, he glanced at the caller ID. His father was calling from Florida. Mickey doubted any emergency to the call; his dad often phoned at odd times just to say hello, inquire about how things were going up in frigid Duluth, or request a prayer for one person or another. He guessed that this call probably had something to do with a Christmas list Mickey had promised to send to his mother but had failed to do. What did he need, or even want? He had no clue. Well, maybe a nice picture frame for the recent school photos of his niece and nephew that Meghan had sent him weeks ago. Or, a small contribution for his 'piggy bank'.

Mickey decided to slip outside and clear his mind rather than clutter it with small talk about any irrelevancies from his parents. It was only a venial sin to ignore your parents when they called, he smiled to himself at the thought: If the matter were anything important they would leave a message or call again later–hopefully not until tomorrow. He closed the door behind him and stepped into a frigid wind that stung his eyes.

The banner on the far west 88th Street railroad overpass at the entry to Benton Park had a banner stating 'Historic past, Bright future'– few who lived there would agree. The Duluth neighborhood of Benton Park surrounding Saint Gerard's Catholic Church was old, blue collar, and becoming more decrepit with every passing year. Mickey's church was a perfect reflection of its milieu: A paint peeling wood-framed structure with a bell tower steeple in need of repair, and badly deteriorated concrete front stoop. In its prime, seven decades and more ago, this same neighborhood was youthful, vibrant, flourishing; today it had become but a shadow of its former self. The church, past and present, reflected the neighborhood. At one time there had been a contagious vitality here and the parochial school affiliated with the parish spoke of its youthful spirit. Youth proffered both a vision and vitality. The school, however, had been vacated for some time before being razed nearly two decades ago. These days, funerals outnumbered baptisms by five to one. A priest friend, upon hearing of his appointment to Saint Gerard's the summer before, offered a humorous insight: "You may go down in diocesan records as the last priest in the history of your parish." Mickey mighty well end up being the captain on a sinking ship.

Mickey still harbored a mild resentment toward the Bishop for this assignment. When he was informed that he was going to Saint Gerard's he believed it was a punishment, a purgatory of sorts. His first two assignments had been inspiring and fulfilling experiences: St. James a few miles east of Benton Park had been his first parish, then a transfer to St. Francis' in the resort community of Brainerd. Both were wonderful fits for the youthful, energetic, if not somewhat idealistic, priest. Both had elementary schools with stable enrollments and a core congregation of committed families. He sorely missed the enthusiasm that his connection with school kids offered and the teaching that was an integral part of his pastoral responsibilities in both parishes.

Saint Gerard's was a test of obedience for Mickey. Perhaps his prayers to beloved St. Joseph helped him cope with the pervasive disappointment. Perhaps, however, it was something even deeper than honoring his vows. Mickey believed that faith was his greatest gift and that if his faith remained strong, his disappointment with the present order of things would turn into a blessing of some sort–what that might be he hadn't a clue.

If both of his former parishes were blessings, each proved to be a curse of sorts at the same time. Controversy shrouded each assignment and put the young priest at odds with the Bishop of the Duluth Diocese, Bishop Anthony Bremmer. Bremmer was said to have referred to Father Moran as 'a loose cannon'. Maybe the bishop was too conservative, maybe Mickey was too liberal. Maybe... maybe it was something even deeper. Mickey had never considered himself to be a philosophical liberal, nor was he possessed of strictly conservative persuasions. If anything, he was a bit too altruistic for his own good. He believed that right would triumph over wrong, good over evil, morality over immorality. On one occasion, or confrontation, the young priest suggested that Bishop Bremmer was a bit 'close-minded'–probably his 'touché' was a grave mistake.

At St. James, Mickey had a group of teenage boys who seemed to find trouble without looking for it. One Saturday night, two of these boys were arrested after a fight with some Duluth East High School kids. One of the East boys was hospitalized with head abrasions and a possible concussion. As fate would have it, the injured boy was the son of a prominent local businessman who was also a prominent member of the bishop's parish.

"Honest to God, Father, they started it," Randy Flynn told Mickey. Jimmy Rossini also swore that they were only defending themselves. Although miscreants in many ways, both teens were former altar boys, and playground denizens who were always up for a game of hoops. Many of Mickey's unstructured hours were spent on the St. James asphalt court playing 'horse' and 'twenty-one' with Randy and Jimmy. Mickey went to bat for his boys with the police and later with the juvenile authorities. The victim's father appealed to the Bishop to put a leash on "that obnoxious priest of yours from St. James." Father Michael Moran had disobeyed his bishop while supporting his boys with the county authorities.

A few months later, the boys invited Father Mickey to a gig they were playing at the Domiano Center with *BABEL*, their upstart rock group. Mickey was having a great time until Randy Flynn introduced him to the young crowd as "Our featured soloist for the evening…!" Embarrassed but amused, he took the stage and conferred briefly with the band members about what he was expected to do. It was agreed that they could accompany him with the spiritual *'He's got the Whole World in His Hands.'* It sounded better than he might ever had expected. The mostly teenager audience sang along with him and, afterwards, clamored for an encore. "Can you do *'Seven Spanish Angels'*?" he asked Randy.

"Can we ever," Jimmy Rossini chimed in, "It's one of my mom's favorite songs." After a dramatic drum roll, *BABEL* and Father Mickey, took the crowd to the 'valley of the sun…' Reveling in the success of his rock debut, Mickey found a downtown pawn shop the following Monday and purchased a used Martin DXI acoustic guitar for $250. A skilled musician, Jimmy Rossini was willing to give him some basic lessons. Although it took some time, Mickey mastered most of the basic chords.

∼

As he walked down the middle of the abandoned Benton Park street and into the brisk wind he could feel its sharp bite, then a spreading numbness across his cheeks. Spotting a small snow chunk near the curb he stopped, disengaged his thoughts of the moment and shifted into imagination gear. As a kid growing up, street tackle football was an activity he and his friends enjoyed. Using an ice chunk for a ball and the bordering snow banks as sidelines, they played a game more akin to rugby than football. Lapsing back to those carefree days he squared up, focused on the snow chunk, took three steps and kicked mightily toward an imaginary goalpost thirty feet away.

"Moran's kick is good!" He shouted into the stillness of the night, raising both arms in an official's gesture for a successful field goal. "Minnesota wins!" He jumped into the air and pumped his fist in mock victory. Having won his Vikings first Super Bowl with the kick, Mickey turned back toward the rectory before his enthusiasm became a serious case of frostbite.

7/ A SECOND DISOBEDIENCE

Turning to head back to the rectory, his thoughts found the thread he had been sewing his frustrations with only moments before–his unmitigated issues with the bishop. The episode in Brainerd two years ago was even more serious and attracted considerably more public attention than the incident in Duluth. Lonny Gregorich was a Hibbing High School classmate and close friend of Mickey's while growing up. Both boys were active in the drama club and school plays. Years later, John became a high school educator and ended up teaching English and directing plays at Brainerd High School. 'Mister G', as the students knew him, was an outgoing, if not blatantly eccentric, teacher, whose sense of humor was widely acclaimed. For the spring play, 'Mr. G' had chosen Neil Simon's, Barefoot In the Park, a comedy with demanding lead roles. Experienced and popular Mandy Baker was everybody's guess to win the leading role of Corie. But, Mandy was not Mr. G's choice for the demanding part. Before the production opened, an attorney from Minneapolis that had been hired by the Baker family petitioned the school board to remove Mr. Gregorich from the faculty pending an 'inappropriate sexual contact with a student' investigation. Coincidently, that student was none other than their daughter, Amanda. In a closed door meeting with the Superintendent, the board caved to the Bakers and their attorney. Lonny Gregorich was placed on an unrequested leave of absence.

"It's bogus, Mickey," Gregorich told his friend over dinner at the St. Francis rectory days after the story was leaked to the press. "I'm screwed, if you'll excuse the reference; it's my word against the girl's allegation. I'm told that a few of her friends are willing to go to the wall for her. It's a classic set-up, Mick. However they want to frame it–it's revenge!"

Father Michael Moran of St. Francis Church was asked to go before the school board as a character witness to support his friend. Lonny's case was a 'small town' scandal and it had sharply divided the community. The bishop appealed to Father Moran to 'let the legal machinery do it's own thing' with a strong implication that the priest was to stay out of it. "It does not concern the affairs of your parish, and you must not allow any friendships to compromise your functioning as it's spiritual leader," Bishop Bremmer insisted. (Bishop Bremmer chose not to mention that Mr. Gregorich wasn't even a practicing Catholic). Despite the bishop's strong appeal,

Father Mickey appeared in court on behalf of his non-Catholic friend.

Months later, the suspended teacher was vindicated when two of Baker's collaborators confessed that they had perjured themselves and that the whole affair was contrived. Although it was now apparent that Lonny Gregorich had done nothing wrong, his good reputation could never be reclaimed. He left teaching and took a job with Best Buy Corporation in Minneapolis.

Father Mickey, who should also have been vindicated as well, was transferred to Saint Gerard's parish in far west Duluth shortly afterward. Although dumbfounded when he learned of his transfer, he remembered six of the bishop's many words from their afternoon conversation: "Humility is a virtue, my son."

Mickey's albatross was going to bat for an underdog in trouble; he had known that from an early age. 'Pick fights that you can win' his father had chided him on more than one occasion. Regardless, he had won twice and ended up losing twice. He coped with his disappointment as best he could. If Saint Gerard's was to be his purgatory, he would accept it as such and, ultimately, he would be all the better for the experience. "It's like a midnight shift in the mines," he once told his friend, Father Mario. "I'll become accustomed to functioning in a dark place, and find ways to thrive in it. It's just the bishop's power trip and a test of my resolve."

"Obedience can be a bitter pill to swallow, my friend," Mario said. "We can only wash it down with faith, faith that His hands always move us to where he wants us to be. Don't ever forget the dark places our Lord passed through on His way to The Kingdom."

But, too often, the dark place was too much for him and Mickey didn't cope as well as he hoped. The demographics of Saint Gerard's were a sharp contrast from everything he had experienced before; predominantly elderly, mixed with low-income and minority families–some from the 'Rez' in nearby Fond du Lac. In his indisputable wisdom, Bishop Bremmer had placed the young priest in the old parish to humble him, to quiet him down, to give him time to reflect.

In his fifteen minutes outside, Mickey's hands and feet were becoming numb, his face red and swollen from the wind. Preoccupied with his thoughts, the priest had mistakenly begun his walk with the wind at his back, which led to his going quite a bit further than he should have. His return took him into the teeth of a stinging wind. The tiny flakes riding in the subzero breeze were like pinpricks on his exposed cheeks. Shoulders hunched, head bent forward, he quickened his pace along the roadside snow banks.

Back inside the warmth of the rectory he noticed the blinking message indicator on the phone. He touched the play mode, his mother's voice: "Mickey, will you give gramma a call. She's having a difficult time with your grampa. I think it's pretty serious this time–so does your father. Lately, grampa's been acting very strangely. Anyhow, when I told her that I'd ask you to call first thing tomorrow morning–after Mass that is–she said something really weird: 'That might not be such a good idea, Sadie' is what she said.

Wish I could tell you what she meant by that. Do what you think is best, son. Otherwise, we're fine and dad will get in touch later. Oh, I almost forgot, it was seventy-four in Naples this afternoon. Thought you'd want to know that. Love ya..."

The second message was from an elderly parishioner. Edward Blazina had been admitted to St. Mary's Hospital with alleged pneumonia symptoms. His wife Lois hoped that Mickey would visit him and bring the Eucharist in the morning. Although the eighty-some year old had moderate hypertension and elevated cholesterol, Edward's greatest health problem was hypochondria. Lois, his constant enabler, called the priest about one thing or another almost daily.

The third missed caller would remain a mystery for some time to come. The caller-ID did not provide a name, but the area code and number indicated the origin was Hibbing, a community seventy miles to the north and the town where Mickey grew up. Anything with a Hibbing connection stirred a thick nostalgia, especially something out of the blue–like an email or phone call. The recorded voice was vaguely familiar and female: "Father Moran…" a lengthy pause, a clearing of the throat, then… the dial tone. It seemed that the caller had changed her mind about something and hung up.

The unread mail next to the phone on the table included a cable TV bill, an oil change coupon, and a letter with no return address. He opened the envelope and read the card's scribbled note:

'Dear Father Moran:

Thank you for your sermon last Sunday. It was good. I have been having truble with some drinking. I was to confession about that last month but I did more drinking again. I'm sorry. Your sermon about respecting yourself made sense to me. You make things clear and help me with my troubles. I will say prayers for you.

Sinserly.
Benjamin Little Otter

Those few words warmed him more than the heat in the room.

8/ AN OLD PHOTOGRAPH

That night, Mickey tossed and turned for an hour or more despite taking three Tylenol PM's. As often happened, events of the day would replay themselves in dreams, incredibly bizarre dreams. His brief football fantasy of earlier that evening was relived on an actual gridiron. Mickey was wearing the navy blue uniform of his high school while his family cheered from the stands. Then, roles dramatically changed; his father Amos, was wearing the football uniform and Mickey had become a cheerleader on the sidelines. A blur of wildly imagined events were followed by the appearance of his great grandfather from somewhere out of the blue. Kevin Moran was being interviewed on ESPN-TV, and was wearing a Minnesota

Gopher baseball uniform.

In an unrelated dream, Mickey was wandering through Black Bear Casino, west of Duluth, looking for Benjamin Little Otter. The Ojibwe Indian was leaning over the bar talking to a man dressed in black with a redlined cloak draped over his shoulders. "Stay away from me!" Benjamin screamed, "I will have nothing to do with you any more." Then with an angry scowl he made a fist, but rather than strike his nemesis, he shoved the devil away from him. Then Benjamin stood, gave Mickey a wide grin, shook his hand and walked tall and proud out of the casino door.

The following morning, Mickey overslept. Upon awakening he recalled the strange dreams and tried to get his head around their meanings, if there were any. In reality, Mickey had never been the athlete that his father had been, or his grandfather Pack; great-grampa Kevin was probably better than both. In fact, after Little League, Mickey never again became involved in organized sports. While in school he loved music and drama and academics, excelling in each of them. He remembered an old, yellowed, photograph he had seen somewhere, probably years before, of his great grandfather in a Gopher uniform. It was the very same perception of Kevin that he had seen in his dream the night before.

The other dream had been inspired by the 'thank you' note of the night before. Mickey made a mental note to look up Benjamin later and see how he was doing with his problem. If there had been one small positive in his St. Gerard's ministry it might be that a few more Indian faces were in evidence at Sunday Mass. Not many, but a few.

After morning Mass and a light breakfast, Father Mickey pondered his schedule for the day as well as for the coming weekend. Busy, always busy! The commitments he'd made to his sister Meg and to his friend Tim, the phone call from his mom regarding Grandfather Pack, the Blazina medical problem–his plate was full. The seminar with Father Mario Morelli at the College of Saint Scholastica, however, brought an easy smile to his face. Mickey enjoyed working with young people, found that their energy infused him, their questions always challenged his spiritual creativity, nurturing their faith gave him a sense of purpose.

The smile, however, was short-lived. He might begin tackling his 'to-do' list by returning his mother's call. Pouring a fresh cup of coffee he clicked the directory on his cell phone. Amos answered, "Is that all I get? A hello Dad, can I talk with mom for a minute? That's a kick in the butt."

Mickey apologized, conjured some small talk–the rumors about the Twins pursuing some free agents, Christmas activities at his church, and, of course; the weather. "Love you, too, son. I'll pass you over to mom, she's sitting here at the table with her morning Sudoku..."

"Wait a minute, Dad. I just thought of something kinda weird. Can you remember an old photograph of your Grampa Kevin wearing an old Gopher baseball uniform?"

His memory tweaked, Amos considered the irony: he had been curious about some old pictures just the day before and one of them was the picture that his son was inquiring about. How ironic! "Yes... I've still got it somewhere, probably up at the house in Hibbing. Kevin was quite the jock in his day, you know..." Amos said. "Why do you ask?"

Mickey searched his thoughts for a long moment. He didn't want a dream analysis from his dad and had no idea where the question could possibly take them. He'd let it go for now.

"Son... you still there?"

"Yeah, I'm here... don't know why I asked... just something that popped into my head, I guess."

Amos' brow furrowed: "Seems kinda strange to me."

Then something slipped out of Mickey's subconscious and into words without his intending them to: "Dad, were you ever disappointed that I never got into playing sports? I know that it kinda bothered Grampa Pack. He was quite a jock–hockey, baseball… played slo-pitch until he was fifty, I think. All you Moran guys were jocks."

"Oh yeah, that's all true enough, I guess–the jock thing, I mean. I'd disagree about the disappointment stuff though. Where in the world did that come from, son?"

Mickey wasn't quite sure how to answer; somehow it had to be rooted in his being a cheerleader in the dream. "That picture of great grampa, I guess. It's nothing–nothing at all, Dad."

"You let that bother you, Mickey? No, for heaven's sake, no! You're not playing ball was never a problem for me or for your mom.

You were always a great kid… we enjoyed watching the school plays and academic competitions as much we would have a baseball game."

Amos felt a twinge of stress. He wasn't being totally honest. Mickey had been small for his age, bullied at times by bigger kids, and would rather be on his computer than watch a Viking game on television. It wasn't until he was a senior in high school that he had a real growth spurt. "Your mom is tugging at my sleeve, she's got a pen and paper ready for… what is it, Sadie? Oh, probably your Christmas list? She wants to…"

Sadie took the phone from Amos in midsentence, "How's my dear Mickey this morning?" His mother had something other than 'what can we get you for Christmas' on her mind. "Gramma Maddie called again last night."

Mickey glanced at the digital clock on his Mr. Coffee to the right of the sink on the kitchen counter. He had a list of items to get done before noon and he'd need to make this conversation as short as possible. His mother could be a long talker: Ask her what time it was and she'd tell you about the inner workings of a clock.

"It's your Grandfather, son." Sadie explained her concerns and those of Grandmother Maddie. Pack was an aging man, fiercely independent, and struggling with his sense of worth. Every classic symptom of depression was manifest in what his mother was explaining. "You've got to give her a call, Mickey. Gramma needs a lot of support. You know how unruly Grampa can be... more than a handful for sure. I know it's a busy time for you..."

His mom couldn't possibly know how busy. He promised to call Gramma Maddie early next week. "I'm swamped right now, Mom. The holidays are almost overwhelming. It's not that I don't care, it's just ... maybe." He scratched his head, "just maybe I can get up there for a short visit next week. I'll do what I can... okay?"

That morning at Mass, Mickey had a lapse in concentration during the *'profession of faith'*. The new liturgy that the Roman hierarchy had dropped on Catholics around the world for this Advent season was an unspoken frustration for nearly every priest in the diocese– probably every priest in the world!

Mickey kept his feelings about the changes mostly to himself, but not entirely. He would probably get an email from Bishop Bremmer regarding his homily the previous Sunday. Departing from his intended message, he let slip that he held little warmth or fondness, but an always dutiful reverence, for Pope Benedict. Mickey suggested that the mandate for the so-called 'new Mass' might well be the new pope's manner of getting his controversial papacy into the Roman Catholic history books.

Mickey found himself reciting the former prayer instead of the new one. It wasn't likely that any one in his congregation was bothered by his misspeak. His lapse was little more than a brief distraction. Since swiping his snooze alarm that morning he had been preoccupied with his agenda of people crises and his weird dream the night before.

Moments later, he began reading the Epistle rather than the Gospel... this mistake, although quickly corrected, would not go unnoticed.

9/ BAD CHOICES

Brian Slade was the youngest of the three Slade children abandoned by their parents and then separated by Ramsey County Social Services in St. Paul. At the time Brian was nine. Beth, the oldest at fourteen was a freshman and honor student in high school. Aunt Hazel was the only relative with an ounce of compassion.

Hazel agreed to assume custody of her niece so that Beth could finish her schooling with as little trauma as possible. Living with Hazel and Charles Broker, however, meant moving to Duluth and enrolling in Denfeld High School. Beth was the easy piece to the puzzle that was the Slade kids. The two boys were another matter: "Ruffians!" was her description of Duane and Brian Slade during an interview with one of many social workers monitoring the well being of the three. "They'd be the death of Charles and me. You folks just do what's best for them."

Duane and Brian ended up in foster care. Duane flourished, Brian floundered. The two boys were as different as fire and ice. Duane, at age eleven, was already a well-developed sociopath and a perfect fit for Mitchell and Brenda Dougherty.

Mitch was an attorney with his own practice–specializing in DUI and drug cases–serving a clientele of reprobates of every ilk. He was good at 'beating the rap' and his reputation on the streets of Frogtown and northeast St. Paul was golden. A closet alcoholic, Brenda had the worst possible personality for her two men; Brenda Dougherty was a codependent enabler.

Brian was a docile child, pleasant and unassuming. He was also a square peg in a world of round holes. The foster care families he was assigned to regarded their charges as a source of income, and an extra body to do the work. One foster father told Brian, "You're worthless kiddo, get that straight. You otta thank God yer not out on the streets. Now get your ass out to the shed and get that lawnmower going. When you've finished that I got plenty more for ya to do." That comment and that miserable day were repeated countless times in his preteen years.

Over time, and despite distance and adversity, Beth Slade managed to keep her brothers connected. Were it not for her perseverance, the three would never have had any sense of a 'biological family'. There were lengthy periods of time when the three were completely detached from one another. Nevertheless, various ephemeral reconnections always seemed to occur. While Beth remained in Duluth beyond graduation, her brothers remained a phone call away in the Twin Cities. Nearly every summer the three Slades had a reunion of sorts–little more than a lunch at Tobies, a restaurant halfway between Duluth and the Cities.

Extrovertish Duane usually found a way to make an easy buck, introvertish Brian usually found a way to lose a buck. There was a grain of truth in the adage that 'people of action are favored by the god of luck'. Most of Brian's bad luck might best be understood in terms of bad decisions and bad associations. His decision to

~

Most of Brian Slade's bad luck stemmed from bad decisions and equally bad associations–both were usually one and the same. The run away from his third foster family at sixteen first got him in trouble with the juvenile authorities. Brian had hitched a ride to downtown Minneapolis with a friend who was going to an Aerosmith concert. Two hungry days later, while wandering through Loring Park, he spotted a woman sitting on a bench and tossing bread crumbs to pigeons. The hopeless part of him coveted the slice of stale bread, the desperate part of him coveted the large canvas purse at her side.

Brian grabbed the bag by its straps, took off running... the burly, black man who tripped him and pinned him to the sidewalk until a squad car arrived happened to be a legal aide with a prestigious law firm. Brian Kellogg was the man's name. The big Brian had the smaller Brian sent back to St. Paul and Ramsey County authorities. Judge Kreig cut the teenager some slack and Ramsey County Social Services found him another foster family–his fourth.

Academics and Brian Slade suffered from a serious case of basic incompatibility. As a junior at Harding High School he was assigned the reading *Two Years Before the Mast*, a classic American novel by Richard Henry Dana. His required book report was brief:

"I hated this book. I couldn't care less about the life of a sailor. It has no relevance. I quit reading at page twelve, before the ship left Boston's harbor. The end."

Mrs. Wrighton, his English teacher gave him an F for his six-weeks grade, adding to his report card a comment: '*Brian seems apathetic and exhibits a negative attitude.*" This might have been the turning point, Brian began failing all of his classes and quit school midway through his junior year. A job at Rainbow Foods earned him enough money to get by on his own. His foster family, Grace and Wally Jansen were satisfied to "leave well-enough-alone" as long as Brian reported home from time-to-time–just enough so they could continue getting their monthly stipend from the county.

At the grocery store he met another dropout, a black kid named Cassius Case. Cassius had been in trouble many times and bragged about his many escapades. Brian became infatuated by his new friend's wild stories. Like Pinocchio, Brian was ripe for an adventure in the 'candy land' of excitement with his new friend. Hanging out with Cass gave him a false sense of self-worth. His adulation and need to impress led to the "I dare you's" that are like a hook baited with chocolate.

"You'ze a candy-ass, Bry," Cass teased. "Betcha can't hit that window there with this here rock," he pointed at the public building behind a row of tall hedges.

"You first. You do it and I will." The two of them were in the alley behind the library at the time. Cassius shattered one window,

Brian another–the experience proved Brian wasn't a candy ass and bonded their friendship. For better or worse; there were no consequences this time.

Later, "Hey Bry, see that car over there?" he gestured toward a red Mustang.

Later, the duo pried a window open, and burglarized a beauty salon. The petty cash drawer had seventy dollars. "We be cool dudes, doncha think?" Cass said as he pocketed fifty and passed a twenty to his cohort.

Cass taught Brian how to hotwire, "Deeze two wires here," he pulled them out of the steering column; "Jus tuch'em to each other and presto…" the starter solenoid turned over. The two teens had a crazy night joyriding through their St. Paul neighborhood. When the lights behind them began flashing, Cass cried out, "Watch dis mother go!" He hit the gas… "I gonna lose doze pigs!"

The chase was a brief one–a corner near Como Park was too sharp, and Cass was too unskilled. A two blocks chase, and two St. Paul squad cars, brought their reckless evening of fun to a screeching halt. Cass stopped after crossing the curb and sidewalk just short of a huge ash tree. The ending could have been much worse.

Cass did time, Brian lucked out.

Enter Joey Dunfy, someone he remembered from high school who was waiting for a bus on University Avenue when Brian walked up to say hello. "Hey Slade. You workin' at Rainbow tonight?"

He was, " What's up man?"

"You know that Judy Franz babe?"

Brian nodded, "Why?"

"Will you pass this along to her when ya see her?" He handed a baggie to Brian.

"What's this?"

"She'll know. Hey, catch up later." Dunfy was ten feet away and sprinting before Brian knew what was happening.

The bus driver saw the exchange, he turned to a man several

rows back, "Say Andy, you wanna make a pinch. Just saw a little dealing going down." Andy Sullivan, an overweight local cop, had had two beers after his shift, and didn't want to get out of his seat. But, what might people think if he didn't do his duty.

Sullivan pulled himself out of his seat, adjusted his gun belt, and charged like an elephant through the side door. Leaping from the step he knocked Brian off-balance, wrestled him to the sidewalk, and pinned the youth against a utility pole. "Don't even try to move, punk." The burly cop put a knee in Brian's groin, then ripped open the jacket pocket where Brian had tucked the baggie.

The bus driver radioed the police department and in two minutes Brian was cuffed and on his way to the juvenile authorities again. The amount of marijuana in his possession was less than 42 grams, his sentence only probation and community service. The minor felony, however, put his name on the books.

Two years later, Brian was twenty, and working for a carpenter who specialized in building the popular and over-priced cedar decks that everybody just had to have. Lofton, the guy who hired him, paid cash on Friday afternoon. Life was good again. Brian had his own place, an old Chevelle to get around in, and some nice clothes.

Reenter, old friend, Cass. "Gotta borrow some cash, Bry," Cassius was out on probation, back on the street, and flat broke. "Just until next week…" A twenty didn't keep Cass away for long. The old nemesis was back in his life and knocking on the door of his apartment.

"Com'on, Bry. I need some help with somethin'. Gimme some help and I pay ya back with an twenty extra. How's that sound, motha? First, ya gotta gimme a ride."

If mistakes were put on a one-to-ten scale, agreeing to help Cass that night was a ten. Cass told Brian to stop at the end of a commercial block on south Snelling Avenue. It was nine-thirty, only half an hour before the liquor stores closed. The two young men got out of the car. "Just walk with me," Cass said.

"No, you go ahead... I'll wait here for ya," Brian said.

Cass gave his a dirty look, "You and me, we'ze pardners, Bry. No chicken shit stuff, okay?"

Cass was intimidating and Brian didn't want any trouble. "What do you want from me?"

The plan was as stupid as it was simple. All Brian had to do was hold the liquor store's door open and holler if anybody came. Both loitered near the curb until the last customer was out the door.

"Now!" Cass shouted and rushed from the sidewalk into the store and down the narrow aisle to the register; "I got a gun man: Jus gimme yer cash, then get down on the floor."

The clerk pulled a stack of ones from the drawer, put them on the counter, then tripped a lever beside the register... the alarm was shrill, piercing... Cass panicked,"Let's get our asses outta here!"

Cass ran down a side street, Bryan toward his car half a block away. Before he could pull out into traffic, he was toast. This felony put Brian Slade in the big house. This time it was five years for Brian Slade– none for Cassius Case.

If Cassius was a bad choice for Brian, Bonnie Potter was worse. Beautiful, gregarious, seductive, Bonnie Potter–a popular television journalist. Bonnie was doing a story for WCCO TV, in the Twin Cities, about the adjustments that ex-convicts had to make on the outside. The state corrections director, Wilson Weber, gave her the bios of several former inmates she might consider profiling–Brian Slade was one of his recommendations. Nice-looking fella, non-violent, personable Brian. Bonnie Potter was a skillful user of people and her strategy was to come on to one of the cons and really get inside his head. Brian was an easychoice from among the seven men whose biographies she had studied.

Brian met Bonnie by accident, he thought, when the lady's car wouldn't start. Potter's Land Rover was conveniently stalled in front of his apartment building. "Hey, ma'am... what's the problem?" Brian said cheerfully. From the simple 'What's the problem? came a series of inevitable calamities that would befall the 'do-gooder' nature of Brian Slade. All too quickly he became totally infatuated withBonnie. His head-over-heels infatuation swiftly evolved into an economic dilemma: The young suitor had spent every dollar of his savings attempting to show her a good time. Skilled with men who were far beyond Brian's league, Bonnie made him feel like a feel like a fairytale prince. After two weeks of deeply personal conversations about his early life and factors contributing to his troubles with authority, she tossed him like yesterday's trash.

But why? Brian tormented. What had he done wrong? When Bonnie Potter's human interest story was aired on regional television the following week, Brian became a local celebrity and the talk of the neighborhood. Although flattered by his sudden notoriety, Brian was a psychological mess–he wasn't too naïve to realize that the local TV personality had used him. Still, he needed to know the details behind the big *why* he couldn't reconcile. . . he needed to talk with her about their failed relationship–were the good times they shared together genuine? Or, was it all nothing more than an act from the very beginning?

Ms. Potter, however, wanted nothing more to do with yesterday's story; turning him away from her door she said: "Brian, we just don't have anything in common. I'm sorry. You're a good person– someone will see that. Now... please let go, okay?" When he sought closure a second time, Bonnie got a restraining order. The next time, he tried to talk to her outside the WCCO studio–she called the police. Brian was booked for stalking, and off to another stint in the Ramsey County jail.

10/ JOHNNY'S CANDLES

It was little more than fifty feet, just a few long strides, from the side door of the rectory to the north entry ramp of St. Gerard's Church. Yet, in the tunnel formed between the two buildings a wind chill of nearly minus thirty brushed across his face like a frozen broom. If he hadn't been fully awake before his jacketless dash, he was now. Once again, Mickey had inadvertently hit his alarm clock's snooze button this morning, half-sleeping through those few stolen minutes from his new day. Hurriedly dressing and skipping the usual caffeine that jump-started most days, his Friday was off on the left foot. Inside the sacristy, he rubbed his hands together and regarded the digital clock: Twenty-five minutes until Mass. Passing the frosted north-facing windows he caught an irritating draft seeping into the room along the old wooden sills. "Brrrr," he mumbled, and resolved to have the churches handyman if he could do some long overdue calking later that afternoon.

Before slipping into his alb, tying his cincture, and draping his stole over his shoulders, Mickey would say his morning prayers. Going to one knee on the padded kneeler, and putting his hands together, he regarded the crucifix on the south wall of the narrow room. He signed himself, closed his eyes, searched his thoughts for a prayer that might lift his spirits and connect him with his God. Within moments he was oblivious to the chill in the air, his surroundings, and his concerns about other people's problems. Being in accord with his Savior placed every worry in a perspective that he could wholly embrace and put his spirit at peace with the world. He petitioned God for greater faith, greater commitment, and a more perfect service. Lately, Mickey had been feeling that his spirituality was not what it should be, that he was too often distracted by worldly and superficial things. At other times he confessed his remorse over allowing the displeasure with his assignment to inhibit the pastoral attentions his flock deserved. He knew that he must try harder, give more, get his priorities better aligned and balanced.

This morning he prayed his *liturgy of hours* in a special way, asking God for those problem-solving insights that had come so easily in the past and had become so elusive of late. The patience that had been a natural blessing for him now tested his resolve to isolate the issue, clarify it, and find a resolution. Come Lord Jesus. Come Lord Jesus. He petitioned in the simplest and most honest of prayers in his repertoire. When repeating this heartfelt appeal, often for long minutes, he could usually quiet the voices competing for expression and provide himself with the spiritual focus he desired. Come Lord Jesus!

Prayer came in a torrent, like rain upon a thirsty bed of flowers. And with prayer came a deep inner peace: The peace that had sustained him since boyhood, and had nurtured his vocation to the priesthood. When he was able to achieve that special oneness with his Lord, he could feel the vitality of surrender and embrace the power that would enable him to make his day a blessing. A blessing that he prayed might become contagious. In addition, with prayer and submission came serenity. He imagined sunshine and warmth and birds and butterflies and abundant flowers and a treasure that transcended this time and place. If, however, his stress was like a mental vice...

"Father..." The bidding came from some otherworldly place. He felt the gentle pressure of a hand on his shoulder. "Father..."

The full-faced smile of Johnny Jawarski brought him back to the drafty sacristy. "G'mornin', John." Mickey glanced at his wristwatch, seven-fifty seven. "Sorry, Father. Din't mean to interrupt yer prayers, but..."

Johnny had been retarded since birth and altar serving at daily Mass was the single highlight of his every day. Mickey believed that John and others like him were the true saints among us, incapable of doing anything sinful and possessing the inner peace that only a person chosen of God is capable of having. "You going to wear your Twins cap at Mass this morning, Johnny?"

John puzzled for a moment, and then realized he hadn't taken off his shapeless and faded cap. "Gosh Fadder...I'm sorry...I din't know."

Mickey couldn't contain an honest and perfect laugh. Blessing himself and rising from his kneeler, he stood and gave the smaller man a hug. Then he smoothed out Johnny's snarled hair. "You saved the day, my friend. I think that my eyes were frozen shut." He made light of being lost in his spiritual realm. "What's the temperature in here anyway? Is the furnace working?"

"Yep, I kin hear'er growlin downstairs, Fadder. But it ain't do'in us much good. Dat furnace, she's kinda old and wore out, I'd say. And, it' sure a bugger out der, Fadder. I'm s'prised anybody came to Mass dis mornin' but I see all the reglars showed up anyhow."

Father Mickey nodded as Johnny left the sacristy to do his favorite morning assignment: lighting the altar candles. One morning Johnny astonished Mickey by saying something so profound that it had to have been inspired by God himself: "When I light dem candles, Fadder... it's kinda like I'm getting' da holy spirit up inta da church. I kin a'most feel it."

While putting on his violet Advent chasuble, Mickey contemplated the 'reglars' that John had referenced. His mind pictured each of them bundled as always in their thick winter down coats and sitting precisely where they sat every morning for the past six months. Only six months, or about 180 days if he counted them, was the length of time that he had been the pastor at St. Gerard's in Benton Park–why did it seem like so much longer? Why did he feel like a sleeping shepherd when his sheep were in need of his guidance? Where had his enthusiasm gone—and why? Why had his brief tenure here drained his spirit and tormented his sleep?

Whenever a serious 'why?' crept into his thoughts, or he had reason to worry about his spiritual health and well-being... Mickey remembered the times and events of years ago that had changed his life in ways never to be undone. Mickey lapsed into a momentary reverie...

During his junior and senior years in high school, Mickey experienced what, in contemporary terminology, would be considered post-traumatic stress syndrome; a condition that caused him months of insomnia and panic attacks. The triggering factors were recurring dreams that defied any logical comprehension. These dreams were not frighteningly nightmarish, yet they were extremely troubling. Upon awakening, often in a cold sweat, he would attempt to interpret their meanings but was never quite able to comprehend them at a level that might enable him to bury them in his subconscious. In their most profound interpretation, the dreams raised an issue that few people ever have to cope with: Was having an earthly existence a blessing or a curse? His trauma was trying to get a handle on the essential 'gift' of life itself. The profundity of his quandary struck him at both an intellectual and a spiritual level.

As a sixteen year-old, while snowmobiling near the family cabin on Sturgeon Lake, Mickey's sled plunged through an unseen hole in the ice. In his dreams, every detail of the experience replayed itself in slow motion–his feet touching the bottom of the lake, his rising toward the surface and striking his head on the hard ice above, his being knocked unconscious. He saw himself floating in the cold black world around him…then he saw what was his 'soul- self' drifting away from the other Mickey.

The memory of this calamity should have been horrific, but it was not. The 'near death' experience had an aftermath that was something beyond surreal. He felt an overwhelming peace along with a profound sense of freedom–a release from every earthly bond. Above him was a window-like opening and from that opening came a marvelous emanation: A corridor of golden light that drew him into an indescribable place. From that place he could see everything occurring below him basked in a white snow that glittered like a bed of diamonds. And, from that vantage unfolded an astonishing scene… his grandfather diving into the black hole… his sobbing father standing helplessly... "Let me be!" Mickey called down... "I'm in a better place... let me be!"... but, no one could hear his appeals.

He remembered his Grampa Pack pounding on his chest, the purge of water spewing from his aching lungs. He remembered his father's reckless drive to the Hibbing hospital, he remembered the 'Code 4!' alarm, the strange medical terminology passing from one doctor or nurse to another: Hypothermia, cardiovascular collapse, defibrillator, and the painful insertion of an endotracheal tube. In addition were vague images of Doctor Callister and the code team working under the bright lighting of a shimmering white room.

Although he could see all these things happening Mickey was unable to make anybody realize he didn't want his life back. "Let me go... I've found my home... please... let me go!" Nobody listened so he lapsed into a deep and overwhelming blackness.

For days he slept but even in his sleep he was aware of the vigil in his hospital room... his parents, sister Meghan and her husband Kenny, his skillful doctors, and Father Mario. He remembered all the beautiful prayers; especially from his priest friend. The entire timeless experience ended with another tragedy–a car accident... the significance of the wreckage and the man that survived it was something he never quite understood.

The insomnia and shortness of breath that followed months after his recovery were especially troubling to Mickey because he feared that his promise to God would never be realized. So, he prayed and prayed–asking Jesus to heal him so that he could be accepted into the seminary and eventually become a priest. In February of his senior year in high school he put his Lord to the test: "If you want me to give my life back to you... heal me of my afflictions by Easter Sunday."

His afflictions gone, Mickey shared his healing experience with the one person who had prayed with him through the entire ordeal.

In so doing, his bond with Father Mario Morelli was sealed for life.

A tug at his elbow, "Shud I pull on da bell now, Fadder?" Johnny asked with a puzzled expression on his face. Fadder Mickey was acting kinda strange this morning.

"Oh, yes, of course," Mickey said.

The bell announced his entry and the beginning of Mass. Blessing himself again, Mickey tried to dismiss every distraction so his mind could clearly focus on the Mass ahead. He had read the scripture passages the night before but had not given any thought to his brief morning homily. Father Mickey would wing it. He'd done it a thousand times before and nobody had ever accused him of not doing his homework. "Come Lord Jesus," he whispered under his breath.

11/ OTHER PEOPLE'S PROBLEMS

After making a deep bow toward the altar and blessing himself with a sweeping gesture, he peered out at his regulars and spoke the greeting prayer with a smile as warm as the cold sanctuary would allow. His weekday morning congregation was, as he had imagined it would be, the same as yesterday, the day before, and–. Behind each familiar face was an equally familiar story. A story shared with the priest in private conversation or in the sanctity of the confessional. And each unique and private story was, in and of itself, an explanation of why each soul in attendance would brave almost any weather impediment to get to daily Mass. He had these devoted parishioners, this flock of sheep to shepherd– needing people for sure, and in many ways, helpless people. People who were damaged or flawed in one manner or another by their heredity or by their life's circumstances, but they were good and decent people none-theless.

If need was a thorn on the stem of a rose, love was the hand willing to bleed in order to pluck the lovely flower. Mickey had plucked but hadn't yet bled. Perhaps, that was the essence of his exasperation these days. He hadn't really helped them, hadn't solved their problems, and hadn't been able make their pains go away. If only he could give them an ounce of the hope they sought... if only! All that he was able to give them was the satisfaction of listening to their problems along with the promise of his prayers. Both his listening and his praying were creditable gifts to give, but he was never able to see them in that light. There had been a time when his prayers had a potency... a potency that had become lost somewhere along the road he had been traveling.

Father Mickey was among the very few outside of immediate family that knew Steven Sundquist had multiple myeloma–a terminal cancer that would take his life in a few short months. Steven suffered without the hospice care his doctor had recommended, preferring to pray each morning from his place at the end of pew four off the left aisle of the sanctuary.

Gladys Barducci's husband had left her and their four children years before. Along with the kids, there had been significant debts and a car that needed major repairs left behind. Gladys' in-laws knew where their deviant son was living and whom he was living with–but they weren't telling anybody. 'Can't take sides' was their misguided justification. Gladys prayed from pew three on the right side of the nave.

Warren Brandt's wife was a closet alcoholic and a fallen-away Catholic. Warren was one of several in the congregation that never smiled, and one of the few devoted men who arrived early to pray the rosary. Warren always sat in the back of the church and left Mass after communion. Whenever Mickey said something he thought was humorous, he would check Warren's face in hope of even the faintest of smiles. So far, Mickey's efforts left him batting zero.

Alice Bergram had taken her daughter to Fargo for an abortion years before. Katie Bergram was fifteen at the time. Alice had told Father Mickey that she would pray for that unborn child every day of her life. She was going on eleven years–more than four thousand days without fail. Alice was not a pleasant woman, nor attractive. She was obese, with dark facial hair and had warts on her hands; she usually sat in pew six while she prayed her daily novena.

Paul and Anita McKay, off to Father Mickey's right, were in their eighties. 'Prayer Warriors' was the term Father Mickey used to describe them. Every day the two seniors prayed for their adult children, grandchildren, each of their living relatives, their friends and their neighbors, the sick of the parish, the hungry and the destitute and the homeless, victims of earthquakes, floods, and other natural disasters… and, for Father Michael Moran as well. Thank God for that. There were times, more lately than ever before, when he found great consolation in prayers said in his behalf.

Ronald Bolger prayed for his pastor, too. But mostly, Ron prayed for companionship. A gay man whose partner had passed away a decade ago, he hoped to find another Christian man to share his life with. Ashamed and confused by desires he believed to be sinful, he had not received communion since his college years. Father Mickey was one of very few that understood him–forgave him, and assured him of God's love. When Ronald could finally and completely be at peace with him self, he would receive the Eucharist he longed for–so he prayed, and prayed some more.

In addition, Mickey still received phone calls from a lesbian woman from his St. Francis parish in Brainerd, emails from a St. James couple whose daughter was in prison at the Shakopee facility for women: Rita Armstrong had been convicted of embezzlement in a very public case. And, Mickey had occasional visits from a suicidal and cocaine-addicted woman that others knew as the 'tattoo lady'. There were many others… too many others. Sometimes, and maybe too often for his own good, Father Mickey's greatest burden in life was that he carried too many other people's problems on his shoulders.

12/ AMOS AND SADIE

Amos mused over the photograph his son had inquired about. Where could Mickey have seen the picture of Kevin in his Minnesota Gophers uniform? He was certain the picture had never left the cedar chest where Grampa Kevin's diaries were stored. To his knowledge, only Sadie knew about the chest and it's contents. Even Pack and Maddie, Amos' parents, had never been told that the diaries existed.

Amos slipped into a reverie, back to a time shortly after his Grandmother's funeral. He and his dad were driving out to Bimbo's for a beer and pizza and then to the Moran family cabin on nearby Sturgeon Lake. That day's excursion returned to his thoughts in such precise detail that he could recall nearly every spoken word verbatim.

After a few rounds of small talk, Amos' father finally asked the question that had hung between them since Gramma Angie's death months before. "What did the two of you talk about for so long?"

While on her deathbed, Amos and his grandmother had talked in hushed tones behind a closed bedroom door for nearly an hour. When his Nana finished what she needed to tell him, she closed her eyes, fought for a final breath and failed. Angela Moran passed from this world with Amos holding her frail hand in his own. Although he had not expected this conversation, Amos felt those last moments belonged to him and him alone. Selfish as it might have appeared, he believed that his obligations to his father ended years ago and he felt that no loyalty debts remained hanging in the balance. Yet, out of respect, Amos did give his father an overview of Angela's feeling about the Moran family's history. "She told me that the Moran clan was star-crossed–that's exactly the wording she used." Amos repeated, "Star-crossed!"

In minimally sharing what he did about the family, Amos was struck with how little his own father knew about the history that preceded his own father, Kevin Moran. The colorful and tragic legacy, written in Kevin's own confident strokes, was a treasure that Amos was finally willing to share. He imagined Kevin's drawing of a family tree beginning with Peter Moran in the early 1900's... "As best I can tell it–" Amos began his story.

For nearly half an hour, over a pepperoni pizza and Budweiser, Amos gave his father a history lesson. Pack wasn't much into his family's lineage and listened in an almost irreverent boredom. As a former cop, Amos had thought that his dad would be inquisitive about the untimely and unresolved death of his own grandfather, Peter. He wasn't. When he had finished, Pack pushed his chair away from the table and said something to the effect of "Water's going to be cold, but we'll have to get the dock secured before we head back home." Sadly, the telling was more of a waste of time than anything else.

~

Amos found himself standing at the kitchen counter with a half eaten piece of peanut-buttered toast in his hand. Where had he just been– before reliving that time with his father years ago?

"What's the matter, Hon?"

"Nothing. Why?"

"You've been standing there with that piece of toast for five minutes. Something's going on in that mind of yours."

"Oh... Mickey... I guess. That picture he asked about. I was just wondering if our son's been snooping around in our attic back home."

"Huh? I think I'm on a different page again, Amos. What picture are you talking about? Did you put something in your coffee this morning?" Her husband had always been a daydreamer and she often had to rescue him from wherever he was at the time. "What pictures have we stored in the attic?"

Amos regarded Sadie looking up at him from a crossword puzzle on the table. The years had been kind to his wife and he fell in love with her over and over again. Her smile, her wit, her intelligence–

and, her beauty—what a blessing he had in this former Flagstaff High School homecoming queen. He forced a laugh, "Oh... its not what you're thinking. It's just an old photograph in the trunk—I was curious about it, I guess."

"Why?'

"Nothing really."

Sadie shook her head: "You and that musty, old chest in the attic. Sometimes I think we should have made a bonfire with it long ago. So what if Mickey's snooped around? I don't understand why you can't just let everybody know about Kevin's obsession with all the family stuff. So what if the Moran's have a weird strain. I think that all families are dysfunctional, it's just a matter of to what degree." She had never bothered to read what was stashed inside the trunk and only knew what little Amos had told her. History wasn't her thing in college—literature and art were. Sadie excelled in both, got her education degree at Northern Arizona University, and then a teaching job while Amos finished his graduate studies at NAU.

Amos always knew when Sadie was provoking him and could easily detect when it was serious and when it was playful banter. "You're probably right about families, my dear. But Nana did want me to do something with Kevin's stuff... I think she had a book in mind. In fact, I know she wanted me to write a book—a memoir, actually." He laughed at a thought, I've considered a title, *'Good Blood and Bad Blood'*, what do you think about that?"

"Catchy, but morbid! Sounds to me like one of those popular vampire books. Like the *Twilight* stuff. To be honest, I don't think your title is very funny at all. As you know, there's enough good and bad on both sides of this family... yours and mine. It's not just those other folks your Great-grampa wrote about in his journals." Sadie was the product of a dysfunctional family of her own. Her two siblings had died tragically and only five years apart; her father needed alcohol and her mother needed Prozac in order to cope with those losses and the life that fate had dealt them.

Despite having a mouth half full of cold toast, Amos could not resist stooping over Sadie and giving her a kiss. "I can't argue with that, my love," he said. He didn't say 'you always do' but he could have.

13/ SATURDAY YOUTH CONFERENCE

Winter months in the Lake Superior port city of Duluth were long and gray but rarely without something to do. Spirit Mountain in the western part of the long, narrow city had become an alpine skiing mecca of sorts, the John Beargrease Sled Dog Races from Duluth up the North Shore of Lake Superior drew mushers from as far away as Alaska, and every weekend found a youth hockey tournament at one of the several ice arenas. The inland lakes attracted ice fishers, the woodlands were crisscrossed with nordic ski and snowmobile trails, and curling bonspiels brought keglers to town on a regular basis.

The Chamber of Commerce had an easy job selling the harbor city and it's many attractions during the summer months when the huge ore ships entered the harbor and the cold waves of Lake Superior lapped upon the long sandy beaches of Park Point. Known to many as the 'air-conditioned' city, Duluth was a welcome respite when July and August heated up. In the wintertime, however, the Chamber staff truly earned their paychecks.

On this Saturday morning, Mickey awoke rested and without so much as a thought of hitting the snooze button. His weekend routines varied only slightly from weekdays; kneeling by his unmade bed his first devotion was a prayer to a special saint of the day, then other prayers and petitions, followed by one decade of the rosary. Today's honoree was one of Mickey's favorite saints. Saint Bernard was a friend and contemporary of St. Francis of Assisi. He scanned the bio from his Book of Saints before heading to the shower.

He would dress casually for his youth conference at Saint

Scholastica today; his faded Levis, an old Zimmy's sweatshirt from Hibbing, and scuffed Nike athletic shoes. In the kitchen, he washed down two granola bars with a glass of orange juice, and found his cell phone. It was early but he knew Sarah Donovan would already be up. Although a gossip and a busybody, she was also the key woman in all matters regarding the cleaning and decorating of the church. Sarah could be counted on to do the things a priest can't or won't bring himself to getting done. Christmas was only two weeks away and Mickey had been negligent in arranging for all the preparations that had to be taken care of from the Nativity display, the altar Christmas trees, and the poinsettia plants. Fortunately, having served many procrastinating priests over the years, Sarah had everything covered: "Don't give it another thought Father, the ladies will be getting all the Christmas stuff done for you." Her voice held the assurance of experience, something woefully lacking in Father Moran to Sarah Donovan's way of thinking. Saint Gerard's greyhead reputation not only described parishioners, but its priests were usually one step away from retirement. That was until Father Moran came along. The young priest was not one of Sarah Donovan's favorites by any means. Too young, she would say, and too darn good lookin' to be a priest. And, asking the folks to call him 'Mickey'... that was borderline sacrilegious!

Mrs. Donovan cleared her throat. "You'll be stoppin' by the bake sale this mornin' won't you, Father. I baked them brownies you like so much."

Mickey checked the calendar on his desk. There it was; the bake sale had been penciled in below the St. Scholastica youth retreat with Father Mario. The reason he didn't see it was because he had also scribbled 'dinner with Meg, Pickwick, 8 PM, with ballpoint in the small calendar box. "Save me some, Sarah. I'll be running in circles today. In fact, I've got to be out the door in five minutes to drive up to St. Scholastica."

Sarah puzzled, swallowing her disappointment like raw garlic.

Father Moran had promised her just the other day–Thursday it was– that he'd be helping out with the fund-raiser. Now, she was certain that he had totally forgotten the commitment, or–worse yet– found something better to do. Young Father Mickey, she thought, has his priorities mixed up these days. Yesterday, she remembered, he even started to read the wrong Gospel, before correcting himself, at morning Mass. Years before, Sarah had telephoned the bishop about a priest that had been 'drinkin' a bit too much for his own good'. It wasn't long afterwards that the priest was transferred somewhere. She guessed, to a treatment home of some kind.

The morning was clear and cold but splashed with an eastern sunshine. Mickey checked his jacket pocket, fingered his cell phone, and turned over the engine. What had he forgotten to do this morning? Oh well, it would probably come to him sooner or later. On the drive east on Grand Avenue, Mickey ran through his motivational message for the youth workshops. He was running late, and the defroster in his Civic wasn't clearing the windshield properly, he leaned over the steering wheel with his gloved hand to rub away some of the moisture. At the last moment he heard the blare of a horn, quickly glancing in his driver's side mirror he realized that he had drifted slightly over the centerline and hadn't seen the pickup truck emerge from his blind spot. Irritated, the driver blared his horn and turned sharply in front of the priest's Honda while gesturing for Mickey to pull over to the side of the road. Mickey eased over to the right, came to a stop behind the driver of the black, oversized Ford F-10.

"What the hell…!" The irate driver leaped out of the cab, striding angrily toward the idling Civic. Only a few feet away, he shouted: "Where the f____!" He cut his tirade short when he recognized the priest. "Oh… Father, Jeeze, I didn't know it was you. Sorry. You kinda scared me when you drifted over. You okay?"

Mickey recognized the man from Benton Park. He wore a

grease-stained NASCAR cap, Sorrel boots, and two layers of wool plaid. What was the guy's name? Mickey searched his memory and came up with a vague recollection–the man worked for the local TV cable company he thought. He made a stab at the name, "Sorry Marty, my defroster's been acting up and I, well I guess I was a little careless. My bad."

The burly, unshaven man shrugged his wide shoulders; "Mike, Father. Mike Rolle. Live down the block from you. I did that concrete work in front of yer church last summer. Remember?"

Mickey had guessed wrongly at the name and occupation of Mike Rolle. Another apology came automatically: "Sorry, Mike. I'm not functioning well this morning. Haven't had my caffeine fix yet." He forced a laugh.

Mike's smile was equally superficial. Shrugging, he turned and walked back to his truck and mumbled, "Where did Marty come from?"

The traffic incident added five minutes to the ten minutes he was already behind in getting to the conference. Finding a parking place on the campus added five more. Mickey grabbed his guitar from the back seat and sprinted across the lot to the fine arts building.

"Better late than never," Father Mario greeted his longtime friend with a mild frown, then smiled and gave Mickey a bear hug at the door. "We had to get started without you, Mick. Not a problem. Grab a cup of coffee and donut. You're in the Business Ed room, number B-12, I think. We've got a great turnout… even some kids you've met before. Good luck, turn 'em on, have fun–all that stuff, Mick."

"Always my best," Mickey assured as Mario hustled off to some event of his own. Mario was in his fifties, short and strongly built. He was beginning to gray around the ears, but still had the ruggedly good looks of Al Pacino. The two priests had a long friendship dating back to Mario's years at Blessed Sacrament Church in Hibbing in the nineties.

14/ ST. JAMES HOOLIGANS

With young people, Mickey was almost always in his favorite element. Having recently taped 'I Am: The Documentary' by filmmaker Tom Shadyak, he planned to use segments of the recording to inspire some deep spiritual contemplation. His plan evaporated when he found his left jacket pocket empty. He had his cell in the right pocket, but– Oh no! he said to himself. He'd forgotten to bring the tape and he didn't have a 'Plan B' for backup. Mickey improvised as best he could, but the passion and eloquence he hoped for were sadly missing in what became a somewhat disjointed presentation. Subsequently, the discussion afterwards left much to be desired.

"Find truth by questioning everything," he said in answer to a girl's question. "Change what's inside and find contentment with who you are. Then–and only then–will meaningful changes around you occur." The girl smiled but Mickey could sense that his answer didn't connect to her specific question. In order for his adlibbed message to strike any meaning with the kids, certain basic concepts had to be understood. Sadly, these bullet points had not been effectively established.

In the small groups he was unable to individualize his main premise and, consequently, he was on a different page than the young people much of the time. His innate charm, wit, and a winning smile, however, enabled him to evoke occasional rapport with the kids. When his Q & A session was finished, Mickey felt compelled to apologize. "I wasn't on my game, guys. I'm sorry about that. Maybe there's a lesson in what's happened here this morning– or, rather–what hasn't happened here. Never begin a race with your shoes untied cuz you're bound to trip and fall and embarrass yourself. While praying together, Mickey recovered some lost credibility by doing something he should have done when he started. He let go of himself and let God work through him. When they all prayed together, their prayers were inspired and meaningful.

Later in the afternoon, the two 'hooligans' from St. James stopped by to say hello. Randy Flynn would be graduating cum laude from UMD in the spring and Jimmy Rossini had a custodial job on the Scholastica campus while he was working on his degree in sociology. Mickey bear-hugged them both, "I'm so proud of you guys–never a doubt in my mind that you two guys had the right stuff."

"Hey, Father… we owe you a little credit for steering us in the right direction." Randy said.

"More than a little credit, Randy. This guy kicked our butts when we needed them kicked and covered our butts when we needed them covered," Rossini said. "We owe you big time, Father."

Randy Flynn gave Mickey a slap on the back, "Amen," he said. Randy topped six-three, wore his auburn hair long, and had an Irishman's quick wit. "Oh, I heard you were trying to play your C chords without a D string–How'd that work for you?"

Mickey laughed, "I've been jinxed all day it seems. When the string broke I was ready to throw in the towel and go home." After the small group meetings a few of the teens had stayed behind and improvised a sing-along with Mickey providing the music. "I think I'd have left my head behind today if it weren't attached." Like the video and a plan B, Mickey had forgotten to put some spare strings in his guitar case.

"Say, I was meaning to ask… are you doing some missionary work down in St. Paul these days?" Jimmy Rossini said. "On the east side, off of the Interstate?" To be provocative, Rossini wore a tattered Green Bay Packers sweatshirt he'd found at a downtown Ragshop store.

Mickey shrugged, "Haven't been down to the Cities since when… last summer I think. St. Paul… gosh, I can't remember the last time. Why?"

"Oh, you remember Jeannie Palazari from our church? Well,

she's a social worker down there… somewhere–she's with some agency that provides services to the street people. I saw her a couple of weeks ago at a concert and she told me she saw you down there–hanging out, talking to some transients; she though you were working the streets like you used to do up here."

Mickey's brow furrowed, "Not me. She must have been mistaken. Say, you guys want to join me for a quick cup of coffee?"

Both declined, 'Maybe later', the boys shook hands with him and headed on to wherever they were going on this Saturday afternoon. Mickey chuckled inside. He had tried to steer both Randy and Jimmy toward the priesthood when they were high school sophomores. Every priest prays that during his ministry at least one of the young men in his flock will become a priest. Mickey remembered each of his inspirations vividly. The first, and probably the most powerful of his motivations, was the miracle when he was sixteen and nearly drowned in Sturgeon Lake.

The other inspiration preceded the near death experience by three years. His father had taken him along on a business trip up the north shore of Lake Superior on an early December weekend in 1993. Amos, well-tuned to his son's fascination with saints told his son, "Mickey, I'd like you to meet a real live saint." He was referring to a former Hibbing priest who served their parish in the early eighties. "When you were just a little tyke, Father Mark and I became good friends. One day when you were two or three he sat you on his lap and played his harmonica. You were mesmerized."

His dad had arranged the Grand Marais business meeting in part because he wanted to visit Father Mark Hollenhorst before the priest died of his terminal cancer. "At every Sunday Mass, Father Mark shares the experience of dying with his parish. His homilies are beautiful testimonials to his love of God."

After spending a Saturday night in a motel near Sven and Ole's and trying the Swede's famous pizza, the father and son attended Saint John's Church the following morning. In his homily, Father

Hollenhorst, integrated the Magi story with an appeal for brotherhood and love. Mickey was mesmerized for a second time by this gentle man. After Mass he had an opportunity to meet Father Mark who leaned over and gave him a blessing, "May God be with you always, Michael."

Father Hollenhorst passed away on 12/27/1993, at the age of 43. His life story is still regarded as one of the most inspirational in the long history of the Duluth diocese. Already nearly thirty years ago, that experience still resonated in Mickey's heart as if it were only yesterday.

Driving back to Saint Gerard's for a second shower and second change of clothes for his dinner meeting with his sister, Mickey was hoping to shake the doldrums. What a disappointing day this had turned out to be. Working with Mario had always been great fun, but this time he had let his friend down. Worse, he'd failed the kids from throughout the diocese, including some from both Hibbing where he grew up and from Brainerd where he had served for two wonderful years. The one bright spot had been reconnecting with his two young friends from St. James. In giving him some positive self-worth vibes, they had saved an otherwise unfortunate day.

In the mildly depressed spirit of the moment, he picked up his cell phone and called Sarah Donovan to inquire about the ladies bake sale at the church that morning. It had gone better than expected. In a subdued voice the old woman reported; "We raised 'bout a hunnerd forty or so. Betty Workman took it all home for countin', Father. She'll get a report to ya after Mass tomorrow."

Mickey thanked her for all she had done for the parish and apologized again for missing the event. "Say, Sarah, how about one day next week, after Mass, you stop by the rectory for coffee and… maybe a brownie or two?"

Sarah hesitated. Was that a proper invitation from a priest? She being a widow and all? "We'll see, Father. Maybe if Mrs. Workman can come 'long, too. Both of us–that OK wit you, Father?"

Patches of ice on the steep hillside winding down to the St. Louis River basin added unwanted stress to his driving. It was only late afternoon and already getting dark along the horizon, the once promising day had turned to dreary gray. Next Thursday, winter would officially begin. The thought, like the nearly spent day, added another ounce of depression. Mickey believed he suffered from something he'd read about called Seasonal Affective Disorder, and was prone to becoming agitated and dispirited during the long stretches of drab, sunless days in northern Minnesota. He thought of his parents in Florida with a mild jealousy. "Get off it, Mick!" He scolded himself, "Don't be adding anything more to an already down day, think positive. God loves ya... He's got you covered." His lips upturned in a wide smile at that assurance. He turned on his radio to Sirius and picked up the MLB broadcast; the Twins had signed a power hitter in Josh Willingham from the Oakland Athletics. Being the diehard fan that he was, the news perked him up. The commentator suggested the Twins stalwart, and free agent, Michael Cuddyer was almost certain to sign with some other team. "Bummer!" Mickey mumbled under his breath, "Why not keep them both? With all of the new Target Field money, the team ownership should be able to keep the two sluggers and Jason Kubel besides." The past season had been one of the worst in Twins history.

Twins baseball was a perfect diversion. As he drove west, he imagined next season's starting lineup. In doing so, his mild depression returned. "We're not going to be very good again this year," he muttered to himself. Minnesota's pro teams had suffered through a dismal 2011 season–with one major exception: The professional women's basketball team, the Lynx were an awesome crew and had won the national championship the previous October.

Freshly showered and dressed in a navy turtleneck and jeans, Mickey hoped that the disappointments of this afternoon would not continue through the weekend. While driving east from remote Benton Park across fifteen miles of the city for the second time that day, he remembered his close call with his neighbor Mike Rolle that morning. He'd have to remind himself to send Mike an apology card of some kind.

The traffic thickened as he exited the freeway and traveled down the main artery, Superior Street. Parts of downtown Duluth looked older, grayer, and more distressingly urban than the city he remembered as a youth. Like people, cities suffered the ravages of age and physical deterioration. Much of the traffic ramped off to his right. The defending national champion UMD Bulldogs hockey team was playing at home tonight against the Wisconsin Badgers at the dazzling new Amsoil Arena attached to the older DECC convention center. The nearby Canal Park restaurants and bars would be bustling both before and after the game. Hockey was second only to religion to many Minnesotans: Hockey was the religion to most Minnesotans living north of Hinckley–or, though it seems to Mickey.

The thought of Hinckley reminded Mickey of his meeting with Father Tim the following night.

15/ MEGHAN'S MISERY

The Pickwick was a comfortable dining establishment overlooking Lake Superior just east of downtown Duluth. Wearing her finest Christmas outfitting of pine boughs, and lights, and bulbs, and candlelit tables, the restaurant was an inviting respite from the cold of the evening. Meghan Moran Williams was seated at a window table she had reserved the day before. Having arrived nearly half an hour early from a superficial shopping foray, she ordered a gin gimlet and stared into the darkness beyond the window. Far out on the lake lights from a mammoth ore vessel moved slowly toward the canal and landmark lift bridge leading to the massive loading docks in the bay beyond. The shipping season was nearly over and dormancy would settle upon the harbor just as the night had settled upon the city. Within a few days, the lake and bay would surrender to the closure of winter's ice. Tonight, the glitter of Canal Park sparkled like diamonds on the mirror of the quiet lake. It was easy to understand the allure of this quaint city.

Megan nervously twisted her wedding ring, still trying to organize her thoughts and determine how she would present her problems to her brother. While growing up she and Mickey were closer than most gender opposite siblings. They had an uncanny ability to communicate their innermost feelings with an honesty that bonded their relationship. As a teenager, Meg was good at unloading problems and, although two years younger, Mickey was an insightfully gifted listener. When she talked through a misbehavior–and there had been many when she was in high school–her brother was able to turn her guilt or apprehension inward enabling her to find a satisfactory resolution of her own. His gift was uncanny. And, his prayers–for whatever intervention– had a potency that bordered on miraculous.

But, that was then, and many years and many changes had passed behind them. Long gone were days when everything somehow seemed to work itself out. Good-times days, times of dancing and laughing and feeling carefree. She thought of the wisdom in the adage, 'youth is wasted on the young' and smiled. Her thirty-four years seemed to weigh heavily on this solitary moment as she sat staring at her reflection in the window. Still very pretty, her eyes betrayed the pain she didn't want to show.

"Meghan," she said to herself, "Get a grip. It's not like you're an old woman. For God's sake, don't wallow in self-pity. Everything's going to work out" she assured. "Mickey will have some answers."

Meg Williams liked wearing black and accenting whatever outfit she wore with something white. Tonight it was a black wool sweater with a wide neck over a stylish white blouse, black slacks, and black boots to just below the knees. Her auburn hair was stylishly cut and the soft light shadowed her features. Like her mother, she had a straight nose, full puffy lips, and perfect teeth. She had her father's deep-set green eyes. When pictured beside her younger brother there was little doubt that she and Mickey were siblings.

Meghan noticed the waitress standing near her elbow, "I'm sorry... was I taking to myself?"

The young woman's nameplate, evenly pinned on a strap of her starched white apron, read Vicki. She was petit, soft spoken, and her smile was genuine. "Not that I noticed, ma'am. Can I...?"

"I'll have another gimlet, please," Meg slid her empty cocktail glass toward the girl. "Make it a double, will you please."

Vickie nodded politely. "Very well," she said, then walked briskly back to the bar in the adjoining room.

Meghan checked the time on her cell, frowned: Mickey was never late. Slowly passing minutes tweaked her apprehension, her gimlet arrived and she stirred the cubes absently. A deep swallow warmed its way down her chest; the bartender here knew how to mix a perfect double. Maybe, she considered, it would be best to nurse this drink until her brother arrived.

How honest was she prepared to be, she wondered? Would it be best to let her head take the lead and allow her heart to follow. Or, should it be the other way around? Or, was the option of saying nothing consequential now a viable one? Her quandary was her vague mental agenda, she knew all too well that it was rarely a good idea to try and script a conversation in advance. Yet, her thoughts were forming like scribbled notes being outlined for psych class.

All afternoon, and for months preceding, Meghan's thoughts had been consumed with her unhappiness. She was at the point now where she had to do something about it, get it out of the closet where she stuffed things she didn't want to deal with. If she were to let this opportunity go by, she would curse herself later–yes, the time had come to be honest. When reexamining those premarital expectations of having a comfortable home in a nice neighborhood, cute kids to dote upon, and a loving husband to support her; she would be hard-pressed to find very much fault with her present situation. Yet, she wasn't feeling fulfilled.

When put under scrutiny, hers was a terribly selfish admission. How many women would give anything to have even a fraction of what she had? When your life is defined by taking care of others, however, it is almost refreshing to let selfishness come through your door... and, once you let her in, you need to feed her, and offer her some measure of comfort–once comfortable, she's hard to push outside where she belongs.

Why did Meghan dump blame on Kenny for frustrations that belonged to her alone? If she started her confession by scapegoating her husband for her discontent, Mickey would see through her, and into her, immediately. Then, her brother would nudge her off the 'pity trip' she was taking and invite her to see things more sensibly. He would nudge, gently nudge–Mickey was much too sensitive to badger or to judge or to pry.

On the drive down to Duluth, Meghan had rehearsed her drama: A misunderstood and underappreciated woman drowning in the depths of mindless tedium. She was unwilling to accept complete responsibility for what was wrong in her life because Kenny, after all, was her co-equal partner. Where was he when she needed him?

Why couldn't he see what was happening right in front of his eyes? How could he continue living his life as if nothing was wrong? Surely, if Kenny really cared about his marriage, Meghan Moran Williams wouldn't be in crisis mode at the moment.

When feeling misunderstood, the lines dividing truth from fiction become blurred. Her husband's success and growing reputation as an up-and-coming architect should have been a source of pride, not a source of resentment. Yet, in her thinking of late, everything in their life seemed focused on Kenny Williams–not Meghan Williams. He was the 'golden one'–his firm was winning design contracts from as far away as Mankato and Madison, he was the vice-president of the Chamber of Commerce, he was an officer on the youth hockey governing board… and, ad nauseum.

"Would you like another?" Vickie and her pleasant smile had returned to the table.

"Please," she nodded, smiled, and checked the time on her cell again. She did a rough count; this would be number four… wouldn't it? "Maybe a bit lighter on the gin–okay?"

What about her own resume? Meghan Williams: Mother, homemaker, transportation supervisor, budget manager, food prep director, community relations manager… responsibilities that didn't add up to very much in the grand scheme of things.

Maybe she could cope with all of the roles and still keep her sanity if– if only there were some occasional 'warm fuzzies'. When was the last time she and Kenny went out for dinner? To a movie? Dancing? On any kind of 'date'? Kenny would say, and had often said: Why go out when Sammy's Pizza delivers? If you want to watch a movie, there's Netflix and we don't have to drive anywhere. Dancing, well–Kenny claimed to have two left feet, and dating to his way of thinking was courtship activity… period!

And, what about the passion, intimacy, making love? If Mickey inquired, she would tell her celibate priest brother, in vague but appropriate terms, of course, that even sex had become unsatisfying. Probably, mutually unsatisfying. But, that, of course, was something she and Kenny didn't talk about. That, along with anything 'delicate' or 'sensitive' was never discussed, these matters were best left hanging in the closet. Hanging along with anything else that might provoke argument, disagreement or discomfort–sadly, the marital closet was becoming crammed to capacity.

Meghan was quite sure that her brother had heard her story, or some version of it, from a hundred married women over the years. Sometimes she wondered if marriage licenses should be renewable every four years–perhaps when one's driving license came due.

Then, there was Jared! Her gimlet arrived. Meghan would withhold Jared's last name. Jared was the trainer at the athletic club she had joined in order to trim up and have a few hours each week away from the house. Actually, Kenny had made a suggestion that she find a hobby, or volunteer for something–do anything to get out and about more often while the kids were at school. As it turned out, Jared Nadeau's schedule– Tuesday and Thursday afternoons– happened to coincide with hers. So did his preference for the treadmills and ellipticals on the south end of the building.

"You're in great shape, Mrs. Williams," he said casually one afternoon. She smiled, brushing off the compliment with slight nod. Yet, those few words from Jared Nadeau meant more to her than anything Kenny had said in the past year. She felt exhilarated and guilty in equal measure. Also, her motivation to workout was given a huge boost by the casual compliment. Later, she became Meg (not Mrs. Williams) and Jared was sharing his personal life as they both pushed themselves on the treadmill. Of course, Jared was single–

"Hey, sis… " Mickey bent over her and kissed the top of her head. One of his favorite scents was shampoo: "Smelling just wonderful, as always… and, looking simply gorgeous."

16/ THE PICKWICK

The drive from Benton Park to the Pickwick on the eastern fringe of down- town hadn't lifted Mickey's sagging spirits. After the earlier conferences that day, he had stayed behind for an hour to hear the confessions of those who were staying to attend the candlelight vigil Mass. Mario would say the Mass by himself so that Mickey could get away early for his meeting with Meghan. For the past six months, most of Mickey's confessions involved older women who redefined the concept of sin: 'I was cross with my husband'; 'I called my neighbor a gossip'; 'I lied about the grocery bill and kept some of the change for myself; 'I lost my temper with my sister-in-law three times: I said 'Jesus' when I dropped a jar of beets!

The confessions he heard at Scholastica were from a far different culture: 'I had sex with my boyfriend three times this week'; 'I had oral sex with my girlfriend'; and from a pretty girl who couldn't have been more than sixteen—". . . it's been more than a year since my last confession, Father... I got pregnant and had an abortion last summer." Mickey could have cried–what could he say to her? You've committed a very grave sin? Why didn't you...? This generation of young people probably was not much different from that of his own while growing up in Hibbing during the nineties. Yet, he could not help mourning the loss of innocence in so many young people. How to heal something one cannot comprehend was a paradox that none of his seminary theologians had been able to teach him. *Judge not lest you be judged*! he reminded himself. But, that fundamental Christian precept failed to provide any measure of solace.

Mickey's poor performance at the conference, coupled with his remorse over the youthful indiscretions he'd forgiven while hearing confessions, festered in his thoughts. Add to that mix the reality that he was dog-tired from a nagging insomnia and stressed over his guilt-inducing lack of compassion relative to other people's problems. He tried to remind himself that stress was a self-imposed malady. That thought was what his seminary profs called 'pulp-psych', so was the idea that he could choose to be happy if he really wanted to–as content as a clam. A clam's contentment, however, was something he'd have to Google later–he hadn't a clue where the expression came from. Regardless, the diversion from self-punishment was welcome. There was certainly a germ of truth in the power of positive thinking–and there was a higher truth in the power of prayer. As he turned off the busy street and into the Pickwick ramp, he said a quick prayer. Maybe visiting with his sister over a great steak would perk him up and save the day.

For twenty minutes the siblings small-talked about family and Christmas and Hibbing gossip, slipping into a comfort zone that made what was to come less intimidating to Meghan. "Yes, we all went out to the Sturgeon Lake property last weekend to cut our own Christmas tree. And, yes, it's just as hideous as the one we chopped last year," Meg said.

Both laughed easily. "I put out that carved wood Nativity set that I found at a garage sale; that's the extent of my Christmas decorating. Thank goodness the church women do a nice job with the altar and sanctuary." Mickey said.

They ordered cocktails, Mickey's a Bacardi and coke, while the siblings continuing with easy topics. Vickie served their entrees. Meghan had chosen the Maine lobster but had no appetite, her fifth gimlet warmed inside..

"So...how are things, Sis?" Mickey looked up from his rib eye steak. "I got the impression you had something important on your mind."

Meghan clutched the napkin on her lap under the table, "Lots, Mick," her expression hardened, her eyes averted momentarily: "I don't quite know where to begin."

"At the beginning, Meg," Mickey's standard rejoinder.

Within minutes Meghan was tearing over her 'woe is me' admissions, and slurring some of her words as she did so. She had decided not to mentioned Jared. Her confession was shallow and self-deprecating–unlike what she had rehearsed in the car on the sixty-mile trip down to Duluth. Everything was coming out wrong and Mickey wasn't helping her at all, in fact, he only listened with a pained, almost jaded, expression on his face. Was he bored? Did he care? What was her brother's problem? Meghan was becoming irritated, confused.

Mickey wasn't quite prepared for a disintegration of marriage conversation. He heard those almost weekly. As he listened a creeping nausea roiled in his stomach. Her husband Kenny was a decent man; their two children–Matthew twelve, and Kathleen eight–were the greatest kids in his world. What Meghan was telling him could be condensed into two words; selfish and irrational. He tried to listen patiently without betraying his emotional pain, but he knew that wasn't coming across. Old memories were creeping around the borders of his sister's lament. As a teenager, Meghan had gone through a rebellion of sorts... and Kenny had been a social outcast. Together, the two of them flourished—as individuals and as a couple. The turnaround in their lives was nothing short of miraculous. Now this!

Meghan was sobbing now—a combination of self-pity and booze. Mickey didn't deal well with either. Rather than get into some of the marriage counseling fundamentals that all priests were trained to use, Mickey's usually good judgment eluded him: "Who's the guy, Sis?" Mickey blurted the question with an unnecessary sharpness.

Taken aback, Meghan swallowed hard, "What makes you think...?"

Mickey forced a smile, "Meg, I'm a pro... remember? It's what I do for a living, that's when I'm not saying Mass or baptizing babies or visiting the sick, or... a thousand other things. I've heard the wife's 'woe is me' lament a thousand times. Not that the sentiment is never justified, often it is. But most couples can fight their way through it, tough it out. That usually works... unless... unless that tall, dark, stranger comes onto the scene. Then everything changes for the worse—not for the better. Then, the foundation really crumbles."

The expression on Meghan's face was more astonishment than anger or betrayal. "What are you talking about? Foundation?"

"Commitment. That's what it's all about, Meg. Not a very romantic word... but that's what marriage is. Commitment!"

Meghan shrugged, rolled her eyes.

Mickey swallowed hard on his own emotions— what he was about to say would cut even deeper. "Let's not dance around the question, Meg. Who's the guy? Tell your brother and get it over with."

Meghan's confidence was shaken to its very bowels; this whole scene was becoming outrageously nightmarish. She had already said enough. This was not the brother she knew and trusted, not any more. This man in his navy-blue sweater, leaning on his elbows across the table was no different from any priest in black garb from down the street. If she gave him a full confession, mentioned Jared, acknowledged that nothing had happened yet, was the priest sitting across the table going to give her five Hail Mary's' and absolution for her sins?

Meghan pushed her chair away from the table, incensed and sobbing: "None of your damn business!" She couldn't believe what she had just said, but she wasn't about to retract a word of it.

Mickey reached across the table to find his sister's hands, "I'm sorry, Meg... really. I didn't mean to accuse you of anything. I just wanted..."

Meghan stood, "Apology noted. I've got a long drive and it's getting late."

"Meghan, don't do this to me. Please, sit down. Be reasonable." Mickey stood, stepped toward her, arms stretched out to give her a hug.

Meghan pushed away, "Christmas is at our place this year. Kenny and me and the kids will see you then. Happy Advent, Father."

With that she grabbed her purse and headed toward the lobby to retrieve her coat. Almost running headlong into the waitress, Meghan pulled her wallet and handed the wide-eyed girl a hundred dollar bill. "Thanks, Vickie. Merry Christmas."

Mickey, he mouth agape, was left standing by the table holding his napkin and feeling almost naked in front of several gawkers at nearby tables. What had he just done? As he turned toward the door to catch up with his fleeing sister, he brushed past Vickie, "I'll take care of this in a minute," he said, referring to the bill. "I've got to find..."

"That's okay, Father. The lady has already taken care of the tab."

When he got to the lobby entrance, Meghan was already gone. He stepped outside and called her name. He heard the slam of a car door somewhere ahead of where he was standing, and then saw the flicker of break lights at the far end of the parking lot. He took a few steps toward the sound of an engine being revved, called out her name to no avail. Off to his right he watched as the pair of taillights disappeared in east London Road.

On the drive back to the rectory, tears stung his face, blurred his eyes. The heater-defroster fan in his Civic still wasn't working effectively, his head was pounding from the tension of failure, and he had difficulty maneuvering in the nighttime traffic. Meghan's sarcastic last words 'Happy Advent, Father' were as bitterly cold the December night. He punched her number on his cell phone: Several rings were followed by her callback message. She wasn't answering. "Please. Meg. I'm so sorry… so very sorry. You mean the world to me and I can't stand the thought of you being angry with me. Please pick up your phone." He tried three more times on the drive back to Saint Gerard's, left three more appeals, but Meg had shut him out. Then he worried. Meg had been drinking before he arrived. He could tell from her speech, and the slight wobble when she stood from the table, that she had gone beyond her limits.

He tried to pray his way through his anguish; tried in vain to find words to help him climb out of this chasm of despair he had put himself into. Maybe his deep sobs and stream of tears were the only and best prayer he would come up with tonight.

Disheartened, he hit the steering wheel with the palm of his hand. What had gotten into him? Meghan was absolutely correct— it wasn't any of his damn business. Maybe there wasn't another guy involved in her problem. Maybe she was just venting pent-up stress that often comes with the holidays. Maybe a lot of things. He'd do his best to repair the damage he had done. If she wouldn't take his calls, maybe a card or letter… send flowers, some gesture of apology was necessary. He'd have to patch things up soon–Christmas at her house was only two weeks away. Under his breath he mumbled another 'I'm sorry, Meg."

Turning off Grand at 88th west, Mickey prayed that Meg would have safe travel and thanked God for getting him back to Benton Park safely. "God, don't let me ruin another relationship tomorrow," he said. He would have to do a much better job supporting Father Tim, his seminary friend, with issues that were probably as thorny as those of his sister. In addition, he remembered that he'd been asked to call his grandmother about his grandfather's problem. Or, problems. When would it all end? Everybody's problems had become Father Mickey's problems. Where could he dump his problems: On his parents, his confessor Father Mario, or on the lap of Bishop Bremmer who didn't like him very much? None of the above… his problems were his problems–he owned them free and clear.

As an afterthought, he sighed, then laughed: "Saint Bernie, you let me down today. I didn't resolve anybody's problems today and probably added a few to my own list. Bummer day! If you're listening to me St. Bernard, I'll give you another chance to do a better job this time next year."

17/ DOUBT

Another night with too many things rolling across his thoughts, one after another, like the concentric ripples from a stone tossed into a quiet pond. On the morning of the third Sunday of Advent, Father Mickey Moran rubbed his swollen eyes, yawned, and stretched his arms out to loosen the joints in his shoulders. His body was tight from too little sleep and too much tension. The night before he had cried tears of self-pity and self-deprecation, something he hadn't done since a close friend of his left the seminary to marry an old sweetheart from his high school days. That was nearly five years ago. Remembering that incident brought to mind his dinner meeting with Father Tim Hagland later that night, and the woman's familiar voice from a phone call on Friday. Priests and designing women presented a dilemma as old as cleric celibacy. The aborted call from Hibbing several nights before had to have been that of Maureen Regan. Maureen was a woman from his distant past.

Fortunately, Father Mickey had outlined his Sunday homily the week before. Every so often he made an effort to stir his congregation from its apathy of too many years of old and traditional priests. Every time he tried, however, he seemed to fall considerable short. What Mickey was planning to say was both honest and timely, and, perhaps a bit too provocative. If he could rouse the nodding heads for once, it might be worth it.

He made quick work of his prayers, showered, shaved and dressed before heading downstairs to retrieve the Sunday paper. The pleasant aroma of freshly perked coffee welcomed him into the drafty kitchen. Whoever had invented the automatic coffeemaker ought to be canonized. His first strong, black cup provided him with the caffeine rush he needed to shake the cobwebs and enliven his weary spirit.

The *Duluth News-Tribune* headlined the U.S. troop withdrawal from Iraq, the sexual harassment problems of Republican presidential candidate Herman Cain, and a three-car traffic accident in west Duluth. He popped some Eggos from the toaster to a plate, spread too much butter, and soaked the waffles in a half a bottle of Log Cabin maple syrup. Skimming the sports he found one big surprise: Albert Pujols was going to be a California Angel next season! Wow! Mickey wasn't expecting the best hitter in baseball to switch over to the American League. Of no surprise, the Twins hadn't made any player deals and UMD had won their hockey game. If he had time later, he'd peruse the paper more carefully and tackle the *New York Times* crossword puzzle.

Mickey crossed from the rectory to the side door of the church with a parka draped over his shoulders. Inside the sacristy he found the light switches, turned up the thermostat, and found his Catholic Saints book where he had left it the day before; next to the prayer book on a table by his kneeler. Saint Bernard's day–yesterday–hadn't turned out too well. Today's featured saint had to do a much better job!

Since his boyhood years, Mickey had been intrigued by the lives of saints, and began the ritual of honoring one for each day of the year. Ironically, since becoming a priest his attention to that detail had become more irregular. Before reviewing his *Breviary*, he paged through the book of saints for December 11 and found a Saint Melchior. Melchior was a missionary in the Philippines before traveling to Japan to care for persecuted Christians in the area of Nagasaki. He was arrested, tortured, and burned at the stake for his faith. Pope John Paul II had beatified Melchior in 1989.

Interesting, wasn't one of the Magi named Melchior? Mickey remembered a clever children's Christmas story premised on the idea that Melchior actually became Santa Claus. He made a mental note to buy a copy of that book the next time he visited a bookstore. Mickey reviewed his *Breviary*, shivered through some memorized prayers, and tried to open his mind and heart to what he would accomplish in the liturgy ahead.

While watching a CNN news program on TV days before, there had been a story that struck him like a stomach punch. A huge billboard near the entry to New York's Holland Tunnel pictured a Nativity scene and was captioned: *'You know it is a Myth'* in bold letters. The sign was sponsored by a local atheist organization. How many thousands of Christians passed by that billboard every day–a million, or more? What kind of thinking did that message provoke?

Christ had certainly been taking a Christmas beating in recent years as every effort was being made to de-Christianize American society. Clerks at retail stores were selling all manner of Christmas items and greeting their customers with 'Happy Holidays'! Oh well, no one could ever stop him from saying 'Merry Christmas'... that would never change. Or... would it? What if the 'religious' season's greeting were to become a misdemeanor and punished with a fine?

There were so many elements of Mickey's Catholicism that went beyond mortal comprehension; only his strong faith sustained him. The virgin birth was one of them. Yet, without that belief, many other elements of his religious beliefs were seriously undermined. Faith! His life was a testament to faith; nothing more and nothing less–without faith, he was nothing and he knew it. For that reason he prayed daily for a stronger faith, not only to sustain him as a priest, but to enrich him as a person. Yet, he would readily admit to doubts and acknowledge his lack of sufficient faith on occasion. But, although there were times when his faith was weaker than it should be, it was always there. What might happen if he ever lost it? That thought worried him more than anything he could think of. For that reason, faith was something he needed to talk about often in order to keep it alive and strong.

This Sunday morning, Father Mickey would raise one of the many paradoxes of Scripture to the scrutiny of his parishioners. Few were more troublesome for him than Matthew Eleven. The theme he had chosen for this morning's homily might take him onto thin ice, and, at the same time, reveal some of his own vulnerabilities. In that Gospel, John the Baptist sent a message from the dark and dank dungeon of King Herod to Jesus: "Are you 'He who is to come' or do we look for another?" John's desperate question evidences not only his desolation, but also his agony of doubt!

Mickey paused after reading the Gospel reference: "Of all the people on earth, John more than any, would surely KNOW that Jesus was the one! His life's mission was to proclaim that fact to the multitudes. No one, not even the disciples, would have had a deeper, or more perfect knowledge of that reality than John the Baptizer."

Mickey could read the discomfort in the faces of several of his parishioners: "Yet, we read in Matthew's gospel that John had doubt. The certainty that defined his reclusive life, the certainty that inspired his pleas for repentance, and the certainty that found an even deeper essence by God's own words as John baptized Jesus in the Jordan River was compromised in his one simple question. John's incredible faith seemed to have abandoned him while awaiting his execution in the shadows of a prison cell. Does this make you wonder?"

At this point, Mickey sensed that he had everybody's full attention: "It makes me wonder!" He paused for effect, looking to his left and to his right, gripping the sides of his lectern, and shrugging his shoulders: "In all honesty, it shakes my faith more than a little." He looked down at his notes scribbled on the back of an envelope. There, under the heading DOUBTS, he had listed some of the Christian truths that were so faith-based that we dared not to explore them too deeply. He recited them, watching disbelief and bewilderment on every face–he ticked off miracles from Cana to the tomb of Lazarus, from feeding the multitudes to the many incredible healings... then, in capital letters: The Virgin birth, and the Resurrection! "We are all challenged by our doubts just as John was, we are weak, confused, and even in denial at times, we are just people–we are of the same flesh and bone as the Apostles were. Oh yes, that funky band of apostles who couldn't even stay awake while Jesus prayed in Gethsemane the night before he was crucified! And, we all know the story of Thomas's doubt don't we."

After bringing the congregation to the depths of doubt, Mickey brought them out of the desert and up onto a mountaintop. "Yet, in spite of that Apostle's doubt, the Lord does not condemn the man; rather, He opens His arms to Thomas–a response demonstrative of Divine Mercy." Mickey finished his homily with an inspired affirmation of faith. "Without faith we are nothing!"

Had Mickey looked from his lectern to the left he would have seen the aghast expression on Sarah Donovan's red and wrinkled face. Her interpretation of Thomas's doubt was totally contrary to that of her priest. To Sarah, Thomas was the least of the Twelve.

At the door where he greeted everybody leaving the sanctuary, Mickey could sense a discomfort among others of his flock as well. Mrs. Watson, who always shook his hand and smiled widely, did an end run past him and out the door. Sarah Donavan brushed past him like a fullback seeing daylight ahead. The sideways glance from Louis Hill was almost chilling. Perhaps, St. Melchior's Day would turn out as badly as Saint Bernard's had been–and, it was only beginning.

18/ "WITHOUT FAITH WE ARE NOTHING..."

Driving back from his dinner with Father Tim in Hinckley, Mickey was psychologically drained. As expected, his friend was teetering, a crisis of faith was how Tim introduced his issues. The two men talked in an endless circle over dinner for more than two hours.

"I was at a total loss for words, Mick. All my training and experience wasn't worth shit... sorry, my bad, I meant to say crap! Can you believe it?–A sixteen year old kid had me babbling like an absolute idiot." Tim looked away from his friend, trying to get a better grip on his feelings, stirring two spoonfuls of sugar into his coffee. Tim's outfit was in sharp contrast to his vocation–he wore an old black Harley-Davidson tee, black denim jeans, with sunglasses propped atop his head, and thick-soled black boots. Even while in the seminary, Tim had evidenced his flare for the contradictory and outrageous. Back then; Mickey believed his friend was obsessed with presenting an impression that was as far away as possible from his farming roots in remote northwestern Minnesota.

Tim's story depicting his encounter with the longhaired teenager was no more than the tip of his iceberg. As he explained it to Mickey, at the insistence of his concerned parents this boy from Tim's suburban parish came into his office for a conference. The boy's name was Gordon Andrews. Gordon had a passion for *Dungeons and Dragons*. All that Tim knew about the game was that it was something evil–like Ouija boards. Gordon told the priest that he didn't believe all the Catholic stuff, all that Catechism stuff that he had been fed since before his first Communion. He went to church because his parents made him go, and he would get confirmed just to avoid another hassle with them. "My folks buy into all that sacrament stuff, you know," Gordon said. "Is this 'infusion of the Holy Sprit' supposed to make me speak in many languages?" His smirk was almost defiant, "What malarkey!"

Tim shook his head at the memory: "I told him that I understood his qualms and encouraged him to continue with his thoughts," Tim said. "At that time I thought I could handle where he was coming from."

Tim added more sugar to his coffee. "Gordon laughed in my face, Mick! 'Com'on Father, like you're not naïve enough to believe all those childish stories... I don't. I can't help it–I just don't believe that a piece of bread is the body of Jesus... that's just over the top. It's like that stuff you do at the altar is just hocus-pocus if you ask me'–that's exactly what he said to me."

Tim shook his head, "That froze me and the kid knew it. If someone doesn't believe in the Eucharist... there's nothing left. I can't make someone believe if they have a closed mind. I just can't– and if I can't defend that essential belief... what am I supposed to do, Mick?"

Mickey felt that he had failed his friend just as he had failed his sister the night before. In trying to jump-start Tim's faith, he only undermined it... "Without faith we are nothing..." he said for the second time that day–probably with the same impact. Tim's faith had been badly shaken and Mickey was unable to get his friend back on track. How many ways could he stress the importance of faith? Whatever he said, and however he tried to say it, nothing was making any positive impression.

Tim left Tobies restaurant as dispirited as when he came in the door more than two hours before.

"What are you going to do, Tim?"

"Don't know. Maybe I'll... I just can't say for sure."

"You want to follow me up to Duluth, hang out for a few days at my church, iron things out? I'll have my friend, Father Mario come over. The three of us can hash things out. What do you say?"

"No... I don't want to do that, Mick. Not at all."

"You going back to St. Lucy's tonight?"

"Probably," Tim lied. "Yeah... probably... thanks, Mick. Thanks for listening. I think I feel better."

Mickey could read the lie as if it were a red tattoo written across his friend's forehead. "Are you sure?"

"Yeah," Tim said without conviction. "I feel better."

Snow flurries in the low beam of his headlights began to mesmerize Mickey as he drove north on I-35 toward west Duluth. If anything, Tim had managed to get under Mickey's skin with some of his exasperating logic. At one point Tim asked, "Who's the smartest person on this planet, Mick? Take a guess. Mickey thought of philosophers, authors, and economists... but came up blank. "I give up," Mickey said.

"Okay, I'll tell you who, Steven Hawking, the physicist from England. That's who! That's what I think anyhow. He's got an incredible mind." Tim became animated for the first time. "Do you know anything about him, Mick? Besides the fact that he's still alive–and that absolutely defies all medical logic."

Mick guessed exactly where his friend was going with his question. "Okay, Tim... enough already. So, he's an atheist, big deal!

Most scientists probably are—either that or agnostics." Both priests and a few million other people had read about Hawking's recent interview with some British newspaper. Hawking had compared the human mind to a computer and claimed that it would stop working when its components broke down. Hawking went on to say that computers don't go to heaven and that heaven is a myth for people who are afraid of the dark.

Mickey could only shake his head. What did Steven Hawking really know about God and His promised afterlife?

The snowfall thickened as Mickey drove past the brightly lighted Black Bear Casino to his left. He shook his head at the sad reality that people could become so highly addicted that their food and utility and medication money could be gambled away– against odds that should discourage anybody with half a mind. How did playing blackjack, roulette, or the slots fit into the faith equation? Something to think about–maybe he could come up with some good stuff for a homily... maybe? Many of his St. Girard's parishioners frequented the casino, spending money they couldn't afford to spend, spending money that could go into the Sunday collection basket.

For the better part of the past forty minutes he had replayed his conversation with Tim. Especially troubling were Tim's references to Hawking's perspective on life and death, and Gordon Andrews' challenging assertions. Teenagers! They could be the toughest group for a priest to reach and minister to. Mickey had been blessed–at least he thought until yesterday's youth conference–with a gift for relating to kids of all ages.

Only the week before Blanche Moyer, a single parent, had brought her fourteen-year old daughter to the rectory for 'counseling'. Blanche called Melissa, her youngest child, 'incorrigible' and wanted the priest to exorcise some demons, so to speak. Melissa had several piercings (without permission) and a snake tattoo on her neck. How many hidden tattoos she had was anybody's guess. Truth be told, the matter was a serious lack of parental supervision and authority as much as anything else.

Mother, however, was concerned with her daughter's use of marijuana. "Next thing she'll be injecting will be, what's it called–oh, yeah, Ecstasy, I think? And all that morphetomines stuff that ruins a person's brain cells. Or, even worse, she could end up getting raped because she doesn't know what's happening to her. I've read a lot about that in the newspapers." Mickey suppressed a chuckle at 'morphetomines'–was that something new on the drug scene? The fact that Melissa was already sexually active seemed irrelevant to the mother. As it turned out, Mickey didn't counsel the girl as much as he educated the mother about drugs and teenage experimentation, and X-generation culture in general– much to the grinning delight of Melissa. The teenager beamed at the priest, nodding often as he explained the way things actually were these days. The bubble of her enjoyment, however, burst when Blanche pulled out a baggy of pot from her purse. "I want you to destroy this bag…this… bag of the devil's drugs, Father. I don't want you to go to the police or anything like that. Okay?"

Melissa winced as the priest put the bag in his pocket, "Let me return it to the person who sold it to me and get my money back, Father. Please!" she begged the priest to no avail. "I'll never use that stuff again–promise." Mickey smiled at her promise, more than likely the girl would use her unearned, and far too generous allowance money to make another purchase. This episode was just a small bump in the road for Melissa Moyer.

Back at the rectory, Mickey checked the messages on his phone. Mrs. Jawarski had called at six, "Johnny's gone Fadda, he slipped on the ice and hit his head… he's gone, Fadda… pleeze come over if ya can. I don know what I'ma gonna do. He's dead for good, Fadder!"

Mickey's eyes teared up, his Johnny, his devoted altar boy… falling to his knees, he blessed himself and cried as he prayed.

From down deep inside, he sobbed unabashedly, his insides were gripped by a spasm of pain, the back of his head throbbed... why... why... of all the people in this mixed-up world, why dear Johnny Jawarski? "Lord, I need to understand this, and I simply can not."

Without removing his coat, Mickey was out the door. He would walk the two blocks to the Jawarski's house on Idaho Street, near the closed down former high school building. Along the way he continued to pray, but his prayers could not mitigate the pain and disbelief that gripped his heart like talons of steel. Then a thought passed through his mind, a thought that should have loosened the grip: Surely, at this very moment, Johnny was in Paradise. But, a counter thought struck like a bolt–a thought that should not have arisen in the mind of a priest–a thought that cast a dark shadow over his hurried footsteps in the snow, was there really a heaven? Or, was Steven Hawking right. Was heaven only a comforting myth for those who were afraid of the dark?

Father Mickey Moran entered a dark and disillusioned funk that night. The bad news didn't end with Johnny Jawarkski's untimely death. There was still more anguish awaiting him when he returned to the rectory near midnight. Two more phone messages: The first from Gramma Maddie in Hibbing, and the other only minutes after from Tim.

Father Tim had called from Bemidji, about three hours north of Hinckley where the two priests had met earlier that evening. The message was brief, "I'm not going back, Mick. Sorry... I know you tried. Pray for me. Please, I need prayers... I'm lost."

Gramma Middies' message was even briefer. "Please call. No matter how late."

19/ PAIN ON PAYNE AVENUE

When Brian Slade slipped into the Catholic Church to get out of the harsh elements, his ears were numb from frostbite. The morning Mass was in progress. Rather than loiter in the foyer, he found a place near the back and settled himself on a scraped and scarred wooden pew. Everybody, about twenty people, was kneeling as the priest held his chalice and a large host in the air above the altar. Brian's memory of the Catholic ceremony came back to him, vaguely at first. After a few minutes, when everyone stood, the priest asked the congregation to offer each other the sign of peace. An older, nicely dressed woman at the end of the pew in front of him reached behind and offered her hand and a smile: "Peace be with you.," she said. Brian returned the gesture, felt an inner warmth.

A strange feeling was creeping through his bones. A good feeling, but hard for him to comprehend. It wasn't the warmth inside the building so much as it was something else. After the Mass had concluded, he sat for a few minutes, absorbing the church's rich ambiance. The sweet smell of incense lingered faintly, the stained glass windows showered multicolored shafts that danced lightly across the long, narrow nave. So much tradition here, tradition that he never understood or appreciated when forced to attend Sunday Mass with some of his Catholic foster families. His eyes riveted on the crucifix hanging high above the altar. He wanted to say a prayer but didn't quite remember the words to the Lord's Prayer; he didn't want to goof it up. That wouldn't be right. Maybe something simple would work just as well: "Jesus," he bowed his head and whispered… I'm not much of a church person… and I've done a lot of sinnin' these past few years." He closed his eyes, what should he say about his unworthiness? Maybe He, God or Jesus, already knew all about that. "Help me, please… if you will… to hook up with my sister Beth for Christmas. She's a regular Catholic so I'm sure it would be better for me if I were with her than down here just hanging out.

And… maybe you could help me to get my act together, too. I haven't had much luck lately, and I'm broke. Anyhow, I hope you'll take these words to heart. Amen." He blessed himself, genuflected in the aisle and walked back to the foyer. He wasn't quite ready to go back outside and suffer the St. Paul streets again so he wandered over to a table displaying various pamphlets and bulletins near the entry door. He browsed the material with little apparent interest. He had become good at finding places to kill time and keep warm, this church was one of the best.

The day held no promise whatsoever; the hours ahead were destined to be the same as the day before and the day before that. He would get a hot meal at the soup kitchen when it opened at eleven, get to the shelter where he slept the past few nights in the late afternoon, and try to stay warm during the time in between. He wasn't eligible for any unemployment benefits yet and had sold his few food stamps for cigarette money and lottery tickets days before.

The church custodian with his bucket and mop in tow entered the vestibule and began swabbing the puddles of dirty brown melted snirt–snow and dirt. Brian decided to leave before he was asked to do so. "Good morning," he greeted the stout man as pleasantly as he could. "Have a good one."

Where next? Outside, Brian pondered the four directions to nowhere in particular. South would take him toward the soup kitchen, west to the 35E freeway, east to his old neighborhood… he wondered if he could get into his former apartment and retrieve some of the possessions he had abandoned. He'd be able to pawn his watch, a microwave, DVD player and a few other possessions.

On second thought, maybe it was not such a good idea. If someone called the cops he'd be in big trouble–again. How bad was that? Maybe he ought to be looking for some kind of run-in with the law. Maybe he'd be better off in jail for Christmas than in the streets without anyplace to go. Lots of maybes… maybe his last girlfriend, Sara Karich would take him back if he apologized to her for the tenth time. Apologized for always being broke, for sponging off of her, for simply being who he was? Sara simply told him one day that she was tired of him and told him to find some other place to live. Maybe the guy she was dating now would drop her just like she had dropped him. All of his maybes added up to nothing. Maybe what his brother, Duane, had told him so many times was true—"Brian, you're a loser!"

He decided to head south, down Payne Avenue to Bumpers, a pool hall and tavern where he could buy a fifty-cent cup of coffee. Maybe he'd hang around for an hour or two—until Bumps, the obese proprietor told him to either spend some money or hit the road. In minutes his feet were tingling from the cold that seeped through the worn leather soles of his shoes and the thin nylon stockings inside. Once his toes began to numb, the chill would work its way up his body and settle in his lower back where it would remain for hours. After three blocks his teeth began to ache from breathing in the icy air, a northwest wind put a sting in his uncovered ears, and his nose started to run. Having no hankie or tissue in his pocket, Brian wiped the mucous away with the back of his bare hand, then from his hand to the side of his gray slacks. "What the hell," he mumbled to nobody but the howling wind.

Glancing at the cracked window of a failed hardware store, he stopped to regard his reflection. Even with his unshaven face and long unwashed hair, Brian Slade was a nice looking man: Maybe even handsome? In the days when he had a decent job and a bank account along with some nice clothes, most women would take a second look in his direction. His complexion was fair and features well defined: Straight nose, square jaw, full mouth… and penetrating, deep set, steel blue eyes. When life had been good, he offered an easy smile, had a confident demeanor, and pleasant personality. His con artist brother Duane had cultivated his own good looks and confidence with far greater success than Brian ever had–or would. Duane Slade was a psychopath who would steal a blind man's cane if he could sell it for two bucks. Duane had no conscience, but money in the bank, and a new girlfriend every other month. Slightly overweight and often unshaven, he was a 'know-it-all' and a braggart and a man who never looked a person in the eyes. In every meaningful way, Brian was a far more decent person than his brother might ever hope to be–but goodness and decency were not qualities that put money in one's pocket.

Brian's sister Beth, the oldest of the three Slades, was the stable, self-made, and successful sibling. She had an honest job and a generous heart. Beth Slade had always been there when Brian needed help, a munificence Brian had taken advantage of much too often. Like Duane, however, Beth had tired of her enabling behavior and made it clear that Brian was 'a big boy and had to learn how to get along on his own'. I always broke her heart and left her with an irreconcilable guilt when she did so. But...

Without fail, it seemed, when Beth had picked him up from the doldrums, Brian had always managed to let her down. Their relationship had become estranged over the past few years. Brian could count on receiving a Christmas card, and a birthday card (with a twenty) in August– that was the extent of his sibling connection. Beth lived in Duluth, about a three hours drive north of where Brian shivered at an East St. Paul intersection. Duluth would be an easy drive for someone who had a car and ten dollars or so for gasoline. From where he stood, he could hear the hum of traffic on the I35 corridor and smell the barrel smoke from under the interstate bridge. He longed to be on the overpassing highway and heading north to Duluth, but was probably much closer to being under the bridge and heading nowhere.

20/ 'O DANNY BOY

Mickey glanced at the digital clock resting on his desk, 12:26 in the morning, where had the past twenty minutes gone? When he first sat down it had been midnight, exactly twelve. His hand still gripped the buzzing phone; whom had he been planning to call? His mind was a total blank. Looking around his small office he saw his winter woolen coat lying in a heap on the floor. It was late, he'd been outside, and he'd started to make a phone call. For a few moments he wondered what was wrong, then it all came back to him. Johnny was dead, Tim was on the run, Gramma was in crisis mode. That was it... Gramma Maddie wanted him to call.

Without considering the lateness, Mickey punched the Hibbing number in his cell phone directory; he'd allow three rings and hang up without leaving a message. Gramma caught the second ring, "Thanks, Mickey... I knew you'd call when you got my message. I've been sitting by the downstairs phone waiting. Grampa is pacing upstairs, back and forth like a zoo animal, so I couldn't sleep anyhow."

"So, what's going on, Gramma? The zoo thing scares me." Mickey hoped for a short conversation; he was physically and emotionally drained.

"More bad news, I'm afraid..."

Mickey sucked in a deep breath and thought to himself: What else was new? Bad news was like a room full of screaming demons on this Sunday... no, it was already Monday. Sure, why not begin the new workweek with another downer. He couldn't imagine anything worse than what he had already gone through in the past forty-eight hours.

Maddie confirmed that Grampa Pack was in a bad way, not physically–he had always been as strong as a bull–but mentally. The former cop was, as his gramma would put it, 'wallowing in a cesspool of self-pity and depression'. Pack's anger and confusion and obnoxious behavior had been going on for weeks. Maddie was beside herself with frustration and worry.

"He won't talk to you, Mickey." She swallowed her pain, "I've got to be totally honest even if it hurts... you seem to be part of the problem he's choosing not to deal with." She went on to explain that Pack had expressed his resentment toward his only grandson. "He says 'you're the end of the line of Morans' and that when you became a priest you betrayed your legacy."

Mickey listened without comment.

"You must realize, Mickey, that he's not himself these days." She did not have the heart to tell him that Pack had also said 'he's (Mickey) wasted his f—ing life'.

Regardless of Pack's disoriented condition, Mickey felt a stab of pain. He knew that with his vows the seed of his father and those Moran men before him would come to an end. He had wrestled with that until his mother offered him her unequivocal blessing. His father, Amos, had never expressed any objections–his approval being more lukewarm. Being the last Moran was not something that preoccupied Mickey's thoughts these days–but maybe it wasn't that way with others in the family. His niece and nephew would never have any cousins, how did his sister Meg feel about that? As Mickey listened to Maddie's description of Grampa's symptoms, he realized that he had no more tears left to shed, what had been stored inside for years had been spilling out like a rain over just these past two days. He had to be tougher, thicker-skinned, less emotionally involved in other people's problems. Maybe his greatest problem was that he carried everyone else's problems like a bag of old fish.

He remembered a metaphor from Father Fabian's philosophy class at the seminary about the traveler carrying a heavy bag over his shoulder as he trudged along a hot and dusty road. A good Samaritan came by with his horse and cart: "Climb up on back, my friend, and let me take you to where you are going," the driver said. The traveler graciously got on board. After a short distance the cart driver said, "My friend you can lay that sack you're carrying in the cart; there's no need for you to keep that weight draped over your back."

The traveler replied, "Oh no, sir... you've been too kind already."

Maybe Mickey was carrying a bag filled with other people's problems and unwilling to let go of the burden. Maybe?

Gramma Maddie elaborated a series of Pack's bizarre behaviors– from his apathy and withdrawal, to his irritability and anger–then added her own resentment with everything Pack had been putting her through. Her portrayal of symptoms seemed indicative of classic acute depression. Grampa Pack's past and present were totally out of sync and he seemed unable to deal with the reality of aging. Pack Moran had been a legend in Hibbing police work. His apprehension of a corrupted cop, after a chase through subzero weather, snow and dense underbrush south of town was the stuff of folklore. Although exaggerated in telling over the years, to be 'as tough as Pack Moran' remained a standard of virility over coffee in many local conversations. But, that was decades ago and Pack had long since retired from law enforcement and had recently retired from a meaningful life.

Pack's withdrawal from Maddie, his lifelong friends, and the world around him came up time and again. Grampa was isolating himself in his den for entire days, sleeping on the sofa downstairs, and disregarding all manner of hygiene. "He hasn't shaved or showered all week, and he won't change out of an old sweatshirt and workout pants outfit. At times he's even locked the door on me, told me to go away and leave him alone. I'm heartbroken and at my wit's end, Mickey. And he absolutely refuses to see a psychologist, won't even talk to Doc Dinter and they've been friends for years."

It was nearly one o'clock in the morning and Mickey's fatigue was affecting his ability to think rationally. He was so close to dozing off that he gave his cheek a sharp slap. After five consecutive "I knows" Mickey was about to say he couldn't stay awake any longer. He'd offer the only logical advise he could muster: "We've got to get him some medical help, Gramma, sooner than later. I know a good psych..."

Then his attention perked, "... playing *Danny Boy*, over and over, all day long..." Maddie was explaining a recent Pack eccentricity.

"What? Run that by me again, Gramma."

She told Mickey that Grampa had locked himself in the den that morning and was listening to his favorite singer, Johnny Cash, on the stereo. She put her ear to the door and heard him crying as the song played, and replayed, and replayed.

Mickey came close to tears again. *Danny Boy* was a lament, as dark and emotionally evocative as an Irishman's soul. Only a son of Erin could have composed lyrics as mournful and heartrending.

Mickey would not sleep that night. The familiar words tumbled over and over in his troubled thoughts:

O Danny Boy, the pipes, the pipes are calling
from glen to glen and down the mountain side
The summer's gone and all the flowers are dying
'Tis you must go and I must abide

But come ye back when summer's in the meadow
Or when the valley's hushed and white with snow
I'll be here in sunshine or in shadow
O Danny Boy, O Danny Boy, I love you so

And if you come when all the flowers are dying
And I am dead, as dead I well may be
You'll come and find the place where I am lying
And kneel and say an "Ave" there for me

And I shall hear tho' soft you tread above me

And all my dreams will warmer, sweeter be
If you'll not fail to tell me that you love me

I'll simply sleep in peace until you come to me…

Mickey wished that his Lord would come to his rescue this night and that he could sleep in peace.

21/ THE SLADE TREE

Hoping that his sister Beth might accept his collect call, Brian Slade decided to give his sister a call. Smitty, the wino in bunk eleven at the Salvation Army shelter, refused to let him borrow the cell phone he had hidden under his pillow. "You din't give me no smokes last week when I askd fer one," was sufficient justification for his refusal. And, the shelter's office phone was off limits–"We break the rules for one and we have to break the rules for all" was the Director's justification.

These days there were probably no more than three or four operational phone booths in all of St. Paul, but he managed to find one of them four frigid blocks from Salvation Army building. He waited through several rings without any answer. He'd need to spend another dollar in change just to leave a message on her answering machine but it was worth a try. Dropping the fourth quarter in the slot, Brian was down to his last three dollars. His message held a tone of honest hopelessness: "Please call me Sis! Please!" He left the phone number of the booth outside the doorless booth and read the graffiti on the walls while he waited, and prayed, for a return call.

Pacing across the pavement within hearing distance of the booth for nearly an hour he rehearsed what he would say. If his desperation had been convincing enough and his sister called back, and agreed to express him some money, he might buy a bus ticket out of

St. Paul for a while. He would tell Beth how much he needed a fresh start, an appeal he had made to her more than once before. But Beth always had a warm Christmas spirit. Beth might be his Christmas angel. For the second time that day, Brian said a prayer that somehow his life would turn around.

Brian shivered as a blast of wind swept down the deserted street. He knew that Duluth was even colder than St. Paul and he wasn't too crazy about spending much time up there. The fact that the Slade family's roots were in the Lake Superior port city made little difference to him. At this moment in late December, Brian Slade felt like he was a resident of no place other than hell.

Beth was forty-one and had been a nurse at Saint Mary's Hospital for nearly twenty years. She had never married and lived frugally in a neat bungalow up the hill from her workplace and not far from the UMD campus. She enjoyed her flower gardens, hiking trips along the north shore, reading mystery novels, and chocolate–usually in reverse order. Since her teenage years, Beth had been self-conscious about her weight and appearance in general. She hadn't dated in years and often took any available overtime shifts at the hospital. She had become politically active while in college and remained a stalwart in Democratic political party affairs, always willing to volunteer stuffing envelopes, knocking on doors, getting people to the polls. She was usually pleasant, but quite opinionated about the government's responsibility to care for the poor and disadvantaged. Barak Obama and Oprah Winfrey were two of her favorite people in the world. She had no love for Republicans, wealthy people, or conspicuous consumption items like Lexus' or BMW's. In fact, in the spring she might join the 'Occupy Wall Street' demonstrations planned in Canal Park.

While in college, Beth Slade did a required genealogy research paper for an upper division sociology class. She was required to trace her family back five generations. The arduous project depressed and confused her; what she learned she wanted to keep to herself. Many of the Slade ancestors would probably be regarded as 'white trash' in the jargon of these times–or, at the very kindest, dysfunctional people.

To her knowledge, the Slades' great, great grandfather had never been identified. Beth assumed the man was probably some pleasure-seeking drifter. Sally Slade, her great, great grandmother, was a alleged to be a promiscuous woman who frequented the taverns near the docks where sailors hung out. The eastern ore-boaters usually got paid in cash before leaving their ship for a few days of furlough in port city. Most would spend their money on whiskey and women, then return to their ship flat broke, having paid dearly for the stories that would sustain them on the voyage back to steel mill cities like Gary or Erie or Buffalo. Sally had a child out of wedlock in 1909, and that son was named Harold. The infant was nicknamed 'Red' in the orphanage where he spent his first two years; Harold was adopted and raised by a family named Myers.

Harold became a delivery driver for a small grocery in the Norton Park neighborhood of West Duluth. Records indicated that Harold married Ardella Niles in 1931 and had a daughter: Martha who died of TB at age eleven, and a son they named John Niles Slade.

John Slade became a meat-cutter and worked at several butcher shops before marrying a Canadian woman named Amanda Janes. The couple moved to Winnipeg where son John Jr. was born. Amanda left John and her young son for another man in the mid-forties. After a contentious divorce, John and son returned to the States and settled in St, Paul where John remarried a much younger woman named Beatrice. John, known to most as Jack, or 'Blackjack', Slade was (at various times when employed) a car salesman, construction worker, and a handyman. He was also a bookie, a carouser and neer-do-well of many stripes. He fathered three children (Beth, Duane, and Brian) with Bea who was a nightclub hostess when she wasn't in a later-life pregnancy. Although quite good at making babies, the couple had difficulty with the responsibilities involved with raising them. They also had difficulty with their vows of fidelity. Jack left their nest first; Bea –and a piano player named Chadley–flew off only a few months later.

Jack Slade was still alive and living in Reno. Beth had last seen her father in '96, fifteen years ago. Her research paper was successfully accomplished with the help of her great grandmother, Ardella Niles, before the woman passed away. There was something ironic that Beth picked up while interviewing the old woman, "Strange as it may seem, my dear, you're not the first person that's asked me all these questions about the Slades. Eight or ten years ago, I lose track of time... maybe more like twenty, a nice looking young man spent an entire afternoon with me. Charming, gentlemanlike fellow, quite wealthy I guessed from his fine clothes. Anyways, I can't remember his name... but I do believe he was from Hibbing, leastwise that's how I remember it." Of the three Slades, only Duane had any connection with their father. Beatrice Slade, divorced and remarried twice, was living in either Charleston or Atlanta, no one was quite sure.

An honest woman to the core, Beth struggled with her final draft of the research paper. What would her instructor think of her and her family if she turned in the truth? After much soul-searching, Beth decided to file down some of the sharp edges with a mitigation here and a fabrication there. When she was finished, she had a much more likable family.

∼

Father Mickey hugged his extra pillow as he rolled over on his side to see what time it was. The last he remembered the digital flash read 2:18. Now it was 4:20 in the morning, and he had been wide-awake for some time. There was no reason to continue tossing in bed any longer; he knew he wasn't going to get any more sleep. Sitting up, rubbing his eyes, he turned on the reading lamp on the bedside table and regarded the crucifix above the dresser across the room. He wanted to pray, but couldn't. Too tired, too stressed, too defeated by life in general. This new Monday morning loomed over him like a storm cloud rather than greeting him with the positive vibes that most mornings offered. If he didn't pick himself up, today would unfold more frustration than inspiration. He had to put the downers of the weekend to rest, pray for a way out of the spiritual dessert he was making for himself. He felt more defeated this morning than any time in recent memory... and Christmas was less than two weeks away.

He plucked his bathrobe hanging on the corner of the half open bedroom door, wandered down the short hallway to the bathroom where he hoped a shower might rejuvenate his usually positive disposition. Standing under the hot spray, Mickey contemplated the fences he must mend that day. His sister was on the top of his list of repairs, Father Mario needed an apology for what had been a lousy performance at Saturday's youth seminar, and Tim... what could he possibly do to help his friend put his life in order. The most difficult task of his day, however, would be helping the Jawarski family with funeral arrangements.

"Yikes!" Mickey screeched as the hot water went suddenly cold! Stepping away from the icy stream, he reached for the faucet and as he did so he felt his right foot slip out from under him. Trying to keep from falling he tried to grab onto the shower curtain but only caught the vanishing steam. In falling, he hit the side of his face on a protruding soap dish, gashing his face near his left eye. The wound bled profusely but he managed to stop the bleeding with a wet towel. "Damnation!" Mickey let out the strongest expletive he would allow himself. Looking at himself in the mirror, he forced a laugh–"If it weren't for bad luck, I'd have no luck at all." He would surely be wearing a shiner to Mass that morning, and for the next few days.

Saying the morning Mass without Johnny Jawarski on the altar along side of him was sad and empty. His mentally challenged friend had been a living angel and had touched Mickey's life and ministry in ways he found hard to describe. The reality of never again tousling Johnny's mop of uncombed hair, never again hearing his 'and wit yer sprite' responses or his long drawn-out 'aaammmens', and never again being warmed by his wide crooked-toothed smile all weighed heavily on Mickey this gloomy December morning. Mickey had special ordered two hundred candles for next week's funeral Mass. The sanctuary of Saint Gerard's would radiate candlelight from it's every nook and cranny, and Mickey would light each one by himself. If Johnny had been correct about releasing the Holy Spirit–Saint Gerard's might be the holiest place on earth that funeral morning.

Usually spiritually connected to every nuance and tradition, Mickey's celebration of the Eucharist this morning was more rote than inspiration–it was as if the wind had stopped billowing his sails. All of the 'reglars' (as Johnny always called them) were into their private petitioning and unaffected by the subpar performance of their young priest. All except for Sarah Donovan at the far left end of the seventh pew. Sarah had talked with her neighbor, Mike Rolle, the previous afternoon. Mike told her about the near accident on Grand Avenue the previous Saturday morning, "He didn't even know my name," Mike said with disappointment in his voice. "Said he hadn't had his nicotine yet that morning." Mike always confused nicotine and caffeine.

Only days before, Sarah's sister-in-law, Blanche Moyer, had confided that Father Mickey flirted with her daughter. "He scolded me and told Melissa that smoking pot these days wasn't really so bad. Told me to lighten up a bit. The nerve... can you believe?"

On a mission of discovery, Sarah Donovan made a few more inquiring calls to friends of hers in the neighborhood. For the most part, everybody thought highly of Father Moran. "He's so funny,"

Millie Lotz said, Dorothy Jasper said, "His sermon on Sunday made me think–I have my doubts just like him." Ethel Goeden remembered: "One night a week or so ago, Harry and me was up late, ya know... I happened to look out the window and there was Father Moran, he was a'jumpin' up in the air. Then, Harry thought he heard him hollering somethin' foolish like Minnesota gin. It was that night that got so terrible cold. Harry and me just laughed so hard. That man is like a kid sumtimes."

Sarah had a mental list of issues, including some mistakes Father Moran had made in saying the Mass, concerns that should be brought to the attention of Bishop Bremmer as soon as possible. While she was at it, she might suggest that the fine people of Saint Gerard's parish deserved an older pastor who could better relate to their needs.

22/ KEVIN'S DIARIES

When Amos and Sadie landed at the Range Airport in Hibbing, their daughter Meghan, their two grandchildren, and Gramma Maddie were gathered at the terminal's large, frost-fringed window waving at them. The thermometer on the side of the building read a chilling minus six degrees. "We've lost about eighty degrees between Naples and here," Amos chided Sadie as they crossed the tarmac to the terminal building to greet the welcoming contingent of family members. Pack wasn't feeling well, Maddie said; and according to Meg, Kenny Williams was out of town. "Hardly see my husband these days," Meg told her father as Amos embraced his daughter. The grandchildren were antsy from waiting for the late Delta flight from Minneapolis but were truly happy to see their grandparents.

"I can't believe how you've grown," Sadie gushed her affection as she approached Matthew. Matthew who was nearly twelve and wearing a navy and white nylon jacket with Hibbing Peewees emblazoned across the front, smiled and accepted his gramma's hug.

"You're nearly as tall as your mother. And, I'm told that you're quite the young hockey player," Sadie gushed.

Matthew beamed, "Got nine goals already, Gramma. Two of 'em last week against Grand Rapids– and we've got a Christmas tournament at the Memorial Building coming up. Teams from the Cities are coming up her to play."

Amos smiled at his grandson, "You're going to be just like your great grampa– Pack was quite a hockey player in his day, you know."

Matthew nodded without comment, and gave his Grampa Amos an awkward hug. He was at an age where a handshake or a fist bump was more male-appropriate.

Ten year-old, Kathleen stood beside her mother allowing her older brother to get first attention. "And look at my little princess," Sadie said. "If you aren't the picture of your mom when she was your age." Katie was wearing a pink Columbia ski jacket, black Spandex pants, and a funky purple wool cap with matching scarf.

While waiting for the unloading of luggage, Meghan got her mother off to the side. Her tone was hushed; "I need to talk with you later, Mom. About Mickey."

Leaning toward her daughter's ear Sadie puzzled, "What about Mickey? I was hoping he'd be here to greet us… is he sick?"

"No… it's more attitude. We can talk… "

Amos called over from baggage claim, "Need some help with these, ladies."

Sadie turned, "Okay, Hon." To Meg, "Later, dear."

As Amos pulled the large suitcase toward the open tailgate door on Maddie's Escalade, his mother caught up with him. "We've got to talk, son. Your dad's been… "

"I know, Mom, Sadie's been telling me. Dad's not been himself lately."

"That's what I tell everybody when they ask about your father, 'Pack's not been himself'. I'm tired of sugarcoating it, of course.

He's in a very bad way and he needs help. I think he needs an intervention."

Earlier that morning when Maddie had suggested that Pack join the rest of the family to greet Amos and Sadie at the airport, Pack shot a profanity blast that might have translated into: "What the hell for? All they care about is themselves. I'm sick of hearing about the weather in Naples." With that he went into the den to watch a sports program on ESPN.

Amos tossed the heavy bag into the cargo space of Maddie's SUV. "How bad is it, Mom?"

"Really bad."

"I'll get over tonight if I can." Amos pulled up his jacket collar to cover his neck. "Don't mention my dropping by for a visit to dad, okay? I want to see him as he is. Do you want me to bring Sadie along?"

"No. She's going to be spending some time with Meghan, I think. Meghan told me that she wanted dibs on Sadie tonight. She's got some issues of her own to deal with… she hasn't confided them to me though."

After the goodbyes and promises to see each other shortly, Amos and Sadie put a few things away and settled back into their home. Meg had stopped by and turned up the thermostats and removed the cloths draping the furniture the night before. Home soothed them both with a cozy familiarity that both missed when they were away. Home was this house in the Homeacres neighborhood, and home was Hibbing for both of them.

It was mid-afternoon and flight-wearied Sadie wanted to take a nap before going out to dinner. "I think Kenny and Meg want to take us out to Zimmy's for a steak tonight." Zimmy's, a popular restaurant-tavern on Howard Street in downtown Hibbing, was named after Bob Zimmerman. Most of the world knew the town's favorite son as Bob Dylan.

"You go right ahead, I want to check out the trunk in the attic," Amos said. "I still can't understand how Mickey knew about that picture of my grandfather. I'm positive that I'm the only person in the world who even knows that that photo of Kevin even exists."

Sadie nodded. When her attorney husband had something on his mind he was doggedly persistent, Amos always needed answers to questions and solutions to problems with a capital S on ASAP!

The attic held much of the outside chill but Amos was dressed for it, having put on a hooded sweatshirt under his denim jacket. The locked trunk was in the far corner among a cluster of boxes, exactly where he'd last seen it. As best he could determine, it hadn't been touched. Upon opening the heavy cedar lid, he saw that the stacks of grampa Kevin's notebooks were carefully arranged just as he'd left them, with the most recent atop the one that were older. About halfway through a collection of old photographs he found the one he was looking for. Yellowed and faded around the edges, twenty-something Kevin had been looking directly into the camera with a stern expression on his face. His 'M' cap sat back on his head, a Louisville Slugger rested on his broad shoulder. Amos marveled at the likeness of Kevin and his own father, Pack. Both were handsome men: chiseled jaw, heavy brows, the familiar intense expression. Amos couldn't help but make comparisons: Mickey's features were less severe than Kevin's or Packs, or even his own, but his son had the same deep-set Moran eyes.

In a large envelope, Amos had drawn a family tree that stretched back to Daly Moran who traveled west to Michigan and then northern Minnesota from Pennsylvania. Daly and his wife, Katherine, had three sons: Terrance, Peter, and Denis. Terrance was an intellectual and ended up teaching at a college out east. Peter was the seed from which came Kevin, Patrick (Pack), Amos, and Michael (Mickey)–the four generations of Moran men. In the same envelope, Kevin had developed an outline of the Denis Moran (Peter's brother) ancestry, but Amos found their tree confusing and much less interesting than his own roots stemming from Peter in early Hibbing. As he remembered, most of Denis' offspring were surnamed Slade and had lived without any noteworthy accomplishment in Duluth, St. Paul and Canada.

23/ SIBLINGS

On the drive to the Northern Transportation (formerly Greyhound) bus depot located on west Grand Avenue, Beth Slade made up her mind to be brutally honest about her feelings toward her downtrodden, brother. No more enabling she vowed to herself. She would make it clear that Brian could visit until after the Holidays–no longer than a week to ten days. She was not going to fall into the trap of being her brother's keeper any more: "You made your own bed," she would tell him, "Now you've got to sleep in it." Beth didn't like that cliché but found that she used it quite often. She should have known that Brian didn't have a bed of his own to make and that he suffered an acute insomnia. Actually, she had no way of knowing exactly how far down her brother had slipped. Nor had she ever been informed about his criminal record or time spent in the Ramsey County jail. All that she really knew was that Brian was broke again and that he wanted to spend Christmas with her. He had told her that he wouldn't be staying long–didn't want to impose. Beth was curious, though, why didn't Brian couch-out with their brother Duane who lived in Roseville? Duane lived only a couple of miles away from where Brian had recently been staying. She knew that both of her brothers disliked Duluth for some reason–visited only on a rare occasion. She swallowed a distasteful reality; they were two of a kind–losers both.

Watching her brother step from the bus, Bethany Slade sighed as she turned up the heater fan. Just the sight of Brian elevated her already high level of stress. Brian was wearing an unbuttoned, unlined, denim jacket over a gray T-shirt and lighting a cigarette with ungloved hands. "Idiot," she mumbled under her breath. Duluth's mid-afternoon temperature was below zero with a serious wind chill. Brian's luggage would probably consist of a large Wal-Mart bag full of dirty laundry and, she hoped, a toothbrush. On his last visit, almost two years ago, Brian arrived with nothing more than his wallet and left with a duffle bag, some new clothes, toiletry items, and a 'loan' of seventy dollars. She remembered a week of frustration followed by an hour of elation when she finally got him out her door and to the bus depot.

With the first drag on his unfiltered Camel, Brian felt the light-headed buzz of nicotine deprivation. "God almighty, this weather sucks," he muttered against the seizing cold. "Where's Beth? I told her about two," he said to a nearby bank of dirty snow. Scanning the lot from the sheltering side of the large bus, he heard a horn honking to his left, and walked briskly in the direction of his sister's idling Solara sedan fifty feet away. Stopping short of her car, he deeply inhaled a final drag before crushing the butt under his shoe. As much as he dreaded this reunion, he'd put his best foot forward and try not to dump all of his personal problems in her lap–at least not right away.

"Hi Sis." He offered a self-conscious smile as he pulled the door closed and tossed his backpack into the rear seat. Leaning across the armrest he gave her a peck on the cheek. "You look great; like your boots," he said. Beth was wearing camel colored Uggs with jeans tucked in, and a matching wool-lined suede jacket. Beth had gained some weight since he'd seen her last. "Thanks for coming down to pick me up. I'm looking forward to my visit." He wanted to assure his sister that he wouldn't be staying too long, but swallowed the thought. He could read tension in the cool return smile she offered.

Beth's smile was forced; she nodded toward her brother without speaking. Brian was unshaven, unkempt, and his clothing smelled of rancid cigarette smoke and perspiration. Looking over her shoulder, she backed up and found an opening in the traffic flow going east. "You look good yourself," she lied. "How's Duane?" Her question might divert Brian from any litany of his own woes. She could really care less about Duane and his warped lifestyle, but at least she had one brother who was capable of supporting himself. Years before Duane had conned his sister to the tune of five thousand dollars with a phony currency investment scam. When she considered what a waste of potential both of her siblings had become, she had to remind herself that they were the only family that she had.

Neither Beth nor nearly anybody else had yet been able to touch or feel the inner goodness of Brian Slade. Perhaps the unfortunate circumstances of his life had caused that light to dim; to become buried somewhere in his dark subconscious. Self-image was like the ember of a fire, without an occasional stoke it gradually dies. While doing his last stint in the Ramsey jail, he learned some valuable things about who he was–and who he could be– through program called 'The Power of People/Silent Cry'. One theme of the rehab was simply: 'We don't focus on what we did, but we focus on why we did it and what we could have done differently'; grasping that concept helped to ground Brian in a reality that he had never quite understood. He finished his term with a positive attitude–his problem was how to sustain any upbeat perspectives in the glum world that he returned to.

By now, months later, Brian's sense of positive self-esteem had lost most of its glow. Most–but not all. Brian kept the thread of a hope that it wasn't too late to rekindle his flame.

"I take it by your not answering my question, that you haven't been in touch with Duane." Beth slowed her car as a careless old man edged his SUV onto Grand from a side street to her right. She bit her tongue rather than lay on the horn, keeping her frustration in check. "Maybe that's just as well."

"Uh huh." Brian didn't want to talk about his older brother. The two of them had parted with some bad blood and just the thought of his older brother put a sour taste in his mouth. "I mean Duane's okay, I guess. Haven't seen him in a while." He smiled, reached across the space between them and gave Beth a light punch on her arm. "How are you, Beth? It's been too long since I last saw ya. Merry Christmas, by the way."

Caught off guard by the pleasantry, Beth softened a bit, returned his smile: "Same to you, Bry. No complaints here–life's been pretty good for the most part." Her younger brother could be a charmer at times, "I'm looking forward to having some time to catch up on things," she said with an ounce of sincerity. Beth decided to take the longer route through the western part of the city rather than ramp up onto the 35 interstate. Taking a few extra minutes together on the trip home might help dull the edge she arrived at the depot with. She searched her thoughts for some small talk; "I see it's been as cold down in the Cities as it's been up here."

"Yep. I mean, it's the wind that gets to ya more than the temperature does. You get a lot of wind up here?"

"Oh yes. Especially up on the hill."

Brian nodded. He knew that downtown, near the lake, had a different climate than the hilltop did. "Hate the wind, Beth." He might have added that he knew the wind's brutality more than most– maybe later.

"I hope you brought some warmer clothes along with you, Brian, it's supposed to stay cold all the way through Christmas." Beth's younger brother seemed to bring out a maternal instinct in her. A need that years before had motivated her career choice of nursing. She could admit that the opportunity to nurture Brian wasn't an altogether distasteful one. Planning a shopping trip to buy some necessities so that he could get back on his feet might actually be fun. She could rationalize that pampering wasn't enabling.

Brian's only warmer clothes were in a closet behind the locked doors of his former apartment. Or, maybe the landlord had deposited them in the alley dumpster by now, along with his microwave and coffee-making machine. Fortunately, he had few possessions and those that were left behind were of little value. In his backpack he had some clean underwear, socks, a couple of T-shirts, another pair of Levis, and his shaving kit. He'd need to pick up razor blades and deodorant at some point. More importantly to the chain-smoker, he'd need to get a pack or two of smokes. The rumpled package in his jacket pocket had only two and a half cigarettes remaining.

"I'll be fine with what I've brought along, Sis. Cold doesn't bother me much," he lied. "I don't want you fussing over me. I'm just delighted you sent me money for the bus tickets."

Beth's middle name could have been compassion. She'd probably have to outfit him again. One of the first things she had noticed when Brian got into her car was that he wasn't wearing the watch she had given him as a Christmas gift three years before. He had probably pawned it, along with the Ipod gift of two years ago. "Don't be silly, Bry. Maybe we can find you a few things later."

"I'd be willing to check out a Goodwill store if it's not out of the way for you," Brian said.

Rather than play at small talk about cold weather or clothing, the siblings traveled for a few minutes without words, Brian had been checking the familiar landmarks along the route: Wade Stadium on his right, Wheeler Field to the left, the Massive network of railroad trestles leading out to the ore docks on the lower St. Louis River. To Brian, Grand Avenue was anything but grand. Previous street sandings and saltings along with occasional snowmelts had painted the crusty banks of snow with road debris in ugly blacks and browns. Chunks of dirty ice, dropped from the wheel-wells of cars, were strewn everywhere potholes jarred them loose. Grand Avenue had plenty of potholes and some appeared large enough to have swallowed an unsuspecting Volkswagen or Cooper.

Brian broke the silence as they turned up the Mesaba Avenue hillside past the municipal buildings: "Hate to bother you, Sis… but, could you make a quick stop at a convenience store on the way to your place."

"Cigarettes?"

"I'm gonna quit, Beth, I swear! That's my number one New Year's resolution. Just getting too awfully *darn* expensive–can you believe Pall Malls are almost five bucks a pack?" Knowing that his sister didn't like profanity–even in the mildest form–Brian eschewed a *damn*. For the next few days he would compensate for his bad habits with good behavior.

Beth could only shake her head in abhorrence to any reference the vile addiction of nicotine. As a nurse she had seen too many cases of emphysema and lung cancer to tolerate tobacco in any form. She mumbled a disgruntled "I suppose."

24/ *A LITTLE LIGHTHEADED*

Father Mickey stepped up to the lectern for his brief Monday morning homily. With a self-deprecating laugh, he pointed to the bandage beside his right eye: "You should see the other guy!" The Torgersons sitting nearest to the altar caught the humor and smiled. Others, Mickey discerned, didn't get it at all. Oh well, probably just another example of the St. Gerard's generational gap. Would he ever be able to coexist with his congregation? Yet, sometimes, he realized that he was a bit too critical of everybody in his flock. The Torgersons were perfectly normal folks as far as he could tell. So were the Johnsons, the Drabecks, Latvalas and… anyhow, there were some, maybe quite a few if he gave the matter proper consideration. Sarah Donovan, he noticed, had an almost horrified expression on her hangdog face. Rather than explain the 'just kidding', he spoke a few words integrating Mark's Gospel into a contemporary setting.

After his 'arrangements' meeting with the Jawarski family later that morning, Mickey retired to his office to make a few phone calls and catch up on some correspondence. Difficult phone calls. He'd try to catch Meg at home so he could make another apology for his indiscretions, connect with Father Tim Hagland–wherever he might be today–and offer Father Mario another apology for letting him down at the youth conference. The thought of each call brought back one element of his weekend failures. A note on his calendar reminded him that his mom and dad would be back in Hibbing today. For the hundredth time in the past several days, Mickey was in touch with how much his personal life had intruded upon his ministry.

He looked for a sheet of church stationery so he could send a nice letter to Benjamin Little Otter thanking him for his kind note and prayers. The thank-you note was paper-clipped at the edge of his desk calendar. He reread the Indian man's thoughtful words–the reality that he had reached someone's soul added a warmth to Mickey's morning. He would assure Benjamin of own his prayers for success in his constant struggles with alcoholism. Feeling a sneeze coming on, Mickey reached behind him for his back-pocketed handkerchief. Too late, a few drops of saliva dotted his desktop. "Where's the box of Kleenex when I need it," he said to an empty room. In a lower drawer he found the box where he had stuffed it along with odds and ends. Resting next to the partially crushed tissue box was a baggie; Melissa Moyer's confiscated bag of pot stared back at him. He lifted it out of the drawer, unzipped it, sniffed the dry shredded contents inside… how long had it been since he'd last smoked a joint? Back in the seminary a few of the guys had tried it on occasion; some liked it a lot and probably still secretly indulged. He knew that Tim did. Mickey hadn't had much of a sensation from the weed but was glad that he'd at least tried it–he felt an arcane satisfaction in having experienced what many regarded as a 'rite of passage' into the contemporary youth culture.

Below the surface of Mickey's conscious was a troublesome persona that sometimes motivated impulsive or unconventional behavior. As a youngster he challenged the class bully–'try picking on someone your own size'– knowing well that he would get himself beaten up. He was. Later he picked another fight with the bully and experienced the same outcome. As a teenager he had two speeding violations in two months while racing against friends on the road to DuPont Lake. On occasion, while serving at St. James, he'd take the bus downtown and hang out with the riffraff of the streets. He could rationalize that doing so was his way of getting a more meaningful understanding of life on the underside, he found that he truly enjoyed the experience–until he was mugged on east First Avenue. Episodes of acting 'out of character' or of disregarding authority, however irrational they might have seemed at the time, enabled Mickey to appreciate the diversity and the complexity of his being.

What the heck, he thought as he locked the door to his office and cracked open a window. Near a votive candle on his credenza he found a book of matches, he tucked the marijuana inside the paper that was included inside the baggie, licked the edge and lit the match; inhaling long and deep into his lungs. The experience became pleasant almost immediately, more so than he remembered from years ago. A little lightheadedness, with an added ease of the tension in the back of his neck, was allowing Mickey to feel more relaxed than he'd been in some time. He took a few more deep drags, leaned back in his chair and was about to put his feet on the desk...

Oooops, Monday morning... Mickey startled at the sound of footsteps on the hallway's hardwood floor outside of his office. He'd totally forgotten, Mary Alice Murray, the housekeeper did her vacuuming and light housekeeping on Monday mornings. He snuffed out the butt in an empty coffee cup, and then fanned the lingering odor toward the open window. The light knock on the door brought a mild panic. "You in there, Father?"

"I'll be out in a minute, Mary Alice."

"Mrs. Donovan is here. She'd like to talk to you."

Of all people, Sarah Donovan! "Just a minute," he repeated. The thickest clouds of pungent smoke were gone.

"Tell her I'll meet her in the church... I'll only be two minutes."

Sarah Donovan waited impatiently… why meet in the church and not in the office? She had come to the Rectory door because the church lights had been turned off after morning Mass. Strange. She had a Tupperware container with a dozen brownies for the priest. She wasn't planning to stay for any coffee unless Mary Alice Murphy would join them. When Father Moran entered the sanctuary, her words had a harsh edge: "I think I promised you… " the statement dropped like a hammer's strike… "What's that smell, Father? It's putrid."

'Oh… the heating system has a burned out bearing, I think, I've been trying to repair it all morning. Must be natural gas you smell." Mickey's convenient venial sin came out of nowhere and brought a small smile of satisfaction. Sometimes he was truly surprised by that deviant 'other' self that surfaced without invitation.

Mrs. Donovan's eyelids dropped into a frown of disbelief but she said nothing further. Did he think she was stupid? That wasn't gas that she smelled. Mickey thanked her profusely for the brownies as he ushered her toward the front door of St. Gerard's. He could not remember ever being more delighted to see somebody leave his church.

Safely back in his office, Mickey scribbled a quick letter to Mr. Little Otter, then paged through his planner and took an inventory of what needed to be done yet today. His notations were mostly done in pencil and subject to change: The Church cleanup and Christmas decorations belonged to the women's altar committee–he put a pencil check beside that item; year-end budget for the bishop's office would be prepared by Orville Orazem and the parish council at their meeting on Tuesday night; a visit with Ed Blazina at St. Mary's; that could be checked off later. Nothing in the planner seemed pressing, so procrastination was a very possible option. Any remaining correspondence could be done later. His usual Monday nursing home visits could be pushed to Tuesday, and the Carmelites afternoon prayer group could get along fine without his making an appearance.

He almost wanted to take a nap and it was only ten in the morning—maybe the pot was still doing its thing in his system. Sometimes when he contemplated things to be done, a siege of inertia would assail him from all sides and nothing could be accomplished.

A half-finished *New York Times* crossword puzzle from the week before was folded under the planner. He penciled in a vertical seven-letter word *sustain*, connected it to the existing four-letter across word, *musk*... and, in half an hour he smiled contentedly, the puzzle was done. Now what? Pick up the Jon Hassler novel that he hadn't touched in days, putty the leaky windows in the sacristy, change the furnace filter? Before he forgot, he thought to take the baggie downstairs to the basement and hide it in the rafters where he once found a *Hustler* magazine. Could one of the 'old' priests who preceded him to the pulpit of Saint. Gerard's hidden the porn? He laughed at the notion, it probably belonged to Mort, the off and on maintenance man.

Today might still be a great opportunity to play hookie. Mickey could stop by Saint Mary's for a quick visit, then catch Mario at the Newman Center on the UMD campus, and still have time to drive up to Hibbing and pay a surprise visit to his folks who had just arrived the other day. He could be up there in mid-afternoon. It might be better to resolve his issue with Meghan face-to-face, he could talk with Tim from his cell in the car... maybe, maybe even spend a few minutes with Grampa Pack. Perfect!

As he flipped off the office lights, and grabbed his jacket, the desk phone rang. Mickey was tempted to ignore it. "Should I?"

He turned back, picked up the receiver, "Father Moran..."

The voice was as familiar as it was unexpected: "And Merry Christmas to you, Bishop. What a wonderful surprise."

Mickey's mouth went suddenly and completely dry. "Just fine, thank for asking. And you?" Preliminary small talk always strained his attention. "Oh, it'll just take a little time, of course." The bishop had inquired about how the new liturgy was settling with him.

"You're right of course. I guess we're all struggling just a little with it– I still find myself slipping into the old familiar words now and again," Mickey said.

"We've just got to be very careful to read every word in the sacramental we've all been given," Bishop Bremmer's instruction was emphatic. "Won't be long and everything will be as natural as before."

"Oh yes, I agree. And, certainly, this is a much better translation." Mickey bit his tongue, grimaced: his second white lie in just the past hour.

"Kinda busy this morning, all the seasonal preparations, you know," another 'whitie' was unfolding. He checked himself, "Nothing that couldn't be put on the back burner, Your Grace." Bremmer deserved honesty and respect, despite some lingering malcontent between the two men.

"Two o'clock? Sure... that would be just fine. I'll look forward to seeing you..."

Mickey hung up, sat down, frowned... he hadn't asked his bishop what the meeting was supposed to be about? Why hadn't Bremmer been more specific? And, why the apparent urgency?

~

At the Kenwood traffic lights, Beth Slade pulled into the lot of Romano's Food and Fuel, a busy corner convenience store near the Saint Scholastica campus on the hilltop not far from her house. "You sure you can't live without them, Bry? This is a perfect time to quit that filthy... You already know that I don't allow any smoking in the house or garage. None!"

"I know. This might be the last pack, Sis. I keep tryin' ya know– then, in a few hours, I get the cravin' real bad, one more and I'm right back where I was before." Brian checked himself in the visor mirror, ran his comb through his long hair, flashed Beth a quick smile: "Thanks for stopping. I'll only be a minute."

The bearded man behind the counter slid the package of Camels toward Brian, "Bad habit, Father." He chuckled and rang up the sale. Brian puzzled, what was so funny? What was with the *Father*? Did he look old or something? Pocketing his change and turning toward the door, he brushed into a young man perusing a *Sports Illustrated* at the magazine rack. He excused himself, and then paused for a brief second, Brian had a strange feeling that the kid with the magazine had tugged at his sleeve–was he being aggressive, or was it merely a mistaken identity–he wasn't sure. No sense in making an issue of it.

Within two minutes Beth was pulling into the driveway on East Toledo Street, just a half-block off of Woodland Avenue. Checking her dashboard clock she noticed that it was nearly three in the afternoon. "I've got a roast in the crockpot and some beer in the fridge," she said. Beth had picked up a six-pack of Michelob Ultra that morning. "I don't know about you, but a beer would be just fine with me about now."

Brian was more than a little surprised; the Beth he remembered abhorred drinking as much as she hated smoking. He returned her pleasant smile, "I've never been one to let another soul drink alone."

25/ PHONE CALLS

His trip to visit family in Hibbing would have to wait until later in the week. When the Bishop calls… all in Catholicdom must obey! Mickey still couldn't imagine what this was all about? His financial reports were current, he hadn't gotten himself mixed up in anybody's legal issues, and he hadn't missed any clergy meetings. So, what? Bishop Bremmer's monotone voice hadn't revealed emotion of any kind–was he upset? Mickey wouldn't spin his wheels trying to figure out the bishop's reasons, he'd make a few calls before heading to Saint Mary's Hospital to visit his parishioner, Ed Blazina, on his way to the bishop's mansion near the Holy Rosary Cathedral overlooking Lake Superior.

His first call was to Father Mario Morelli.

"You're too hard on yourself, Mick. It wasn't that bad at all. Some of the kids I talked with after you left the conference felt they had really picked up some good ideas from your workshop." Father Mario thoughtfully and skillfully mitigated Mickey's self-deprecations. "And those two young fellas from Saint James think the world of you. The taller one, Randy... I think, anyhow, he said he still 'owed you one', whatever that meant. Sounded positive, though."

Mickey laughed, "That would be Randy Flynn. I helped him out of a jam a few years back." He shared the story. "Got myself in hot water with the bishop over that. Randy's never forgotten the episode. Nor has Bremmer." Mickey went on to mention that he would be visiting with the bishop that afternoon. "Strange. He wouldn't say what he wanted." Mickey promised to fill Mario in on their meeting later in the afternoon.

As expected, the call to Tim Hagland, found his seminary friend in Roseau visiting his parents. "I called the honcho's at Saint Lucy's after we talked yesterday. They've got everything covered through Christmas, told me to take some R&R up here for a week or so."

"You're planning to go back then?" Mickey said.

"Not sure, Mick. I'm still a little bent out of shape. Feels really good to be away from all the church crap. Sorry, I... "

"Don't apologize for feelings, Tim. It is 'church crap' to you right now. What are you planning to do up there? Just hang out?" Mickey knew that Tim was not on good terms with his father, a farmer who thought religion was best kept to one's self. Nor with his stern border agent mother."

"Yeah, hang out mostly: Watch some hockey games, see some friends. You know... Oh; your old high school's team is up here for a weekend series with both us and Warroad. Hibbing's supposed to be pretty good again this year."

Mickey hadn't followed the Hibbing High School Bluejacket sports teams in recent years but knew that hockey had always been the school's athletics claim to fame. In recent years the Hibbing girl's volleyball teams had made quite a reputation as well. "Just have a good time, Tim, kick back, chill out, forget all that 'crap' back at your parish. Okay?"

Mickey knew that Tim had been in a long-term relationship with a girl named Bonnie LaPatka before enrolling at the Saint Paul Seminary. Bonnie liked guys and Tim was only one of several. Possessive by nature, Tim couldn't cope with the competition. Some seminarians believed that the priesthood was a dramatic compensation for his broken heart when Bonnie dumped him. To Mickey's knowledge, Bonnie was still unmarried. He wouldn't bring up her name and invite upsetting his friend. "Let's keep in touch, my friend. Merry Christmas."

"Same to you, Mick."

Mickey couldn't help but wonder if he was failing his friend by not suggesting that he consider getting some help. Tim's metro diocese must have some excellent psychological counseling for struggling priests. He made a mental note to investigate the matter and get back to Tim–maybe after the first of the year. R and R was probably the best therapy for his friend right now.

His sister, Meghan was either not at home or still not answering Mickey's persistent calls. His hope of patching things up with her before the Moran family gathering for Christmas would have to wait. He'd try reaching her again later. His next call, before driving out to the east end of Duluth for his meeting, was to his parents who had arrived in Hibbing for the holidays.

"Merry Christmas, Mom… and welcome back to paradise."

Sadie laughed at his twisted humor. For nearly ten minutes, his mother talked grandchildren, and more grandchildren. Mickey guessed that she and his dad would probably be willing to forgo the remaining winter months in Naples if Meghan just hinted that they could babysit the two kids for a few weeks. Mickey understood their attachments, he loved his nephew and niece nearly as much. "Yes, it's hard to believe how fast they grow." Mickey agreed. Other small talk included Pack's 'not being himself', Matthew's hockey tournament, Katie's piano and ballet lessons, Kenny's new design contracts, and Gramma Maddie's frustration with Grampa.

"What's with you and Meg?" Sadie asked. "She told me that you really blew her off when she drove all the way down to Duluth to visit you. She called you 'Almighty and Merciless, Mickey Moran'– and she was heated-up when she said it. What did you do to upset her so? I think she's started smoking again and that's simply terrible."

"She didn't tell you what we were talking about, Mom?"

"Not in much detail, really. I know that she and Kenny have some issues–he's gone an awful lot, you know. Meg's got a full plate with the children and all of her commitments."

Mickey wasn't going to blow any whistles. "I'm sorry she feels that way, Mom. I'll give her another apology."

"Your father's here, I'm passing the phone… can't wait to see you here for Christmas, son. God bless."

Amos, like Sadie, was enjoying time with the grandkids. "Matthew's a real Moran–that's for sure. You'll have to see him carry the puck down the ice…" Amos dropped the thought.

Mickey winced, a 'real Moran'… was that meant to imply that *real* Morans were jocks.

Amos, realizing his son's sensitivities, deftly changed topics: "I plan to stop by and see your Grampa this afternoon, son. You've probably already heard, but your grampa 'hasn't been himself' lately."

Eddie Robinson was a UMD junior and part-time bartender at a Central Avenue tavern, near Raleigh Street, in west Duluth. He was a close friend of Jimmy Rossini who was having a Coor's on tap. Eddie was explaining the episode at the convenience store up on Kenwood near the UMD campus. "I swear he walked right by me like I was a piece of shit, Jimmy. Me! One of his altar boys at Saint James. How in the hell does he forget something like that in what is it, four or five years? I tried to catch his elbow, you know, to say 'hi' but he just gave me a sour look and pulled his arm away."

Jimmy shook his head, "Not Father Mick, Eddie. He'd never snub one of us guys."

"Five bucks, Jimmy. I got five that says you're wrong. I think our old padre might have become a stuck up jerk since he left here."

"Don't say anything like that when Randy's around, he'll kick your ass from here to sundown."

With a fifty-dollar loan from his sister, earmarked for the purchase of some warmer clothes, Brian Slade browsed the racks of the Goodwill shop on First Avenue. An older lady who had a cart full of children's clothing caught his attention. "You getting some things for the poor, Father. God bless you… and Merry Christmas."

Brian smiled, "I'm sorry ma'am, but …" Before he could ask her what she meant, the woman was moving down another aisle away from him. *Father*? That was the second time someone had mistaken him for another person. A priest? He laughed to himself, what an outrageous mistake. Brian Slade, a priest!

Beth was one aisle away looking over some hooded sweatshirts and overheard the woman's comment and Brian's incomplete response. Curious, she caught up with the lady: "Excuse me, maam, is that man over there a priest?" she gestured toward Brian who was trying on a fur-lined parka.

"Father Moran, honey. Used to be at Saint James, maybe five years back, maybe less, can't quite remember. Nice man, always a pleasant smile for people. Went someplace else, though. Ain't seen him in a while."

"Father Moran, is that what you said?"

She nodded: "Young folks always called him Mickey."

Beth wished the lady a Merry Christmas and filed the information away for the moment. She would go online later and see what she could find out about this Father Moran.

26/ UNUSUAL BEHAVIORS

Bishop Anthony Bremmer was a short-legged, long-trunked man with a stomach that hung over his belt. Every feature accentuated his size; round head, thick neck, bulky shoulders. The only incongruous feature was a pinched nose that seemed to pull his cheekbones toward the center of his wide face. A renowned theologian, and avowed conservative, his intellect could be intimidating. His reputation as a scholar had enabled him to travel frequently to the Vatican in Rome. At fifty-two, many considered him to be a rising star in the Catholic hierarchy.

The bishop's office was ornately furnished in dark leathers and rich mahogany, his walls adorned with countless diplomas and photographs with church celebrities–his favorite with a smiling Archbishop Timothy Dolan. Bremmer's large desk was situated upon a scarlet-carpeted platform, an island near the center of the spacious room, about six inches above the surrounding ceramic floors. The windows were heavily draped.

Mickey smiled, bent to kiss the Bishop's ring, said: "God bless you and Merry Christmas, Your Grace," then accepted the smaller man's cool embrace.

Bremmer had an immediate confirmation of the phone call that precipitated this unscheduled meeting. The smell in Father Moran's clothing was unmistakable. He wouldn't say anything yet; maybe not at all. Offering his pudgy hands, Bremmer suggested they say a prayer together. The two men said an 'Our Father, Hail Mary, and Glory be…'

"Please sit down, Father, and make yourself comfortable," the bishop slid a large leather chair near the front of his platform and stepped up to his desk. "Quite a bruise you have Father, did you take a spill on the ice?" Mickey's explanation about slipping in the shower only brought an uplifted eyebrow. In the back of Bremmer's thoughts was a concern about alcoholism or drugs, or both. He'd withhold any suspicions for the moment. "Having difficulty with balance, Father?" Bremmer frowned, "Have you seen a doctor? Could be otitis or labyrinthitis –I'd suggest you have your ears checked. Will you do that for me?"

"Sure…" Mickey let it drop with a shake of his head. Sitting below the bishop was discomforting; perhaps the bishop's posture of authority was designed to humble him.

"So, how are things at Saint Gerard's, Father?"

The open-ended preliminary was expected and Mickey explained the parish activities in simple detail. Always of concern to His Grace were the weekly receipts and bank account. Of course the bishop already knew that contributions were considerably down from those of Father Dorsher who had preceded him. "Are you stressing yourself over finances, Father? It must concern you– as it does me– that Saint Gerard's requires sizable financial subsidies from the diocese. Is your congregation aware of the assistance our diocese must provide just to keep your doors open?"

Mickey admitted that he had probably been somewhat remiss in pressing his flock for more money. "Benton Park, as you know, is a depressed area. Nobody's got much money."

"I know the demographics quite well, Father. For your benefit I could probably recite the median income of your parishes' families, the percentage of single-parent households, school dropout figures… whatever." Bremmer's scowl matched his sarcasm. "And, Saint Gerard's only managed to contribute a paltry three hundred and forty one dollars, and sixty-four cents to the United Catholic Appeal drive this year. The poorest effort from a single parish since 1984, when Good Shepherd Church in west Duluth gave less." Of course Bremmer didn't need to mention that Good Shepherd had been closed down for years.

Mickey wondered if the purpose of this meeting was to give him a heads-up on eminent closing Saint Gerard's. If so, he would find it difficult to argue against that economy. He was about apologize for the bleak economic picture, when Bremmer continued…

"Perhaps a few more homilies on stewardship and tithing along with a few less sermons on doubt… on your personal doubts about the greatest mysteries of the Christian, not just the Roman Catholic faith." Bremmer actually leaned forward and rose slightly in his chair as he spoke. His voice elevated an octave.

Mickey felt a throb in the back of his neck, the first symptom of a headache, he swallowed hard, would he be able to bite his tongue and avoid disrespecting his superior? He would try to avoid any unnecessary confrontation. "I don't think you quite understand my… "

Bremmer would not allow him to finish an explanation. "Just a moment, Father Moran. Just a moment, please." He smiled, rose from his chair, stepped down from the platform and slid his sizable frame into a matching leather chair next to Mickey's. Placing his small hand on Mickey's forearm, he patted as one might do in order to comfort a reprimanded child. "But, I do understand, Father. I understand very well, from personal experience–I have a brother who had great difficulty overcoming his stress. Fortunately we recognized the symptoms in time, got him some help, and saved him from any further incapacity. Without our intervention…?"

How could the bishop know about his stress, Mickey wondered? It was personal and private and certainly not something that required any medical attention. "Incapacity? Intervention? I'm confused… what makes you think that my stress is a problem, Your Grace? How does stress relate to my homily on doubt?" Before Mickey could explain either his health or his theology, the bishop shushed him like a first grade teacher would do to a little misbehaving Johnny.

Bremmer removed his hand from Mickey's arm, retrieved his wire-rimmed reading glasses from his coat pocket along with a folded page of his personal stationery. "I've had several conversations over this past weekend, Father. You have many dear friends who are quite concerned about you–what a blessing that is. Vickie, that lovely little waitress at the Pickwick restaurant, is a member of our Holy Rosary parish. The episode with that attractive young woman the other night–I believe it was Saturday–anyhow, that scene was quite disturbing to her. She was the first to bring that matter to my attention; some other patrons witnessed the disagreeable scene as well.

Fortunately, you were not wearing your collar–that would have been scandalous. Anyhow…"

The bishop had a list of Mickey's 'unusual behaviors'–"Let me share some other recent matters that have been brought to my attention, Father:"

-Skipping out of a commitment–actually a promise I'm told– to the parish ladies for their Christmas bake sale;

-Reading the wrong gospel at Mass;

-Forcing a man off the road, on Grand Avenue, I believe it was;

-Running in the streets late at night in subzero weather and shouting profanities;

-Something about a fight you had and beating up another man– that admission, I'm told, occurred this very morning;

The bishop considered mentioning the marijuana suspicion of earlier this morning but withheld any comment for the moment. He knew that if he did, Father Moran would easily discern the source of his list of misbehaviors. He would pass that information along to the rehab people. He would also refrain from rehashing the previous 'issues' between them.

"I don't believe anything is gained by going into these matters in any more detail, Father. Suffice it to say that I am concerned for your physical and emotional health." He paused, stood from is chair, and walked to the far wall of the large room, he straightened a picture frame, stared out a window for a minute or two, hands folded behind his back, then turned back to Mickey. "I understand that your parents have a place in Florida for the winter months... in Naples, is that correct, Father?"

Mickey nodded, "I remember them–Amos and Sadie, if I'm not mistaken–met them both at your ordination here... what has it been, seven years already?" He smiled, "Yes Amos and Sadie Moran, fine people."

Mickey nodded, a defeated smile crossing his face. How terribly misconstrued the bishop's information was–worse, how incredible his surveillance! He wouldn't get into his sister's issues, couldn't explain kicking a snow chunk in the street to a man who probably didn't know a football from a hockey puck, nor would he explain the humor of his 'other guy' remark this morning to a man who had little or no sense of humor. He had no doubt about where the leak in his sinking ship had come from, all for the love of a brownie! He suppressed a smirk over the misinformation surrounding his 'stress problem', wanted to use a favorite line from an old movie–*"what we have here is a failure to communicate"* said the warden to 'Cool Hand Luke', played so well by Paul Newman.

"Uh, yes, sir... Naples," he answered weakly, straightening himself in the uncomfortable chair. "Wonderful people, mom and dad."

The bishop's decree was not open for discussion. Mickey would begin a temporary leave of absence sometime around the first of the year. Father Graham, long retired priest living at the seminary in Onamia would replace him at Saint Gerard's for the time being. Mickey would 'rehabilitate' while assisting the priests at Saint Leo Church in Bonita Springs, Florida–a short distance from Mickey's parents in Naples. While on leave of absence, he would undergo a structured counseling regimen. The Diocese of Duluth would absorb the expenses and oversee his recovery. "Your specific program and routines will be determined, and supervised, by Bishop Cordoba in the Venice Diocese."

Bishop Bremmer had met Cordoba at a liturgical conference years before. Both men loved chess and Medieval history and spent hours playing and conversing. Cordoba had written numerous papers published in various Catholic journals on the stress problems of clergymen. His diocese happened to include Naples where Father Moran's parents resided in the winter. The coincidence of friendship, expertise, and geography was striking.

Bishop Bremmer gave Father Mickey his blessing as he showed him to the door. "I would prefer that you keep this matter completely confidential, except for your immediate family, of course. I will explain things to your friend, Father Mario at the Newman Center; so you needn't burden him with this issue. Is that understood, Father?"

Defeated and confused, Mickey was speechless. All he could do is shrug his shoulders in resignation.

22/ PLAYING HOOKY

When Mickey left the mansion it was shortly after two in the afternoon. Frustrated as much with himself as he was with Bremmer, he felt as if he'd allowed the bishop to run roughshod over him. The headache had traveled down into his lower back. He had been blindsided, betrayed, and browbeaten with lies and innuendos without putting up a word in his own defense. Why? Was it obedience, reverence, apathy? Maybe, his silence was rooted in all three in one manner or another. The apathy part of the equation was most troubling. Had he allowed himself to be dressed down because he didn't really care? If so, he did have a problem and might need some counseling. Until this very moment Mickey had never questioned his vocation or his vows–not even when being disciplined by Bishop Bremmer in the past. No, Mickey loved being a priest. He couldn't imagine himself being more fulfilled doing anything else. There had to be a reason for what was happening. He tried to pray for insight but found all his networks clogged.

Rather than head west, back toward Benton Park, Mickey turned north toward Highway 53. "What the hell!" he said to himself, "If my bishop thinks I'm a wacko, I might as well walk the walk."

He called Mary Alice, Saint Gerard's parish receptionist, office manager, housekeeper, and occasional cook to report his whereabouts. Mary Alice Murray answered the second ring. Mickey explained: "I'd like to visit my grandfather in Hibbing, it's kinda like a family emergency but not quite, and I wanted to check with you and make certain that nothing pressing has come up since I left two hours ago. And, would you please check my calendar, too?"

"If you wanna play hooky, Father, it's fine with me." The little woman had a big heart and an Irish humor. "Nothing here that you really need to take care of. Mrs. Blazina called about her asking you to visit her husband. Well, wouldn't you know it, he's not at Saint Mary's no more–between you and me, Father, I think he's a hypochondriac."

Mickey grinned; Mary Alice was a keenly perceptive woman. "So you think I'm playing hooky? Shirking my responsibilities? Shame on you, Mary Alice," he chided.

"Just calling a spade a spade, Father."

Mickey couldn't contain his laughter, "Okay, I'll admit it's not really an emergency. Don't tell anybody, especially the bishop. I think I'm already on his black list."

"Not a word, Father. If Sarah Donovan comes snooping again, I'll cover for you."

"You do that."

"Ya know something, Father... there are people who bring happiness wherever they go… others whenever they go. What do you think about that?"

Mary Alice's wisdom was great tonic for the moment; she had pegged the culprit without saying so. "I think it a jewel. I'll use it in my next homily. Thanks for the uplift–I needed it."

Mickey put away his cell phone, smiled to himself. It was not at all surprising to him– it had to have been the busybody, do-gooder, Sarah Donovan, he mused to himself. Every parish has it's Judas, or Judasina. "Your condemnation is much too harsh, Father," he reprimanded himself.

Mickey's trip to Hibbing didn't turn out as he imagined it would. Famished, he stopped first at the MacDonald's on Highway 37 and had a quarter-pounder with cheese, fries, and a strawberry malted milk: A calorie blitz that he hadn't indulged in quite some time. From his booth he scanned the restaurant for familiar faces. Some of his father's friends, Whalen, Perfetti, Lolich, and Bolf were clustered at a corner table; probably talking golf, politics, or Twins baseball. Mickey had attended high school with some of their kids. Finished with his food, he smiled and waved to the men as he left.

He took the ramp off of Highway 169 and onto First Avenue, then drove northward toward Howard Street, the downtown commercial artery. Returning to his hometown was always a nostalgia trip. A myriad of bittersweet memories rushed into his thoughts, sending him back in time. He had stocked shelves at Cobb Cook Grocery to his left. Maureen Regan's family lived in Greenhaven off to his right. The old 'haunted church' on the corner of Twenty-eighth had finally been razed, leaving an empty corner patch of snow. The former church reminded him of his own Saint Girard's; only a tad more deteriorated. He wondered if anything would ever be built on the lot–on any of the empty lots around town.

Taking a right, past an abandoned gas station and another empty lot on Twenty Fifth Street, he headed east toward Seventh Avenue, then north again. He pulled to the curb and turned off the ignition in front of the Blessed Sacrament Church. Gazing at the impressive edifice, a surge of memories inspired prayers of gratitude. It was here where he was baptized and confirmed, trained as an altar boy, and here where he discovered his vocation. Adjacent, and attached to the church, was the remodeled and expanded Assumption School where he attended years before. Inside, at some desk this afternoon, his niece and nephew were current students. He considered visiting Father Rosati, the well-liked pastor, then decided against it–he didn't want to explain anything to anybody today, including his family.

On the next block was the massive Hibbing High School campus. The sprawling complex was unparalleled in its architecture and amenities and legendary in the education it had provided over the decades. Growing up, Mickey had thrived in the companion environs of church and school. He was bombarded with images of classmates and teachers, lockers and hallways, Bluejacket ball games, trophy cases on the corridor leading to the ornate auditorium. It was here, in his beloved HHS, where he had been an honor student, Key Club president, thespian, and the knowledge bowl team captain leading his teammates to the state tournament in his junior and senior years. It was here in the old gym where he went to Friday night dances, and attending the junior prom…what wonderful times they were. Why did everything seem so deeply buried in the past? Had it really been that long ago?

Choked up from thoughts of times lost and gone forever, Mickey continued north to Howard Street, then turned left past Shubats garage, then passed Zimmys and the Sportsmans on the right, the Androy opposite and assorted shops to his left and right. The Androy had once been a major enterprise of his Great Grandfather, Kevin Moran, and the anchor of downtown Hibbing. A few years back there had been several empty storefronts evidencing a seriously depressed economic climate. Conditions seemed improved on this December, 2011, afternoon. When the huge taconite operations were pushing out iron content pellets at full capacity, times were great on the Mesaba Range. If the economy was solid this year–and it was–just wait… unfortunately, the industry was terribly cyclic, boom times were often short-lived, and bad times led to massive out-migrations. Over the years, the plants had retooled, costing thousands of jobs. Sadly, the Iron Range had lost several generations of their best and brightest youth as men and women alike moved from college to jobs in distant cities.

Taking a right on Third, passing the post office, he noticed that the Sunrise Bakery had moved to a new location across the street, over the railroad tracks were Checcos and Palmers, popular watering holes in Park Addition. Looping back around Bennett Park, then the Muni golf course east of the road leading north to the Massive Hull-Rust Mine, he drove past his grandparents' house near the Frank Hibbing statue. He didn't stop. Nor did he stop at his parents' house in Home Acres. Making amends with Meghan, giving Grampa Pack some encouragement, and saying hello to his parents– all of these intentions were abandoned. Mickey would wait until the family Christmas, one week away, to reconnect with everybody.

Before returning to the beltline, Mickey pulled off to the side of the road in the tourism building's parking lot across from the police headquarters and county offices. He had the phone number from the other night on his phone. He cleared his throat: "Is Maureen home, please, Mrs. Regan?"

A long pause, a quizzical voice: "No, she's at work this afternoon…" Then, "Who's calling, please?"

Mickey felt his tongue twist into knots, why in the world had he made this call? It was so stupid of him. "Just and old friend… I'll try again later."

"Is this that Roger, again? I have a mind to…"

Mickey was no longer on the phone.

He ended his afternoon journey with a heavy heart and a lump in his throat. The thought of being estranged from his priesthood was beginning to weigh more heavily on his thoughts. Again he chastised himself for not having protested the allegations the bishop threw in his face. Every absurd charge could have been logically explained. Why had he just called his old prom date? Why the complete neglect of his family members when he was only blocks away? Maybe all that was happening now was part of some diving scheme? He realized that his cheeks were warm with tears, he prayed for greater faith, greater understanding, a greater commitment to his Lord. He remembered a poster from Brother Andrew's classroom at the seminary: 'If God brings you to it; he will bring you through it'. For the first time, and for nearly an hour, Mickey prayed himself through the network of questions. By the time he was back in west Duluth, he was finally at peace with himself.

28/ *'JOY TO THE WORLD'*

Christmas morning arrived in a classic arctic-style blizzard.

Brian Slade shoveled the sidewalk from the side door to the garage and then the driveway out to East Toledo Street. The driveway was lined with snow-laden Norway pines, he breathed in their sharp pleasant scent. The hilltop air was so clear and fresh that he couldn't help a comparison with the toxic-smelling air where he might have been this morning. Payne Street and the neighborhood around it were choked with smells of gasoline exhaust, alley garbage, and sewer stench. He paused, leaned on his shovel; these past days had been his best in years. Sticking out his tongue to catch a dancing snowflake, he looked up into the white freefall–maybe there was a God up there, and maybe that God had a better life in store for him. This Christmas morning was the most beautiful he'd ever seen. Brian felt the warmth of tears on his cheeks, "Merry Christmas, Brian Slade..." he said to himself.

His back ached and his uncovered ears tingled when as stepped out of his boots and shook the snow off his parka in the small foyer off of the kitchen. His sister had fried some bacon and eggs and brewed a second pot of coffee. "Thanks for shoveling, Bry. Have some breakfast and change clothes before Mass."

"I'm really not up to it, Beth," he said to his sister who was putting plates on the kitchen table next to the Sunday paper. Beth had been nagging him to go with her to Christmas Mass before he went outside to clear the snow. "Besides, nobody should be driving in this storm."

Beth Slade had Googled the Diocese of Duluth homepage after returning from the Goodwill store days before. She had located a roster of parish priests and their current assignments. Father Michael Moran was listed as the pastor of Saint Gerard's; the address was in Benton Park. No photograph accompanied the brief listing. "Oh, Brian, it's Christmas! What's more, wouldn't it be something to check out this priest in Benton Park."

If what Beth told him, and his recent bizarre experiences, were actually true, his presence at the church would be a distraction, and maybe an embarrassment to all. He didn't want that... nor did he want to disappoint his sister. A quandary. They had talked about it the night before and left the matter unresolved. "Beth... I just want to take a shower and kick back today. I might even shave." Brian rubbed his hand across the side of his face; he wore a week's growth. "You okay with that? I mean I'll go if it's that important to you–even though I'd rather not."

Beth didn't want to spoil the day by insisting that her brother go with her–but, she did want to see this priest for herself. "Will you shovel the front sidewalk while I'm gone?"

"That's a deal," he leaned over and gave his sister a peck on the cheek. "Maybe we can go another time. By the way, I like your dress–green is a great color for you."

Flattered, Beth said, "Maybe... but I'm going to drive out to Benton Park for Mass this morning."

Although he and Beth had agreed to skip gift-giving this year, they had trimmed her artificial spruce tree and listened to Christmas music the night before. Beth had made a huge bowl of popcorn, drenched it in butter, and opened a bottle of inexpensive champagne. Brian hadn't had a more pleasant Christmas Eve in recent years. He was going to keep a good thing going. "I'll get to the last of the shoveling before I shower."

"Don't overdo it, Bry. Take a break, have some coffee before going out again." She regarded the wall clock, "Oh my, I'd better be getting along myself. It will take a few extra minutes with this storm."

Brian reached into the hall closed and handed his sister her Ugg boots. "Sis, if I haven't said so yet... thanks for everything. Merry Christmas." On the tip of his tongue but left unsaid was an 'I love you' that would have made Beth's day even brighter. But Brian couldn't quite get the words from his heart to his tongue.

"You too," she blushed. Guess I'll be off now. Thanks again for the shoveling." She might have added an 'I love you' before leaving, but didn't know if Brian truly shared the sentiment. Regardless, having Brian around was becoming more pleasant with every passing day.

"Pray for your bro," Brian said, as he gave his sister a hug at the door. "I'll say one for you while I'm shoveling."

"Thanks. I'll pray for both of my brothers," she corrected, "let's not forget to give Duane a call later today. If I remember right, he likes to sleep in and doesn't appreciate being wakened before noon."

"Especially when he sleeping with some bimbo," Brian mumbled under his breath. His revulsion toward Duane left a bad taste in his mouth, but along with it was the germ of resolve to try and make things right between them. The spirit of Christmas did wonders for his disposition.

"I'll get back before noon, Bry. Need to find someplace that's open so I can pick up some groceries. You're eating me out of house and home." Beth gave him a kiss on the cheek, "Don't take that wrong, it's been nice having you here," she said. For the second time in minutes, Beth realized how much a simple 'I love you' would have meant to both of them.

~

Father Mickey was truly in the Christmas spirit this bright, crisp, and white December morning. He and Mort Shea, the less-than-part-time custodian, who lived just down the block, had been up early to clear the walkways, Mort with his 8-horse Toro snow blower and he with an old aluminum shovel.

The storm had kept many at home so the Vigil Mass the night before was sparsely attended. In that many Catholics went to Mass only twice a year (Christmas and Easter), he was certain that the two Masses this morning would be crowded. Perhaps the collection baskets would be full, to the delight of his parish council, and to 'Big Brother', his new reference to the ever-observant Bishop Bremmer. Mickey often believed that the revenue aspects of his church and his ministry were the primary measures of his competency. A good priest, to many in the hierarchy of his church, was a priest whose receipts were greater than his expenditures. A great priest was one who had built a substantial nest egg for the diocesan coffers and for future pet project of the bishop. By the revenue yardstick, Mickey had had only one successful year of service, out of his six since his ordination: His first year at Saint Francis in Brainerd showed a four percent increase in revenues. "Quit being such a cynic," Mickey chided himself. "It's Christmas! Christ's birthday! Rejoice!" Checking himself in the sacristy mirror, he smiled: "Merry Christmas, Father Michael Moran."

Mickey followed the four altar servers up the wet, creaky aisle toward the altar, singing 'Joy to the World', smiling widely, and greeting parishioners along the way. As expected, quite a few faces were unfamiliar to him. He was aware that some of his congregation seemed surprised at his appearance. For the past few days, Father Moran hadn't shaved. And, he was a few weeks overdue on getting a haircut. Add to that, his right eye had a purple and yellow ring around it. Mickey was feeling a sense of freedom. He had come to regard his impending leave of absence as an opportunity for spiritual growth. Time away from the problems of other people so that he could focus on his own relationship with Jesus.

He stopped to shake hands with Mike Rolle, "Merry Christmas, Mike," he said to the concrete worker. Near Mike were Blanche Moyer and her daughter Melissa, he greeted them warmly as well. In the pew ahead, a woman he'd not seen before, was staring at him with an intensity that almost made him feel uncomfortable. "God bless," he said in passing.

The snowplows had been clearing since three in the morning and the major streets were passable. Beth hadn't been this far west in the long, narrow city for years. Benton Park was a neighborhood with an interesting past, blighted present, and bleak future. In bygone years the steel plant here employed more than a thousand men. Nearby Riverside was like Benton Park, it's blue-collar twin, where during the WWII years it had been a prominent shipbuilding facility manufacturing cargo ships and tankers for the war effort. The pair of once prosperous sites, nearly two generations ago, was evidenced today as huge, empty, and overgrown eyesores.

Following the *MapQuest* printout taped to her dashboard, Beth found the old wood-framed and white-steepled Saint Gerard's church with little difficulty. She parked nearly a block away and rushed, head down into the west wind, hoping not to be late for the ten o'clock start of Mass. Inside the crowded sanctuary, she found a space on the aisle, blessed herself, knelt down for a quick prayer. Inside as well as out, Saint Gerard's was well past its prime. In former years it had prospered and vestiges of a former life were still in evidence. The altar was ornately carved oak with gold leaf, the colorful stain-glass windows depicted Biblical scenes, the statuary at the side altars were of quality marble. The age and wear were most evident in the sagging wooden floors, scarred wooden pews, worn leather kneelers. The organ music concluded, the murmur of conversation ceased, the congregation stood, and the choir began singing its opening hymn.

Beth followed the 'Joy to the World' lyrics in her songbook, noticed the alter servers passing to her left, heard a 'Merry Christmas' greeting just behind her, then turned...

For just a fraction of a moment, their eyes met. Beth gawked, felt her throat constrict, her knees weaken. Oh my God! she said under her breath, I can't believe what I'm seeing. This priest, this Father Moran, was her brother's duplicate! Not only in his features, but–as she watched him walk up the aisle–in his casual stride as well. The next several minutes were a blur as a dumbfounded Beth Slade tried to comprehend what she was witnessing. When he stood at the lectern to read the gospel, she studied every feature: Father Moran had the same longish sandy brown hair, squarely defined jaw line, full mouth... his deep-set eyes– she couldn't tell if they were blue as Brian's were. His frame was similar, perhaps the priest was a bit thinner, and his voice a bit deeper. If she didn't know better, she would swear that this priest was her brother.

Father Mickey was animated this Christmas morning. This homily would be his last at Saint Gerard's for how long... he had no way of knowing. He wanted to explain his circumstance, defend his misconstrued behavior, but more than either, he wanted to say 'good-bye' to his flock. He could not. Instead, he spoke with eloquence about God's gift to mankind with his beloved Son. "Celebrate our wonderful Gift–give your love to another who needs it. Today is a day of great love." Then about human imperfections, the call for repentance, and the opportunity afforded by this holy season to renew our commitments to our Lord and to our faith. Borrowing from the controversial Irish playwright, Oscar Wilde, he reminded: "Every sinner has a future and every saint has a past"

29/ A MORAN FAMILY CHRISTMAS

Duane Slade and his current squeeze slept late on Christmas morning. The two had celebrated their Christmas Day earlier than most– from midnight until three in the morning– with three bottles of an inexpensive pinot noir. Duane would have nodded in agreement to the New York billboard near the Holland Tunnel suggesting that the Bethlehem story was a myth. His Christianity began and ended with his Baptism–which he gave no consent for– at seven months of age. He viewed all religions as clever business ventures and was often tempted to organize one of his own. His Roseville condo exhibited no hint of the season. He had read somewhere that the average American family spent $800.00 on gifts and decorations and all the trappings of Christmas. He had spent $25.00 on the wine and cheese– so he was a solid $775.00 to the good.

The ringing phone woke Duane at 11:45 in the morning. Without waking Dianne, he wandered sans pajamas to the kitchen where a plate of dry cheddar slices, cracker crumbs, and empty wine bottles littered the counter top. He located his cell under a paper plate. "Merry Christmas to you, too, Beth." He put a cup of day-old coffee into the microwave, pushed the one-minute button, sat his warm bottom on a cold vinyl kitchen chair. "What wouldn't I believe, Sis?" Still only half awake, Duane tried to process what his sister had just told him. ""Like our Brian? That's crazy... a priest you say?" He laughed at the notion. "Did he look like a deadbeat?"

Duane apologized for the slam, "Since when have the two of you become so tight? I've found that our dear brother has become a very lousy investment. I've quit counting all the red ink from my redistribution of wealth program."

Dianne, wearing nothing more than sheer bikini panties, came into the kitchen, sat on Duane's knee, and nestled her head of snarly brunette hair on his shoulder. "No one you'd know, love," he said to Dianne as he pushed her off his knee, stood and retrieved his steaming cup of coffee.

"What's that you said? A perfect double...? So, what does Brian think? Maybe he missed his calling, there's probably good money in being a priest these days. Other people pay for your housing, food, and pay all your bills. Just like the taxpayers of Ramsey County do when you're in the slammer." He laughed at his clever metaphor, then apologized again. "Don't mean to be so hard on bro, he's had some bad luck along the way." Rather than go on for an hour about all the bad decisions Brian had made, Duane let his sister believe that Brian's poverty was more 'bad luck' than 'bad behavior'. "Okay, sis, let me talk to him."

"Not a big thing," Brian said, "Beth gets hyper over things like that. Maybe I'll get out to Benton Park one of these days and see this priest for myself. See how much she's exaggerating."

The brothers talked for a few minutes. "No, Bry... I didn't mean it that way–Jeeze, I call myself a loser all the time." Duane wasn't artful at making amends. "Any time ... you're my brother for God's sake, you're always welcome here." He bit his tongue, "In fact, I've got a little holiday gift for you when you get back in town," he lied. Already the devious mind of Duane Slade was contriving.

~

After the ten o'clock Mass, Mickey was free for the day. Highway 53 going north to the Iron Range was slippery and traffic moved cautiously. Mickey counted four cars in the ditch by the time he reached the Hibbing cut-off at the Highway 37 off-ramp, a two-lane skating rink heading west for the final twenty miles of his trip.

He had mixed feelings about the family celebration and wondered if anyone had heard of his being in Hibbing earlier in the week and not connecting with any of them. To admit that he wasn't 'in the mood' would float like a lead balloon. He had finally gotten a hold of Meg on Wednesday night and somewhat defused the stressed situation between them, but still had the feeling that the truce was a shaky one at best. His Christmas gifts for every member of his family were tucked neatly in his jacket pocket. Gift cards were the godsend of apathetic shoppers.

Mickey couldn't decide on which parent to confide his banishment from Saint Gerard's and his upcoming residency in their Gulf Coast paradise. Probably dad. Amos had thicker skin than Sadie, but, on the other hand, his mom had a greater sense of empathy. She would cry and console, dad would rationalize and reason. In the past, his best advice came from mom, so did the best chewing out. On closer scrutiny, however, it seemed to him that the best option would be to keep the rehab business to himself for now. Why put a damper on the Moran family's Christmas celebration. His parents would probably be around until after the first week of January so he'd have ample opportunity to explain before they returned to Florida. Procrastination was always the best friend of those with doubts. Doubt–Mickey's nemesis!

The day could not have been more delightful. Meghan and Kenny outdid themselves as hosts to the three Moran generations assembled in their comfortably spacious home. Pack was clean-shaven, and wore the pine-green cardigan sweater he had always worn for Christmas occasions. He seemed like the 'same old Pack' to all, playing Monopoly with Amos and the children. In his typically strong voice, the senior Moran was chiding and cajoling, wheeling and dealing, and losing all of the early money he'd accumulated from rent on Baltic and Mediterranean Streets. When Pack was being himself he could totally capture a room. Maddie spent most of the day nervously watching her husband as if on guard for any sudden changes or relapses into his depression.

A wreath and candle centerpiece adorned the meticulously set table. Centered on the white linen was an enormous turkey surrounded by all the trimmings one could imagine. Meghan and Sadie had worked all morning to make the meal a masterpiece; the men played ping-pong and pool, enjoyed cocktails, and relaxed. Ever vigilant Gramma Maddie flittered between the women in the kitchen and men in the downstairs rec room trying to keep her apprehension in check. After Mickey led the hands-held-together grace and everybody around the table gave the person beside them a kiss on the cheek, the serving trays were passed from Pack, at the head, clockwise toward Mickey at the other end. Anxious to impress, twelve year-old Matthew cleared his throat and turned toward his uncle Mickey, "Do you know why Santa is so jolly?"

Mickey leaned back in his chair, gave his nephew the serious look of deep thought: "Oh... let me see... he likes giving toys to good little boys and girls, that would be my guess." Mickey said.

"No," Matthew had won everybody's curious attention at the table. Amos took a similar guess, then Sadie, "I'd say that Santa loves chocolate chip cookies," Kenny ventured.

Matthew had them all stumped, "I'll tell you why..." He had picked up the joke at hockey practice the day before. "Santa's jolly because he knows where all the bad girls live." His laugh was met with a deafening silence.

The frowns from around the table were enough to make the youngster want to melt away under the table. Not quite knowing what to say he could only shrug his shoulders and offer a defeated half-smile. Maybe they didn't get it–he hadn't, the other boys had.

Mickey saved his nephew from drowning in an ocean of embarrassment. "That's a good one, Matty. Santa's one smart guy–he knows where all the good girls live, too. Doesn't he."

Rescued by his uncle, Matthew smiled, looked toward his frowning mother across the table from him, "Sure... he's gotta know where everybody lives... Right? Mom, would you pass the dressing, please."

After the momentary lull, eight year-old Katie picked up the ball, "He knows where the bad boys live, too. Right Uncle Mickey?"

After overindulging, two servings of turkey and dressing along with a mountain of mashed potatoes, and jellied cranberries, Mickey found an opportunity to visit with his grandfather. Kenny had offered the men some Cuban cigars he'd picked up on a recent trip to Winnipeg. "You'll have to smoke in the garage, but there's a small heater under the workbench," Kenny said. "I'm going to wait until later, maybe have mine with a bit of brandy. Anybody...?"

Amos declined the offer and Pack accepted. "Wanna join me, Mickey? It's not a sin for a priest to smoke an illegally smuggled cigar, is it?" Pack put his heavy hand on Mickey's shoulder.

"I believe I read somewhere that it's only a venial sin, Grampa. I'm allowed three of those a week. Just don't ever tell the bishop I go over my quota quite often." Both men laughed. "Say, Kenny, maybe I'll have that brandy after all. Can't let my Gramps drink by himself."

Mickey hadn't smoked a cigar in years, but the opportunity to spend a few minutes with his grampa was not to be missed. The north wind had picked up in the late afternoon and the walkway to the garage was drifted over with snow. Since his arrival just after one, several inches of powdery snow had fallen. "You planning on driving back to Duluth tonight, Mick? I'd think, maybe you otta spend the night with me and Gramma–we've got lots of room, ya know."

Mickey nodded, "Thanks, Grampa. I'd enjoy that, but I really should get back to Saint Gerard's tonight. I'll probably have to be heading back in an hour or two. We, I mean a group of fellows from the parish and I, have a meeting to do our bookkeeping on Sunday nights. I'm hoping we made a haul today." It would have been nice to tell his grampa that he wanted to go out of Saint Gerard's with a bang.

To Mickey's surprise and delight, Pack opened the door to a meaningful conversation with a choked-up admission. "Getting old is a bummer, Mickey. Downright cruel! I find myself trying to relive the past, you know–the good times, I had lots of 'em. But ya jus can't do that." Pack's voice was subdued, his words well thought out. "What's almost worse is that you find yourself thinking about what your obituary ought to say about the life you've had." Pack sniffled, looked away, took a long pull on his cigar, sipped at his brandy. "Suppose you heard that Chub Maki passed away a few months back."

Mickey had sent his grampa a sympathy card when he learned about the death of his grampa's closest friend. He'd probably forgotten. "Hadn't he been pretty sick for quite a while, Grampa?"

Pack nodded. "Yep. Cancer. Maybe it was a blessing... but God knows how I miss the guy." The emotion of the memory was more than Pack wanted to talk about. He continued: "Getting' old's a bummer all right," he repeated. "It's not so much all the aches and pains–and there's plenty of those– as it is the feeling... the feeling that you've become worthless. Worthless as an old worn out shoe. You can't imagine... "

Pack would not allow himself to cry–too much out of character for him. But, Mickey could tell that his Grampa was close to tears. Knowing that his grampa was trying to swallow a thick emotion choked him up as well.

If Mickey were to break down under the weight of the moment, Grampa would surely lose it himself.

"I know it's tough." Mickey would try to keep their conversation as non-threatening as possible under the circumstances. If he could do that, Pack could maintain his dignity. Yet, emotions ran deep between the two of them. Years before, this once fearless man had saved Mickey's life by plunging himself into a hole in the ice of Sturgeon Lake where Mickey's snowmobile had sunk. Years before that, this once feared cop was the Chief of one of Minnesota's finest police departments. Mickey's heart ached in seeing his balding grampa in such emotional pain. What could he possibly say? To suggest that they pray together would be the ultimate turnoff. "Come Lord Jesus," he thought to himself.

Mickey swallowed hard, he had a good idea of what Maddie had tried to do with her despondent husband–she cajoled, suggested help, scolded, and probably, without intending to, enabled as well. None of those ploys would float a boat. He would have to take a different tack if this opportunity was going to be taken advantage of– he would take a risk!

"What do you want from me, Grampa? God has blessed you with reasonably good health… you're seventy-four and could probably still skate circles around Matthew who's only twelve. You could probably still kick my dad's butt on a golf course if you took your clubs down from the attic. I still couldn't beat you at arm-wrestling– not even if my life depended on it. You've still got a ton of tenacity and grit and guts–I could see that all afternoon. And, you've got that sense of humor I remember from growing up." Mickey tried to smile, Pack only stared.

"You lost all of your Monopoly money like you always do, and you returned every slam that my dad hit on the ping-pong table. There's nothing wrong with you–okay! Get that in you head, please. Don't quit on living your life, Grampa. That's the worst possible thing you could do. Let me worry about writing an obituary for you, you get your butt out of the house. Get up in the morning and get at it–whatever 'it' happens to be. Shower, shave, splash on that Aqua Velva you've always used and hit the new day like a punching bag."

Pack nodded without speaking. Tossed down the last of his brandy.

"I'm told that you shut yourself in your office for hours feeling sorry for yourself. That's bullshit! If you're ready to throw in the towel, have Gramma check you into the old folks home up by Bennett Park. They play a mean game of checkers up there." Mickey had his grandfather's heart and spirit in his hands. "I don't think you wanna call it quits yet. I think there's too much piss and vinegar left in Pack Moran."

Pack flinched at the bold language, frowned at the mention of playing checkers in an old folks home, then smiled at his grandson, the priest. Maybe he had misjudged Mickey… maybe the young man dressing him down wasn't a wimp after all.

Mickey felt his edge: "Take out those Bauer skates you have hanging in the basement, have them sharpened, and bring young Matthew over to the Greenhaven rink next week. Show him that slapshot of yours–he'll light up just like I used to. Better yet, volunteer to help his Peewee coach with some practices. Join the old-timers and their card games at the Memorial Building on weekday mornings. If nothing else they will confirm what a bummer it is to be getting old. The difference between them and you is they can kick-ass laugh about it." Mickey surprised himself with the passion behind his words.

Mickey put down his cigar, lifted his brandy glass in the gesture of a toast: "To the Pack Moran we dearly miss." He swallowed the last of his liquor and stepped closer to his Grampa.

Pack, met his eyes with a riveting stare. Mickey didn't know how to react. Had he really screwed up again? Almost ready to apologize for hurting his Grampa's feelings, Mickey found himself smiling with a confident satisfaction. He had put it all on the table, there was no possibility backing off now.

Pack stepped closer and gave Mickey a bear hug. "Who told you about shutting myself in the office? Maddie? Bless her heart. You know, she's the very best thing that's ever happened in my life. I'm so lucky to have her, Mick." He began to tear for the first time and turned away to compose himself. "Doesn't she look beautiful today?"

"She always looks beautiful. Have you told her that, Grampa?" After twenty additional minutes in the garage, talking about sports and politics, and composing themselves, the two shivering men were ready to return to the warmth of Meghan's kitchen for a cup of hot chocolate. "Ya know, Mick, I think I can still skate–it's been quite a while–but? Maybe I should go down to the Memorial Building and practice a bit before joining Matt's Peewee friends. Think that's a good idea?"

"Great idea, Grampa. You might even consider that seniors bowling league you belonged to a few years ago, there's gotta be a team that needs a former 170 average bowler."

"Just a minute, make that a 172 average, thank you very much!" Both men laughed until their stomachs ached.

Maddie was passing plates with servings of warm cherry pie to Sadie who scooped a dollop of Cool Whip and set them on the countertop. Pack stepped behind his wife and gave her a pat on the bottom, then gave her a peck on the cheek, "I love you," was all that he could get out of his tight throat.

Later that day, Pack would tell Maddie that he was happy that the Moran's had a priest in the family. Later that evening, Pack would tell his wife that he wasn't going to sleep on the couch in the den any more.

As the afternoon wore on, Mickey found time to talk with his brother-in-law. He suggested that Kenny give their mutual friend, Larry Huber a call. Larry was a marriage counselor–and a good one. Kenny seemed surprised at first, then nodded: "You've talked with Meg about our marriage, haven't you? That's what's been eating at her for the past two weeks?"

Mickey had promised his sister that he would not interfere in their relationship. He had a feeling that breaking that promise was simply one of his three allowable venial sins for the week. "She's in love with you, Kenny. But, you've become like a ship passing in the night of her life. I'll risk being out of line in saying that your priorities are seriously out of whack."

Later that night, Kenny told his wife that he was going to take a few days off from work. They hadn't been to the Twin Cities together in months so he'd book a room at the downtown Marriott

City Center Hotel and take her to the Guthrie to see the acclaimed Dickens classic, *A Christmas Carol*, which was ending the next week. Meghan loved theater. "Mom and Dad would like to have some time alone with the kids…" he said, his voice betraying his emotions, " More than that… I'd like some quality time alone with you, just the two of us."

It was nearly four in the afternoon when Mickey began making the rounds and saying his goodbyes. He promised his parents that he would see them before they went back to Naples. Meghan caught him at the door as he was leaving with a package of leftovers, "I know how much you love cold turkey sandwiches, and I've included dressing and pumpkin pie to go with it."

"Love ya, Sis. Once again, I'm sorry… you know… I'll keep you in my prayers."

"I know, Mick. And I'll keep you in mine. Merry Christmas." She gave him a hug and teared up as she did so, "Thank's for breaking that promise you gave me. Kenny's been his old self this afternoon. I think that maybe, just maybe, he loves me again."

The snowfall had diminished to a random swirl of flakes and the wind had subsided. The return trip to Duluth was not nearly as treacherous as driving to Hibbing had been earlier. Mickey listened to an old Elvis CD he had borrowed from his mother long before. No one, Mickey was certain, had ever sung the traditional Christmas carols like Elvis Presley had. As he sang along with Silent Night, his eyes became moist. After years of being an emotional stoic, Father Mickey Moran was becoming an emotional wuss, he laughed at himself: "If my Grampa Pack can cry, anybody on earth can cry!" He reminisced about each of his family members and thanked God for blessing his life with them.

30/ MARIO'S INSIGHTS

Duane Slade was beside himself with curiosity. "What if everything his sister had told him was true? What if Brian did have a double? A priest for a double? What were the possibilities of taking advantage of that situation?

Opportunities must never be taken for granted, they must be greeted with an anticipation of potential friendship. He sent Dianne home so he could concentrate and contemplate. Her constant parading around half-naked was a walking distraction. When Duane sniffed any opportunity to make a quick buck, regardless of how remote or absurd, his mind automatically went into overdrive. It was like the smell of blood to a hungry shark. The simile struck Duane as profound, more than anything, he considered himself to be a shark.

After an hour on his computer, Duane was unsatisfied with what he had learned about this Father Michael Moran of Duluth. The diocese website was no help. The photos he managed to glean from a seminary yearbook, an ordination news clipping, and various parish bulletins did not meet the exactness that his sister had claimed. A fair resemblance, yes... but, Duane would probably have to see the priest for himself in order to be convinced. What excited him more than anything was the biographical information on the Moran family of Hibbing. Clearly there was significant wealth in the estate and various trusts and foundations they controlled. How was he going to go about getting some of their money–not all of it; only a million dollars would do just fine. He laughed to himself, maybe he was becoming a tad conservative with age. Not long ago he would have wanted it all.

Duane Slade liked nothing better than a challenge, especially if the rewards were worth the risks. He reviewed the notes he had outlined on the yellow legal pad beside his computer. Benton Park and Saint Gerard's parish, where the priest lived and worked, evidenced a destitution that offered little incentive. Economically and demographically, Moran's former parish of Saint James wasn't too much better. Brainerd, however, was intriguing. Mega-resorts lined pristine lakes that attracted wealth from throughout the Midwest. Duane had spent golf weekends at both Craggans and Maddens resorts on Gull Lake in the past.

Sundays always depressed Duane, holidays even more so. He envied people who had families, friends, neighborhoods where people cared about each other. Standing at his living room window he peered into an enveloping gray where shadowed oak trees lined a ridge above the slowly crawling traffic along the Highway 36 corridor. Only a few inches of slushy snow had fallen, not nearly as much as further north. It struck him as odd that Beth and Brian seemed to be having a pleasant time together. Why hadn't he been invited to join them? In a moment of remorse, Duane felt alone and unloved. Although he had he never felt any honest affection toward either of his siblings he somehow expected them to like him. He recognized the strange contradiction and smiled inwardly. "Ya get what ya give," he reminded himself. Checking his Rolex clone, a thought crossed his mind. It was just after two; if the highways were clear enough he might be able to drive up to Duluth and be at his sister's place before dark. What a surprise that would be–Beth would go bonkers to have the 'family' together on Christmas.

Without giving the matter any more thought, Duane became a part of the Highway 36 flow, exiting 36 at 35-E and turning north toward Duluth. He had packed in a hurry knowing that if he decided to stay more than a day or two he could buy additional clothing at the mall near where Beth lived. How long he might visit depended on a scenario he hadn't quite figured out yet. The Moran money was enticing; his mouth watered as his imagination played devious games in the back of his mind. He found himself thinking outside the proverbial box: Abduction, extortion, fraud... a foolproof scheme of some kind would come to mind if he didn't force it. Relax, he reminded himself as he loosened his grip on the steering wheel. Just let things come to you–don't chase after them. How might he exploit the sexual vulnerability of a priest?–that seemed to be the favored scheme in the cesspool of his thinking. Any plausible strategy was fine, but something sexual had an irresistible flavor.

An attractive young woman in a red Lexus coupe glanced Duane's way as she sped past him on the left, splashing salty slush onto his windshield. By now the road crews had salted and sanded the highway and he was making better than expected time. As the Lexus turned up the Hinckley ramp, Duane felt a pang of hunger, fueled in part by a pang of curiosity. Sure enough, the woman was pulling into the parking lot at Tobies restaurant.

Inside, as he watched her eat, the idea he'd been mulling over returned to him. Celibate priest meets beautiful girl, beautiful girl hits on celibate priest, celibate priest's repressed hormones rage, priest's celibacy compromised. What if the entire episode were carefully staged, then caught on tape...? A bar scene... a hooker... a motel–how to put them all together? Who did he know that could help him stage everything? This scenario might well be something to think more seriously about. His thinking, however, was suddenly interrupted: "You stare too much, mister. Get a life!" The Lexus lady brushed by him on her way to the register. Before Duane could react, she was pushing open the glass exit door.

～

Mickey was passing the empty parking lot of the Miller Hill Mall in Hermantown, north of Duluth, when it occurred to him that he wasn't really needed at the church for the processing of the morning's collection receipts. The financial committee had taken care of that task for years, long before Mickey ended up at Saint Gerard's. His appearance whenever they met was purely social–he didn't have much more than an ounce of accounting aptitude to contribute to the process. It was just after six in the evening, so maybe he could connect with Father Mario yet tonight. The UMD campus where Mario lived was a short side trip from where he was at the moment. He tried his friend's cell phone and after the third ring greeted him in a schoolboy's Italian he had picked up from Mr. Gabardi at the Lincoln School years before: "Hey, Buon Natale, amico mio... "

Mario chuckled, returned the Italian greeting, "Not bad for an Irishman, Mick–you'll have to work on your enunciation though." Like Mickey, Father Mario was returning to Duluth after visiting with his family in the small town of Deerwood near Brainerd. The two priests decided to meet for coffee, in an hour. "Meet me at the Perkins on the Interstate beyond the Central exit, I think it's open 24/7. You still hungry? Maybe we could get a turkey sandwich," Mario joked. The restaurant was nearly empty and the two men settled into a corner booth. Mickey, despite being told not to, gave his friend a detailed recap of his meeting with the bishop–from the chunk of snow field goal one frigid night to Melissa's confiscated baggie of pot one recent afternoon. "So, Bremmer has exiled me to Florida. Some R&R in paradise for his wacky, wayward priest. I guess he's buddies with a bishop down there."

Mario listened patiently, without interruption or comment. His own pain etched in lines along his eyes and across his forehead. Reaching across the table he took Mickey's hand in his own, "I'm sorry, Mick." He paused for nearly a minute before saying anything else: "I must correct you on several points, my friend, please don't take what I say the wrong way. First, I wish you would stop regarding Saint Gerard's as some sort of purgatory, or punishment, and realize once and for all that the bishop is not out to get you. He's concerned. He loves you, Mickey, and has the greatest respect for your integrity. I know that for a fact because he's told me so–more than once. Secondly, and more importantly... there is a reason why that woman went to the bishop with her crazy allegations–however unfounded they were. Neither you nor I know why she did, nor do we know why the bishop, in his wisdom, decided to place you on leave... We don't even know how much of the crap he actually believed. Maybe less than you think. If he smelled pot on your clothing, like you suspect he did, then that's another situation all together.

"If old Mrs. Donovan could smell it, he probably could too. If he did he didn't say anything about it."

Mario paused, gave Mickey's hands a squeeze. "Whatever. I'm convinced that there is a higher reason for what's happening. I've always believed that you have special gifts, gifts that are probably not being utilized very well in the setting of a traditional parish–at least not at this point in your ministry.

"Something is out there. I have no idea what that something might be, or where it is, or when it will manifest itself. There may be a trial of some kind, a test of your faith, your own personal Calvary of sorts. Who knows? Mickey, don't ever forget that you have been chosen–I emphasize that word, *chosen*. Were it not for a miracle many years ago, you would not be here tonight, and in all likelihood, I wouldn't either. More than likely, neither one of us would be a priest." Having drained two decanters of coffee, Mario checked his watch. "Enough said. I don't mean to patronize or pump you up... just letting my heart pour out."

Mickey nodded his understanding of Mario's love and concern. Both men had talked about the Sturgeon Lake near-drowning episode on many past occasions. Their bond was solid. He let go of Mario's hands, stood as if he was ready to leave.

Mario said: "One other thing. You said you can't explain why you just sat there while the bishop 'chastised' you–that's your word, not mine–and you didn't offer a word of self-defense. Why, Mick? You of all people, always a fighter for what's right and true. The bishop knows that. Is it possible that when you sat there and took what he dished out without so much as a whimper, that he became convinced that something was wrong with you."

Mickey could not dispute his friend's insights. "Thanks, Mario," was all that he could say.

"Just pray for discernment, Mickey. You can be assured that I'll be praying as well."

Two delightful messages awaited Mickey when he checked his office landline.

From Gramma Maddie: "Did you really tell your Grampa to 'cut the bullshit'? If so, I've got a big thanks for you, he's been wearing a smile all day. Hugs and kisses, Mick."

From Meg: "Thanks. I love you again!"

Mickey's Christmas night wore a crown of gold. He was ready for the next chapter.

31/ GREEN EYES

Monday morning's Mass at Saint Gerard's was like any other, except for the regulars; Sarah Donovan was not sitting in the seventh pew, left side. Mickey couldn't remember a time when Mrs. Donovan had missed a daily Mass. Guilt, he reasoned, was a powerful deterrent. Instead, in the seventh pew were a well-dressed stranger and a woman he had seen recently but couldn't quite place. Following his final blessing, Mickey announced the Tuesday evening wake and Wednesday funeral Mass for Johnny Jawarski. He did not mention that on Thursday, Father Graham would be saying Mass. He smiled to himself, how sweet it would be to make the announcement that one of their own would be replacing him soon–Father Graham was the personification of pleasant senility. Swallowing his quick smile, Mickey chastised himself for another venial sin.

"I'm speechless!" Duane told Beth when they got back to his Lincoln. "I can't believe what we just saw. It's unreal!"

"I told you so."

"Father Moran and our own Brian Slade–two peas in a pod. You could have knocked me over with a feather." Duane liked clichés, thought them to be the signs of rich intelligence.

"Why didn't you want Brian to come with us and see for himself? I thought that was rude of you, Duane. He's sitting home alone fighting that urge to light a cigarette. It's been four days... I'm so proud."

"Four days–he's got it whipped by now."

"You didn't answer my question."

Duane gave his sister a playful tap on her shoulder. "Believe me, I've got my reasons, Beth." Duane had not confided any potential schemes to his siblings. Beth lived on a moral high ground and would never knowingly be party to any kind of dishonest behavior. Brian, on the other hand, was in a desperate spot these days and might be willing to do almost anything for some money. Whatever, he would be careful to keep his ideas to himself for now. How did people put it–silence is golden.

"What do you mean, you've got your reasons?" Beth persisted.

"Maybe I'm jealous. Maybe I just wanted some one-on-one with my sister." He lied. "I'll probably be going back to the Cities tonight, and we haven't had a chance to talk– just the two of us, I mean– in a coon's age. I thought going to Mass, then stopping somewhere for breakfast would be a nice idea. Give us a chance to bond with each other like you and Brian seem to have done already."

Beth was flattered, "I had no idea you felt that way, Duane. What was it you wanted to talk about?"

"Nothing specific, I guess. Just that I've been thinking that we've all grown too far apart over the years. And, I've realized how important family is, and religion, too. We've all had our share of family issues to deal with, I just think we Slades need to stick together more than we have. Blood, after all, is thicker than water."

Beth smiled at the sentiment, "I'm surprised to hear that coming from you. I've always had the feeling that you wanted nothing to do with me or Brian."

"And, I apologize, Beth. I know I've given that impression, but we all share the blame in not communicating better. That's got to change, and I'm going to get the ball rolling. I've started saying the rosary before going to bed and getting to daily Mass once or twice a week."

Beth beamed her approval.

Over breakfast at a Denny's restaurant, Duane further shared his newfound values of faith and family with his adoring sister. "I'm delighted, Duane. It's a miracle how much you have changed.'"

Duane always marveled at human gullibility.

The following morning Duane went to Mass for the second day in a row. This time he brought a small Sony recording devise that he purchased at a Wal-Mart on his drive out to Benton Park. Beth had been correct, the priest's voice and inflections were different from Brians. In order to find out the color of Father Moran's eyes, he would have to get much closer to the priest.

After Mass, Duane approached the priest, "Good morning, Father," he offered his hand. "Adam Gordon, from the Cities. Visiting family over the holidays."

Mickey took the man's hand, "Very nice to meet you Mr. Gordon. Does your family belong to Saint Gerard's?"

Duane shook his head. "No, they live up near UMD."

The two men found very little more to talk about, and excused themselves to get on their way. "Just wanted to say hello", Duane said in an apologetic tone. "Have a great day."

Mickey returned the greeting, yet puzzled over why this Mr. Gordon would drive from far eastern Duluth to Benton Park for morning Mass.

Mickey had packing to do. Duane had driving to do. As he drove south, Duane Slade played the taped Mass over and over. Brian's voice had a noticeably higher pitch, and the priest had green eyes: Two minor discrepancies that might require attention.

PART TWO

32/ ON THE ROAD

Although his sleep had been fitful once again, Mickey arose at just after 4 AM on Thursday morning feeling remarkably refreshed. Resting upon the duffle bag near the closet was his Catholic Saints book. He took a moment to pick one of the saints listed for this day, December 29. He was partial to saints that had been beatified by his favorite pontiff, Pope John Paul II, and found a recently anointed saint near the top of the page. Saint Galvan Bermudez, he learned, had led a wild and abusive life with loose women and liquor before reentering the seminary that had expelled him years before. He was later executed for ministering to the poor and was canonized in 2000.

Johnny Jawarski's funeral the day before had been Mickey's last official duty at Saint Gerard's–but only he knew that reality. Early that morning he lit all two hundred candles spaced inches apart across the alter, then spent an hour in prayer. He could feel a presence in the quiet sanctuary, an uplifting and inspiring presence. Johnny had probably asked the Holy Spirit to help Fadder Mickey conduct his funeral. When blessing the casket, he said his silent goodbyes–first for his departed angel, and then for the parishioners he would be leaving.

Mickey's Civic had been packed the night before and all of the last minute details he could think of were accomplished. His car afforded little cargo space so he had to make some difficult decisions. His collection of books would be left behind so that he could stuff his Martin guitar in the trunk space. In a small duffle bag he packed his wrinkled blacks–suit coat and slacks–along with his Roman collar. His most difficult judgment was whether to take along the black leather case containing the chalice and paten of his ordination. He chose to leave the case behind, locked in a sacristy closet. Father Graham had arrived the previous afternoon, been given a superficial briefing about the parish, and retired to his bedroom after the six o'clock news. The substitute priest had no idea about why he was here or how long he might be staying. As a tidbit of parting advice, Mickey suggested: "If you have any problems, Father... Sarah Donovan will be most helpful. She's been my right hand."

Within half an hour, Mickey was crossing the Blatnik Bridge into Wisconsin where he would make his first coffee stop. The morning sky was star-filled, the air crisp, the highways worn dry of snow and ice. Once on Highway 53 south, he set the Civics' cruise at fifty-eight, only three miles per hour over the posted speed limit—Wisconsin highway patrol officers had a well-earned reputation of feasting on Minnesota drivers.

Mickey continued with his morning prayers as he motored through the awakening Wisconsin countryside. With the storm of thoughts swimming through his mind it was hard to concentrate on prayer, "Come Lord, Jesus... just ride along and enjoy my company. Keep me safe and keep me in your loving arms always." He slipped an Oak Ridge Boys CD into his stereo system, closed his right fist into a mock microphone and sang along with the country band... within minutes he was singing *Elvira* at the top of his voice.

A serenity had settled on Mickey's shoulders as he absorbed the feeling of freedom on the open roads that lay ahead. If nothing else, the unknown was liberating—he could feel something stirring in his chest. Maybe Mario was correct in suggesting that God had a special calling for him. He would be open to whatever that might be. Passing Madison four hours into his trip, he was singing along with Neil Diamond's *Sweet Caroline.*

By early afternoon, and two more coffee stops, Mickey was cruising the toll highway outside of Rockford, Illinois. He had promised his dad that he would call sometime today; mom and dad were the third click in his cell directory. In the past week, Mickey had not said a word about his rehab 'sabbatical' to anybody but Father Mario. He might keep it that way for a while longer and allow his dad to believe that this road trip was no more than a post-Christmas vacation of sorts. With cell phone communication you could call from anywhere and say you were somewhere else. He could tell his dad that he was spending some time in Iowa if he wanted. That, however, might be hard for anyone to believe–Iowa? Mickey had a feeling that there might be quite a few venial sins–little white lies– between where he was now and where he would end up in a few days.

Amos and Sadie were watching their grandson's hockey game in the Memorial Building arena and the resounding echoes from inside the huge building made conversing too difficult: "I'll call later, Dad. Say hello to all for me." The abbreviated conversation was perfect– later was vague– later could be next week. Along the way he had promised phone calls to Mario and to Bishop Bremmer; instead his next call would be to Father Tim: A call that he had procrastinated for more than a week. Mickey had kept his seminary friend, in his daily prayers but the fear of bad news had kept him from calling. No answer. He left a message for a return call.

He said a prayer before his next call. Molly Matonich, Bishop Bremmer's secretary, put his call through without pause. "Father Moran, so good of you to call, hope you had a wonderful Christmas." Bremmer was in fine spirits this day and his small talk was pleasantly spirited, an air quite unlike their past conversations. Eventually, the bishop's voice dropped and octave as he redefined the basics of Mickeys rehab program. Mickey was to first report to the Diocesan Bishop Cordoba in Venice, Florida, Cordoba already had made arrangements, and then... a passing semi tanker hauling ethanol momentarily drowned their connection... who was the pastor of Saint Leo Church in Bonita Springs, just north of Naples. Mickey might have asked the bishop to repeat what he had just missed, but, for some reason, didn't. "You'll like the church, it's a vibrant community from what I've been told and it's an easy drive from your family's place." Bremmer had made a few changes from the earlier plan, "Bishop Cordoba has made suggested some changes relative to your housing and counseling. We both think that it's probably best if you don't stay with your folks as earlier planned… of course you will be able to visit them on occasional weekends." After fifteen minutes and scant additional detail, the bishop and Mickey said a prayer together, then Bremmer blessed his travel.

"I will look forward to seeing you soon, Mickey. I've got great hopes for you." Mickey almost went off the highway and into a cornfield–Bishop Bremmer had just called him Mickey!

That was all. Mickey was left with an enigma. What else had the two bishops talked about? What did Bishop Bremmer mean by *'great hopes'*?

∼

Beth Slade passed the phone to her brother and resumed preparing the chicken alfredo hot dish that would be their evening meal. The kitchen phone rang–

"It's Duane, again. Wanted us to know that he got back to Roseville safely." A smile crossed her face as she thought how considerate her brother had become. "He wants to say hello to you, Bry."

Brian got up from the table, passed the can of Diet Pepsi from his right to his left hand and took the phone, "Hey Duane, what's up with you?"

The two men talked for only a few minutes, Brian mostly listening. He cradled the receiver, gave his sister a strange look, "He wants me to come down, stay with him for a while. A month ago he kicked me out, now he's all palsy-walsy. I don't get it, Beth."

Beth's smile was almost matronly, "Duane's done a lot of growing up, Bry. He's changed. We had a chance to talk yesterday and I was almost in tears. He's found the Lord, and he's got a whole new attitude about family. He's remorseful about how he's treated you; both of us for that matter."

Brian considered what his sister was saying, "He claims he's got a job for me. Can you believe that? A job! God knows I've got to work."

"I'm not surprised he's found you a job. That's Duane for you; when he sets his mind to something there's no stopping him."

Brian nodded without comment.

33/ ". . . SOME KIND OF SALES..."

The nearly treeless central Illinois countryside, with its snow-blanketed farmlands and occasional grain elevators, offered an endlessly boring diversion as Mickey chewed the miles southward. Just south of Effingham, Mickey pulled to the side of the I-57. To his left stood the largest freestanding cross he had ever seen, illuminated by ground lighting, the symbolic cross cast it's glow over the landscape. What an impressive testimonial to Christianity he thought. It was already dark and the early evening chill stood. After stepping out of the Civic and gulping some fresh air, he said few prayers before continuing his journey. The brief stop refreshed him even more than the Twinkies and Diet Coke he had been snacking on.

Nightfall came early in December and Mickey was seriously road weary after nearly thirteen hours of pounding the highways. Mount Vernon looked like the perfect place to end his first day on the road. He checked in at an Embassy Suites motel, kicked off his Nikes and sprawled on the king-sized bed.

Before finding a place to eat, Mickey would make a call to an old Hibbing friend who lived in Chattanooga, his next planned overnight stop. His former classmate, John Christopher, was a pharmacist and had been working at a Walgreens store there for the past two years. Mickey had loosely planned his travel itinerary so that he would pass through Atlanta on an early Saturday morning. Every Midwestern snowbird he had ever talked to absolutely dreaded Atlanta's urban canyon experience. Some took much longer circumventing routes simply to avoid the congested snarl of multi-lane traffic in the sprawling megalopolis.

John was delighted to hear from Mickey and promised to show him the town when he arrived the following afternoon. "You'll see why we love it down here, Mick," John promised. "Think about staying over on Saturday as well; that's New Year's Eve, you know."

Somehow, Mickey had spaced that out. "I doubt it, John. But it would be fun to go out on Friday night with you and Susan."

After talking with John, he tried to catch Father Tim again. He left a second message. After a shower and a change of clothes, he walked to a Pizza Hut down the street from his motel. Whenever in doubt about what kind of meal he wanted, pizza always seemed to win out.

It was comfortable to be wearing jeans and a sweatshirt, his collar and black clothing might have to be put into storage for quite some time. His thoughts about that remained very mixed–would he be a practicing priest or a patient of some kind? Father Michael Moran was spiritually prepared for whatever lie ahead–the 'let go and let God' reminder from his friend, Mario, was making better sense the more deeply he embraced the idea.

His waitress was a flirty and thirtyish blonde named Naomi. She took a more than necessary interest in helping Mickey make a menu selection. "The large is probably more than you could eat, that is if you want to keep your... your athletic shape." She laughed and leaned over the formica tabletop exposing her ample cleavage. "Or... just right if your girlfriend is going to be joining you."

Mickey amused, "Oh, no... I'm very single," he added a devious wink to his smile.

The restaurant wasn't too busy, so Naomi could safely pursue the dialogue, "I find that hard to believe–'very single', I mean– you're not a bad lookin' guy–but, I'm sure you've been told that before."

"That's what my mom says, but she's, you know, kinda prejudiced."

Naomi laughed, "Nah, I'd say she's jus tellin' it like it is. What brings you to Mount Vernon? Most strangers this time of the year are snowbirds. I'd say you're much too young to be retired."

"I could be young and rich enough to not have to work anymore. That's possible don't ya think."

"Yah, wouldn't that be somethin'–young and rich!" She rocked back on her heels and gave an appraising stare; "You don't look rich, though. Are you a some kinda musician?"

"Do I look like one?"

"Kinda. Like a country singer."

"Sorry, I can't sing a note."

"I'll bet you could," Naomi laughed, looked over her shoulder, craning her neck to see if the manager was watching. Coast was clear. "Okay, I give up–you'll have to tell me what you do?"

Mickey would take their flirtatious banter one step further, "Why don't you take a guess?"

"Sales… you're in some kind of sales."

"Great, how could you tell?"

"You've got a good, honest face. I'd buy something from you, probably anything." She giggled, "What do you sell?"

Mickey was enjoying himself but his charade had gone just a bit too far and he had a squeamish feeling, "I sell God, his son Jesus, and the Gospel."

Naomi frowned, puzzled she said: "Bibles? You sell Bibles?"

"I sell what's in them. I'm a Catholic priest."

Naomi blushed at first, then her demeanor changed completely, her voice took and entirely different tone; shaking her head she said–"Medium pepperoni, mushrooms, and a Diet Pepsi. Will that be it?"

Mickey nodded, and a red-faced Naomi retreated to the kitchen. When he was finished with his pizza, a waitress named Sandy brought his check. "Would you please pass this tip on to the blonde woman who served me?" His conscience was seriously guilting him over his playful, but turned-bad, ruse. He gave Sandy an extra ten-dollar bill to pass along to Naomi who was probably hiding in the kitchen.

Back at the motel he plopped on the wide bed and flipped on the TV remote. Surfing the channels he paused for a moment on bombastic Bill O'Reilly's 'no spin zone', then to college hoops on ESPN, before settling on a Law and Order episode. Just when the program got interesting, his cell phone rang.

Tim had been drinking and admitted so, "Mick I'm plastered and I'm sorry. I think I'm going to hell… really… I've been–Oh my God, Mick, I've been verrry baaad," he slurred. "I'm sorry… what can I say, Mickey, I've really screwed up my life." Tim began sobbing, his breath coming in heaves, "Really screwed up, big time."

Mickey tried to calm his drama-prone friend, "Get a grip, Tim," his tone emphatic, then conciliatory. "Anything you've done can be forgiven, you know that. God loves you… regardless of anything you could possibly do."

"No He can't, at least not any more. You wouldn't believe what I've done… Mick, Oh, Mick… I've really slipped away." He caught his breath, paused for a long moment, "Will you hear my confession? Even if I'm kinda out of it right now."

"I don't think I should, Tim. I can listen and reassure and pray with you… but give you absolution… maybe not right now."

A long pause, "I guess I understand. It wouldn't be right. Maybe I shouldn't have called–at least not in this condition."

"No, you did the right thing, Tim. How about I forgive you as a friend but not as a priest. Will that work for you?"

However unorthodox, one suspended priest listened to the 'sins' of one of his fallen colleagues. Mickey was more pained than surprised as his friend opened his soul over the phone. The old girlfriend, Bonnie LaPatka, separated from her husband, was as vulnerable as Father Tim. "Just once, Father, I felt so terrible that I couldn't live with myself. I wanted to step in front of a train and end it all. I swear, I could never do it again." Tim had already left his family's house in Roseau and was staying in a Bemidji motel where he'd been for the past several days. He had been drinking almost continuously.

After unburdening himself, Tim promised Mickey that he would contact his bishop in Saint Paul and his pastor at Saint Lucy's, "If they won't take me back, I don't know what I'll do, Mick. It's taken this experience to convince me... I want to be a priest more than anything. A much better priest than before."

Mickey searched his mind for consoling words, something clicked:

"Tim, remember at our ordination... remember the story Father Jim Scheuer shared with us?"

"Only vaguely... what was it you remember him saying?"

That day the old priest, now deceased, told the congregation that years ago, when he had been ordained to the priesthood, a friend of his came up to him and said: 'Congratulations on joining a group of holy men.' Father Scheuer corrected his friend's perception, 'I'm joining a group of men struggling to be holy.'"

After a long silence, Tim said, " He was a wise man, wasn't he."

Mickey couldn't let his friend suffer alone. "Just between us, Tim, I've got a confession of sorts myself... " He disobeyed his bishop's directive again, and confided his own story. Maybe hearing that he had issues of his own to work out might give Tim a little boost–maybe misery does love company. That night, despite his physical and emotional fatigue, Mickey slept poorly. The venial sins and the disobedience were weighing heavily on his soul. How far astray form his own priestly vows was he heading? His friend's contrition was both deep and honest–was his own?

34/ 'I BELIEVE IN ANGELS...'

Standing at the counter of his narrow kitchen and looking into his simply furnished living room, Duane Slade splashed water into his glass of bourbon, then ambled across the carpet. It had taken him twenty minutes to outline the details of his plan, and he hoped that the impression he conveyed was one of confident assurance. Perspiration, however, beaded on his forehead, and his hounds-tooth sport jacket, a few sizes too small, pinched under his damp armpits. "I've done my homework, we can pull this off," he appealed "And we can do it with minimal exposure or cost to you. Once we get their money we'll split it right down the middle: fifty-fifty. Slick as a whistle!" he added with a breeze to his voice. David Rossman, stood up from the fabric-worn sofa and walked to thewet bar across Duane's living room. He poured another two fingers of vodka into his glass, grimaced–"Damn cheap liquor you got here." He stirred the cubes with his finger. "Maybe," was his only comment after hearing his friend's scheme.

Both were shysters, neither trusted the other. "Just maybe," he repeated, turning back to the sofa and plopping his substantial frame into the cushions. "What kinda guy is this brother of yours? You sure he's gonna go for this?" Rossman being in the role of a potential investor, the deference of the plea-maker gave him a sense of power. And, to be a wise investor one had to be a skeptic as well. "Lots'a ifs ands and buts, Slade."

Duane squirmed: "Brian? Nice guy, naïve, and on the skids these days. I already told him I've got a job for him and he seemed excited. The way I've planned it so far, we're gonna keep him in the dark as much as possible. It's best if he doesn't really know what's going on."

"Ya, that's what you already said. He must be a gullible SOB if you think he won't have any questions."

"Gullible? That's his middle name. And Dianne? You've already met her... "

"Yeah, Dianne the body, she's as dumb as a stump." Rossman felt a stir in his groin at his lustful thought. He pulled himself out of the spring worn sofa, then stood and slipped out of his pinching white vinyl shoes. His left sock had a hole in the toe. Scratching his head, he crossed back to the bar, leaned over his elbows and regarded Duane with apparent unease. "Yeah, yeah, maybe you got somthin' here. Maybe not... maybe I'm being hustled just like your brother. Hard to tell. What's the timeframe, Slade? When can we get our cast together? Go over what we're gonna do?"

The 'we' of Rossman's comments inspired Duane. "Brian comes in tomorrow. Let's see...that's Thursday...how about Friday night; we can get together here at my place?"

Duane had given his plan considerable thought. David Rossman, a businessman who owned three single-star motels that rented rooms by the hour when requested, also laundered drug money, and was the critical link in Duane's pulling everything off. David was like Duane in two important ways: He had an undeveloped conscience and he was always open to a con if the odds were reasonably favorable–better than sixty-forty.

In their planning and feasibility meeting, Duane had outlined three ideas, saving his favorite for last. Plan one involved having Brian impersonate Father Moran and withdraw funds from various church accounts. With this plan, both exposure and risk were high–but tolerable. The primary liability was that too much depended on Brian's willingness to take part in a blatantly criminal activity.

Similar to plan one, plan two involved soliciting money from wealthy parishioners under the pretense of building a youth drop-in center, a home for unwed mothers, or a school in Botswana; something to pique the compassion of the rich. Several people, from three different parishes, were likely candidates and could be discreetly approached.

Duane had composed a list of elderly widows that he deemed to be especially good marks. Again the risk factors were high... and again, Brian wasn't likely to go along. Any workable plan would require deceiving Brian. Thus, the third plan. Clean, quick, low risk: If Rossman agreed to partner with him, the project could easily be completed over a few hours on a single weekend.

~

After an entertaining Friday night with John and Sue Christopher, checking out one Market Street nightspot after another, the threesome reveled in lively downtown Chattanooga until nearly midnight. Mickey was up early the next morning and ready for the third leg of his trip. "I've had a blast with you guys, but I'm going to pass on staying over for New Year's Eve."

John had wondered, but hadn't directly asked, why his friend was going to Florida. He guessed it was a vacation, but Mickey seemed a bit high-strung at dinner the night before. "Well, safe travel, buddy–and please keep in touch with us. You'll be able to get through Atlanta before nine and Saturday morning traffic should be tolerable," John said.

Mickey said his thanks and goodbyes to John and Sue over coffee and toast, waved as he pulled out of their driveway, and wound down the narrow, hilly back road to the Interstate. He pulled onto I-75 at six thirty.

The last day of 2011 in Chattanooga, Tennessee was a balmy fifty-two degrees. As he crossed into Georgia's western mountains he realized that this would be his final state before entering Florida. He'd made remarkable time but had pushed himself more than necessary. "Relax", Mickey chided himself. "And, catch your breath for heaven's sake. This isn't a race." His morning prayers calmed him.

Atlanta was always busy. The northern suburbs passed by quickly and even travel through the center city went rather smoothly–but south of downtown approaching the airport, traffic suddenly clogged. Nearly an hour of bumper-to-bumper congestion passed, and Mickey was on his way to the I-75 Macon bypass. By late afternoon Mickey was passing through the green pastures of horse country around Ocala in sunny northern Florida.

Aside from the stress of Atlanta, the third day was relaxing and reflective. The freedom of the road had settled in so deeply that he felt he could go on for days. Anticipating balmy weather ahead, Mickey had dressed accordingly in beige cargo shorts, a light nylon Twins jacket, and a 'What, Me Worry' Alfred Newman tee shirt. The transition from tundra to tropics in three days was exhilarating. Mickey had always been infatuated with flowers and Florida bloomed in abundance year around. He decided to get off the interstate and take some of the backcountry highways. If it took him three more days to get to Venice, or neighboring Bonita Springs, he would still be on time for… whatever?

Rolling down his car window and hanging his arm out over the door, he breathed in the warmth of the day. Above, and to the west, were fair weather wisps of clouds, beside the highway clusters of dense palmetto, ahead the orb of blinding sunlight.

The open road offered a marvelous sense of freedom, a release from the times and places that dropped off behind like autumn's leaves in the wind. Mickey listened to songs from his Ipod he'd plugged into the Civics' stereo system. Many of his favorite songs were BeeGees hits dating back to the disco days when he was in junior high school. He still enjoyed dancing, and Sue Christopher had been a great partner the night before. While dancing she teased him: "If you weren't a priest, I'd bet that you could have your pick of any girl in the place." Laughing at the memory, he contemplated her words more seriously. He wondered if he might stumble along the way as Tim had. He was heading almost blindly into uncharted territory.

Days before when driving around Hibbing, he had called his old girlfriend, Maureen Regan–just to say hello–then rudely hung up on her mother. Who was this Roger guy? Was he a boyfriend or, judging from the tone of Mrs. Regan's voice, a pest? What if Maureen had answered and told him the reason she had called without leaving a message two weeks before? What was the reason? He did drive by her house in Greenhaven before leaving Hibbing. The disco music inspired memories, the memories inspired thoughts that had long been repressed. Father Mickey had cause to wonder about his vulnerability. An ABBA CD got his head bobbing again as he strummed a pseudo guitar with his free right hand and wailed 'Fernando' into the Florida countryside. Then… he mellowed and found himself singing along with 'I Have a Dream'–his favorite ABBA song:

> *'I have a dream, a song to sing.*
> *To help me cope with anything*
> *If you see the wonder of a fairy tale*
> *You can take the future even if you fail…*
>
> *I believe in angels…*
> *When I know the time is right for me*
> *I'll cross the stream… I'll have a dream.*

As Mickey sang the refrain, 'I believe in angels', over and over, his thoughts went backward to a more recent time and place–to Johnny Jawarski. He found himself crying and singing the refrain. For as long as he could remember, Mickey had had a devout sense of an angelic presence in his world. "Pray for me up there, Johnny…"

Putting aside his Ipod, Mickey prayed for strength, faith, and a greater love of his Savior, his one and only true friend, the one he had vowed to serve until death. More than any music, his prayers inspired a passion to be more open to the unknown opportunities that Mario had imagined for him.

'*I believe in angels*' he sang.

35/ THE FILMMAKERS

Brian Slade chose a glass of chocolate milk over the Miller Lite his brother offered. He had arrived at Duane's Roseville apartment an hour before, unpacked his freshly laundered and ironed clothing, and checked himself out in the full length mirror beside the dresser. Not only had Beth outfitted him in some stylish new clothes, she had fattened him up some. He hadn't eaten so well in years. For once he had left his sister's house with an open invitation to come back any time; it had been a mutually pleasant visit.

Sitting across the living room from Duane, he shook his head: "I thought you said a job! My idea of a job is going to work and putting in a forty-hour week. This is stupid, Duane. I'm not an actor and I don't want to be an actor. If you had told me this earlier I wouldn't be here now. A role in a movie? Get real for heaven's sake."

Duane had just finished giving Brian an overview of the project that he and Rossman had devised. "You telling me you want to turn down an opportunity to make an easy $250? For a couple hours of work? And, with the potential for a lot more in the future?"

"You got it, Duane–that's exactly what I'm telling you. I'm not getting into any porn film–whatever you say this guy's willing to pay. No way, Jose!"

Duane had expected that he'd have to cajole his brother some, but he wasn't prepared for a flat-out, emphatic no! Perhaps Rossman could be more persuasive. "The director will be stopping by after supper, Mr. Rossman can give you a better idea of the project. Just listen to what he has to say and don't screw it up for me, Brian. I've lined up some investors for the film."

Brian gave him a doubtful look, "Investors?"

"Yes… investors. Rossman is not a small-timer, he's got connections with Paramont and MGM, outfits like that. We're looking at royalties, you know what royalties are?"

Brian had leaned forward on the sofa and evidenced some interest, he nodded: "Yeah, I know what royalties are–who doesn't?"

The brothers talked filmmaking and royalties for another ten minutes. Having had enough, Brian rose, "Still not interested, Duane. I'm hungry. And, when I'm hungry, my craving for a cigarette gets really bad." Brian had eschewed the habit for eight days–and counting!

"How about I give Rossman a quick call–tell him to pick us up a pizza on his way over here?"

"How long's that gonna be?"

"Less than an hour. Have some cheese and crackers for now."

"I don't see any cheese or crackers. Not much of anything in the fridge or cupboards. Don't you ever eat in? All I can find is a box of Frosted Flakes, a carton of sour milk… some rancid take-out Chinese. Yuck!"

"Quit complaining. I'm not your fat-assed sister with fifty thousand calories in every cupboard." He no more than said it and regretted it.

"What did you… ?"

Duane retracted, "Beth's a sweetheart. But we both know she's got to lose a few… right? For that matter, so do I."

Rossman wore a one hundred dollar Men's Warehouse suit, a loudly stripped shirt, a red and navy paisley ascot, and a heavy amber-studded necklace. He looked the part of a carnival lord and would play the role of a Hollywood insider, dropping names like Mike Lukas and 'Stevey' Spielberg while using every movie business cliché that he could imagine. The three men finished their pizza and small talk about recent box office successes. Rossman lauded The Girl With the Dragon Tattoo, Duane had no recent favorites, Brian admitted to loving westerns but rarely having the money to go to the theater. Beth had rented True Grit, both he and his sister enjoyed the movie and lauded Jeff Bridges' acting. The men retired to the living room, settled back to relax with a glass of the Reunite wine that Rossman had brought with him.

The director belched, then farted, and laughed: "I remember when we were filming *Jaws* a few years back, that's what got me hooked on making movies. Stevie Spielberg, everybody knows who he is–anyhow, he wanted me to help with the filming of a few other flicks before I went out on my own. That might have been the best decision I ever made. You guys ever see *Doctor Zhivago*?" Without pausing for an answer, Rossman continued: "Well, that was the movie that got me my first Oscar nomination." (Nobody in the room seemed to know that the Zhivago film had been released a full decade before Jaws debuted in 1975).

Brian was overwhelmed, Zhivago was one of his favorite movies ever. "You filmed *Doctor Zhivago*?" Although he never quite understand the plot, he fell head-over-heels in love with Lara, played by Julie Christie, and he thought the scenery was breathtaking.

Rossman wondered if he'd carried his bullshit a bit too far, "No one person films a complex film like Zhivago. That's gotta be obvious. I did the…" he coughed, excused himself, and tried to come up with some memory of the film, "… the Siberia parts. That's what I did, Siberia."

When Duane filled their glasses a second time, the downstairs buzzer rang. "That would be Dianne Montez," Duane announced. Dianne had been well rehearsed by Rossman earlier that afternoon. Some of the rehearsals were behind closed doors. Bedroom doors. Like Brian, she was being conned for the easy $250; unlike Brian, she was ecstatic about being what Rossman called the next Garbo. She had promised Rossman to charm Duane's brother if he remained to be reluctant about committing to the project. "I ain't gonna let no jerk ruin a career for me!" she said.

When Duane went to the door, Rossman leaned over to Brian's ear: "She's what we call a starlet in show biz lingo. Looking for that one big break, you know. Marty Scorsese recommended her to me."

Dianne Miller was a dark skinned, dark eyed, beauty. She wore a miniskirt with mesh stockings, a skin clinging purple cotton blouse, and gold cosmetic jewelry. Her preparation for the role of Dianne Montez consisted of watching *Bus Stop* with Marilyn Monroe three times. Heavy, musky perfume pervaded the room when she stepped inside. Nearly tripping in her stiletto heels, Diane accepted the highball Duane handed her. Then, the busty 'starlet' walked over to Brian: "Helllooo, Dahlin… so nice to meet'cha." As she sat down beside him, her lovely booty brushed against his thigh.

Brian didn't quite know what to say or do in the presence of these Hollywood people, "Hi." He said, moving a bit more toward the empty end of the sofa.

"This your bro, Duane? The guy that's gonna play the priest I fall madly in love with?"

Duane nodded. "Like you sweets, it'll be his first role in a feature film but I think he can handle it. Right, Bry?"

All Brian could do is nod in agreement.

"Not a bad lookin' guy if I say so myself. We otta get together and practice some stuff… whatta you say to that?"

"Nothing. I mean, nothing." Brian's face reddened.

∼

The next day was Sunday, New Years Day of 2012, and Mickey found Saint Jude Catholic Church on Marion Oak Drive, in Ocala. He had spent the 'Eve' in a hotel room watching an offense-overloaded Chick-Fil-A Bowl football game: Auburn routed Virginia. He didn't know any of the players and frequently nodded off to sleep. When awakening at nine, he felt more refreshed than any morning in recent memory. After prayers and a few sips of a microwave-warmed cup of yesterday's Burger King coffee, Mickey headed to the tiny bathroom shower stall. Speaking into the shower's nozzle he half-sang: "Happy New Year, Michael Moran–Father Michael

Moran, I should say! Happy New Year to yooooo." Laughing out loud he added, Who woulda thunk it two weeks ago–a priest from Duluth, Minnesota taking a New Year's morning shower in Ocala, Florida and having no clear idea why he's was here and not there. Bizarre!

The priest saying the 10:30 Mass was young, looked to be Hispanic. Mickey hadn't attended Mass as a spectator in some time and felt as if he was only getting a small fraction of the satisfaction he was accustomed to. He would have to get used to his changed status–whatever that status might be. He felt as if he were in some kind of limbo, waiting on an appointment with a bishop he'd never met, and some rehab plan he knew nothing about, in a place he'd had not visited in years.

As his destination neared, his doubts were becoming a dense cloud in his mind. Up until now he had allowed himself to be more tourist than penitent. The more he thought about the future, the more confused he became. Mickey swallowed hard on the concept of rehabilitation: What for? He'd done nothing wrong. He was as healthy as any priest he'd ever met–more so than most. This is so unbelievably stupid! He mumbled under his breath. I don't think I can go through with it. Despite the nearly three weeks since the bishop's unfounded decree, it was disturbingly obvious that he had not reconciled anything yet. He was a little boat stranded on a vast sea without oars or anchor– at the mercy of the winds. Is that what his loving God wanted to put him through?

Mickey resolved to talk with Father Mario before reporting to the Venice dioceses' Bishop Raoul Cordoba, the following day. Today, he planned to drive from Ocala south to Tampa, get onto the Tamiami Trail at some point, and then follow the Gulf of Mexico coast toward Naples. He would find a place to park his car and spend an hour or two walking the beaches… letting the wind blow through his hair, letting the waves roll over his feet. The thought of aqua water and endless sand brought back wonderful memories of the family's Florida vacations in Naples when he was a teenager.

After Mass and the Eucharist, Mickey felt like a half-empty glass as he ramped back onto I-75 south. "Get used to it, Mick," he said to the dashboard as he set the cruise control at seventy. Minutes became hours, he crossed over Interstate-4 marveling at the Sunday traffic passing between Tampa and Orlando to the east. He had managed to put his issues out of mind and become engrossed in the lush greenery. He tried to count the different species of palm trees along the highway, gave up at twenty-something. Florida was pleasantly intriguing–especially after much of the country he'd traveled through. The mountains of Tennessee, however, had been a beautiful respite from everything else until his arrival in Florida.

Mickey was beyond Tampa by mid-afternoon when he ramped off the interstate at a Bradenton exit and found Highway 41–the Tamiami Trail- going south through Sarasota. He planned to drive the last few miles and spend the night in Venice, and then...?

36/ VENICE, FLORIDA

Mickey's shoulders burned from being too long in the sun that afternoon. He had walked the Venice beaches–south from the municipal parking lot to Caspersen Beach–for nearly three hours. The baggy pockets of his cargo shorts were filled with a variety of colorful shells. Sundrenched and weary, he found a beer and burger joint, ate too much, and found an inexpensive motel near the Tamiami highway. He would have to watch his spending money as he had no idea what his finances would be like for the next... however long?

Then a stroke of reality passed between his ears causing him to laugh at himself: "Oh yeah, like I'm going to be hurting for cash with my folks only a few miles away."

That evening, Mickey put an aloe cream on his shoulders and his back as far as he could reach. He found the novel he had been reading about a runaway teenager who ended up witnessing a murder in

Flagstaff, Arizona. The Minnesota author was one of Mickey's favorites and the story was absorbing. In an hour, he turned off the bedside lamp, and immediately dropped off to sleep.

Monday morning. Mickey had until Wednesday to contact the bishop of the Venice diocese and still had no idea what kind of report had preceded his arrival. Had Bishop Bremmer diagnosed him as and addict, a deviant, a sociopath–or simply a misguided soul? He was none of the above, so what kind of program might he be forced to participate in? Stupid! How many times had the word stupid come to mind in just the past few days? A hundred? More? Probably every time he thought about where he was and why. Yet, another word cropped up in equal measure–*obedience*!

The city of Venice had a pleasantly relaxing feeling to it so Mickey decided to spend the day knocking around, walking through neighborhoods of lushly landscaped yards, and letting the time whittle carelessly away. Shady and pleasant Castile Street took him to Amanda Road and then to Harbor Drive. A stiff southwesterly wind the night before had peeled long fronds from the tops of palm trees, littering the boulevards and sidewalks. A coconut-laden palm had shed some of its hard-shelled fruit as well–Mickey couldn't help but wonder how much damage the coconuts would cause during a hurricane. It would probably be much like a barrage of cannon balls flying in every direction. And, from forty feet above the walkway, a falling coconut might cause a person to suffer more than a huge headache. Looping back toward Venice Avenue with aching feet and sweat-stained tee shirt, he vowed to get himself in shape while living in the tropical paradise that was southwest Florida.

Bonita Springs, if that was to be his destination, was less than two hours south on the Tamiami Trail and he still had two days–after calling upon Bishop Cordoba– to get there. Off of South Harbor Road he found the city pier, Sharky's, a quaint Tiki bar, and more beautiful sugar-sandy beaches. The Gulf was showing her deep blue-green colors under the radiant globe of sun. He couldn't help thinking of back home in Duluth or Hibbing where winter had been wearing her drab gray colors for two months already–and would be wearing her winter white for three more.

A brochure at the Motel 6 where he had spent the previous night detailed places of interest in Venice, restaurants and taverns, and everything a visitor should know about or want to see. For lunch he decided on Carney's Irish Pub on the palm-lined main street, then found a parking lot behind the building. Even at two in the afternoon, the restaurant was busy and the mood jovial. It was definitely the 'tourist season' on the Gulf coast and everywhere he looked he saw white skinned legs, grey hair, and cameras dangling like heavy necklaces.

Mickey ate at the bar and tried to ignore the staring woman across from him. She had to have spent a fortune on making herself look fifty. Once she noticed Mickey's attention, she lifted an empty highball glass in his direction. Was that an invitation to buy her a drink? He didn't know so he ignored the gesture. She gave Mickey a few moments to acknowledge her invitation, then turned her attention away from him and looked about the bar for another man to hit on, or hit up–whatever!

Unable to finish his over-sized corned beef sandwich, he accepted a doggie box, paid his tab and walked back out into the brilliantly sunny late January afternoon. What to do with the rest of the gorgeous day? He felt as if he were a stranger lost in a paradise without any idea how to kill his empty time. How sad was that? He was still sore from too much beach walking the day before, he wasn't up for sitting in an air-conditioned movie theater, bars were places best avoided, and he hated to shop–despite the many trendy shops on Venice Avenue. So, what to do? Standing in the shade of some Royal Palms, he contemplated options. The one he was favoring was the one he hadn't allowed himself in years–a nap.

Getting his bearings, he turned the corner toward the parking lot where he had left his car. Spotting an empty beer can resting a few inches from the curb, he gave it a soccer-style kick toward an imaginary goal post thirty feet away. His field goal attempt was way wide. The memory of a similar childish moment on a frozen street in Benton Park weeks before brought a nostalgic smile. He was truly a misunderstood man.

Tomorrow he would see the bishop, and then what? Maybe the best thing to do would be to find the Epiphany Cathedral, the bishop's church, and say a few prayers–ask his Father in heaven a few questions, like: 'What in Your divine name am I doing here', 'how long are You going to have me stay', and 'what then… when I've finished whatever it is I'm going to be doing'? It almost seemed laughable. Yet… he was feeling a need, powerful at times, to keep himself connected to his vocation and a need to keep his fickle faith from slipping away from him.

Everything else put aside, Mickey's next decision boiled down to one of two options: the bishop's church or the motel's air conditioned room and king-sized bed? In the heat of the moment, the latter felt better.

About fifty feet away from where his car was parked, in the shadows behind the building, he heard the soft whimper of someone crying. A boy of about twelve was standing over a mangled bicycle. It appeared as if the bike's front wheel had been run over by a car. The rim was badly bent out of shape. On closer look, the boy was in some physical pain and holding his left elbow. The knees of his pants were torn and his knuckles bleeding. "What happened, son?" Mickey called ahead as he hurried toward the boy.

"My bike…" he sobbed. "Ruined. I don't know what to do, it's ruined." The heartbroken boy spoke in clear but heavily accented English. "What am I to do now?"

"Forget about your bike… you're hurt. Let me see," Mickey stepped toward the boy.

The boy backed away. "I'm okay!"

Mickey allowed the frightened lad his space, went down on one knee about three feet away: "Will you tell me what happened and let me look at your elbow? That's all. I want to help you if I can."

"I'll be okay."

"I know you will." Mickey wanted to be careful so as not to intimidate the already frightened lad. "Can you tell me your name?"

Reluctant, the boy said, "Miguel. Miguel Olivio."

Sobbing more heavily now, and rubbing at his sore elbow, the lad explained his dilemma and the accident that caused it. Miguel was bringing a bag lunch to his father who worked in the kitchen of the restaurant behind where he was standing. "My father will be so upset with me," he held the smashed brown bag in front of him. Looking down at the bike, Miguel said, "Worse, it's my brother's bike–not mine. His heart will break."

The twelve year-old admitted to being careless and hitting a curb two blocks away. The bike careened into a fire hydrant spilling Miguel onto the sidewalk where he landed on his elbow and knees. "I tried to bend it back," he said kicking the mangled bike rim in frustration. "Maybe you can bend it," he smiled weakly and for the first time. Miguel had perfect teeth, and an engaging smile: "You are very strong man, no?" Not only was the rim destroyed beyond repair, two spokes were snapped, a pedal had been half torn off, and the handlebars twisted askew. Mickey had tools in the trunk of his car but nothing that would enable him to put the bike in riding condition.

"I could try bending the rim but I don't think that will do you much good," Mickey said. He straddled the bike and gave his best effort, but even with Miguel's help he couldn't bend the rim back into shape. He shrugged in disappointment, "Sorry, Miguel. Now what?"

Shaking his head in dismay, Miguel dragged the bike toward the back door to the restaurant, "I must tell my father–he will be very angry."

"Don't worry about your father or the bike. You are hurt, Miguel.

Please, ask him if I can take you to the hospital."

Miguel's dark eyes widened in fright, he shouted his protest—"Oh no! No hospital!"

The back door of the restaurant was ajar, at Miguel's 'Oh no!' a dark haired girl looked out: "Miguel!" she hollered, "What's happened?".

In a moment, the young woman was joined by a small, gray-haired man. "Miguel…" the man cried as he raced from the doorway to the boy's side. Mickey guessed that the older man was Miguel's father. The two spoke rapidly in Spanish as the lovely girl stood near Mickey. The father flexed Miguel's elbow back and forth, still speaking rapidly; then bent down and examined his bruised knees. Satisfied that the boy was probably okay, he bent over and kissed the boy's forehead. Once again, they talked in Spanish.

Miguel wiped at his tears with the back of his hand, smiled at his father, then at Mickey: "Papa's not angry," he said.

The father then spoke at length to the girl, probably in her twenties, in staccato Spanish before offering his hand to Mickey.

The young woman, Miguel's sister Maria, spoke in nearly flawless English. "Alexi" she put her hand on the older mans arm, "thanks you for your concern. The boy is not seriously hurt but will need a ride back home. We have no phone to call ahead… and must stay here until seven. He asks a great favor of you, sir… will you please drive my brother home?"

Mickey nodded, "Absolutely… anything I can do to help."

Maria bowed her head, "We are very grateful you were here. Thank you for your kindness." Her smile was warm but subdued.

The Olivio family and more than one hundred other Hispanic families lived in an enclave called 'TriPalms' outside of Venice proper. To most, the isolated and out of sight, community was known as 'Little Haiti'. Turning east off of North River Road the blacktop ran out after about five hundred feet, giving way to a quarter mile of pot-holed gravel. Mickey had never visited a third world country but could only imagine that TriPalms was a slice of the barrios found in Port au Prince or Manila. Dire poverty was everywhere in evidence, from the substandard housing to the apparent lack of sanitation. The putrid smell of sewerage and decaying refuse hung in the languid air. Black plastic bags of refuse along with old mattresses and other trash were piled at the far end of a dirt field near the entry to the village. Tall wooden utility poles with their sagging power lines stood in conspicuous rows like teeth on a comb. What seemed to be the main street, Calle de El Cid, offered a Mobil gas station with a dingy Quik Pik convenience store attached, a few storage-type buildings in serious disrepair, a long tin-roofed garage with a sign reading 'Rico Repairs' and several white Isuzo trucks parked outside, and little else of note. Turning to his left, a huge repair shop was abuzz with activity. An HME sign identified what appeared to be a repair shop for small engines. Behind a chain-link fence were fifty or more trailers, along with half that number of riding mowers. In the open garage door were countless workbenches with assorted blowers and trimmers and other landscaping tools. If nothing else impressed, HME seemed to be a prosperous enterprise.

Miguel had been dreading his older brother's anger over the accident and was quietly somber on the three-mile drive from downtown Venice to his corrugated metal house in TriPalms. Miguel told Mickey to turn right on La Calle Decimo and, after two blocks, to stop adjacent to his house. After parking off to the side of the street and turning off the ignition, Mickey unloaded the damaged bike from his trunk.

Miguel stood awkwardly, brushed away a tear, and backed away from the car. "I am ashamed, sir. This is my home. My shame hurts me more than my arm."

Mickey had a lump in his throat that he could hardly swallow. What could he possibly say to that? More importantly, what could he do about that?

Miguel paused at the open doorway of his house, "You do not want to come inside, I think. Thank you, sir. God bless."

Mickey realized that the boy had never asked him his name or anything else. "Miguel, please call me Mickey. Father Mickey–I am a priest."

The boy's eyes widened, he quickly blessed himself with a sign of the cross and bowed reverently, "God bless..." he said again. "A holy priest... my goodness!" The lad scooted inside and closed the torn screen door behind him.

Before the inside door slammed shut, Mickey said, "I'll come by and see you tomorrow, God bless..."

As Mickey drove slowly away he replayed the scene he had left behind in TriPalms. Why had he told the boy that he was a priest? Of what relevance was that to a twelve year-old boy? Where did his 'I'll come by and see you tomorrow' come from? More than anything else, Miguel's shame about his family's home stabbed into his heart. He fought against tears. Mickey had just been into and out of another world without any opportunity to get a handle on what he had seen. His head was swimming with conflicting emotions. Had something profound just happened? Was grief... or guilt... or some sense of empathetic compassion eating at his soul? Or, was the combination of these and other feelings causing him to distort a reality he had not imagined before.

Passing HME again, then crossing Calle de El Cid, Mickey shook his head, "I'll come and see you tomorrow"... the words had arisen from somewhere in the depths of his soul without a prethought of any kind. As the dust billowed behind his car, the village became obscured. He found himself slowing down for some reason. Focusing his eyes on the side mirror of his Civic he felt a dizziness behind his eyes, the floating cloud of powdery dust raised by his car took an unusual form. Mickey thought for a moment that he discerned a face in the cluster of brown particles, an apparition? No, no... it was a face! A face so familiar that Mickey almost lost his breath. Signing himself he spoke more words that came from somewhere inside: "Thank you, dear Lord. I won't leave you back there." His breath was coming in measured spasms, his words from his soul: "I believe that this simple village is where you want me to be…" He slumped over the steering wheel for a long minute, sat up, then wiped perspiration from his brow: "Now, Lord, I need to know what you want me to do here."

He fought against tears of sadness for the Alexi Olivio family, and others who shared their poverty, but tears came anyhow–tears of melancholy that were mixed with tears of joy for this miraculous revelation. Some yet unknown and mysterious opportunity was beckoning… he could feel it settling deeply inside… he was being called by his Lord to make a difference.

37/ 'SATAN'S WINDOW'

David Rossman dropped Brian Slade off at the corner of Hennepin and LaSalle in downtown Minneapolis with instructions to try on and pick up the costume rental he'd ordered in advance from an internet site. He would meet Brian in an hour or so at Duffers, a trendy pub two blocks away. The priest's black suit fit Brian as if it were tailor made. He appraised himself in a full-length mirror, "Can I wear it home? You know, just for the fun of it? Put my other clothes in a bag?"

And, it was fun! While walking the downtown sidewalks of Minneapolis in the black and collar, passing people nodded respectfully, smiled approvingly, and greeted him with "Good afternoon, Father." What a trip, he thought, this is so totally cool! For the next two days, Brian wore his costume often, justifying his infatuation with the newly discovered status with the logic: "I've got to practice being a Catholic priest for the movie." Despite the buoyancy of pseudo-priesthood, Brian simply could not comprehend why a Hollywood producer would chose him, of all people, for a role in a major picture. Duane assured him that, as important and connected as Rossman was, the producer owed Duane some big favors.

Rossman assured Brian that the novice actor wouldn't have to memorize any lines; "We'll dub in what we need later," he said, while offering another insider's perspective on his high-tech 'business'. Rossman was thoroughly enjoying playing the mentor to an aspiring underling: "You see, in most movies there are people you've never heard of, 'character actors' is what they're called. There are thousands of them–some get noticed and make it big. I'll be honest with you, Brian, the chances of you becoming a Brad Pitt or Robert DiNiro are rather slim. Hollywood, you see, is kinda like dreamland. Lalaland... they call it–a thousand would-be Marylyn Monroes arrive there every day. 'Tinsel town', my favorite nickname, is also a heartbreak city to most. The smart ones find a day job, but there's nothing wrong with taking bit parts now and then if the money's there."

David Rossman and Duane had been explaining their project in detail to Brian and Dianne. Rossman portrayed the plotline as being an 'epic romance-drama. One of the main scenes, and their roles in making it, involved a priest and a prostitute: "The editors will splice-in our footage with other film being shot in Ireland and Boston, and–voila– a major movie is born. Film editors are the magicians of the industry." He noticed Brian's scowl over arms folded tightly to his chest and remembered Duane's caution that his younger brother was 'naïve but sensitive'. "But, if you're wondering about the big picture, the priest does find a redemption of sorts in the end. He..." The wheels in Rossman's mind were turning. "... He eventually repents and rises to become a Cardinal." Brian seemed even more perplexed, a Saint Louis baseball player he thought: Gimme a break? Maybe he'd been listening to Rossman's crapola too much, and not enough to his own better judgment and conscience. Something about the producer and the project was beginning to sound almost nonsensical to him. Was he getting himself into something he'd later have regrets about? He had promised his sister before leaving Duluth that he was going to keep his nose clean from now on. "I'm not doing a porn flick, if that's what you're thinking, no way in hell!" Brian blurted as he leaned forward in his chair. "That's all there is to it!" He looked toward Rossman and shook his head, then to a scowling Duane. Dianne Miller stood up from her chair, pointed a long finger at Brian; "Don't you dare mess it up fer all of us! My career? Mr. Rossman's fine repetition with the Hollywood people? Jeeze…"

Rossman swallowed a laugh at her use of the wrong word, then put a sympathetic hand on Dianne's bare shoulder, "Don't worry, sweetlips, you've got star power written all over ya. We'll get you a priest if you need one."

Duane's mind raced, Brian was the key to the entire scheme—without Brian, they had nothing! "Come on, bro." He bent down so that his eyes were level with Brian's, "You've got my word… this ain't no porno thing. Okay?"

Brain shook his head, "I don't believe you—but even if I did, that's not all that's been bothering me. What if Beth finds out? What's she gonna think of me doing this. She thinks you found me a real job, Duane."

Disgusted, Rossman slammed a sheath of papers and a clipboard on the coffee table, then stood up to leave: "That's it folks. I've had more than enough. I'm outta here. There are lotsa people out there just dying for an opportunity like this." Glaring across the room at Duane, his voice boomed for maximum dramatic effect: "F—-it all, I've had more than I can tolerate of your little brother's whimpering, Duane." He turned and glared into Brian's face, "You're nothing more than a flat-assed busted loser, kid—just like your brother told me you was. Opportunity of a lifetime comes along and you chicken-out. 'What will my sister think?…For god sake grow up, get a life! If it were porn, would your sister spend her money to see it?"

Rossman turned his back on the room, took a long stride toward the door, "I've got better ways to waste an evening. C'mon Dianne, baby… let's blow."

Dianne's eyes burned into Brian like a blowtorch, she leaned over and said, "Yer a wuss, a dickless wuss… I've got half a mind…"

"Just a minute," Brian leaned back in the chair, then stood up and returned her glare. "I ain't a wuss, don't nobody say I am. Okay! He ran his fingers through his longish hair, considered what to say or do next. Maybe Rossman was right about something, Beth would probably never ever see the movie. He certainly wasn't going to tell her anything about it. "How much money can I get up front for this so-called job? I mean, like, right now?"

Rossman stopped short of the door, pivoted: "A light finally go on, dimwit?" When producer David Rossman plunked two one hundred dollar bills on the kitchen counter, and promised Brian another fifty later, the film *'Satan's Window'* was about to be born.

Rossman's Pipers Motel, off Snelling Avenue, would serve as the primary shooting 'location'. Room 108 on the ground floor had a shear taffeta draped window that provided a false impression of privacy when the interior lights were dimmed. From a second story window in an old, two-story wood-framed quad that Rossman also owned on the adjacent lot, camera one would be able to film the motel's interior room scenes below. Camera two would be set up in the motel's narrow hallway. The cast would include four of Rossman's motel clerks, three of whom would be playing roles as 'Johns', and the other as a bartender. Each of the Johns would be filmed entering room 108 for a massage with the sultry 'Dagmar', played by Dyana Marsh– Dianne Miller's new stage name. Dagmar would be wearing a scanty negligee. No one had any lines to memorize and only Rossman had a copy of the faux script.

Camera one, in the apartment building window, was equipped with a rented Cannon XF100 camera and 10x lens and would be manned by Duane Slade. Rossman would direct from the hallway and operate camera two. To establish the right mood, Rossman explained the character role each would portray. Dagmar (Dianne) would unabashedly display her everything in each scene. "Your body is your ticket to stardom," Rossman assured.

Father Francis McGill, played by John Ray Black (Brian) was the story's protagonist. Brian liked the Hollywood moniker Rossman had chosen for him and was beginning to believe that he may, however remote the odds might seem, have a future in the industry.

38/ MODERN DAY ROBIN HOODS

The filming of 'Satan's Window' was accomplished in three hours on a late December Saturday afternoon. Pains were taken to assure that the recording maintained an 'amateurish' quality. As the three men reviewed the final cuts the following night in Duane's apartment, they were unanimous–the video's quality was first rate. Dianne wasn't able to join her coworkers because she had a date with one of the Johns she had met on the motel set the day before. Only the three segments depicting Brian and 'Dagmar' were on the edited DVD they had been watching. One segment was Father McGill (Brian) and Dagmar (Dianne) having drinks at the Piper Motel bar– the meeting of priest and prostitute was shot from a table at right angle from the bar with Rossman's camera two. As agreed, only rarely was a quick full-face shot of Brian filmed. His acting instructions were simple: "Just remember that you're nervous about being recognized by someone, okay. You look around from time to time, okay... " The cut of the bar scene worked quite well, Father McGill looked highly agitated and nervous. Next were clips of Father McGill at the door of Room 108. The priest, after looking surreptitiously down the hallway, took Dagmar by the shoulders as an excited Dagmar gave him a wet kiss and pulled him inside the room. Brian had trouble with Dianne's wanton nakedness. His protest that "She rubs them against me too much" did not fall upon deaf ears. The directors went out of their way to keep Father McGill happy.

"Take it easy with the boobs on the holy man, Sweets," Rossman said with a quick wink.

Another related compromise evolved from some professional coaching from director Rossman: "Okay, after you look briefly down the hallway toward the camera, you can turn your shoulder back slightly... that will block out the boobs a bit, then, if you want to, you can close your eyes for a moment. Dianne, don't overdo the seduction thing. He's, Brian–I mean Father McGill– he's supposed to be the hungry one." The second take was not first-rate, but adequate.

Finally, the close-up shots from camera one in the window of the house next door were reviewed. Dagmar was in her panties while taking off the priest's jacket and collar. Brian had refused to fully undress so the concluding shot was from behind with him in his underwear. Even at that, the scene left little to the imagination. When Father McGill turned the bedside lamp off, the tape ended with a fuzzy gray-blackness...

After the edited preview session, Brian went to his bedroom to read a magazine article on the Demi Moore tragedy–if he had a gun right now, Brian might go out and shoot Ashton Kutcher for his infidelity. With some of his new wealth he had purchased nearly every Hollywood magazine at a local convenience store and was becoming increasingly intrigued by a Hollywood lifestyle; a culture that might be his one day soon. He couldn't help imagining John Ray Black... walking across the red carpet... the cameras and the adoring throng. Something broke his reverie. "Don't worry, damn it! Moran will get the money!" His brother's voice was high-pitched, insistent. The bedroom door had been left slightly ajar and, when he strained, he could make out the conversation between the two movie moguls. He put the magazine aside, put his ear to the opening and picked up the thread of what the his brother and Rossman were talking about. Suddenly, he stormed into the living room. "I heard that," he shouted. Brian Slade was furious! Pointing his finger at Rossman, he hollered:

"You can't do that! We'll all go to prison. Gimme that CD, right now." Realizing what Duane and his sleazy partner were planning to do with the DVD, he lunged toward the DVD player. In the moment it took him to eject the disk, Duane had his large hand on Brian's elbow. He yanked Brain off balance and, violently twisting his brother's wrist, he rescued the disc. "What and the hell do you think you're doing?" Duane shouldered Brian to the side of the room. "This ain't your property, Brian. Belongs to Mr. Rossman and the studio."

"What bullshit–there is no studio. I'm not as dumb as you might think. You did this to blackmail that priest... go ahead–tell me that's not what I heard you talking about. Go ahead, tell me another lie!"

"You misunderstand everything, Bry. Get real for a change. Think outside the box for once." Duane's voice had a calming tone. "In this day and age it's all about money–first, how to get it and second, how to spend it. Understand? To get it, sometimes ya bend the rules a bit."

Rossman chimed in, his tone angry: "You don't really have any clue about what we're doing here. You're too naïve. Put this in your pipe and smoke it Brian: we're taking a little money from people that have lots more of it than they need... we're talking lots of dough here... and we're just planning to redistribute some of it. The money we take is the same money they took from folks like us in the first place. We're kinda like modern day Robin Hoods if you think about it."

Brian laughed in Rossman's face: "Stupid Brian, huh? He'll swallow anything, right? That's what you guys think–but you're wrong, dead wrong. You guys lied to me–you used me, and you're not going to get away with it. Just wait and see." He assessed the situation, Duane was only an arm's length away, Rossman sitting deep in the sofa. "I would never... " He suddenly grabbed Duane's hand, yanking as hard as he could, trying to wrestle the disk from his brother's grip. "Give it to me, damn it!"

Once more, Duane's bulk and strength were too much for Brian to overcome. Forced to let go, he stepped back, "I'm not going to be involved in any blackmail scheme," he said. "What you're planning to do is sick and it's criminal, too–I don't care what kinda spin you put on it. We're a bunch of Robin Hoods?–how lame is that? I've lived with cons day and night for three years–I've heard some wild things, but nothing as crazy as that. You guys are no different from them, you have a way of thinking you can do anything–just don't get caught. Well, I'm not going to be a part of it."

Duane had given up trying to cajole his brother, leaning into Brian he laughed in his face, "You already are a part of it all, bro. You saw the video, stupid, you're one of the stars! Use your head for a change, we're all in this together–all four of us, like peas in a pod."

Brian took a sudden and wild swing, Duane stepped aside, and countered with a sharp right to the jaw of his brother. Brian staggered back, regained his balance, then lunged a second time with both hands going for Duane's throat, "You bastard!"

Rossman pulled himself off the couch with the speed and agility of a frightened hippo, stepped behind Brian, got a hammerlock on the smaller man, then bent him over and pressed him onto the carpet. "Like Duane said," he was puffing heavily, "you're part of it all, kiddo–just like me and your brother. Makes no dif if you like it or not, okay...?" The bulky man was breathing heavily from the exertion of wrestling Brian away from Duane. "We all sink or swim together, Slade."

Fearing a heart attack, Rossman lifted himself off of Brian, allowing Duane to take his place keeping Brian subdued: "Don't you ever come at me like that again... I'll break your goddamned neck!"

Undeterred by the threat, Brian again swung recklessly at Duane's face, caught the side of his head above the ear. Duane swore and punched Brian twice in the face, "Take that! Want more? Come at me again... " he taunted.

Bloodied and beaten, Brian's voice was more whimper than warning; "Gimme that CD, Duane. I'll go to the cops. I swear I will . .. I'll tell'em everything..."

Duane only laughed at the threat: "Go to the cops? You stupid ass, you'd just be asking for more time in the Ramsey pen. You keep adding to the pile of dumb that you already are. You got a track record with them... me and Dave are clean as whistles. Your word against ours–figger it out."

Rossman, the peacemaker, stepped between the irate brothers like a referee, "Let's just settle down; both of you. Nobody's going to the police. Got that, Brian?"

Brian's nose was bleeding, tears welling in his puffy eyes. "Why did you guys lie to me? Hollywood... what crap that was... and I almost believed it. I guess you're both right,–I am stupid!"

Duane offered his hand, "No you're not. I didn't really mean what I said. Rossman didn't either. Just cool down a bit and listen to reason. Okay? In the end we're all going to be rich. Probably much more so than if this was really a second rate Hollywood movie.

Brian shook his head, "You guys might get rich, not me... I'm outta here." Dabbing at his nose with his handkerchief, he walked into the bedroom, took his duffle out from under the bed, and stuffed his clothing and shave kit inside. He'd leave the movie star magazines behind. He was done with the fairy-tale world. Hanging on a chair beside his unmade bed was the rented costume he hadn't yet returned, just for spite he threw that into his bag as well. Minutes later he stormed across the living room carpet to the door, he glared back at the two men sitting on the sofa: "I'd rather be a fool than a blackmailer. I hope I never see either one of you again."

"You rat us out, Brian... you're a dead man. Got that?" Duane said.

"He's not kidding you... we got people..." Rossman left his threat hanging.

Disregarding the grim warnings, Brian Slade slammed the door.

After assuring Rossman that Brian could be trusted to keep his mouth shut, the two men returned to the details they had been discussing. It was agreed that they would send one copy of the video to Father Moran at Saint Gerard's parish in west Duluth along with their extortion note and a demand for one million dollars.

"Hell yes, the Moran's have got it," Duane reassured his partner. "I've done my research. They're loaded–they have their own foundation and give money away. A million will be easy as pie for them. We can go after more later if we wanna."

Both agreed to meet again after the mailing. The enclosed letter would let the priest know that if he went to the police there would be dire consequences. The letter and the CD would be cleaned of any prints and handled with latex gloves. Duane Slade and David Rossman had seen their share of crime stories on television and weren't about to be tripped up by some foolish mistake. "The priest will go to his parents for the money; probably concoct some kind of story as to what he needs it for–a charity most likely. He gonna be scared shitless."

Their follow-up contact would be on a phone that couldn't be traced. They would tell the priest when and where to make the money drop, and insist that the bills be in small denomination that could not be traced. Duane would mail the CD and letter from a post office in Minneapolis the following morning. Then, they would wait a week or ten days before the call. Both Duane and Rossman would each keep a copy of the video for themselves. The two men shook hands and clinked their highball glasses. "We're gonna be in the money, Ross," Duane used a nickname for the first time. "What'cha gonna do with your half?"

Back on the street that night, Brian called his sister. "Beth, the job down here didn't pan out," he said. "Think I can find something in Duluth?"

~

That very same January night in Venice, Florida, Mickey found a Trek bike store, visited with the mechanic in the repair shop, and negotiated the purchase of a twenty-dollar rehabbed Schwinn bicycle. At a Walgreen's near the motel, he made a second purchase–a disposable cell phone. In the morning he would check out of the Motel 6 and travel to TriPalms with the bike. If everything went as he prayed it would, he might become a resident of Little Haiti for some time to come. His appointment with Bishop Cordoba in Venice would have to be put on hold, Mickey was embarking on a rehab project of his own definition; he would work his hardest at becoming the priest that he believed his God wanted him to be. Later, he would share his decision with Mario... his parents would have to be kept in the dark for now.

Mickey's plan, however well intended it seemed to him right now, was not without incumbent stress. He was violating his vow of obedience again. He prayed to Saint Joseph for some sign that he was doing the right thing, but Saint Joe wasn't about to give him an immediate answer. He knew that what he was choosing to do would have consequences–probably dire consequences. Whatever... his mind was made up.

39/ STUNNED, SHOCKED, AND STAGGERED!

In late January, millions of Americans from Berkeley to Bangor, to Branson and every 'B' in between, were fervently awaiting the Super Bowl. Judging from the two weeks of hype, this event, more than any other secular or religious, defined contemporary American culture. In one generation this football extravaganza had surpassed Independence Day. Sunday Super Bowl parties respected no limits in terms of expenditure. The amount of food consumed was second only to Thanksgiving Day. An NBC report predicted that 1.25 billion chicken wings would be consumed, 11 million tons of chips, enough beer to fill twenty Olympic-sized pools, and a total of 1800 calories would be consumed by every American–man, woman, and child, whether watching on a jumbo screen TV somewhere or a hundred miles from the nearest set. A male child born on this Sunday would likely be named Eli or Tom or Brady... a girl... maybe Manning?

In Saint Paul, Duane Slade and David Rossman shared a mutual stress of another kind; not over bets they had placed on the big game, but rather over a carefully designed plan that wasn't working anything like they had expected. The CD package had been sent to the Saint Gerard's parish rectory on January 13th–that was already two weeks ago. Father Moran had not been in contact with them. Duane's theory was that the priest needed more time than they had originally thought in order to get the million dollars released from the family foundation without raising any suspicions. (What lies that priest was going to have to tell!) Rossman worried that the Feds had been contacted and the two of them should lay low, maybe even skip town for a while. "You give me half of the seven bills I've already laid out for this farce and we'll call it even," Rossman said. "If you want to pursue it further, you can go ahead without me."

"Maybe we should'a sent the CD to this priest's parents, a guy named Amos... can you believe that, Amos? Strange name, like the cookies."

Duane's laugh was nervous, his brow deeply furrowed. He was nearly broke, half of $700 was about $300 more than he could get his hands on. Finances were so tight that he would be hard-pressed to cover *any* share of Rossman's alleged costs. He actually wanted to borrow some money from his partner to pay this month's rent.

Rossman contemplated his edgy partner; there was neither honor nor trust among thieves. He smiled crookedly, "Maybe we could give that idea a shot–get the parents involved, play the shame game on them. Wouldn't hurt, I guess– maybe this Amos guy can round up the money easier than his kid can." David Rossman was anything but a fool, there was no way that a scoundrel like Duane Slade was going to beat him out of his share of a million bucks. Taunting his partner for half the expenses was an attempt to see how cold Duane's feet were getting.

"Nothing ventured, nothing gained," Duane offered a fitting cliché.

What the two did not know wouldn't hurt them. The package did arrive at Saint Gerard's on the 15th along with a few letters addressed to Fr. Moran. As he had been instructed, substitute pastor, Fr. Graham, dispatched all the mail to the bishop's office. Most mail directed to the bishop's attention was opened and sorted by Molly Matonich, the office secretary with nearly twenty years of service to the Duluth diocese. Molly immediately brought the package to the bishop, as Father Moran had become a 'missing person' of significant concern to His Grace.

The whereabouts of the wayward priest remained unknown. According to the last report, Father Moran had registered on schedule at a Motel 6 in Venice–already two weeks ago. The package, simply addressed to Father Moran and postmarked from Minneapolis, was a curiosity to the bishop. He cut through the thick bands of scotch tape, and retrieved the plastic case. A sticker affixed to the case was marked with 'XXX'. He opened the envelope attached to the CD first and read the typed message:

'If you do not want this video to get out to the public, round up $- 1 million dollars in small bills. You will be contacted soon. Do not call the cops or you will really be in for trouble.'

Bremmer puzzled at the unsigned threat. He slipped the disk into his computer, clicked on the icon, *'Satan's Window'* appeared on the screen. What the bishop saw in the next seventy-two seconds stunned, shocked and staggered him more than anything he had seen in all his years. He heard a gasp that wasn't his own as Molly Matonich clutched the half open door to keep herself from falling to the floor in total disbelief. All Bremmer could say at the moment was, "Don't breathe a word of this!" Speechless, Molly could only nod as she pulled the door closed behind her.

As intelligent and resourceful as he was, the bishop was in a complete quandary about what he should do. He read and reread the letter demanding one million dollars without giving thought to the fact that he was contaminating vital evidence with his fingerprints. The scholarly bishop was too overwhelmed to be thinking coherently. He had called Amos Moran twice during Father Michael's absence, and now felt compelled to call him again–with more devastating news than previously. He took several long minutes to collect himself before placing the call to Naples.

The bishop did not begin the conversation with any small talk or pleasantry. "Mr. Moran, this situation has tested my patience beyond capacity. I must locate your son immediately! Surely you have heard something from him… ?"

"Your Grace, I've only spoken to my son twice–as I've already told you. In his last call, from Venice, and I was shocked to learn he was on some kind of sabbatical–he wouldn't give me any details. But, I've already told you that. He assured me that he was fine and not to worry." Amos was mildly frustrated with the bishop. "I'm not aiding and abetting my son if that's what you are implying. He's a grown man...if he's under great stress right now–as you claimed in our last conversation– you couldn't tell it by me. He sounded just fine on the phone and was in wonderful spirits at our family Christmas."

Christmas had been one month before and all that Mickey had told his parents days afterward was that he was going to take a vacation–a road trip of sorts, and that he might even have an opportunity to visit them in Naples after they got back to Florida. "No he hasn't been to our house. We're as puzzled about that as you are, Bishop."

Bishop Bremmer had no tangible reason to disbelieve the Mickey's father, and apologized profusely: "Please don't think I'm accusing you of any complicity or misbehavior, Mister Moran. Nothing could be further from the truth."

"I understand, Your Grace," Amos said.

A long pause brought a repeat understanding from Amos.

"I'm afraid that I have some... rather... devastating news to report. Are you by yourself, ahhhem...?" Bishop Bremmer cleared his throat.

"No... my wife's here... why?"

"What I have to tell you is... very sensitive."

"If this concerns my son, Sadie has every right to know. What do you mean? Sensitive?" Amos' voice tightened.

The bishop explained the video and read the letter of demands.

"Someone is playing a horrible practical joke... what you're describing is so far out of bounds that it hardly warrants a response."

"That is not my Mickey!" The voice was Sadie's standing nearby her husband. "Maybe some pervert looks like my son, but that is not... I repeat, that is not my boy that you are talking about. How can you even think... ?"

"I can only tell you what I've just viewed on my computer, Mrs. Moran." The bishop expected initial denial. He would not push the issue any further at this time. "I'm only reporting, Mrs. Moran–don't kill the messenger. " I'm not making any accusations. I hope you understand that."

"This whole business about my son is really beginning to weigh on me, sir. I can only wonder what you, or the Catholic Church, have done to Mickey. He is not a deviant of any sort. He's the most sincere, genuine, loving person…". Sadie's emotions were getting the better of her, she passed the phone back to Amos, "You take over for me, hon."

Bremmer felt the tension as if it were an electricity passing through the airwaves. "Is this Mister Moran again? One more question needs to be raised."

"We're both listening," Sadie said. "You can speak to both of us, bishop," Amos said. "This is quite sensitive and personal… please forgive my asking, but does your family have that kind of money?"

Amos answered quickly and succinctly, "Yes. Next question."

∼

Only two people outside of TriPalms knew where Mickey was and what he was doing. Father Mario was one of them. Larry Wheeler was the other.

As a teenager, Mickey met Larry while his family was vacationing in Naples. The Morans had rented a three-bedroom stucco bungalow on Banyan Boulevard, the Wheelers lived a block closer to the Gulf beaches. The two teens bonded immediately and spent most days hanging out together at Lowdermilk Park on the Gulf–only three blocks from where they lived–often sneaking onto the golf course behind their houses, and bicycling throughout the city.

Mickey was Twins fan, Larry loved the Red Sox, and the two of them often took a bus up to Ft. Myers to watch their respective teams during spring training. Bragging rights almost always belonged to Mickey's friend.

Over the years, the two had kept in touch with a phone call from time to time, or an email–usually their conversations centered on baseball and childhood memories. The previous fall, Mickey's Twins had lost 99 games after winning the Central Division the year before. The Red Sox had collapsed in September and missed the playoffs entirely. Both had good reason to razz the other, it was just a matter of which of their respective teams had had the worst season. An answer to that question would probably challenge a panel of baseball pundits.

Larry's family owned Wheeler Development, one of southwestern Florida's largest real estate contractors. After his father's untimely death, Larry–a Notre Dame graduate–took the reins of the fledging company with every intention of growing what his father had started. Larry, his wife Lori, and their two children, now lived in a modest Port Royal home in a fashionable area of Naples. They might easily have purchased the largest home on Galleon Drive, but instead lived in one of the least conspicuous. Lori had grown up in Spencer, Iowa and her small town values infused her family. The Wheelers were well known in Naples for their civic involvement and benevolence; their family Foundation made annual grants to nearly every charity and worth cause in Collier County.

40/ A BUMP ON THE ROAD TO TRIPALMS

Becoming a resident of TriPalms would not happen without overcoming a few bumps in the dusty road that led to the Hispanic immigrant enclave. Before taking the new bicycle to Miguel, Mickey decided to respect the family headship of the boy's father, Alexi Olivio. It would be inappropriate and counter-productive to do otherwise.

In the morning, before the downtown Venice restaurant was open for business, Mickey parked his car and went to the same back door of Carney's Irish Pub that he had visited the previous day. After knocking several times. Maria opened the kitchen door a crack and saw Mickey standing there with a wide smile on his face.

"What do you want...?" Maria did not quite know how to address this man whom her brother had said was a priest. He did not look like any priest that Maria had ever seen.

"Good morning, Maria. Buenos dias, Senorita." Wearing a grin of satisfaction with his Spanish, he added, "May I speak with your father, please?"

Maria looked over her shoulder into the kitchen with obvious embarrassment and discomfort. The reality of talking to a Catholic priest in an alley doorway was the stuff of cheap fiction. Again, she had serious doubts of her brother Miguel's claim. She spoke to someone–probably her father– inside the bacon grease smelling kitchen. Mickey waited patiently, keeping his confident smile, as the staccato Spanish conversation inside played itself out. He wished he had taken Spanish in college instead of music appreciation and other electives of questionable merit.

The evening before, when Miguel told his family that the wonderful man who had given him a ride to TriPalms was named Mickey, and was a Catholic priest, he invited unwanted skepticism. Alexi Olivio found the news to be confusing and disturbing. "Are you certain that this priest, as you say he is, said that he would see you tomorrow, Miguel?" Alexi asked his son in Spanish. "Or is this more of your imagination." Miguel was often known to exaggerate things, and make up stories to get attention. "Look at me and quit your daydreaming, son. I will put you over my knee!"

"Yes, father–that is the truth." He said in Spanish.

Maria scolded her younger brother, "Speak Inglais to your father." The household rule was that every child spoke English when in the house.

Miguel reaffirmed what the priest had said: "Honest to God, Father!"

The boy knew immediately that he had misspoken as soon as he said it–to use God as his witness was profane.

"To bed with you, pray for God's forgiveness. I will tolerate no more of this nonsense!" Alexi barked, waving his hand in dismissal.

Fifteen year-old, Livan Olivio, whose bike had been damaged, attempted to support Miguel, "Papa, Miguel would not lie about this. I can tell when he is dishonest." Livan's heart ached with empathy for his younger brother.

"Enough of this." Alexi looked from one face to another at his family crowded around his chair in the living room. His wife, Octavia, stood, nodded to her husband: "Excuse me, I must get to my chores." The children: pouting Maria, saddened Livan, confused Cali and Carissa–the seven year-old twins–looked from one to the other not knowing how to react to their usually mellow father's angry demonstration.

"I have things to do as well," Alexi said. "I'll be back later."

Alexi met with his older brother, Alberto, and several other adult men in the Hector Munoz trailer that often served as a village meeting place. It was early on a sultry January evening and the men, as was their patriarchal privilege and custom, would get away from their crowded family quarters for an hour or two to chat and smoke. It was important for them to discuss matters of the day without the distraction of their womenfolk and children.

"Your son imagines too many things, Alexi. Remember when he had us all believing that there was a twenty foot boa constrictor near the frog pond?" They all had a chuckle over the memory of the invisible snake. The village men seemed to believe that the stranger Miguel had brought to the village was nothing more than a good gringo Samaritan. They told Alexi not to worry. The man, whomever he was, wasn't likely to come back to TriPalms. "It would be an embarrassment to all of us for a holy priest to mingle with our simple villagers," said Alberto, an outspoken elder. "If what my nephew says is true, and this man does come here again, you must ask him to leave us alone, Alexi." Alberto spoke with authority and Alexi listened with deference. His older brother was his benefactor and the one person most responsible for getting his family from Puerto Rico to America. All of the elders nodded their agreement with Alberto's instruction. To a man, they wished that Hector Munoz were with them to confirm what Alberto had ordered. Munoz was held in the highest esteem by every soul in TriPalms. His decision on any matter was indisputable, he would know what to do about this or any stranger to their community. Unfortunately, Hector Munoz was in Tampa on business.

Jose Parada, one of Munoz' employees spoke: "What if this man is an ICE agent? What if he is here to find illegals, to check papers? Then what?"

The federal agency, Immigration and Customs Enforcement, was more dreaded than the devil himself. With Parada's questions, the elder's conversations took a more somber tone.

Mickey had been waiting for long minutes and was about to poke his head into the kitchen when Maria reappeared at the door. "Papa thanks you again for helping Miguel yesterday. That was very good of you. What more do you want?" Maria didn't like the rudeness her words might have conveyed. She knew that this man had become Miguel's 'super hero' but she also knew that her father didn't want the boy's infatuation to go any further than it already had. Her father's wishes were inviolate.

"Can your father find me a place to live in TriPalms?"

Maria felt a constriction in her throat. Live in TriPalms... why in God's name would he want to do that? She could have answered 'no' to such an absurdity on her own, but she posed the question to her father.

Alexi came to the service doorway, he spoke to his daughter without making any eye contact with Mickey. Mickey could imagine what Alexi was saying by the unsympathetic expression his face.

"My father says it is not possible. Nobody has any place for a boarder; every home is overcrowded now. He is sorry that you have no place to live."

Mickey laughed discretely, "That's not the problem, Maria, not at all. I already have a place where I can live, but it is my hope to get to know your people better. Maybe I can help with some…" He didn't want to disparage what he knew to be their substandard living conditions so he let his sentence drop. What he wanted to say wasn't coming off very well.

Maria frowned, Alexi looked to his daughter for a translation. "Que el hombre?"

Mickey would go out on a limb of sorts, "Tell your father that I am a Catholic priest without a parish at this time. He would be doing me a great favor if he could help me serve our Lord in your village. A great favor…" he repeated. Was there a better word than serve to describe what he hoped to accomplish in TriPalms? Having no clear idea about what he might be able to do, he hoped to avoid any direct questions. If they were confused by what he was trying to say, Mickey was even more so.

Serious, even heated Spanish dialogue between daughter and father gave Mickey a bad feeling, a feeling of being an unwanted imposition on their lives. Maria broke away from her Spanish: "He is sorry that he cannot help you, sir–I mean Father." With a pained expression on her lovely face, she said: "We are wanting to apologize, you must go now please and we must get back to our work." She turned away and closed the door.

The sun baked the landscape to a dryness of such severity that a spark might ignite a massive forest fire. Mickey had driven out to Tri-Palms but pulled off to the side of the dirt road about fifty yards before the first row of trailers. He would wait there all day if necessary, until someone offered some hospitality or invited him to come in. Most of the people who passed by were on road-battered bicycles; men and women who were adept at avoiding potholes which might send them flying over their handlebars into the bordering palmettos. None of the cyclists stopped yet each offered Mickey a wave along with a curious smile. Most of the incoming traffic consisted of landscaping trucks pulling trailers of various sized. The few cars that passed by had seen better days.

It was just after seven in the early evening when Mickey spotted the headlights of a crowded white van, the transport that the Olivios shared with several others from the village. Mickey waved as it rattled past him, leaving another thick cloud of dust in its wake. Having spent the last six hours at the roadside, Mickey wore a coating of brown and had probably eaten a pound of dust. He would prove to be more determined to get into TriPalms than the villagers were determined to keep him out.

Darkness had settled like a blanket over the cooling evening. Somewhere after eight o'clock, Mickey watched as several people approached him from the village. Two of the men leading the procession held Coleman lanterns, Alexi, walking off to the side, was focusing the beam of his flashlight on the road ahead of him. The group stopped only feet from where Mickey was leaning against the fender of his Civic. A man that Alexi called Alberto seemed to be the party's spokesman, "We do not wish to disrespect a man of God, sir. Not in any way." His English was passable but not nearly as good as Maria's. "Is it true that you are… a priest of God?" The others pressed closer to hear an answer. "Have you any kind of identification?" From the crowd Mickey heard someone ask, "Can you say the holy Mass?" Then, mumbling.

Mickey nodded with noticeable reservation. The second and third questions were sticklers–he couldn't lie. "Yes, I am Father Mickey, Father Michael Moran, from a place in Minnesota that you have never heard of. I don't yet know if I can say Mass… I would have to get permission from Bishop Cordoba to do that." Mickey reached for his wallet, "My drivers license gives my name as Reverend Michael Moran."

Alberto waved his dismissal, "Papers... You know... like we, each of us, must have papers to work? To be legal."

"No. I'm sorry." Mickey didn't know how he might explain the concept of a sabbatical leave to the men, so he let the matter float for the moment. He wished now that he had chosen to pack his chalice and paten instead of his guitar, perhaps they would be a convincing verification.

More conversation went back and forth among the men. All were looking at one another and shrugging their shoulders in apparent confusion. "Why do you want to live in TriPalms? You have already seen that ours is a very poor place to live."

Mickey's eyes met Alberto's dark stare: "I want to live among good people, Alberto. Good people like you... and Alexi, that's all. And I want to live where I can serve God in a different way than I have in the past."

Apparently, Mickey had answered the question well enough to evoke a smile for the first time. Alberto said, "Yes we are different from you, but we are good people."

Mickey's comment had been partially misconstrued. "Yes, you are good people–I am the one who is different."

Alberto laughed, the others joined him without knowing quite why. Two of the men gestured for Alberto to come over to the side of the road where they had huddled together. Several of them talked amongst themselves for nearly five minutes while Mickey waited.

Alberto and Alexi stepped forward together. Alberto said: "Come in our village tonight. Hector will be here tomorrow. Maybe he will find you a place. It will be for him to decide."

Mickey thanked them, "Gracias..."

Following the parade into TriPalms in his car, Mickey couldn't help but wonder what was meant by 'Hector will be here tomorrow'. Who or what was Hector?

On his first night in TriPalms, Mickey slept in the front seat of his Civic, declining an invitation to stay with Alberto Olivio's family.

41/ GOALS OR A BULLDOZER

The two oldest residents of TriPalms were Arturo and Lucia Placencio. Out of respect for their age, the two Cubans enjoyed a one-bedroom trailer to themselves. Arturo had been a legendary baseball player in the Cuban leagues years before the American majors had been integrated for Latino players. Neither spoke more than a few words of English but their love and hospitality expressed a language of its own. Rarely had Mickey been more warmly received by strangers.

For the first two days, Mickey remained an anomaly to everybody. The villagers were respectful and pleasant but had no idea what his presence among them was supposed to accomplish. Of course there were rumors passing among the men and women of the community. Some believed that the Church had excommunicated him; others that he had committed some heinous crime and was on the run; and in some minds there was the suspicion of a combination of both. In that it is human nature to add one's own embellishment to something when passing it along to the next person, eventually the portrait of Father Mickey became quite distorted. Many held the simple belief that he was a good man but not a priest at all.

Yet, on the other side, there were some who perceived him as a priest—sent by God himself to help the people of the TriPalms. This distinct minority found scant support those early days when Mickey did little more than hang out with the children—playing their games, reading books to them (he couldn't read the Spanish, so he improvised stories to go with the pictures—much to the delight of all) and teaching them a few words of English while he was at it. If the adults mostly kept their distance, the children were far less inhibited. Miguel had younger twin sisters, and several first cousins who helped to break the ice with all the others. When with the children, of course, the eyes of the parents were always alert for any untoward behavior.

Amidst the apparent confusion regarding his true identity, one resident accepted him without reservation. To the locals he was simply 'Tortuga'–a name that Mickey would later learn meant some form of the word turtle in Spanish. Miguel told him that nobody knew where the dog came from or how long he'd been around. "We've always called him Tortuga because he never runs and moves fast like a turtle." The boy laughed along with Mickey at the description. Tortuga was as devoted as only a dog can be. The limping, old mongrel was a mixture of Labrador, Whippet, and some breed that contributed a long and furry tail. Whatever his unique genetic combinations, Tortuga (Torts, to Mickey) was an adoptee of the entire community who shared his days and nights with many different families. It seemed, however, that Torts was becoming most comfortable when relaxing in the shade beneath the back bumper of Mickey's Civic. When Miguel why Tortuga always lingered at Mickey's heels, he suggested: "I think he likes the smell of my feet."

Miguel's next question, "Did you ever have a dog, Father?" inspired a lengthy conversation and a warm nostalgia. When Mickey was seven or so, his father brought home a two year-old English bulldog–a surprise birthday gift for Meghan who had wanted a dog since she was a little girl. 'MacArthur' had worn out his welcome with the Versich family from Keewatin. "He's the most lovable dog in the world," George Versich told Amos as he accepted a check for $200. 'Mac' was truly loveable, but... "After the dog chewed his fifth pair of my moms shoes, destroyed my dad's favorite chair in the rec room, added countless yellow stains to the basement carpet, and once even pooped under the dining room table when my parents were entertaining guests..." Mickey told the boy that Mac was given to a family in Chisholm whose bulldog had passed away the month before.

The Olivios, among the predominantly Catholic populace, were considered by most to be Mickey's host family. Being that Alexi Olivio's family was held in considerable respect, Mickey would not remain a stranger for very long. Yet, nobody including Mickey himself, had discerned exactly what he was supposed to be doing in Tri-Palms. An old adage that he had picked up somewhere seemed to fit his circumstance perfectly: 'Don't push the river, it flows by itself.' At times he felt as if his prayers were bouncing off some unseen barrier between himself and his God, and ending up back in his lap.

On his third day, Mickey was invited to participate in a game of soccer with some boys of Miguel's age. On the west edge of the community a large dirt patch served as their playing field. Mickey succumbed to the heat and dust after about half an hour of running up and down the concrete-like surface. He was called for infractions several times—mostly illegal touches with his hands—and, despite his size advantage, was unable to distinguish himself in any aspect of the game. Of the five times he kicked the ball, two went to an opponent and one forced his own goalie to make a remarkable save. The other two accomplished little more than getting rid of the ball to someone who knew what to do with it.

Miguel plopped down beside Mickey and Torts in the spotty shade of some starving live oaks. "Next time we will let you try playing goalie, Father. I think you might have good hands and feet for that." Mickey laughed to himself. In the subtle manner of a respectful child, Miguel was suggesting that he might be less of a liability standing out of everybody's way at the end of the dirt field.

Mickey sipped some tepid water that Lucia had boiled for his canteen that morning. Today might offer his best opportunity to find out what he might be able to accomplish here—being a nice guy to the children didn't go far enough and probably raised some suspicious eyebrows. "Miguel, if you and your amigos could have anything they wanted, what do you think that would be?"

Miguel pondered a world of possibilities for a long moment. "Anything at all, Father? Even if much money is needed?"

Mickey nodded, "Si…"

Scratching his head, Miguel's eyes suddenly flashed: "Goals."

Mickey shrugged, "Goals? You mean like… what you want to become? Aims?"

Miguel laughed, "Oh, yes. We need to know what we want to be some day, but… goals! You know, goals?"

Mickey shook his head in ignorance.

"Father, the soccer field has no goals."

Mickey laughed at himself. The children played with two crooked poles at each end of the field. "Are you sure, goals more than anything else you can think of, Miguel?"

"Yes. Can you get us some goals?"

He told Miguel that he could probably do that. "Now, what I mean by anything is… you must use your imagination, okay?… something almost impossible. Something that you might only dream about."

Miguel thought hard, his brow was furrowed, then a quick smile crossed his brown face; "A big swimming pool! That would be so wonderful." Then his smile faded, "Papa says that in the city many, many families have a swimming pool of their own behind their big houses. Is that really true?" Sometimes Miguel asked questions that he already knew the answer to. Every twelve year old in TriPalms knew that there were two worlds–their world and that of the wealthy white people. It had always been that way and would always be so.

Mickey's assessments of what TriPalms needed would be a Herculean challenge to accomplish. An elementary school of their own was probably out of the question, but maybe the construction of a small library would be a possibility. A library could serve as a pre-school venue that might attract a Head Start program as well as provide a meeting place for adults. Why not? Why not build a community center with a library and a classroom and… a gymnasium? Scratch the gym–that would add too much additional cost. As exciting as the project seemed, there were other basics that might have to take priority. Life and death and community health matters like a new well for fresh water and an adequate sewerage disposal system. These were less conspicuous but critical necessities as the entire village infrastructure was woefully inadequate.

Later that day, Mickey was sitting in a lawn chair in front of the Placencio's small trailer with a thick Malachi Martin novel. The heat inside was unbearable and within minutes, he would become headachy and nauseous. He waved at Maria, five trailers down and across the narrow gravel roadway. It was a day off for her so she was babysitting the neighborhood girls who adored their 'big sis'. At the moment, Maria was playing a jump rope game with her little sisters and another girl about five. "Come over later," he called down the street. "I've got something I want to ask you."

Maria nodded and within about ten minutes slowly made her way to where Mickey was sitting with his book and fanning himself with the brim of his Twins baseball cap. As everybody did, the petite Latina leaned over to give Tortuga a good scratch behind his floppy ears, causing the dog's shaggy tail to make a sweep across the sandy ground. As he tried to lick her hand, Torts groaned his pleasure at the attention.

Maria was in her early twenties, with dark hair that flowed over her delicate shoulders, a long neck, and a slender but shapely body. She was easily the best looking young woman Mickey had seen in TriPalms. He had always believed that Hispanic women married young, had lots of children, and lost their youthful shape by the time they were in their thirties. He immediately chided himself; ethnic and cultural stereotypes were the relationship barriers of small-minded people. As she approached he reminded himself–Maria's life is none of your business! Mickey had been careful not to say or do anything that might be considered flirtatious–yet, he could tell by her subtle glances that Maria was probably mildly infatuated with him.

Yet, while he found a warm acceptance from her parents and from the Olivio children, Maria remained noticeably distant.

"Maria, I have a question for you, he said as Maria stood several feet from him. "I asked your brother the same question earlier today."

Her expression was unreadable. "What?"

"Okay, here it is. If I had a million dollars to spend on something in TriPalms, what would you tell me to buy first?"

Maria was both smart and articulate when she wanted to be; she had been an honors graduate at Venice High School. Mickey sensed that her parents did not think it appropriate for her to go to college—maybe, when they were of age, the sons would be permitted to go on for more schooling, but not the daughters. Maria also had a clever wit, her response was quick and emphatic: "A bulldozer!"

42/ THE PRIEST IN THE MALL

Beth Slade once dated a fellow nurse at Saint Mary's Hospital named Barry Holgate. She sensed that Barry still liked her and that he might be willing to do her a big favor if she were to ask. Barry's father was a maintenance superintendent at the large Duluth hospital and supervised crews of skilled craftsmen—plumbers, carpenters, masons and electricians—along with the large custodial staff. Beth was more determined than ever to help Brian get back on his feet. He had been scanning the want ads that morning and was planning to make a few phone calls while Beth was at work. "It's not what you know, it's who you know," she told her brother, "and I just happen to know someone who knows someone…"

Since arriving on the bus three days before, Brian had not been himself—not the same brother she so enjoyed over Christmas. Something was bothering him but he shut her out when she began to pry. Of one thing she was quite certain, he'd been in a fight of some kind as his right eye was swollen and his jaw wore a purple bruise. Her calls to Duane were not being answered and she feared that Brian was in some kind of trouble.

"I think that I'm finally getting to know some things, Beth," Brian confided as he stirred his coffee while sitting at the kitchen table. "I never really thought much about what kind of person I was before–I thought my screw-up's were probably some bad genes I had. That made it a lot easier to explain things like getting in trouble... you know. That was foolish, but I've been a fool for most of my life." He might have explained the program he went through in the Ramsey County detention center but decided against getting into that chapter of his past.

"Now, I think that I'm starting to make some smart choices–not just quitting smoking, other things. And, I'm starting to like the face looking back at me in the mirror. That's good stuff, Beth. I'm feeling... hope, yeah... that's what it is–hope. A new start. If you know someone, Beth, just tell'em that your brother will do a good job, that he's a hard worker, that he can be trusted. That he won't disappoint anyone that's willin' to give him a chance."

Beth swallowed hard, fought back the tears that would ruin the mascara she had just applied.

"If I can just get a job, then a lot of things can happen–like getting a car, getting my own place... I'd be on cloud nine."

Beth stepped behind him, leaned over and gave him a hug around the neck. "I don't know what happened in the Cities, but I can see you've changed. Anyhow, I'm really glad you're back with me. Back home. We'll put our two heads together and come up with something... okay?"

Brian smiled, "I love ya, Beth."

That afternoon while Beth was at work, Brian took the city bus to the Miller Hill Mall dressed in the priest outfit he had taken from Duane's apartment. He couldn't remember the last time he did anything just for the fun of it. Some guy on Doctor Phil's show on TV that morning had talked about laughter and health and told his audience to find things that make you happy–made you feel good about yourself. To Brian, that advice seemed timely and sound. Bored with the doldrums he had been stewing in these past days, and feeling in a funky mood, he was game for doing almost anything that might be foolish and fun.

Just as it had been in downtown Minneapolis, the reaction of people to a man of the cloth was an enjoyable ego trip for Brian. Strangely, however, once again there were a few people who approached him familiarly–two even called him Father Moran. Apparently, both Beth and Duane were right about the double stuff. If people wanted to mistake him for Father Moran, that's what he'd give them.

"Yes, I'm doing just fine, thanks for asking..." he would reply to the greetings. After pausing to converse with a woman named Lucy Meckola who remembered him fondly from the Saint James years, Brian was at his best. Upon listening to a fond memory of Lucy's, he responded: "Yes, I remember it well, Lucy." He smiled graciously, "I remember as if it were only yesterday."

Not everybody was pleasant. A few people thought that Brian, or Father Moran, should know who they were, and they seemed upset that he didn't. Can't please everybody, Brian thought. Just smile and be pleasant, say hello to everybody... most people seemed delighted to be greeted by the young priest.

Beth would have been outraged by his impersonations, so he kept his other lives–porn actor and priest–to himself. One afternoon, his sister was the bearer of wonderful news: Brian would begin his custodial training at Saint Mary's Hospital on January 19th. If all went satisfactorily, he would be assigned to an afternoon shift from four to midnight, with one–Friday through Monday–long weekend off each month. He was elated at the opportunity and determined not to screw things up again. Beth intended to help him find a place of his own and offered him a loan of some up-front money for a deposit and one month's advance rent. "No, Beth, I can't thank you enough for all you been doing for me, but I don't want to start a new life with a loan–especially from you. I'm going to do this by myself. It might take me until April, but that's fine with me." Beth was delighted at her brother's attitude, and equally delighted about a bit of related good fortune. Barry Holgate had accepted her invitation to work on the Obama reelection campaign, and further, she had accepted his invitation for dinner and a movie the following weekend. Neither had seen the film, Help, and both were looking forward to reacquainting themselves with each other.

Meghan and Kenny Williams spent five days in the Cities. Both were sports fans and two of Minnesota's winter pro teams were in town during their extended vacation. The Lynx' new season hadn't started yet. At the state-of-the-art Xcel Energy Center in Saint Paul, they watched the Wild defeat San Jose in a shoot-out; at the Target Center in Minneapolis, they watched the Timberwolves lose to a weak Cleveland team. Meghan shopped 'til she dropped', while Kenny visited some of his college professors in architecture department at the University. (He had some new design plans along with him and wanted their insights on how to lowball his budgeted estimates.) They dined at the best places every night and went to the Walker Art Center and the Guthrie Theater during the afternoons. All this occurred after their second session with their marriage counselor. Things were good, very good– and getting better!

Father Mario was finding himself in an increasingly awkward situation and was having qualms about where his allegiance needed to be. He prayed… and prayed, and asked his friends to pray for his 'special intention'; but the torment would not go away. He had to tell somebody before he went half-crazy, but who? While in Hibbing years before he had come to know Mickey's parents quite well. He knew how close Mickey was to them—maybe he could feel them out, see what they knew about their son's activities and whereabouts. Regardless of what they may or may not know, he felt they could be trusted with any confidence he might be willing to share with them. Mario's call to the Morans in Florida came the day following Bishop Bremmer's lamentable introduction to the world of porn, and his sharing of that information with Mickey's parents.

"I don't know, Father... Amos and I are beside ourselves with worry," Sadie said. "It's been almost two weeks since we've heard anything." Sadie Moran had taken his call as Amos had gone to the driving range to practice hitting his new Ping G-20 driver.

Sadie knew that Mario was probably her son's closest friend, both in the clergy and out. She knew him to be trustworthy and discreet—she would confide everything she knew: "Have you talked to the bishop, Father?" She would feel him out before divulging anything.

"Not recently... and not about Mickey since... since when he didn't report to the bishop down in Venice as he was supposed to do. Why... has the bishop learned where he is?"

"Hold on to your chair, Father..." Sadie told Mario about her conversation with Bishop Bremmer and the repugnant details of the CD along with the threatening letter that came with it. "We don't believe that Mickey could ever... you know, but we can't help but wonder if he is in some kind of danger. We simply have no idea what to think."

Mario knew Mickey as well as anybody, his friend would never—under any circumstance, including being at gunpoint—ever engage a prostitute. "I agree, Mrs. Moran, that's not Mickey—no way in... " he almost chose the wrong word but caught himself, "the world!"

Mario was digging in his memory for something elusive, then—like a bolt— it came to him. "As strange as it may seem, Mrs. Moran, there must be someone out there who could pass for Mickey. I remember reading something about doppelganger in a psych class.

It's a German word that defines the concept of having a double–the idea suggests that we may have a duplicate out there somewhere. I know it's a bizarre thought, but…" He was trying to remember an occasion when someone thought they had seen Mickey in an east Saint Paul neighborhood. And, there had been a student he'd talked with at the UMD Newman Center who claimed; "Your priest friend spends lots of time hanging around the Miller Mall." Mario had many priest friends and didn't give the comment much thought at all. "I thought that priests had more to do than loiter at the food court."

Mario laughed. "The pay sucks but it's a pretty good life, you might want to consider it for yourself." Both laughed. "I'm serious. I'm free to talk about it any time."

Mario wouldn't have connected the shopaholic priest to his friend, Mickey–Mickey was in Florida. "I just wonder if there's something paranormal going on here, Mrs. Moran? Stranger things have happened."

"Both his father and I know that he's in Florida but that's about it. I wish he'd call again and let us know more about what he'd doing. I'm more worried than Amos… but I can tell he's getting a little apprehensive, too."

Mario took a deep breath, "I'll get in touch with him, Mrs. Moran. I think that I can convince him that the secrecy business needs to come to an end."

"We'd certainly like to hear from him, but don't want it to be forced, you know. Mickey doesn't go for that kind of thing. Do you know–is he well?"

"I can assure you that he's never been better."

Mickey had been gone from Duluth and Saint Gerard's for nearly a month. During that time Mario had talked with him four times. He was probably the only person who knew precisely where Mickey was living and what he was doing. Yet it would be very difficult to explain to another party in any logical way–was he hiding–yes; was he doing the Lord's work–absolutely; was he rehabilitating–yes… just not in any prescribed manner. Maybe the time had come for him to quit circumventing his bishop. One of the most fundamental ethics of the priesthood was obedience and both Mario and Mickey were violating their vows. He resolved to contact Mickey and tell his friend that he was feeling duty-bound to confess his complicity to Bishop Bremmer. And, suggest that while he was at it–give his folks a call.

~

"I still miss him, Emma," Lucy Meckola confided to her friend, "Such a handsome young priest." Lucy was sharing the wonderful conversation she had with Father Moran at the Miller Mall earlier that day." Lucy had a wide circle of acquaintances in her west Duluth neighborhood and she liked to 'keep in touch' with most of them on a daily basis. She told Emma Zdon, and several others, about running into Father Moran at the Mall . "He remembered the Driscoll funeral when we served the full reception buffet with all the trimmings when the widow wanted nothing more than cake and coffee. We both laughed…"

Emma would mention Lucy's incident at the mall to her husband Walter, a KC officer at Saint James. One of the Knights in his brotherhood was Lenny Odegaard, formerly of Hibbing where Mickey Moran had grown up. Odegaard's sister-in-law was Sandy Graber who lived next door to Molly Matonich in the Ordean neighborhood of eastern Duluth. Molly Matonich was Bishop Bremmer's personal secretary… Gossip chains can be amazingly intricate, injurious and, at times, insightful.

43/ A COMMUNITY CONCERT

"That simply cannot be," the bishop's denunciation was emphatic. "He's on the lam somewhere in Florida. He'd never sneak back to Duluth... much too risky... and, if he were foolish enough to do so, he would not be wearing his collar in any public place. You must be mistaken, Molly," he said to his secretary when she explained what she had heard.

When she answered her phone that morning, Lucy Meckola almost fainted–the Bishop was on the line! Bremmer had thoroughly walked the rumor back to its source. At the bishop's insistence, Lucy retold the Miller Hill Mall incident exactly as she remembered it happening. Within minutes of the telling she had broken down in tears, the bishop wasn't believing her: "I'm positive, Your Grace... absolutely. He remembered something that only Father Moran would remember."

Bishop Bremmer was stressed. This good woman would never deliberately mislead him, but she had to be mistaken–regardless of her strong conviction. Maybe this situation had evolved to the point where it needed to be aired publically? Maybe there were people out there who had useful information to offer? Up until now he had treated the 'Moran Affair' as a Catholic Church matter and refrained from allowing any disclosure to the local media. Maybe a very discrete news story would be helpful in locating his missing priest. He placed a call to Harold Grant, the diocesan public relations person.

~

Mickey had made only two trips into Venice during his first month in TriPalms. One was to a used books shop where he spent thirty dollars on children's books; the other for some OTC meds at a Walgreens– several kids had sharp coughs and runny noses. Today was his third. He would be meeting his old Naples friend, Larry Wheeler, for lunch at a Burger King on Tamiami Trail. Mickey and Larry had talked by phone several times since Mickey's arrival in Florida, and the two had met once in TriPalms to eyeball the pipedream. The contractor had made some contacts of his own and was getting even more excited about the plans the two of them had been discussing. "I'm ready to roll,' Wheeler said in his last conversation with Mickey. "Get it? Ready to roll?"

"Yeah… me, too," Mickey said.

Larry Wheeler let his pun fly over the head of his priest friend. He'd connect the 'Wheel and rolling' later; when his priest friend didn't have his mind over-loaded.

One breezy late-January evening, Mickey took his Martin guitar out to the trunk of his Civic and began strumming some of the chords he had learned while at Saint James years before. He tuned the strings and hummed some familiar melodies to himself. Within minutes several curious children were beginning to congregate, in another few minutes the parents slowly wandered toward the Placencio trailer where Mickey was playing his music.

"Does anybody here know the words to *Michael*?" He sang, *"Michael row the boat ashore… hallelujah… Michael row the boat ashore…Hallelujah…"* Alberto Olivio was quick to pick up the rhythm and lyrics, then his brother Alexi chimed in… then others followed their lead. *"Sister help to trim the sail… Hallelujah."* Then the women came on board, clapping their hands to accompany Mickey's strumming. The improvised concert moved from the trailer to the soccer field where blankets and lanterns added to the festive spirit of a 'sing-along'. Later, Mickey introduced an old favorite of his, the ballad, *Tom Dooley*. In no time everybody was singing… *"Hang down your head, Tom Dooley…"*

With simple C and C7 chords, Mickey played a tune that was a favorite of his parishioners at Saint James Church in Duluth. *"He's

Got the Whole World in His Hands..." Unexpectedly, Mickey was able to win the hearts of any remaining doubters on that starry January night. For days afterward, TriPalmites were humming Michael and *Tom Dooley* as they went about their daily routines. Someone was watching over him when he packed for his rehab assignment. Someone had insisted that he make room in his trunk for the Martin guitar. It had taken Mickey these few weeks to realize that his Maestro was orchestrating every step he had been taking.

His weeks in TriPalms had been the most rewarding of his priesthood. The children had been his natural bridge to the adult world. Many of his little ninos were learning English in the public elementary school in nearby Nokomis and beginning to teach their parents some vocabulary when they shared their evening meal. Every night, Mickey made the rounds, one trailer to the next, to visit briefly with his students and their parents. Each day he sent along three new English words for the children to memorize. Many of the words he chose had religious connotations: Faith, beauty, trust, honesty, charity–others equally useful in day-to-day interactions: loving, learning, sharing, working, cooperating... Each vocabulary word would inspire a story from Mickey's vivid imagination. His personally involved approach enabled him to learn some Spanish and French while teaching some English–everybody, of every age, was the better off because of his involvement. Every family in TriPalms hoped that they might be lucky enough to get a visit from 'Padre' after their mealtime.

Eventually the mothers and wives were meeting each morning in the large trailer initially provided by Hector Munoz for use by the village men. Only the village men! They wanted a place to visit with each other, probably gossip a bit, and a work on their blooming English vocabularies. Change was not without controversy and Mickey was in the center of a gender confrontation. Cleverly, Mickey identified the most vociferous men and the most indignant women;

then, without their having any idea of what he was trying to accomplish, he called them together on the soccer field one night. Before the meeting was over, he had cleverly formed the first TriPalms community choir. In practicing and harmonizing, both sides came to appreciate how much better a song could be sung with the blending of voices.

In the minds and vocabulary of the locals, Mickey had come to be known as the secreto padre and, more recently, as the pacificador (peacemaker). In a first ever town meeting held one cool, moonlit evening on the soccer field, Mickey, wearing his Roman collar for the first time, introduced the choir, led them in some songs, then addressed all of the adults. With the endorsement of Hector Munoz, the village's most prosperous and respected citizen, he spoke about the importance of citizenship and community and equality for women and men. To the astonishment of all, he saved the best for last. After a closing hymn, and prayers for a world of peace and justice, he unveiled a drawing of the community center that was moving rapidly from planning to actual construction. There were the ooohs and aaahs of astonishment followed by a long, loud round of applause.

But, the town meeting was not over. When the crowd had settled down and Mickey had everybody's full attention, he cleared his throat and made boldest pronouncement yet. In rehearsed Spanish he said: *"Los catolicos confiesan sus pecados a un sacerdote. Yo soy tu padre!"* He told his flock that he was their priest and that he would begin Catechism classes for First Communion, begin Confirmation training for teenagers, perform baptisms and marry properly prepared couples. In addition, he would hear confessions by appointment.

With the tall Cuban, Hector Munoz, standing erectly at his side, Mickey's credibility was insured. Munoz owned three landscaping companies and employed nearly two hundred men on a near-regular basis. His HME services employed seventy more in his TriPalms small engine shops. In addition, he had significant investments in a large commercial cleaning business and was part owner of the areas largest roofing contractor. Munoz ran a tight ship; only those who had papers were on his permanent payroll; for those less fortunate, he found day-to-day cash jobs with other employers where and when he could. For those who were fortunate enough to have full-time employment with Munoz' enterprises, there were two inviolable rules: work to the best of your ability at all times, and treat everybody with respect. To all, Hector Munoz defined what success could be and was the role model for every youngster in the village. To Mickey, Munoz was part pillar and part patron and always his most valuable ally.

As the days turned to weeks, Mickey's network expanded. Using his untraceable phone, he was in contact with Father Mario, his brother-in-law, Kenny Williams in Hibbing, Larry Wheeler and Sarasota County Commissioner, Barbara Knox. Sadly, his parents had remained out of the loop. Excluding them was painful but necessary. If Catholic Church bureaucrats along with two bishops were actively searching for him, Amos and Sadie's Naples home, computer, and cell phone may be under some kind of surveillance.

"I really like what he's come up with," Larry Wheeler told Mickey in a corner booth over a burger and fries in a Venice Wendy's. Larry had been in frequent contact with Kenny Williams' architectural firm in Hibbing. Mickey's brother-in-law had provided Larry with several innovative ideas. Kenny had agreed to design an all-purpose community center with amenities for Tri-Palms. "If your brother-in-law ever decided to settle down here in Florida, I'd be able to find a thousand jobs for him. My own architect, Del Saccoman, gave his prints a thorough look-over–'two thumbs up' is what he told me, way up!"

Larry had his late father's good looks– he was tall, lanky and had a longish floppy head of golden blond hair, sky blue eyes. In his day, the senior Wheeler had often been told that he bore a striking resemblance to every woman's heartthrob–popular actor, Robert Redford. In addition to a physical likeness, the son had the father's easy smile and disposition. The ambitious TriPalms undertaking was going to be a pro bono project for Wheeler's construction firm.

Larry had filed all the necessary paperwork with Sarasota County and permits would be forthcoming. Barbara Knox was an expert facilitator of everything Larry sent her way. Together they had greased all the necessary wheels to put the plan on a fast track. Further, the contractor had a larger master plan and promised other TriPalms improvements to follow the initial construction phase. The county officials were friends of Larry's and had agreed to keep the community building under wraps from the media as best they could. Also, needed infrastructure improvements were being scheduled for mid-June, four months down the road.

"When are you going to contact your Dad, Mickey? He's got to be one seriously stressed guy these days… and your Mom," Larry shook his head, "Sadie's gotta be a basket case by now."

Mickey nodded, "It's breaking my heart. Maybe in the next week or two. I know dad's going to want to be involved in what we're doing here."

"He'd be a great addition to our team, Mick"

"He's a good man, Larry. I love him to death…" Mickey found himself at a loss for any more words.

"I know that, my friend–he's your father and that says it all for me.

In the back of Mickey's thoughts was a dark lining of guilt–and out of the guilt came the seeds of doubt. Could his disobedience be honestly justified?

What unforeseen consequences were down the road? Where and when would this marvelous adventure end? Was there a balance between the good and the bad: the good deeds he was accomplishing in TriPalms, and the bad feelings he had been sowing with many of those he loved? What portion of the pie he was making was selfless service to God's less fortunate's, and what part was serving his own ego? Was he being honest with himself about that? Did everybody do good things in order to feel better about themselves? How wrong was that? He struggled with his conscience and his motives; wondering deeply–were any of us, in all honesty, capable of selfless acts?

There were times when Mickey would pray and find that he had unknowingly been crying. There was a pain deep inside him that he could neither comprehend nor resolve. A part of Father Mickey wanted to walk away from everything he had started here, as well as everything else he had ever done as a person and as a priest–to take off by himself to some remote place where he could be alone–isolated on some unknown island. That part of his nature was what Brother Sebastian in his seminary theology class termed the 'Trappist Syndrome. Sebastian believed that most religious had a subconscious wish to be a cloistered contemplative and live a life of silence and complete devotion to God. Whenever Mickey recalled that 'syndrome', he was able to get a better grip on who he really was and what he truly wasn't. Mickey wasn't cut out to function in any order that required a strict observance to silent prayer and devotion. But, he was learning some valuable lessons here–lessons that would serve him well as a servant of God. Christianity is community, service to God is sharing, love is giving, holiness is placing God above self and all else. If this experience was a mountain to climb, it would prepare him to cope with the valleys that would surely come later in his ministry.

One morning while sitting in a lawn chair outside the Placencio trailer and saying his prayers, with his eyes closed he asked God to confirm what he was trying to accomplish: "Send me a sign of some kind," he implored… "Anything… let me be touched by Your Spirit so that I know that You approve of what I'm doing here. I need to feel..." Mickey's prayer was distracted as he felt something wet on the side of his face–Torts was looking him in the eye and giving him an affectionate lick. "Are you my sign from God, old fellow?" Torts' tail began to wag as he offered a soft groan of affirmation.

44/ A PROWLER IN HIBBING, MN

The Twin Cities coconspirators had agreed to meet weekly while their extortion plan was evolving. Each time they met their patience was put to another critical test of wills. The acrid tension between them kept tightening its grip.

"Almost three f—ing weeks, Duane... that's what its been... and still nothing! I'm getting my ass outta this mess as of now. E-n-o-u-g-h... this woulda, shoulda, coulda crap you keep feeding me has worn me down. I'm cuttin' bait." David Rossman paced, his arms folded tightly across his barrel chest, "It's about time you paid me what I'm owed."

Duane Slade tipped back his Budweiser bottle and drained the last few ounces. His apologies and excuses were getting thin and he was close to admitting defeat. "Quit pacing and sit for a while, for Pete's sake. I'll get us another round." He and David Rossman were meeting at the Collegian Bar near Hamline University on north Snelling Avenue in Saint Paul. Duane scratched his head, they had been through this 'cut bait' issue before, he was even more broke today than last week. He had made three calls to Saint Gerard's Church since the preliminary mailing and had talked with some foggy-voiced guy named Graham. All Graham would tell him was that Father Moran was not available.

Graham had identified himself as a priest. When pressed further, Graham would only say, "I am not at liberty to tell you anything about Father Moran. You may contact the bishop if you'd like." Graham sounded old, and Duane assumed, he was probably the second pastor at the church.

"All right, what say you give me one more week to get this figgered out. If I can't get us back on track... then, I'll pay up. That a deal?" Duane appealed. "One week–I'll leave no rock... " he couldn't remember how the cliché went–overturned, underturned?

"What you gonna do in a week that ain't been done already?"

"I'm gonna tighten the screws on the Morans. If I have to... I'll get smack in their face. This CD is a ticking time bomb for them– I'm going to make damn sure that every one of them knows the consequences." Duane had no clue about the 'what' and 'how' of his bold statement, nor any idea of how he might go about making good on his promise. "Just another week, one more is all I'll need to get the ball rolling again, Duane. "I'll rattle their cages... no more of this bullshit!"

Rossman nodded, running his fingers through his mop of greasy black hair: "I suppose one more week won't make much difference. Let's meet here next Saturday afternoon. For the last time, okay? No more excuses, no more stalling. If you don't have some good news; bring me the money you owe... I hope you damn well know that I can tighten screws, too." He ran his pudgy index finger across his throat, smiled the smug smile of the powerbroker. Rossman was the alpha dog and he knew it.

A mutual accord was reached. Duane had another week. He would return to his apartment to organize his scattered thoughts and come up with a revised plan of action. He'd been too passive for too long and needed to get off his butt–it was time to confront the Morans. As much as he didn't want to, he'd drive up to Duluth, pay a visit to Saint Gerard's, and lean on the old priest If necessary, he might use force to get Moran out of hiding, if hiding was what the priest was trying to do. Force was the Glock he had locked in a safe in his bedroom closet. He'd never used the firearm and never hoped to. The more he thought about the gun, the more leery he became– using that kind of force was not in his nature. Besides, if everything went south on him, a gun would add ten years to whatever sentence a judge might hand down. Surely, his very best weapon was the video, he just hadn't maximized it's potential yet. Lingering in the back of his thoughts were the police, maybe even the Feds. What if they were lying in wait for him to do something rash? Confrontation was a risky ploy, but time was running out on both him and the plan–'nothing ventured, nothing gained' he reminded himself. Despite the risk, Duane Slade would go to the church in Duluth, then–if necessary–drive up to Hibbing where the Moran money was probably sitting in some bank account.

Father Graham was, indeed, an old man. Ancient! He could hardly support his frail frame as the wind whipped and whirled at the rectory door. "Sorry, Father Moran is not in today."

"Or yesterday, or the day before, or the day before that! I know, cuz I've been calling and getting the same song and dance for two weeks already. This is an emergency, sir... Father, I mean. A family emergency!"

Graham wondered, might this insistent man know anything about Father Moran's whereabouts? It seemed clear that nobody else had a clue so any tidbit could be a priceless piece to the puzzle. If he could garner any information from this stranger the bishop would be very pleased. "What kind of an emergency?"

Duane expected the question; "All I'm allowed to tell you is that I've been sent by his father... Amos Moran. The emergency has to be a hush-hush thing–understand?"

Graham posed another question. "When did you last see Father Moran?"

Duane quickly fabricated, "Two weeks ago, maybe less... what's that got to do with anything?

"Where?' Graham ignored the heavy man's question.

"You deaf, Father? This is all hushed-up... how many times do I have to tell ya?'

Graham cleared phlegm from his throat. "I'm sorry, sir. You

should see the bishop about this. Let me get you his private phone number and the address of his residence."

Duane was not about to see any bishop. When the priest retreated inside to find the address, Duane hustled back to his parked car. This old man didn't know shit from shinola He would shift into the Plan B he contrived on the drive to Duluth. Now, somewhat annoyed, it appeared that he'd have to extend his trip by another seventy miles and drive up to Hibbing, a place he had never been to before. The road trip could be an interesting diversion from the stress that tightened in his back; maybe even educational. He'd heard lots of things about Hibbing, like trivia things. Bob Dylan came from there–everybody knew that. Fewer people, however, knew that Dylan's real name was Bob Zimmerman. But, Duane was one of those few who did. He'd enjoy seeing the house where Dylan grew up. And, that basketball player for the Celtics a few years back. . . McHale, Kevin McHale… he was also from Hibbing. And, there was someone else, Duane pressed his mind… yeah, "Rudy Perpich", he said the name aloud. Rudy had been the governor of Minnesota for two terms. Tumultuous terms in the minds of many, but Rudy was a favorite of Duane Slade's. Rudy and Jesse Ventura; two movers and shakers, guys who could think out-of-the-box. He smiled to himself, now Minnesota had another unorthodox character in high political office: Al Franken was his state's junior senator in Washington. Franken, like Rudy and Jesse, was a clever dude to his way of thinking.

Duane was pleased with himself, he knew lots about lots of things–music, sports, politics… you name it! He'd often wondered how successful he might have been if he'd finished high school. Damn teachers, they really screwed him up: division, denominators, fractions, ancient Egypt, Rome, planets… book reports and homework. They, the teachers, stifled him with all their crapola–Duane knew more than they did about the things that really mattered; about how to make a buck. They sure weren't making much money.

Maybe they were teachers because they couldn't do anything else.

As Duane Slade made his way up the steep hillside to Highway 53 north, he passed within two miles of Toledo Street where his sister Beth lived. He would see her another time, maybe on his return trip–maybe not. She had called a few times but Duane hadn't answered, she probably wanted to know how Brian was doing. He hadn't heard from Brian since his brother stormed out of his apartment two weeks ago. Where was he these days? You can pick your friends, but you're stuck with your family. Hell, what family? Duane's 'family' was no more than three individuals who happened to be related by birth.

Driving north in light traffic, he rehearsed what he might say to the father of this elusive priest. Duane had an extra copy of the video with him and considered giving it to this Amos Moran guy. That would get the ball rolling for sure. Hell, Duane might even leave Hibbing today with a million bucks? Maybe Amos Moran would walk right down to the bank and withdraw the money, in small bills of course, and hand it over to him in a suitcase. Then, Duane could be back on the road–a rich man for the rest of his life. Maybe? Stranger things have happened.

Nobody came to the door of Amos Moran's Home Acres neighborhood residence. Duane walked through the snow to a side window and peered through a narrow space between the drawn drapes. The living room furniture had been covered with drop cloths. From what he could tell, the occupants had obviously been gone for some time.

"Can I help you?" The question startled him. The Moran's neighbor–a lady named Arles Jackola–was watching him from a driveway next door.

Embarrassed, he tried to keep his voice even and casual: "Oh, I'm an old family friend... in town, you know. Where's Amos?" Duane shook the snow from his pant cuffs and loafers.

Suspicious, Arles said. "The Morans aren't home. I didn't get your name."

"Anderson, Tom Anderson. Went to college with Amos."

The neighbor lady wished she knew where Amos had gone to college so she could catch this man in a lie. If he were from out of town he'd have called before stopping at the Moran's house. She didn't like window peepers. "Maybe you should see his daughter, she lives down by the Frank Hibbing Park."

The daughter would be the priest's sister, Duane reasoned–he hadn't thought about any other relatives: "Sure. That might be a good idea. I know I've met her, somewhere... just can't remember her name."

Arles Jackola would call and alert Meghan as soon as this guy left, then she would call the police. Maybe the police first. "Missus Williams lives in the big colonial across from the Frank Hibbing monument. Know where that is?"

Duane shook his head, "No, ma'am, haven't been up here in years."

"Address is in the phone book, under Kenneth Williams. Should be 900 something–Minnesota or Michigan Street," she said. "Can I call and tell her that you're stopping by?"

"Won't be necessary..." Duane wasn't sure how to complete the thought or what he might do next. "Well, thank you... you've been most helpful." He turned, walked as nonchalantly as possible toward his car.

Now where? So far he was batting zero for two. As he drove away he saw the neighbor in his rear view mirror; she had darted into her house.

Duane decided to backtrack to the MacDonalds he'd spotted on the highway coming in to town. He'd get a cup of coffee and think things out. Finding the Dylan house or checking out the Hull-Rust mine view today wasn't a priority. Duane was certain that the neighbor woman had seen his license plates and called the cops.

Amos was out of town somewhere–maybe his priest-son was with him. Whatever, he wasn't going to learn anything helpful up here. The sister's name was Williams; at an address in the 900's–he might check that out later.

Sure enough, Duane hadn't driven four blocks before there was a bank of flashing blue lights on the car closing in behind him. Small town, he thought, everybody knows everybody and if you're not from here, you're up to something no good and a person of interest. He pulled off the busy street and into the Walgreen's parking lot near the Highway 169 beltline.

Officer Hyduke looked as if he had wrestled in high school and eaten a couple testosterone donuts with his morning coffee. "Driver's license, sir. And an insurance card, please," Hyduke said through the scowl on his square-jawed face. The officer took them, said "Back in a minute."

While in his squad, Duane knew the drill: Hyduke would run a background check on him and find nothing. Then a meeker cop would return his license, maybe even apologize. Five minutes became ten. Sure, he'd gonna let me sit for a while, they like to let you stress as much as possible.

Hyduke knocked on his window and Duane rolled it down, letting in a rush of cold. "You tell a lady back there," he turned and gestured, "You're a friend of Amos'?" He returned the license and insurance card.

"Yes, sir."

"Tell her your name was Anderson?"

"Yes, sir."

"License says you're Slade, Duane Allan Slade."

"Yes, sir."

"Why the lie?"

Duane swallowed hard, "Sir… to be honest, I… I just didn't think it was any of her business. I mean… she writtin' a book or sumthin?"

Hyduke stood for a long minute without saying anything more. Duane sweated.

"This your address in Saint Paul?'

"Yes, sir." Duane said.

"Mind if I look around in your car?"

"No, not at all–go right ahead." Duane's mouth was dry and is voice too high pitched. "Should I get out?"

"Not necessary." He walked around to passenger side of the car. Looked into the back seat, then gestured for Duane to put down the window. Can I see what's in your glove box, sir?" Hyduke's search was deliberately superficial. "Will you open your trunk?"

Duane breathed a sigh of relief as the cop rifled through his trunk... what if he had packed his Glock before leaving the Cities? That would probably get him a trip to the local police station, maybe even an overnight.

"Are you leaving town now, Mr. Slade?" As much as Hyduke didn't like strangers from the Cities, he despised liars. Slade's license and insurance were current and his record was clean, but he had a look about him–maybe the eyes. Hyduke cleared his throat, "I asked you a question, sir. You on your way out of town?"

"Yes, sir. Maybe stop for lunch… I saw a MacDonald's out on the highway." He wasn't going to find this Williams woman today. Maybe he'd find her phone number–if she had a landline–and give her a call later. For now, retreat seemed like the best strategy.

"Keep your seatbelt on, drive carefully." Hyduke tried to smile, didn't do very well. He'd made a note of Slade name for any future reference, but didn't have grounds for an arrest. "You can go now. Enjoy your lunch," Hyduke's parting sarcasm gave him a little charge.

Duane could feel the perspiration in his armpits as he signaled and drove carefully away. His appetite had vanished and he wanted to get as far away from Hibbing as he could. He hadn't seen any of the sights. Maybe another time. Meghan Williams gave Officer

Hyduke her parents phone number in Naples. "I think your dad ought to know about this Slade fellow–I didn't have a good feeling, Meg." Hyduke and Meghan had been classmates at Hibbing High School. "Tell Amos to work on his short irons down there," he added. Hyduke had beaten Amos for the fifth flight consolation championship in the previous summer's Vern Fryklund golf tournament.

45/ THE TRUNK IN THE ATTIC

Since the call from Bishop Bremmer, three days ago, the Morans had been on edge. Their son's strange disappearance was one thing, the video and extortion demands quite another. Being an attorney by training, Amos had a good sense about what to do and what not to do. But doing nothing was killing him!

"That was very strange, Sadie," Amos said. "Jimmy Hyduke, you know, George's oldest son... the cop, he just called."

Sadie dropped the *Newsweek Magazine* she had been reading on the living room sofa, "Something about Mickey?" she said.

"Don't know." He rehashed the brief conversation with officer Hyduke to his wife. "Don't remember any guy named Anderson from college–do you?"

Both had graduated from Northern Arizona University in Flagstaff where Sadie had grown up, "Not that I can remember."

Amos frowned; "What about Slade? Ring a bell?"

"Don't think so. There were some Slades that my folks knew in Flagstaff, lived somewhere out on Soliere Road." She stood, fully attentive, "I've got a gut feeling, Amos; this has something to do with our son."

"Hyduke said this guy lives in Saint Paul." Amos shrugged, "Maybe he knows something. But what? I just don't know how to connect it with what little else we've got to go on. I've never felt so lost in the dark."

As he slipped his cell phone into his trouser pocket, Amos felt a light flash on in the back of his memory. Slade? The name had a germ of familiarity. Slade... Slade... Slade... He repeated the name trying to find a thread, to get a picture of a face to go with the name; it must have something to do with something he had read. A novel? A sports magazine? He felt sure that it hadn't been that long ago.

"What's the matter?" Sadie said.

"Trying to remember something... that name, Slade... I'm trying to attach it to something, but I don't know what." He stepped forward, gave Sadie a hug, "It'll come to me, sweetheart. It's probably nothing– just not as sharp as I used to be. I'm feeling more like the infamous Inspector Cluseau these days." Both laughed at the reference to the *Pink Panther* comedies. When he needed to think at the deepest level, Amos would often take a walk and allow his mind to wander before pressing for a specific focus. The day was typically gorgeous as he headed down Banyan Boulevard toward Lowdermilk Park and the Gulf beach. He paused to watch a cluster of white ibises feeding in the dry grass below a live oak tree. Above him, gray beards of Spanish moss hung like fluffy boas from the branches. A silver Porsche convertible passed to his right, the driver–a man surely in his seventies–was bobbing his head to some song on his radio. Amos never quite understood an aging process where men turned to diamond ear studs or gold loops and ponytails, women to Botox treatments and facelifts. Was that anywhere in his or Sadie's future? A gruesome thought passed behind his eyes, how many of these wealthy seniors had come to Florida for a final fling at living before the big nap.

Distracted, Amos refocused on the reason for his walk to the beach. He'd find a bench, wriggle his toes in the sugary sand and soak up some sun. Slade? He ruminated on the name once more, trying to make a connection of some kind. At the beach he found an unoccupied tiki hut, kicked off his flip-flops, and breathed deeply of the salty air. While living in Naples he never failed to think of how close this climate was to the virtual Paradise of everybody's imagination. Nearby was a large gathering of Hispanics enjoying an outing on the beach, the men relaxing under colorful umbrellas while the women spread picnic sandwiches and sodas on a card table, and the children carried buckets of wet sand from the gulf shore to the beach for castle construction.

To his left was a cluster of forty-foot Queen Palms swaying in the southern breeze; beyond the shoreline and gliding across the aqua water, were a pair of sailboats. To his right, a college-aged woman lying on a beach blanket was writing in a notebook. Amos mused, he'd always wanted to write a book–he'd even half-promised his beloved Nana that he would write a Moran family history from the notebooks of his grampa, Kevin. Years ago he started writing a memoire, it was going to be titled The Moran Diaries, and it was…

It struck Amos like a stomach punch, almost taking his breath away–the diaries! Grampa Kevin's diaries! Over Christmas he had been looking for the picture that Mickey had inquired about. While browsing in Kevin's old trunk he couldn't help but reread some of the old journals. Yes. Slade. That mysterious uncle… Denis Moran… he had fathered an illegitimate son… the mother's surname was Slade. That name had continued through two or three generations. Slade? There had to be some kind of connection… but what? In his mind he tried to recreate an image of the family trees that Kevin had diagramed. His focus was back!

Amos literally leaped from the bench, passing the girl on the blanket he smiled, "Thanks for keeping a diary… you don't know how much that has helped me."

The girl gave him a 'what kind of crazy are you' look, "Dah?" was her pithy response.

Half-running east on Banyan Boulevard, Amos cut across his front lawn and into the house. He grabbed his cell phone from the kitchen counter where he'd left it, touched the screen, and had

Meghan on the line in seconds. Amos took a minute to catch his breath, "Meg, you've got to do me a favor– right now!"

Sadie muted a 'Studio B' Fox News program she was watching, gave Amos a curious look. "What's going on, hon?"

Meghan explained her father's strange request to her husband. "I'll be back in an hour or so, Ken." She had her parent's house key on her key ring. Kenny Williams was one of the few people who knew the whats and wheres of Mickey Moran's new life. His drawings, along with Larry Wheeler's expertise, were bringing her brother's dreams to fruition. He had been tempted to share what he knew with Meghan many times–but felt honor-bound not to do so. This had been the second suspicious call in the past hour: First Officer Hyduke, now Amos. Both concerned a man named Slade. Kenny pondered the name but couldn't connect it with the Tri-Palms project or anything else. After Meghan left the house, he would try to reach Mickey or Larry and see if the name Slade made any sense to them. "Take your time, hon," he said to Meghan. "I'll pick up Matthew at the arena after his practice."

Meghan had not been in the attic of her parent's home since childhood when she and Mickey played hide-and-seek there. Nostalgia was everywhere around her: Old clothing her mother had saved, toys she'd forgotten she'd played with as a little girl: Barbie's pink jeep, a shelf of Nancy Drew and Hardy Boys books–memories galore raced across her mind. The key to the trunk was exactly where her father had said it would be.

"Okay, Dad...I'm here." As instructed, Meghan had her cell phone with her. "The chest is open, tell me what you want me to look for."

She ruffled through the papers but couldn't locate the family trees that her father wanted. "Okay, forget that... to your left about halfway down the stack you should find four or five green-covered notebooks."

Meghan found them and paged through the one on top. "Let me see, Dad... Yes, there is an Elizabeth Slade; she was only seven at the time your grampa was writing this. Let me see... yep, there it is–Beth Slade has a younger brother named Duane."

"That's the information I needed, thanks Meg. Thanks a ton. Now I've got to figure out how to follow up on this."

Meghan puzzled, "There's more here, Dad. The youngest Slade is named Brian. Looks like they were all born in Duluth. How old would they be now?"

Amos remembered the diaries ended sometime in the late seventies. The Slade kids would be close in age to his own children. Interesting. But, Amos didn't quite know how to process what he was learning. It would appear as if the Slades were shirttail relatives of the Morans. If this guy, Duane Slade, was the same guy that Hyduke had stopped in Hibbing earlier that day, then Amos had a distant relative who was looking for him? Should he call the Hibbing police with this information? The bishop? What could they do? His challenge would be connecting a random field of unnumbered dots in some way so as to make a pattern out of them.

"Dad... you still there?" Meghan said.

"Oh... yes... sorry, I was just thinking."

Sadie had been standing silently and curiously at his side. "Are either one of you going to let me know what's going on?"

"Yes, here, say hello to Meg for a minute, hon."

After his brief conversation with Meghan, Amos was on his computer and entering Google. He found the Saint Paul white pages, jotted some phone numbers on a tablet, got on his iPhone, and started calling down the list without success. The D. Slades were Daryl, David, Deward, Donna, Doreen–none of them he talked with knew of any Duane Slade. If this mysterious Slade had a cell phone, he'd be harder to locate by conventional means. Maybe, Officer Hyduke could find a phone number using the sophisticated system that law enforcement had access to. First, out of curiosity, he checked the Duluth white pages for an Elizabeth Slade knowing full well that she had probably married and left her maiden name behind. Or, just maybe...

Amos' second call to a Duluth phone number was answered by a woman. "Duane... you must have the..." Beth was caught off guard by the question, "Oh, I'll bet you're looking for my brother Duane? Duane doesn't live here, never has... he's in the Cities."

"Yes, I have his number... " Beth paused, just a minute, sir... May I ask who's calling and what this is about?

Amos, feeling a rush, already had his next question ready to fire: "Do you also have a brother named Brian by any chance?"

"Just a minute!"

Amos slowed the pace, "I'm sorry, Ms. Slade, ma'am... I should have introduced myself properly. I'm Amos Moran, my son has been missing for some time." Here he would improvise a fabrication. "My son and Duane are old friends and I'm looking for any help I can get."

Beth's enormous empathy surfaced. "I'm so sorry, Mr. . . excuse me, did I hear you say Moran? By any chance are you related to Father Moran?"

Amos' knees almost buckled, heat rushed up his spine. Maybe he'd found the proverbial straw in the haystack. "Yes. Father Mickey Moran is my son, my missing son. Do you know him?"

"Not personally... I've been to his church in Benton Park though."

As the conversation concluded, Beth told him that yes, she did have a brother Brian as well and that he and Father Moran looked remarkably alike–"It almost blew me away," she said. Brian, she told Amos, was not home at the moment but she'd ask him to call if that might help.

"That won't be necessary–at least not for now. But I will call your brother Duane," Amos said.

"I'll keep you and your son in my prayers, sir... Mr. Moran."

Amos thanked the pleasant woman, pocketed his cell. "Bingo!" He had the Saint Paul cell number for Duane Slade. Now, what to do with it? Through the ups and downs of his sixty-two years, he had learned that there is no such thing as coincidence. There had to be a connection of some kind between Mickey and the Slades. What escaped him in the elation of the moment was the obvious: Beth Slade had told him that her brother looked remarkably like Father Moran. "Sadie, we've finally caught ourselves a break," he shouted from the kitchen. In the back of his mind he wished that his grandfather, also an attorney, were here to help him unravel everything.

46/ THE TRIPALMS TEAM

By his fifth week, Mickey had learned more about humanity than he had during all his years in college and seminary. More about human destitution and deprivation than he thought possible. And more about love, too. Mickey had always considered himself to have a well-developed sense of empathy and had always found folks that he met to be interesting, unique, and worthy of respect; yet his experience here added a dimension to each of these perceptions–a dimension that he might never have considered. Every person in TriPalms had a story–often a harrowing one. Etched deeply in their psyche was their experience of getting here–by legal or illegal means. Never again would he take any human being for granted. Never again would he use the words common, regular, typical, or normal to describe another human being. The escape stories of Juan Estrada and Diego Vargas would read like an adventure novel, the stories of Bonita Mendez or Abulla Ortega would break one's heart. In every respect, TriPalms and its citizens, had enlivened his spirituality and taught him things that no seminary in America could ever hope to teach him. And, everything here was both a 'hands-on' and 'in your face'.

In addition he had met another saint, maybe two... Hector Munoz was a tall man with a sun-weathered face, a head that seemed a bit too small, ears that seemed too big, eyes that could see into your soul, and a heart of pure gold. Through a simple handshake, one could feel his gentle power.

Mickey had been curious as to why TriPalms wore the label of 'Little Haiti' when the great majority of the 3400 residents were of other Hispanic origins–most of them Puerto Ricans, Cubans, and Dominicans. Incredibly, there were fewer than three hundred Haitians, and most of them were under the age of ten. Their stories were both familiar and tragic. The earthquake of January, 2010, which took more than 300,000 lives and devastated the island nation also left millions homeless and orphaned. When he saw the first news clips from Port au Prince, Haiti, on TV, Hector Munoz chartered a helicopter and had his work boots on the ground four hours later. He had no idea of what to do–except help others in any way he could. One tireless month later, Munoz had circumvented immigration red tape and begun airlifting orphans and infants with surviving parents out of the anguish and squalor that was Haiti. Munoz would cash in a decade of favors owed to him in order to accomplish his humanitarian endeavors. His brother Hugo, in Miami, handled some of the logistics from his end of the Haitian pipeline. Hugo Munoz worked with Lutheran Social Services, Catholic Charities, and both Dade and Broward County Social Services to find homes for nearly a hundred of the evacuees; Munoz relatives in Tampa also opened their doors to some of the children; while others were placed through an ingenious plan that began with two of Hector's employees in Ft. Myers.

"I'll take two of the little girls, Boss," said Willie Rivas... "My wife has been praying for a little boy for years," said Juan Alico, "That little boy with the broken arm is the answer to our prayers." From Willie and Juan came an inspired plan. Hector then held meetings with his employees at several locations and offered a unique incentive: Any employee who would take in an orphan and raise them as their very own would be given a sizable monthly stipend along with their regular wages. The response was overwhelming.

Another element in the resurrection strategy was importing bilinguals to help with the settlement of families and children. Most Haitians spoke French. In Ft, Myers he found eleven women with Haitian roots who were willing to relocate to various communities where they could be of assistance–some in Miami, others in Tampa, Lely, Cape Coral, or Naples. Four of the women were already living in TriPalms. Whatever the reward in heaven for saving nearly three hundred souls from death by starvation or disease, Hector Munoz had earned his halo and wings.

"When I was a small boy of four in Baracoa (southeastern Cuba) a hurricane struck without warning," Munoz spoke in measured tones. "My parents were working in the field of a property they once owned but had been confiscated by the Castro government. Anyhow, my gramma was knocked unconscious by a table that was thrown across the room. Not knowing what to do, I screamed for help until my lungs ached. A stranger heard my cries above the howling storm and raced into what was left of our house. He pinned gramma against a wall so she wouldn't blow away and held me in his powerful arms–he saved our lives that morning. I'll never forget that incident and I'll always hear a call for help. That stranger's hands would be my hands for as long as I live."

Larry Wheeler was another story of selfless generosity and kindness. Fully 25% of his business and personal income went to his church, charities, and a foundation that provided day care for the working poor–mostly mothers with below subsistence wages. The TriPalms community center project was something that gave him great pleasure. One hot afternoon, he sidled up to Mickey who was trying to teach some English vocabulary using his limited French with a small group Haitian children. *"Oui, je peux vous comprende,"* he said. The girl had correctly said 'I am a smart little girl' in English—Mickey had told her that he understood. As always, Mickey's improvised classes were accomplished with the help of Miguel Olivo, his diligent and devoted assistant, who was becoming a valued trilingual.

"Mick, I can't thank you enough for getting me involved in this project. I've never been so excited about building something before." This from a man who's father's company had developed MaryEllen Oaks, an elegant Naples residential community near Livingston and Pine Ridge in the eighties, and Crosswinds Plaza, one of the top commercial districts in Naples. Since his father's passing, Larry added to a list of achievements that would touch upon the unbelievable. "My Mom, bless her heart, taught Sunday religion classes in the small library room of our church. I can't help think that she's watching over this project—I'd be delighted if she was."

All Mickey could say was, "I have it on good authority that she is, Larry." He nudged his friend playfully, "Glad you're having fun. When you can enjoy your work, please you mom, and make points with Saint Peter at the same time; you're way ahead of the game."

Larry laughed, "That's what I figgered? Do you have a pipeline to Peter's place up there," he pointed skyward, adding "I mean you being a priest and all?"

"I'd like to think so, but getting 'up there' to collect our points is a long way off for both of us—at least that's one on my long list of prayers."

"Whatever. I'm glad you came along, Mick. I needed something uplifting and this has been the perfect medicine."

"I'm glad I came along as well. I probably needed more uplifting than you did. Whatever, God bless you, Larry. You're a good man." Mickey's comment came with a hug that wrinkled and dirt-smudged Larry's starched white shirt.

When Kenny Williams faxed his preliminary plans for the three-room, 1600 square foot building, Larry asked him to add another classroom, adding an extra 700 square feet and a few thousand dollars to the project costs.

On Monday of the fifth week since Mickey's arrival in TriPalms, the materials began arriving like an army invasion. Wheeler construction workers had already begun putting down the footings so above ground construction could get started. The entire community was an audience in awed disbelief of the rising concrete block construction. The word that spread around the community became exaggerated with each telling, it was said that the three men–Mickey, Hector, and Mr. Wheeler–were building them a castle.

Hector Munoz was a man on a mission. Like Larry Wheeler, he knew how to organize and get results. As a ninth-grader ready to quit school, his math teacher told him: "If you give up now it will be that much easier to give up the next time something difficult comes along. Soon giving up will become second nature. When that happens, you've defined yourself as a coward–one who's afraid to fail." Mr. Arneson's wise counsel had kept him going to this day. He owed most of his success to being a dogged competitor.

Munoz had been a key advisor in the Marco Rubio senate campaign in 2010, and a significant financial contributor as well. That campaign, like everything else he did, was accomplished from the background–Hector did not look for, nor would he accept any public recognition. Carefully studying the prints, he determined that an outside patio area would enhance the 'community-gathering' concept they wanted to achieve. To Mickey he said, "As you know, I've been quite successful as a landscaper–I often have more clients than I can handle. I only brag to people I respect and trust without reservation."

Mickey nodded without response.

"And, I'm invested in some other companies; one installs underground irrigation systems."

Mickey smiled, "I know. And I know that most of what you do

is known to God alone–He's pleased with you, Hector." Mickey was probably the only person outside of family members who ever called him Hector.

"I hope so. He's the only one I'm hoping to please." Emotion tightened the tall man's voice. He looked away for a moment, then said: "Do you know why I don't live here in TriPalms?"

"I might guess, but tell me."

"Long ago I realized a need to have some degree of separation frommy employees. Never wanted lines of authority getting tangled with personal relationships. Anyhow, I have family, friends, and a host of relatives here and I visit the community three or four times a week; I've been doing that for as many years as I can remember."

Mickey could sense the emotion of his friend's disclosure, and he wasn't about to interrupt .

"Can you imagine my guilt, Father?" Hector was one of the few who had been mildly standoffish, or business-like, toward Mickey these past weeks. Before this moment, the young priest had never had much more than a perfunctory conversation with the tall and intimidating entrepreneur.

"Guilt?" Mickey shook his head.

"Yes, guilt. The guilt I get whenever I look at all the dirt, dead grass, litter, and the few sickly trees along the edges. So, for years I've closed my eyes and thought that 'it is what it is'–not 'it isn't what it should be'. I've been remiss..." he let the thought drop without completion.

A tight laugh escaped from the mouth of Hector Munoz. "See those three brown Imperials out there," he pointed toward the palm trees beyond the soccer field to the south. "They are the namesakes of this place. Pathetic, don't you think?"

Before Mickey could comment, he felt Hector's huge hand on his shoulder: "Gotta run," he said abruptly. "I'm getting emotional." Hector didn't say anything at the time, but the private vision he was contemplating would beautify and rejuvenate the community; giving the people of TriPalms a sense of pride they had never experienced before.

~

Mario's phone call woke Mickey from a fitful sleep in the unbearably hot trailer where he had been living. "What's up, bro?" Still groggy, Mickey used the favorite slang of his young lieutenant, Miguel Olivio. "You guys out shoveling snow this morning?"

Both laughed. After brief small talk, Father Mario blurted the reason for his early call. "I can't take being in the middle any longer, Mick. Sorry. Last week the bishop called twice, he thinks I know more than I've told him. He's perceptive. I can't keep covering for you with lies of omission."

"I know. I've really put a strain on you, Mario. I'm sorry."

"I've got to come clean with the bishop, Mick. Can you be okay with that? Will you forgive me?"

Mickey was choked with empathy, "It hasn't been fair to you nor to a lot of other people who are dear to me. I know that more than you could possibly imagine, Mario." A long pause preceded his next words: "Please, give me one more week–even five more days. Okay? I'm so close to accomplishing what I set out to get done here. As much as I hate to, I'll have to say my goodbyes sooner or later." It pained him to admit that all good things must come to an end. It pained even more to put a timeframe to his project. He had been blessed beyond anything he might ever have dared to hope for. "Then, Mario… then I'll contact the bishop myself and face the music."

Mario considered his friends proposal, "Okay. That works for me. Can I tell the bishop that I heard from you and that you are planning to contact him next week? That would help me a lot."

"Yep. I'm okay with that. Tell him that I'm fine, that I've been in a spiritual rehabilitation program, designed by God himself, here in Florida. Give him something to feel good about... tell him that I give him all the credit for whatever's being accomplished down here because he's the one who banished me to Florida in the first place."

Mario laughed, "I'll let you tell him those things yourself."

"And I will. It's true, you know. A divine plan was behind all the stupid things I did– and he misconstrued. I truly believe that, so why wouldn't Bremmer?"

Mario didn't remind his friend that he knew the Lord's fingerprints were all over what Mickey was doing before anybody, including Mickey, had so much as a clue. "The bishop will put a nifty spin on your story for the media. He's always loved to see the Catholic Church getting some positive print with all the negative stuff going on these days. If he can get his name squeezed into the story, all the better."

The bishop had been an outspoken critic of the news media for sensationalizing the deviant priest stories. Both Mickey and Mario had talked about the pedophile issue on many occasions, both felt that a thorough housecleaning along with a total disclosure had been delayed far too long–and, in too many case covered up by the Church's rigid hierarchy. "Mick, one more thing," his voice became subdued: "The last time we talked you said you were going to be calling your parents. Have you done that yet?"

Mickey's guilt settled in the back of his head, an ache shot down to his shoulders. If he had caused Mario great tribulation, his parents stress must be off the charts. "No. I've come close a couple of times, but no, I haven't. Look, no BS, I'll call them tomorrow. I've gotta start putting my own house in order before it's too late."

"Promise?"

"Word of honor."

As much as he would like to see the end result of his plans and prayers, it just wasn't meant to be. Mickey knew that reality from day one. This paradise was not home. Home would always be his beloved diocese in gray and frigid northern Minnesota. What would be harder for him to do: to leave TriPalms behind, or to face Bishop Bremmer's discipline?

47/ SADIE THE INTERROGATOR

Amos stared at Duane Slades phone number scribbled on the notepad at his elbow. What to do? Should he call the Saint Paul or Roseville police? Or, confront the man himself.

Sadie didn't like indecision and her husband was waffling. "Are you going to find out why this Slade guy was prowling around in our yard?"

"I'd really like to do that but if he's involved in this ugly extortion business, we might be pushing him into a corner; no telling what he might do then."

Sadie cocked an eyebrow, "If the police get involved, it might endanger our son. That note was emphatic– don't call the police."

"That's true enough, but extortionists always say that, hon. That being the case, however, you are right–I'm just overly reluctant to do anything that might put Mickey at risk I guess. Yet, on the other hand... " He hated indecision as much as his wife did.

Amos' face reddened, he slammed his fist on the tabletop: "That video still drives me crazy. What kind of pervert could even think of doing a thing like that? If I get my hands on him..."

"Only an absolute sicko would do something like this, and there are millions of them out there." Sadie stepped behind Amos, massaged her husband's shoulders, "How about if I make the call to this character, hon? Women have a way of putting things that put men off balance. Besides, sometimes I feel like I'm the third wheel."

"I have no problem with that, Sadie. I might lose my cool and do something stupid. Just wait a sec, let me get that little Sony recorder from the desk drawer in my office. If this Slade guy is involved, I want to get him on tape. Be right back."

Sadie punched the numbers on her iPhone, 1-651-5505, and let it ring a third, a fourth...

"Yeah, what's up, Duane here?"

Long pause, deliberate...

"You there?" from Duane.

Sadie's voice was two octaves lower than normal: "Yeah, this is Mrs. Moran–Mrs. Amos Moran. You stopped by our house in Hibbing when we weren't home the other day–what were you looking for, Duane?"

"Damn... finally! You damnwell know what I'm looking for. Don't get into playing games, lady... I want the money for crissakes!" Duane sensed he had the upper hand now; he'd handle this woman with ease. "I've been waiting weeks to hear from you. Don't you give a damn if your son's reputation goes down the toilet? What kind of mother are... ?"

"Whoa, just a minute. What are you talking about, Duane–I hope it's not about that joker who's playing a priest in the video you mailed out?"

"You in denial? Is that what it is, lady?"

"Screw you, denial... that's not my son and you damnwell know it, you pervert!"

Duane Slade laughed tightly, "Me a pervert? Did you see your son and the hooker on the video? He's the pervert, not me."

"You crack me up. There's no need for me to see it. I know enough to know that it's bogus. Those that have seen it–I should say the *experts* who examined it frame by frame–say the same. They all agree that is not my son." Sadie amazed herself at pulling that fabrication out of thin air. "A fair look-alike, but not Mickey. Sorry, you're not getting any money from me for your sleazy scam."

Sadie wondered if she was pressing Duane Slade too hard. "Sorry, we're just not in the market for porn these days. The only reason I called was to let you know that we aren't buying the crap you're trying to sell."

Duane felt a pang in his chest, a shortness of breath. He considered hanging up and retrieving his Valium in the medicine cabinet. This was all very strange. Where did this woman get his name, his unlisted phone number? Who were these 'experts' she mentioned? Who was she–really? Was she actually the priest's mother… or was Rossman putting a squeeze on him? It could be the police, too. They were clever. But, so was he.

"If you're really the priest's mother, you wouldn't be such a smart ass. You'd want to save your son's reputation. We've got the goods and we're ready to share them with the media. Can you imagine how the people in Duluth will react when they see the tape on the local news–no, I take that back, it's much too explicit for television. The internet is another story. One way or another, I think you'll find that everybody will see the truth–your son's just another f--ed up priest, they'll say. People are getting used to seeing that kind of stuff in the news these days. They'll think that your son just got caught in the act."

Amos smiled from over Sadie's shoulder, his wife was handling the conversation more convincingly than he could have. Maybe she should have been the lawyer in the family. "Do you know what else people enjoy seeing in the news, Duane Slade?" She used his surname for the first time. "They love seeing con men like yourself getting thirty years in the Stillwater pen without parole. Have you ever been there, Duane? Stillwater is just a few miles east of where you live on Highway 36… nice little town, Stillwater, but their prison is the absolute pits. Your friends, if you've got any, might drive over to visit for a few minutes on a Sunday afternoon. Otherwise, kiss the outside world goodbye!"

Duane knew more than he wanted to about Stillwater. The lady was right, if this scheme went bad he could spend a lot of years there. Yet, he clung to the notion that the ball was still in his court. "Tell you what, we'll send you a copy of your son and the hooker he hired.

You can be the judge, okay? I think you'll change your tune; I think you and your husband will want to make a trip to your bank and make a withdrawal. That's what I think. Then we can talk again about the details of where the money should be delivered. How's that sound, bitch?"

"That's enough," Amos cringed at the vulgarity, wanted to take the phone from Sadie and tell this jerk his days were numbered.

Nonplused, Sadie kept her grip on the phone. "Nah, you just save the postage money, Duane–buy a bottle of mouth wash. You eat with the same mouth you talk with?" Sadie wasn't going to let this jerk get under her skin. "Then, once you've cleaned the filth from your trap, you can go to your bank and withdraw some money. You'll probably need all you can get your hands on for defense lawyer fees. Oh, you might also remind your accomplices about life in Stillwater, Duane... see if they still want to sail on your sinking ship."

"That was great, hon," Amos whispered out of range of the speaker setting and tape recorder.

"What are you talking about... accomplices? Where'd you get that crazy idea from?"

"You just told me, more than once I believe. *We* this and *We* that."

Amos scribbled a note on a napkin, I think we already have enough to nail him with on the recorder.

Sadie nodded. "Well, Duane, that should do it for now. We'll meet you in court one of these fine days. Probably sooner than later– okay?"

"Funny lady. You won't laugh when all your friends hear about your son, the lustful priest. You can bet that the news is gonna break everybody's heart."

Sadie laughed, she had said enough. She handed Amos the phone. "Say Duane... Duane Slade of Roseville? Amos Moran here, would you be interested in making a trade... our tape of this conversation for your copy of the bogus video? Just kidding..."

The line went dead.

48/ A MILLION DOLLAR POOL

Father Mario called to assure Bishop Bremmer that his lost priest had never really been lost. "He told me last night that he would contact you in one week. He's finishing up with an important project. I have his word, Your Grace –he will call you."

"You've deliberately kept this from me, Father?"

"I have, Your Grace."

"Is he alright?"

"He's better than ever."

Bremmer breathed a sigh of relief, smiled to himself. He knew of the two men's friendship and didn't want to prejudge their deceitful behavior. Asking Father Mario how long he knew about Moran's whereabouts, or the extent of what he knew, would serve little purpose at this point–it might even prove to be counterproductive. Bremmer knew some things that Mario did not know, and he would keep them to himself for the moment–withholding information was a two-way street. Just knowing that Father Moran was not in any trouble or danger was enough for now Bremmer would say nothing about his conversation with Bishop Cordoba the night before, nor would he divulge a word about the controversial CD. Two could play the same game.

Bremmer cleared his throat: "Okay. I can be fine with that. Father. I've managed to get by without hearing from your friend for several weeks already–I guess I can wait one more. Tell me more about what you know of this program of his."

~

Family news finds its own predictable network. Sadie confided what she knew about this Duane Slade character to her daughter, Meghan.

Meghan then explained the extortion video and everything her mother told her to Kenny. Kenny, in turn, would relieve himself of the burden of keeping Mickey's whereabouts from his wife. He explained, then apologized; "It's been a secret I've kept from you, and everyone else, for a couple of weeks. Sorry, hon... your brother wanted it that way."

"I've got to tell my parents what Mickey's been doing. They have no idea and they're worried sick."

"I feel for them," Kenny said. "Let me suggest that you call Mickey first, tell him that I've spilled the beans, then get his permission to tell your folks what he's been up to. He has his own reasons for keeping his life hushed-up. He might want to tell your folks himself–I know it must be killing him to shut out his loved ones."

"Good idea. You've got his tracphone number, don't you?"

Kenny nodded, pulled a slip of paper from his billfold.

Mickey had told Kenny the day before that he would be finishing up with his part of the project in just a few days. "You going to tell him about that CD? Or, leave that up to your parents?" Kenny asked.

"I don't want to do that, I'm not..."

"Not what? What's that strange look, Meg? You don't think...?"

"I don't know what I think anymore. Everything and everybody is going bonkers around me. You and your secrets about my brother, my parents totally in the dark about their own son, a frustrated bishop in Duluth, extortion letters from this Slade weirdo? What else might be going on?"

"Meghan, don't be foolish! You're not thinking that Mickey...? There's gotta be some imposter out there." He laughed to himself, how could Meg even consider the possibility.

Meghan had not told her husband about her pre-Christmas meeting with Mickey in Duluth; another spousal secret. Her brother had been mean-spirited and holier than thou. Despite all the apologies and the wonderful time they had all shared at Christmas, she still hadn't completely buried those feelings. It seemed as if everybody had a secret, but acknowledging hers could wait for another day. Within a few moments, things settled down and her brief irritation faded. Meghan rehashed the barrage of information she had been given in the past several minutes. Something was stirring in the back of her mind... but what?

Suddenly, it struck her. The name Slade! In less than a minute, she had her mother back on the phone. Sadie confirmed that the Duane Slade she was inquiring about was the same Duane Slade that she had uncovered in grampa Kevin's old trunk. "Yes. The sister lives in Duluth, your father talked with her this morning. He said she was very pleasant and helpful."

"I've just picked up Mickey's phone number from Kenny–a long story there, I'll fill in the blanks later. I'm rushing, Mom... I'll let you and dad bring Mickey up to speed on this CD business. Okay? 'Til later, here's Kenny to give you the scoop as only he knows it."

When the family ship is on rough water, everybody on board wants to grab an oar and help in whatever way they can. Megan's mind was racing. She took down the phone number her mother had given her and called Elizabeth Slade from the landline in the living room. The woman, however, didn't answer and Meg wasn't going to leave a message. "Kenny, can you take care of the kids for a few hours? I'm driving down to Duluth." As she pulled on her winter coat, she explained what she hoped to find out. Kenny was totally supportive. "Good luck, hon... keep me posted."

Megan was out the front door and her Escalade out of the garage before Kenny could pick up the remote and off the mute button of NBA game he'd been watching on the TV before the flurry of phone calls.

Amos contacted the Minnesota Bureau of Criminal Apprehension in Saint Paul, explained what was happening in detail to a detective named Lucas Davenport. He was instructed to bring his recorder to the Naples police: "They've got pros down there, we'll get transcripts from them," Davenport assured. The Bureau would have an agent at the Roseville address of Duane Slade within the hour.

~

After clicking off his phone, Duane Slade began packing his suitcase. His train had just been derailed by that Moran woman, he cursed her as he emptied his underwear drawer, "Damn that woman!" he repeated several times. In five minutes he was out the door, and behind the wheel of his Lincoln two minutes later. He smelled trouble and wasn't going to stick around until the cops came. He'd crash at David Rossman's place for the time being–maybe head up to his sister's in Duluth later. But… Rossman would be furious if he learned what was going down–maybe he should keep everything to himself for now? Did Rossman share in the blame for a scheme that had somehow gone suddenly south? No, it wasn't suddenly at all, he realized–the plan had been going in the wrong direction from the start. As it stood now, he needed another plan; a plan of escape without consequences.

He checked his speed, seventy– ten over the posted limit. "Be careful, Duane" he mumbled. The last thing you need right now is a highway patrolman pulling you over". He slowed, his mind racing: Maybe, just maybe, Rossman could help. Misery loves company. As unpleasant as it would be, he'd have to tell Rossman the bad news, he'd open the can of worms that was their present predicament. But, then again, maybe he should have more fear of Rossman than of the police? The back and forth of his dilemma brought beads of perspiration to Duane's furrowed brow–where to go, what to do? He found himself traveling west on I-494, in the direction of Rossman's place. "If I can get my sorry ass out of this mess, I'm going straight. No more of the get-rich-quick stuff for Duane Slade."

"Preposterous!" Mickey cried in disbelief. "I've never heard of anything so totally absurd." Having finally found the courage to call his parents, he was hearing about the extortion CD for the first time. Sadie, at Amos shoulder, was on her phone to their daughter, Meg, taking notes, warming coffee in the microwave, and trying to keep abreast of Amos' conversation with their son– a veritable mistress of multi-tasking.

Amos said, "I know its crazy, son."

"The bishop can't possibly believe this crock…" Mickey said.

"The bishop wouldn't say what he believed."

"I hope mom doesn't…" From Mickey.

"No, not for a minute."

"Who's behind…?"

"I've been on it already. Some guy named Slade? From the Cities? Your mom's already let him have both barrels." Amos confided.

"She talked to this guy?"

"More than talked; she reamed him!"

A pause from Mickey's end. "Then he knows that you know?"

"Yeah. I think your mom scared the hell…Slade hung up on her."

"You're kidding… mom did?"

"It's on tape, listen for yourself." Amos played the recorder for Mickey. "I've already played this for the state police in Minnesota and I'm bringing it to the Naples police when I get off the phone with you."

"You think this Duane Slade might already be in custody, Dad?"

"They will keep us posted."

"Tell mom she's an awesome interrogator." Mickey said.

"She knows that already."

Mickey laughed, cleared his throat. "I've got a lot that I need to tell you about…"

"I'd say so," Amos's voice was tight. "What in God's name have you been doing with yourself for the past few weeks? Meghan told us something about a place called Palmtrees... said that you would finally fill us in."

"I hope it's been *'in God's name'* as you just put it, Dad. Mickey briefly explained his life in TriPalms, his plan to have a 'tell all' conversation with Bishop Bremmer, and his plans to return to Minnesota. "We've got the most wonderful team you could imagine working on our project."

"I'll–I mean, we'll have to get up there–your mom and me. Maybe tomorrow, will that work for you."

"That's great. You'll both see an old friend of ours–he's part of our team."

Amos remembered the Wheelers well, "I'm not surprised that Larry stepped in to help. I know his father would have done the same. Great people."

After a few minutes of updating for his mother's benefit, Mickey steered back to the Slade CD, "You think that guy is dangerous?"

"No. Con artists are opportunists, people without conscience–sociopaths, " Amos said. "Cowards as well," Sadie added.

Mickey returned to his work in TriPalms. "The folks here are really excited about everything. It's just great to see." In describing the project he had set the table for a question–already knowing how his parents would answer. "Say, ... hypothetically, would you be able to cough up that million bucks without taking out a major loan? I mean, if my life were in some kind of danger?"

"You know better than to ask that, son. We've been blessed with Grampa Kevin's inheritance for years." Amos said. "I don't even know much we've got. That's your mom's department–she's the accountant, not me."

"But... you've got that kind of money–a million dollars–if you needed to get it."

"Sure we do," Sadie said, from her husband's side where she was listening intently. "What are you driving at, Mickey?"

The living room phone rang, an anxious Sadie rushed to get it.

"It's Meg again," she called to Amos in the kitchen. "Keep Mickey on the phone until I'm done here."

Meghan had her own agenda going forward, "I'm turning onto Highway 53, heading for Duluth right now." She explained her plan, then said a quick goodbye. "Oh, tell my brother I love him."

Racing back into the kitchen, Sadie took Amos' phone and playfully shoved him to the side. "I'm back, what's this about a million dollars? Do you want us to pay off that sicko? That would be an admission of guilt." Sadie's forehead developed deep furrows.

Amos whispered to his wife, "He was beginning to say something about a pool he's in–I think." "

"You've lost that much money in some kind of pool, son?" Sadie said. "You've been gambling? Is that it? Is that real reason that you haven't called in so long? Mickey, you ought to be ashamed!"

Amused, Mickey explained that he wanted them to consider building a pool in TriPalms, not pay off any debts.

Still confused, Sadie said, "For heaven's sake, we've got a nice pool in the back yard." Looking askance at Amos, she said "Doesn't he know that he can come over for a swim any time he wants."

"I think I need a drink," Amos said after saying goodbye to his son. "I believe we should have a toast to our wonderful son."

"And to our wonderful new investment," Sadie added.

"I'll drink to that."

Sadie gave him a hug, "Me, too. From all that Mickey's told us, I'd have to agree–we've made two very good investments: our son and the children of TriPalms."

Amos splashed tonic over the gin and ice cubes, handed a glass to Sadie and raised his own: "To an olympic-sized swimming pool for the fine folks–not only the kids– of TriPalms, Florida. We've got to do a road trip tomorrow–can't wait to see Mick… see his project."

Sadie nodded and was about to say something when Meghan's

special ring filled the room.

"I'll get it," Amos said as he reached for his cell on the kitchen table. Upon answering he said to Sadie, "I've got you on speaker."

Meghan was following her GPS instructions, ""I'm almost to the mall, turning on, like, Arrowhead Road now," she said. "Did Mom tell you what I'm up to?"

"Uh huh, good luck."

"I'll see if I can, like, learn something from this Slade woman. You talked with her, does she sound... like, okay, you know."

"She's *like* okay, Meg. Why do you talk like that all the time."

"Talk like what?"

"Punctuating every sentence with 'like'."

"If I didn't, your grandchildren wouldn't be able to understand a thing I said. Like, that's just how it is, Dad. I mean, like, we're already twelve years into a new century. Like, get with it before it passes you by."

When both Moran parents had finished a second gin-tonic and rehashed their conversations with their two children, Amos reached across the glass table on the outside patio where they had retreated for fresh air. Taking Sadie's hand in his he said, "Did I tell you how great you were on the phone with Duane Slade today?"

"You might have and I couldn't agree more. *Great*, however, is a bit mild. I think stupendous is more like it."

"Stupendous works for me."

"How'ze 'bout a thirrrd, m'dear," Sadie purposely slurred, laughing at herself. "It's been a wunderfullll day."

Amos chuckled along with his wife, "We've got something wonderful–make that stupendous–to celebrate. Our prodigal son has been found!"

"That too," Sadie giggled like a schoolgirl, "but I still can't help myself from thinking about our becoming the proud parents of a million- dollar swimming pool."

49/ REALITY CHECK

David Rossman did not mince words with his former associate; "Duane, get your ass outta my sight. I don't ever want to see your stupid face again. When they catch up with you, and they damn well are going to, you had better keep your mouth shut! Zip-zip! Got it? You give them my name and you're dead meat. You won't have a place in the world to hide from me–not even the Stillwater pen."

Duane held his hands in front of him, in deference to the larger man's threats. His voice was low, conciliatory: "Com'on... I'm no rat–you know that. Give a guy a break, Dave. How about if I hang out in your motel for a few days? Only two, maybe three, I promise. Nobody will ever know that I'm there. Please! I won't be no trouble. I gotta come up with a plan of some kind. Gimme a little break, damn it!"

Rossman laughed, "I'll give you a break, all right, you ain't outta my sight in one minute, I'll break your f—ing neck!" With the warning, the bulky filmmaker grabbed Duane by the arm and steered him toward the apartment door.

~

Megan almost fell off the porch when Beth Slade opened the side door of her neat bungalow. Beth's brother Brian was sitting at the kitchen table eating a powdered sugar donut. "Oh my God! I can't believe what I'm seeing."

Brain stood, smiled at Meghan: "I'm Brian. Beth told me I look like your brother" –even his smile was Mickey! "It's nice to meet you."

Still speechless, all Meghan could do was shake her head in an astonishment she was in no way prepared for. Blinking as if what she was seeing was an apparition she mumbled *impossible* under her breath.

Brian felt a surge of relief as he stepped forward and offered his hand to the stylishly dressed woman standing in a frozen pose near the entry door. This was going to by his moment–his charade would end here and now. When Beth had told him that the priest's sister would be visiting them, he searched the closet of his conscience where the junk was being stored. It was time to clean the closet. Brian would need to take a step or two backward in order for his life to move forward.

Brian's forehead furrowed, his eyes averted: "Lot'sa people down here think I'm a priest. Think that I'm your brother–Father Moran. It's been kinda fun for me. I didn't mean any harm by it–honest. I mean, by wearing my priest outfit now and then. But I knew it was wrong, too. It was like… for the first time in my life, I felt like somebody. Like somebody people could respect."

He looked at his sister standing with an expression of surprise that was equal to that of the woman named Meghan. "I shoulda said something before now… I know that. I'm sorry… sorry to both of you."

Now Beth was confused, "What outfit are you talking about, Bry?"

Brian's expression was sheepish. "Don't get mad at me, Beth–okay?"

"What okay? Maybe I will get mad."

"Well I didn't want to tell anybody… but maybe I should have. I mean now that the priest's sister is here." He gestured for the two women to sit at the table, then pulled out a chair for himself. When they were seated, Brian took a deep breath: "Without meaning to, I let myself get hooked into one of Duane's stupid schemes."

Not only did Brian explain the *'Satan's Window'* scam but he explained what his older brother and this Rossman character were planning to do with the video. "When I learned what they were up to I tried to get the CD away from them. It ended up with me getting beat up a bit–two against one– but, I got in a lick or two." He smiled weakly, making eye contact with Meghan. "Anyhow, I took off–came home... I mean, came to Beth's house. I didn't want any part of what they were up to."

His eyes moved to his sister sitting at his elbow, he voice was no more than a contrite mumble... "I'm sorry, Beth."

Beth stroked the back of her brother's hand, the disappointment slowly leaving her face. "You did the right thing, I'm proud of you, Bry. Very proud."

Brian felt the burden melt from his shoulders as he fought back tears. His lips quivered, he sniffled, rubbed at his nose... he wanted to hug his sister, wanted to thank her profusely for those few kind words...wanted to affirm that what she had just said was like having the filth of his indiscretions washed away. He didn't have those words but he did have a smile of relief that spoke even more eloquently.

Meghan, overwhelmed with empathy, confirmed that Brian had done the right thing. She told the Slade siblings that their brother Duane's insidious plot had been exposed and that the police were probably already out looking for the pair of extortionists. "You've been through a lot, Brian. I really appreciate your candor. Much of what you've told us might be helpful–like, I didn't know that your brother had a partner in crime."

"Oh yes, a guy named David Rossman." Brian said. He didn't mention Dianne Miller's name because she, like himself, was more victim than instigator–albeit a most willing victim.

Meghan nodded, continued her side of the story. "The CD made it's way to the bishop's office here in Duluth. My brother only learned about it earlier today. He's been in Florida since shortly after Christmas."

"Oh my! The bishop, Bishop Bremmer, knows about this," Beth was stupefied.

Meghan nodded without reply.

"I knew this was going to happen," Brian said. "There's no such thing as easy money. I should have learned that by now. I guess we all–the three of us–are going to have to pay the price." He turned his head away from the two women, felt a throb at the back of his head. "I'm a part of the whole miserable thing, even if I quit when I knew what it really was. Two hundred lousy bucks and I'll end up in jail again. I have the damndest luck! You know something else," he turned to meet Meg's eyes, "I just got a decent job at the hospital where Beth works. I thought that finally, finally I would start getting things right. Now I'm screwed..." his thought trailed off to a realm of complete, self-loathing, remorse.

If Beth remained in shock over the disclosure, Meghan was still shaking her head in disbelief. How could any human being be a near perfect replica of another? Brian Slade was a veritable clone. Even Brian's display of emotion was Mickey-like. Incredible!

Beth, seated across from the Hibbing woman, was feeling the pain of her brother. The thought of Brian's going to prison was heartbreaking. Brian was crying now. Beth took Meghan's hand in hers; "I'm sorry, Mrs. Moran; sorry beyond words. Your poor brother having to go through this... this mess. I saw him once, last Christmas, he seemed like a very decent man, a spirit-filled man." She took a Kleenex from her sweater pocket, dabbed at tears. "Excuse me a moment, let me get you a cup of coffee. It will only take a minute."

Meghan gave Beth's hand a gentle squeeze, then released it. "Thanks, I'd like that."

As Beth busied herself at the counter, Meghan's gaze returned to Brian. Brian, seemingly lost in his thoughts, had stopped crying and was staring vacantly out the kitchen window. She almost felt as if she was staring at her own brother, as if Mickey was suffering some grave disappointment. As she was about to say something consoling to the man... she was struck with a realization...

Before she could speak, Brian turned toward her, "I'm sorry for what I've done. I hope you can believe that. I hope that your brother can too. I could tell you were staring at me... are you angry?" Meg shook her head, "No, not with you, Brian. And, I do believe that you are sorry, sincerely sorry. And, yes... I apologize for staring. But, I've just realized something– you have blue eyes, Brian. Mickey, Father Moran, has green eyes. Were it not for that... ?

"Duane told me that my voice wasn't quite the same. He had some tape recordings of Father Moran saying Mass.

Meghan frowned at the admission of tape recordings. "Maybe that's true–but, with everything else so identical, who would really pay any attention to the voice?"

~

The next morning, Amos and Sadie drove up I-75 from Naples to Venice. The two were still trying to get a handle on what Meghan and Mickey had told them the night before. Amos had gone to his trusty computer and searched for information on the phenomenon of genetic doubles. He found the word he probably hadn't considered since reading a chapter on parapsychology in a psych textbook back in college–doppelganger. He reasoned that the connection between his son and this Brian Slade probably went back five generations to Denis Moran and a woman named Sally Slade. Bizarre but plausible! That being the case, this Brian Slade had legitimate Moran genes. Incredible!

When they pulled off the highway and into Venice, Amos stopped at a 7-Eleven convenience store. When he asked for the directions to TriPalms, the nearly toothless woman at the counter glanced at the silver Lexus parked outside, shook her head: "Me thinks you got sum bum infermaton, sir. Youze don wanna go out dere."

The community of Tri Palms was a depressing site, but exactly as Mickey had described. Mickey greeted his parents with a hug. "Isn't it crazy? Me having a genetic double! I've heard of this doppelganger thing, but never thought I'd see the likes of this. It's like the paranormal stuff you hear about on late-night radio."

"Coast-to-Coast? I know, I've listened to their programs when I can't seem to fall asleep," Amos said. "Interesting stuff, some great interviews."

Hector Munoz came over and introduced himself, "Welcome on board, Mr. Moran, Missus Moran. I'm glad you can see all this before we're too far above ground. When we are finished with everything, you won't recognize the place."

Larry Wheeler joined the group, smiling widely. "So good to see you both. It's been years. You haven't changed a bit."

Amos and Sadie each took his hand, reciprocated his comment: "And you look just like the teenager we remember so well, Larry," Sadie said. They had missed the recent funeral of Todd Wheeler, Larry's father. Mrs. MaryEllen Wheeler had passed away years before. Sadie squeezed Larry's hand, offered belated condolences: "Your parents were such wonderful people, Larry. We miss them so."

Larry acknowledged the sentiment with a nod. "So, your son has hooked you two just like he hooked me."

"The first disciples were fishermen, weren't they?" Sadie said.

"Point well taken," Mickey said.

Larry shaded his eyes from the sun with a clipboard he was holding. "I can't do enough for these folks. There's a great feeling going on here. Your son has been a human dynamo; the people here, young and old alike, simply adore him–and, rightfully so."

"We're delighted to finally get a chance to participate, Larry," Amos said, more to his son than to anybody else.

Mickey noted the emphasis on 'finally'. He let it pass. "Truth be told, these guys do all the work here, I just enjoy taking credit for it."

They all laughed, "Let our 'number one' slacker show you folks around while we get back to work. Mickey's been checking his wrist watch for the past five minutes," Larry said. "That means that the break time he allows Hector and me is over for this morning. Right, boss!"

The footings already outlined the dimensions of the new community center. Two rows of concrete blocks were in place and stacks more were awaiting mortar. "Hector is going to build a large patio over there and the pool, your pool…" Mickey gestured ahead toward a large rectangle of stakes delineating the approximate size and shape of the pool. "Your pool should be situated like so. A brick patio will surround it and extend to over there." He pointed toward an area staked out nearly thirty yards from where they were standing. "We'll squeeze a kiddy pool out of the funds, too. That will be separate– a few yards beyond. Over there to the left."

Amos saw what lay beyond the 'over there' of his son's sweeping gesture. A row of dingy trailers with little space between them and surrounded by hard-packed dirt. He shook his head. "Almost makes me upset in the stomach, son. How can a family live in housing like that–raise their kids? We just don't realize that there are places like these only a stone's throw from the highway."

Sadie felt a shame of her own. The two of them lived in Old Naples, one of the most luxurious residential areas in all of Florida. Two people with two thousand feet of space. On Thursday of every week, crews of Hispanics like those she could see here in TriPalms, cut their grass, trimmed their shrubs, and hauled off the debris. Nice people. Always pleasant, always a smile, always busy–never sneaking away to a shady spot or taking an unauthorized break from their toils–not even to cool off in temperatures in the eighties with a matching humidity. "I just never gave it any thought, son. Where these people lived, how they lived… I would have… " She didn't have the right words to express what she 'would have'; her emotions of the moment said enough. For Sadie the 'reality check' of two different worlds would leave a lasting impression.

Mickey could intuit his mother's thoughts by reading the expression on her face. "Over there," Mickey pointed toward the trailer his father had referred to. "That's where the Rodriguez family lives. Extended family, I should say. Elderly grandparents, Luis and Monica and their four children, Monica's sister and her husband Juan Casilla–they have three children. Three small bedrooms and thirteen bodies."

Amos shook his head, "That shouldn't be."

Mickey agreed, "It is what it is. In time, maybe we can change it some. In time… maybe?"

50/ SAYING GOODBYE

After saying goodbye to his parents, Mickey visited with his two committed benefactors at a card table under the shade afforded by a tent awning. With the generous assurances from Amos and Sadie Moran, their vision for the people of TriPalms was well on its way to becoming a reality.

"Well, guys… it's that time for me."

Larry Wheeler looked into the dark eyes of Hector Munoz, then into the deep-set green eyes of his friend. "What's that supposed to mean, Mick?"

Father Mickey had never completely shared his story with these two men, these two dedicated and generous friends. "I have a confession to make. If the two of you will hear it and give me absolution I'll feel much better."

Both men looked one to the other, shrugged in mutual confusion, and then nodded. Mickey emptied his soul. "So, I've been persona non grata in my diocese up north these past six weeks or so. I talked with my bishop the other night and smoothed things out a bit–at least I think I did."

Neither man knew quite how to respond to the story they had just been told. "I've done all that I can do here, fellas. Now it's time for me to go home."

Larry slid his chair next to Mickey's gave his friend a hug, "I knew that one of these days you would be leaving… but… " His sentiment was left hanging as his throat constricted.

Standing up from the table where they had been sitting, Hector Munoz folded back the cover of the blueprints folder from the blueprints on the table. A man of emotional stoicism and few words, Hector swallowed a lump in his throat, then walked behind Mickey's chair and placed his large hand on his friend's mop of unkempt hair, "May God always walk at your side, Father." With that sentiment the tall Cuban walked away.

Mickey had circled February 15 on his calendar. Over the six weeks of leave from his other life, Mickey had been a dropout in every sense of the word. He hadn't read a newspaper or watched a news program on TV since the day he set foot in TriPalms. He didn't know that his Twins had lost two of his favorite players in Michael Cuddyer and Jason Kubel. Nor, that pitchers and catchers would be reporting to spring training camp in Ft. Myers in a few days.

Nor did Mickey know that a Catholic man named Rick Santorum was currently the leading Republican candidate. Mitt Romney, a Mormon, was close behind. Key primaries in Michigan and Arizona were ahead.

The Middle East remained a boiling kettle with speculation that Iran's nuclear program was dangerously close to threatening the entire region. Many wondered if Israel would take a military initiative and bomb the Irani research facilities. Syria was close to outright civil war and gas prices in Florida were escalating toward $4 a gallon. President Obama's hair, like that of his predecessors, was becoming grayer with each month of his presidency.

There was more than a grain of truth in the adage: The evening news is where network anchors Scott Pelley, Brian Williams, or Diane Sawyer begin with 'Good Evening' and then proceed to explain why it isn't.

Mickey would have time to consider how irrelevant so much of what he had always thought to be important really was. He could do little to make his Twins contenders in 2012. His one vote for president in November might be important, but certainly not critical–especially in Minnesota where voters loved the donkey. And, world politics were in hands of people whose motivations were largely unknown to him. The sum total of all the news he had missed was a point or two over zilch.

His six weeks in this remote and largely unheard of Hispanic community, however, did have relevancy. His time and efforts did make a difference in the lives of more than three thousand good people. Mickey had good feelings about what had been accomplished there. Back at Saint Gerard's, in his absence, Sarah Donovan and all the others were probably doing just fine. If he had been there, instead of here for these past several weeks, he probably wouldn't have changed much of anything in the lives of his aged parishioners. With the attitude he had at the time of departure, he might have effected changes in people's lives in the range of two or three over zero.

Mickey paced and prayed and tried to cope with a melancholy deeper than any he had experienced before. His work at TriPalms was done for now–probably forever. He could stay longer and help with the construction, but that wasn't the kind of service he needed to do. He missed saying Mass far more than he ever thought he could. As rewarding and enriching as everything in TriPalms had been, the emptiness inside him was pervasive. Being a day-to-day priest was far more important than being a social worker extraordinaire. Mickey Moran was getting in touch with the reality that he had become, in the words of an old Kristofferson song, a walking contradiction. Perhaps that was the greatest epiphany in his young life.

Mickey's confession to Bishop Bremmer was now behind him and he seemed confident that, with due diligence, the burned bridges could be mended. All the puzzle pieces of his recent life appeared to be in place for now. With a heavy heart he surveyed the village that had been his home for six weeks–six weeks that seemed so much longer that it was hard to comprehend. Evidence of the community building rising from the dirt, soccer goals at each end of the field, the old trash dump no longer evident, the smell of fresh paint hanging in the air. The spirit of beautification was contagious and competitive as well, with weekly donations of paints and supplies from the local hardware store where Alberto Olivio worked, nearly everybody was becoming a part of the transformation.

Mickey had never been very good with goodbyes so he hadn't said a word to any of the residents of TriPalms about his impending departure. As much as he would like to slip away into the night, doing so would not be respectful to those he had come to love. Yet he would not allow any kind of farewell fete or recognition.

Having told Larry Wheeler and Hector Munoz of his plans, he would pay a final visit to the Olivio family the night before his departure. There were many tears shed among friends that last evening in TriPalms. "We cannot thank you enough, Mickey," Alexi said in the broken English he had been working on every day.

Mickey smiled: "My thanks will be the prayers you say for me, okay?"

Miguel, so sad he could hardly speak, tried to get words through his swollen throat: "I will pray for you every day and... maybe, if I work hard in school... maybe one day I can become a priest like you."

Maria remained dry eyed and somber throughout the emotional

farewells. "Will you pray for me, Father?"

"Absolutely, Maria–every day of my life."

The tension that had been welling up inside the lovely young woman finally vented. Her eyes were downcast and her voice cracked as she spoke: "I would like for you to pray that my parents allow me to go to college so I may become a nurse."

Now that her consuming sadness was out in the open for the very first time, Mickey could understand Maria's hurt. He looked toward Alexi who looked to his daughter for an accurate translation of what she had told the priest.

"Miguel, will you tell your father what Maria has told me?" Mickey said.

The boy beamed, turning to his father he stirred a rapid conversation that caused his sister Maria to suddenly begin sobbing. Alexi stepped over to his daughter and embraced her, patting her long hair. "Lo siento... Lo siento..."

Miguel offered a translation that Mickey would have understood in any language. "Papa is sorry."

Mickey nodded, "Miguel, will you please tell your father that my mother would be honored to pay the tuition for her schooling."

As the boy spoke to his father, Alexi shook his head, told Miguel to tell Mickey that he had been saving for Maria's education for the past six years quietly and patiently, a few dollars at a time. With her father's admission, Maria's quiet weeping became deeper sobs.

Mickey would leave the Olivios with every confidence that one way or another, Maria would go to college, and the other children would follow in her footsteps. He would leave TriPalms knowing that he would have their prayers, and the prayers of many others, to sustain him in good times and bad. And, he might hope that maybe one day in years to come, he would be able to pray with a young Hispanic priest named Father Miguel Alberto Olivio. He would leave it at that.

51/ ABANDONMENT

When Duane Slade was pushed toward the door of Rossman's apartment, he spotted a set of car keys on the counter near a chrome toaster. As he pushed back at the larger man, he slipped a hand into his trouser pocket and found his Lincoln's keys. Rossman tried to knee Duane in the groin, hit his thigh instead–Duane bit at his adversary's shoulder, then kicked Rossman above the ankle, Rossman buckled slightly, allowing Duane the moment he needed to deftly made the switch of key rings.

"You sonofabitch!" Rossman screeched in pain, "I'll break your neck." He hadn't seen Duane's hand swipe his keys off the counter behind him. He grabbed at the hair on the side of Duane's head, yanked. "You ever…"

Duane was able to get a grip on the door handle, jerking his head back and with all his remaining strength, kicking Rossman's leg again. "I'm outta here!" he cried.

Behind him he heard Rossman bellow, "You bastard! If I never see you again…"

Adrenalin pumping, Duane hustled down the hall, down one flight of stairs, and out the side exit door.

Rossman's black Beamer was in the front row of parked cars. A push of the middle button on the key panel brought a flash of headlights and the click of an unlocked door. Within two minutes, Duane Slade was on the 494 ramp leaving West Saint Paul and heading west. Why west? Where was he going? In his panic he wasn't thinking clearly. The last he had heard, his father was living somewhere in Reno, his mother in Atlanta or Charleston. Dianne Miller's apartment in Richfield would probably be the first place Rossman, or anybody else who might be looking for him, would check. Yet, maybe she had some money he could borrow… maybe she could even be smooth-talked into taking a road trip with him? Dianne was usually game for anything.

Duane could only guess at how long it would be before Rossman realized his car had been stolen. Since the swap of his Lincoln for this older model BMW was nearly a wash, he wondered if Rossman would even report it stolen to the police? He doubted that–David Rossman might already be on the run himself. The BMW had a half tank of fuel. If the police were already looking for him, his credit cards would be too easily tracked and too risky to use. He had three twenties and some ones in his wallet. Not knowing what to do next brought a spike to his already high blood pressure and beads of perspiration across his brow. Spent testosterone from his scuffle and the stress of his situation was an obnoxious odor in his damp armpits.

South on 169, the lure of the Mystic Lake Casino in combination with his crushing indecision created a desirable pocket of asylum. Duane Slade always found relaxation sitting in front of a spinning and blinking and pinging slot machine.

~

Mickey's final assignment before leaving Florida was set for the early morning on Wednesday, the fifteenth day of February. In their recent conversation, Bishop Bremmer had asked him to visit the Venice bishop and set things straight with him. After embracing his hosts, the Placencios, and giving them the Saint Jude medal he had worn for years as a token of his gratitude, and rousing Torts from under the back bumper of his car, Mickey was ready to begin living the next chapter of his priesthood.

The sun was just rising over his shoulder in the eastern sky as his dusty Civic headed down the dirt roadway from TriPalms and toward the city of Venice. He had vowed to himself not to look back on the village; knowing that his heavy heart would break. But, TriPalms couldn't be left alone–Mickey blessed himself as he adjusted his rearview mirror. "Thank you Lord for blessing my life so beautifully. I pray your blessings on those I leave behind… and those that are ahead of me. Thank you for changing me in ways I would never have imagined. I promise to serve you better and love you more for as long as I live." The feelings of exhilaration and melancholy were competing emotions of the moment. When times were good, or when they were bad, he had always used his friend as a sounding board. Never did he feel disappointed with the advice he received. He mashed Mario's number on his iPhone.

"Hey, my friend, what's up." Mario knew more than Mickey did on this bright Wednesday morning.

"I'm headed north, Mario. One last stop and I'm on I-75."

"I know. I'm happy for you. I'll say a prayer that your meeting with Bishop Cordoba goes well."

Mickey puzzled, "How do you know about that?"

"I know lots of things, Mick. I'm in the loop, you know."

"What loop is that?"

"I know all the honchos, they like me, that's all."

Mickey laughed to himself, Mario was a master BS'er. "So, what is this Cordoba like? I've heard good things–really good things. I don't think he's anything like our Bishop Brenner?"

"You'll see for yourself."

"Thanks. Well, I'll check in with you later, I'm almost there. It probably won' be more than a few minutes. Kinda like as courtesy call. He's probably a busy guy."

"Say, I want to tell you something that everybody else seems to know and you don't quite have a handle on. Okay?"

"Shoot. I've got another minute."

"Mick, I want to congratulate you."

"Yeah... "

"No, just a minute. There's been a miracle–*a passage of redemption*. Think about that, okay? You've been given a gift from the Guy upstairs."

Mario's words brought him back to the Christmas night coffee conversation when Mario had told him that God had something marvelous in store for him. Perhaps it had been a miracle. "Thanks, Mario. You had the scoop quite a while ago."

"Welcome, Amigo. Be prepared for some surprises before the day is over. I've got the inside scoop again."

"What do you mean by that?"

The phone was dead.

One block from the bishop's residence, Mickey saw blinking lights in his rear view mirror and pulled over. He swallowed a cuss. He'd been careful to observe all of the traffic signs and had made a complete stop at the last intersection.

"Was I speeding officer?"

The unsmiling trooper cleared his throat. "No. The citation I've got here says 'abandonment'–what's that about."

Mickey shrugged, "I have no idea, sir."

"You leave something behind in TriPalms, Father?"

How did this cop know he had driven from TriPalms? "Not that I'm aware of, sir." Mickey had double-checked everything late the night before. "No, I couldn't have."

"Well, says here you did," the officer examined his ticket book.

Then Mickey heard a loud bark coming from the back seat of the patrol car. He turned, looked over his shoulder. Tort's head was hanging out of the window.

"Folks said this here's your dog, Father. You'd better take him back to Minnesota with you. Buy him some warm blankets; I'm told that you've still got a few more months of winter up there."

52/ THE BISHOP OF VENICE

Torts came with a leash, a bag of Iams dog food, and a water bowl. Mickey stroked behind his ears before hooking him to the back bumper where there was ample early morning shade. "Back in a few minutes, Torts. Then we're off to a place where shade will be the last thing on your mind for a long, long time.

What an amusing and thoughtful surprise the dog was. He would have Torts to remind him of the love he was leaving behind. Once again he was choked with emotion. Mickey found himself fighting back tears. He counted to ten, hoping to grasp a measure of composure as he stood outside of the Epiphany Cathedral. The notion of turning around and going back to TriPalms tugged at his heartstrings.

"Suck it up, Mick," he told himself– saying 'I'm sorry' is a lot easier than saying 'good-bye'! His apologies had begun with his own bishop, would continue here, and would find a completion of sorts back in Minnesota. He signed himself, swallowed, stepped into the church's foyer and prepared to meet a man whom others he knew had called 'holy'. Mickey realized that Bishop Cordoba had been caught somewhere in the middle of a controversy, a vague disciplinary action of other peoples making. What more could he possibly tell this bishop than 'I'm sorry'?

Mickey regarded himself in a long mirror that hung near a statue of Saint Anthony in the waiting area. Mickey's tanned face was a Spanish brown and he had lost a few pounds but his black suit fit him better than he remembered. Lucia Placencio had pressed his slacks and washed his collar until it virtually shown. Wearing his priestly garb for the first time in weeks allowed him to feel the strength of his commitment to God. When ushered into the bishop's office by a lanky priest named Eduardo, Mickey found a small, brown-faced man of unexpected youth sitting in a chair near a massive stained glass window, reading glasses were propped on his wide nose. The bishop rose, stepped toward his guest, spreading his arms widely.

"Father Michael... or should I call you Mickey," his smile spread wrinkles across his round face as he embraced the taller man. "Or, maybe, the *secreto padre*, as you have been called by my people in TriPalms?" Cordoba's smile was disarming and Mickey's liking of the man was immediate and absolute. What did this man already know? What had Bremmer confided? The hug was genuine in its affection. "Please come and sit with me," the bishop gestured toward the pair of chairs.

The two men talked for nearly an hour about what was being done at TriPalms. "I've known all along that you were there, Father; doing God's work in the long-overdue manner that it was supposed to be done. It just never occurred to me to tell my friend, and your bishop, about it. As far as I was concerned, you had improvised your own rehabilitation program—one far better than any I might have come up with myself." Mickey laughed along with Bishop Cordoba.

Then, there was a pause, something almost magnetic had bonded the two men, each could feel the genuine affinity. Any pretences or status constraints had melted away. Mickey met the Bishop's searching dark eyes. "What? Is there something that I . . ?"

A radiance shown on Cordoba's face, "I'm curious, Mickey." The bishop had become comfortable with the nickname. "What you have done these past weeks is highly unusual to say the very least... Why, why did you do what you did?—what was the motivation to immerse yourself in a culture that you knew nothing about? And, as I understand it, a community that didn't offer you a very warm welcome when you arrived?"

Good questions. Mickey considered his response for a long moment. "Like Your Grace, I guess... some time ago I received an invitation—an invitation to follow Him. Jesus wanted and I heard His calling. I have to believe that on that January afternoon when it all began to unfold, it was He deciding precisely where I would park my car, and precisely when I would return to the parking lot. It was Him who led me to a little boy who had just had an accident, and... from that moment, I simply followed His will without giving it too much thought. I know that's kinda trite, but I can't describe it any differently. Some might consider it to have been a coincidence, I have no doubt that it was Divine intervention."

"Well spoken, son, it was pretty much as I thought. There's no better way to understand it. And, like yourself, I don't believe in coincidence when it come to spiritual matters." Cordoba took Mickey's hand in his. "An invitation to follow Jesus... you put it very nicely."

"Thank you, Your Grace." Mickey wondered if the bishop's touch was a subtle invitation of his own–an invitation to say a prayer or maybe to conclude the meeting. "Well, I suppose..." He was about to rise from his chair and thank the bishop for his kind words.

Cordoba squeezed, then released Mickey's hand. "Another moment of two–I'm enjoying myself immensely. Am I keeping you from something?"

Mickey flushed, "No, your Grace. Not at all. I'm feeling blessed beyond words."

"As am I, Mickey." Cordoba's expression became more somber than at any time in their meeting. "My silence has been golden–that is until last week when I learned about this video nonsense from your bishop in Duluth. A very nice man, and a friend of mine for years. A man who thinks far more of you than you can possibly realize. We had a long chat, Tony and I, and I learned much about your colorful, if not somewhat checkered, history up there in Minnesota."

Mickey nodded, chuckled to himself–not only at reference to his 'checkered' past, but even more at the reference to Bishop Anthony Brenner as 'Tony'.

Cordoba noticed the chuckle, understood it, continued, "He told me that most of that more recent business at Saint Gerard's parish has been cleared up. A nice fellow named Little Otter along with a few other parishioners visited with the bishop about some woman who had been stirring up the nest at your church for years. Anyhow, that's another story and I'm sure he will want to tell it to you himself."

"Are you saying that Bishop Brenner knew what I was doing down here before I called him the other night?" Mickey's eyes betrayed his surprise.

Cordoba nodded genially: "He did–I had already given him a rather detailed report. When he got his head around your work down here, he decided to allow you to make your own decision about when to leave. Oh, we both wanted to let you tell the TriPalms story yourself."

"Are you telling me, Your Grace, that he would have been okay with my staying here, in TriPalms, longer? I can hardly believe…"

"I was certainly of the impression that the timing of your departure was, at very least, a negotiable matter, Father. Would you like to stay longer?"

His stomach gripped. He was not prepared for this invitation. Without any searching of his soul, Mickey's answer was as impulsive as it was emphatic: "No… my work here is done, Your Grace. I'd only be a bystander. It's all been wonderful… but…

"I understand and accept that." Then the bishop's eyes and expression changed from that of mirth to that of melancholy. "I want to continue what you have started in TriPalms and expand my own ministry to TriPalms… and, to every Hispanic community in my diocese. There are more impoverished enclaves than most people realize, all of them facing similar challenges to those you encountered." His forehead furrowed in heartfelt sadness, "I have failed my people, terribly, I'm afraid. I can't plead ignorance either. Apathy–yes, for sure. For that I pray for yours and God's forgiveness. But no longer will my eyes be closed–I intend to assign a priest to TriPalms when your community center is completed. Thanks to you, the Spirit is alive there now."

Mickey's eyes widened. "A priest? The folks will be ecstatic."

"The deserve far more than they get from my Diocesan office." Cordoba's admission deeply inspired him and the bishop's promised commitment to other communities like TriPalms was beyond anything he might have imagined. "God bless you, Your Grace."

"I hope he will, Father. In fact, I think He already has."

Mickey was ready to stand for the second time, to excuse himself, and receive the bishop's farewell blessing. This meeting had surpassed anything he might have imagined. "Thank you…"

"Oh, one more thing before you head back to Minnesota."

Mickey settled back in his chair.

"Your friend, Mr. Munoz, has a church on his drawing boards already. Did you know about that, Father?"

"No, Your Grace." Larry Wheeler had confided to him that Hector had 'something else' in the works and Mickey thought that would be a public works project of some sort. "Mr. Wheeler said that there was some 'secret' wish of Hector's—but, that was about all he told me. We both know that Mr. Munoz keeps most things to himself. I guessed that it was something further down the road."

"That may be. It will take some time but we also know that Mr. Munoz has a way of making things happen that is almost miraculous," observed Cordoba.

Mickey nodded, his smile was one of affirmation.

"He really has a passion, that man. And, I've found that he's far better at expediting than compromising."

Mickey's grin widened, "You've got that right. He's been a big part of everything we've got going in TriPalms, Your Grace. His respect is unbelievably awesome, not only there, but everywhere. Everyone's been energized. What's been happening is nothing short of miraculous."

Cordoba agreed. Standing up from his chair and taking Mickey's hand in his own, the bishop said: "You don't know this, and it won't be official until we get word from Rome—our Catholic bureaucracy loves nothing more than total oversight along with a mind-boggling set of regulations and restrictions. But, you more than most, know that hurdles make achievements more satisfying.

Mickey was astonished. "A church? That's incredible!"

Cordoba let the news settle in, beaming at Mickey's delight. "But those hurdles…" Cordoba reminded. "The major hurdle being—"

A long pause. "Mister Munoz insists that the church be called Saint Michael's. Can you imagine dictating his terms to the Vatican?"

Mickey stood speechless, his spine tingly, knees rubbery.

"That's not all, he is equally insistent that the church's dedication stone be inscribed with the words: 'In recognition of our beloved priest Fr. Mickey Moran'.

The End

EPILOGUE:

August, 2012

Before going to press, I would like to tie up some loose threads to this story. There are many. Thusly, my characters bow out of this story.

Duane Slade decided not to run. On February 16th, after losing his last few dollars in the slots at the Mystic Lake Casino. Broken and tearful, he presented himself and the stolen BMW to the Roseville police. The local cops called in the state crime bureau people to assist in the interrogation of their disoriented suspect. Despite having an assigned attorney in the room with him, he chose not to 'remain silent'. In his three-hour confession, he admitted to being totally responsibility for the entire scheme. Intense cross-examination did not trip him up. "The people in the video were hired and paid by me; told what to do by me, and led to believe that the project was nothing more than a porn flick. None of them had any idea about what I intended to do with the CD–they all are completely blameless," his final written statement explained.

Duane would go to his grave without naming his accomplice. Pleading no contest to felonies lesser than extortion in the Minnesota criminal code, Duane's public defender was able to get him seven to twelve with potential parole in four. He is currently serving his time in Stillwater. Beth and Brian Slade continue to make a monthly trip from Duluth to Stillwater to visit their brother. Nobody else has paid him a visit.

Film director and entrepreneur, David Rossman, married Duane's former girlfriend, Dianne Miller, in a Las Vegas Wedding Chapel. For an extra $125, Dianne had her name legally changed to Dagmar. From Las Vegas, the newlyweds traveled to Los Angles where they continue searching 'Tinsel town' for an agent with legitimate connections in the movie business.

Father Timothy Hagland was a broken man and unable to make a readjustment to the priesthood. He prayed fervently for an inner peace but, sadly, his hopes proved to be too elusive. It wasn't until he totally accepted the passage in the Lord's Prayer–"Thy will be done"–that he was able to go forward with his life. Being more comfortable with numbers than with people, he found employment as an accountant with the Koochiching County land department. On the upside, International Falls- like Roseau–was hockey country. At the local arena he found some joy in his otherwise empty life while watching high school hockey on a frigid winter Friday evening. From a distance he would follow his old friend, Father Mickey, cope with celebrity.

Brian Slade passed his probationary period at Saint Mary's Hospital and joined the employee's union. By August he had his own apartment on Woodland Avenue within walking distance from the UMD campus. He is currently taking some pre-ed classes, driving a decent car, and has a girlfriend named Kathy. Katherine Roddy is a good Christian woman with two children of her own. Her kids adore Brian as much as he adores them. Brian Slade and Katherine have arranged to be married by Father Moran in the spring of 2013.

Yes, the doppelganger pair did meet. Bishop Brenner's curiosity would not be satisfied until he met Mr. Slade in the flesh. Not surprisingly, the bishop arranged the meeting at his mansion and invited a select representation of media people for the occasion. The story provided such uniqueness that YouTube videos attracted national attention. Brian did not wear his priest's outfit for the PR session, nor has he worn it since.

Father Michael Moran would not return to Saint Gerard's parish. The bishop informed him that the old church had seen it's better days and would be closed forever before the end of this year. After numerous meetings with Benjamin Little Otter of Saint Gerard's parish and the Fond du Lac reservation, the bishop was planning to create a new branch in the Diocesan bureaucracy.

In his first meeting with Father Moran, he posed a three-part question. He began with: "What would you like to do, Father? I'm considering three options..." Mickey was taken aback, this from a bishop who always called the shots; all the shots! Brenner unfolded: "With Easter coming and the fine folks at Saint Gerard's anxiously awaiting a young priest with some fire, you could return there and help me with the process of consolidating with your former parish of Saint James. You would be perfect for that."

Mickey smiled his appreciation at the unsolicited complement.

"Or, I'll frame a second choice as a question: Would you like to return to the Venice Diocese and work with Bishop Cordoba in expanding his Hispanic ministry and getting that new church built in TriPalms? A lot of people would be delighted to have you return."

Mickey nodded without responding.

"The third option is a rather innovative but still a quite nebulous position." Which would you prefer, Father Moran?"

Without so much as 'What is the new position?', Mickey said: "When do you want me to start my next nebulous project, Your Grace? I'm ready to go right now."

The large Diocese of Duluth served five separate Anishinaabe (Ojibwe) Indian reservations: Bois Forte, Fond du Lac, Grand Portage, Leech Lake, and Mille Lacs. Bishop Brenner had long envisioned a closer integration of the American Indian community with the goings-on of the wider diocese. He was delighted at Father Mickey's enthusiastic willingness to accept the challenge. Somehow, the bishop never doubted that Mickey would accept the new position. As it would turn out, Mickey was to have a hand and voice in all three of the bishop's options.

In early August, the bishop announced that he was granting Father Mickey another 'sabbatical' (the word he used with the media to describe Father Moran's time in Florida). The newly christened Saint Michael's Church of TriPalms would be celebrating its first Mass on Easter Sunday of 2013. As Hector Munoz had done with the Haitian refugee children, he did with the construction of the new church–he pulled every string necessary to get what he wanted.

And, the other Morans. I've been through five generations of the Hibbing family and continue to enjoy sharing their lives. Meghan and Kenny are pretty solid these days and have had a 'date night' each week for several consecutive months. Both would readily admit, however, that marriage is commitment more than anything else. When that commitment is firm love can flourish. It's been flourishing in their household.

Back in April, Grampa Pack had a wonderful experience. Playing in a Police versus Firefighters benefit hockey game, he broke his ankle while making a turn in front of the net. His cast was signed by the fifteen Peewees he had helped coach that winter. To Pack, the cast was a badge of macho.

Embarrassed by the amount of accrued revenues in the Moran's various foundations, Amos and Sadie began a process of structured liquidation. From Naples, the Morans would help Bishop Cordoba with his mission and finance projects similar to those in TriPalms. In addition, the Sadie Moran Scholarship program would provide financial assistance to five deserving high school graduates to attend an accredited college of their choice.

Incidentally, this author likes to toss out a red herring here and there. The missed phone call from Hibbing–remember the familiar woman's voice? And, remember Mickey's swing past Maureen Regan's house while on his meaningless road trip home to Hibbing. The storyteller forgot to mention that Mrs. Regan followed up that December call with a brief note several days later:

December 21, 2011

"Mickey,
Our 15th class reunion is nearly upon us–August 11-13 is only months away. We all would like you to be our MC for the evening. As you've done in the past, we'd also appreciate if you would do our banquet invocation. More information will follow. Call if you have any questions. Tom and I and all your classmates look forward to seeing you then.
Maureen Regan

Mickey not only accepted, but also did a marvelous job.

~

To this day, the village of TriPalms is a small Eden with flowers and shrubs and green everywhere. The community center-library is the hub of cultural life and education and easily the greatest source of pride to one and all. The dirt field has been sodded (and irrigated) and is a major venue for numerous community outdoor activities. The Wheeler Foundation is gradually (a new manufactured house each month) improving the overall living conditions dramatically: streets, street lighting, sidewalks, sanitary sewers, and water lines have been dramatically upgraded. The Sarasota county health department will have a fulltime nurse and an office in the soon to be completed Administration building–next to the office of Alberto Olivio, the recently elected mayor of TriPalms.

A Passage of Redemption

A final note...

With the publication of *A Passage of Redemption* I have completed my tenth book–seven novels and three children's stories–an achievement well beyond my wildest imaginings of a decade ago. After a dryspell of four years, I began this story. It didn't take long for me to realize how richly rewarding the telling of a story is to me. So, why am I sharing my joy of writing with you, my cherished readers? I'm already thinking about what Father Mickey might be up to next. The best way for me to share my literary meanderings and allow you to keep up with Mickey Moran will be through my website. Follow along and I will keep you posted: patmcgauley.com

A Passage of Redemption

OTHER WORKS BY THE AUTHOR...

'The Mesabi Trilogy'
To Bless or to Blame (ISBN: 978-0-9724209-0-7)
    An historical drama, romance, set on the early Mesabi Iron Range.
    Ruthless and driven, entrepreneur Peter Moran is bigger than life in the rowdy mining hub of Hibbing in the early 1900's. A "compelling debut novel" and NEMBA award finalist.
    Trade paperback (2002). $18.95

A Blessing or a Curse 978-0-9724209-1-4)
    Sequel. Ambition runs in the Moran bloodlines. Obsessed to achieve what his unscrupulous father never could, Kevin Moran plunges into a political battle against the established Iron Range power structure. An historical drama, romance.
    Trade paperback (2003) $19.95

Blest Those Who Sorrow (ISBN: 978-0-9724209-2-4)
    Sequel. A psychological thriller completes the Mesabi Trilogy. Kevin and Angela Moran are swept far from their familiar Hibbing roots in a page-turner of deceptions and delusions. "A deftly crafted drama!"
    Trade paperback (2004) $16.95

Other novels
The Hibbing Hurt (ISBN: 978-0-9724209-3-8)
    Murder mystery set in Hibbing, 1956. A racial abduction/homicide stirs the conscience of the ethnically rich Iron Range community. Pack Moran is hard-nosed cop who unravels the complex conspiracy.
    "There are no heroes in this tragedy."
    Trade paperback: (2005) $14.95

'Flag' (ISBN: 987-0-9724209-4-0)
Angry and conflicted, 18 year-old Amos Moran is a runaway who ends up in Flagstaff, Arizona. Connected to earlier novels, this forth generation Moran is a compelling character. Amos witnesses a murder, falls in love with a spirited coed, and risks his own life to save that of an innocent Navajo man. "Action packed!"
Trade paperback. (2006) $13.95

Saint Alban's Day (ISBN: 987-0-9724209-5-2)
The consummate political thriller with a wide Minnesota scope. Amos Moran accepts a controversial political appointment while coping with a psychopath from his past. The prison escapee had threatened his family. Drama builds in McGauley's most provocative story.
Trade paperback. (2007) $14.95

Children's books
Mazral and Derisa: An Easter Story (ISBN:987-0-9724209-9-0)
A spiritually uplifting Easter fantasy involving a mouse and a dove in ancient Jerusalem. A Resurrection miracle occurs in a cave on a Calvary hillside. Trade paper. (2004) $12.95

Santa the King (ISBN: 987-0-9724209-8-3)
An incredible fantasy in which one of the Wise Men is spiritually led to the North Pole where he becomes Santa Claus. The story combines the 'real' Christmas with the delights of Santa. "A delightful story for young and old alike." Hardcover. (2005) $13.95

The Midnight Hour (ISBN: 987-0-9724209-6-9)
A mischievous elf named Nathan almost ruins Christmas for all of the children of the world when he puts a sleeping potion in Santa's hot chocolate. A story that provides a positive message of redemption, and a story that will not be easily forgotten. Hardcover. (2011) $14.95

*Autographed copies of all titles can be ordered through author's web site: patmcgauley.com

A Passage of Redemption

Minnesota author Pat McGauley is a former Hibbing High School teacher. Born in Duluth, Minnesota, McGauley grew up in Hoyt Lakes. He graduated from Winona State University (BS: '64) and the University of Minnesota (MA). A former political candidate, iron mineworker, regional historian, and state agency commissioner under Governor Albert Quie, McGauley resides in Hibbing and Naples.

A Passage of Redemption